I0708520

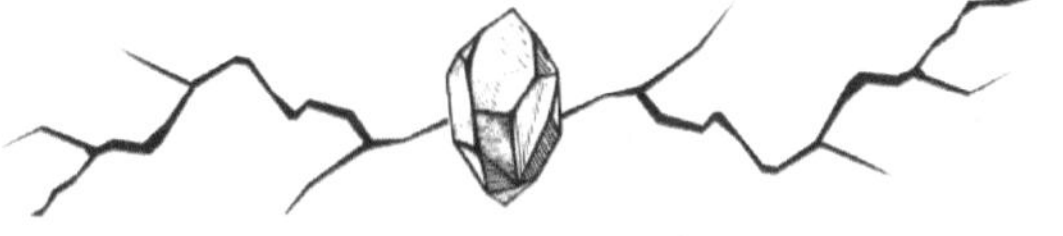

Also by

The Ambient Series: Sam

Salvation's Fall
Ambient Height
Desolate Seasons

The Ambience Series

Her Latent Charm
Provenance Of Power

Short Stories

Grim Imperative
The Smile Before The Sword
Searching For Fortitude

The Gloom Sundered

A Tale Of Celuthia

Dana C Brentson

Content Warnings

This book is an adult fantasy novel. Some Content may not be suitable for all readers

- Violence (gore, death, blood, mutilation, physical assault, torture)

- Drowning

- Imprisonment

- Grief, anxiety

- Explicit sexual content (female-female, female-male, female-male-female)

- Discrimination, segregation

- Drug use

- Human experimentation

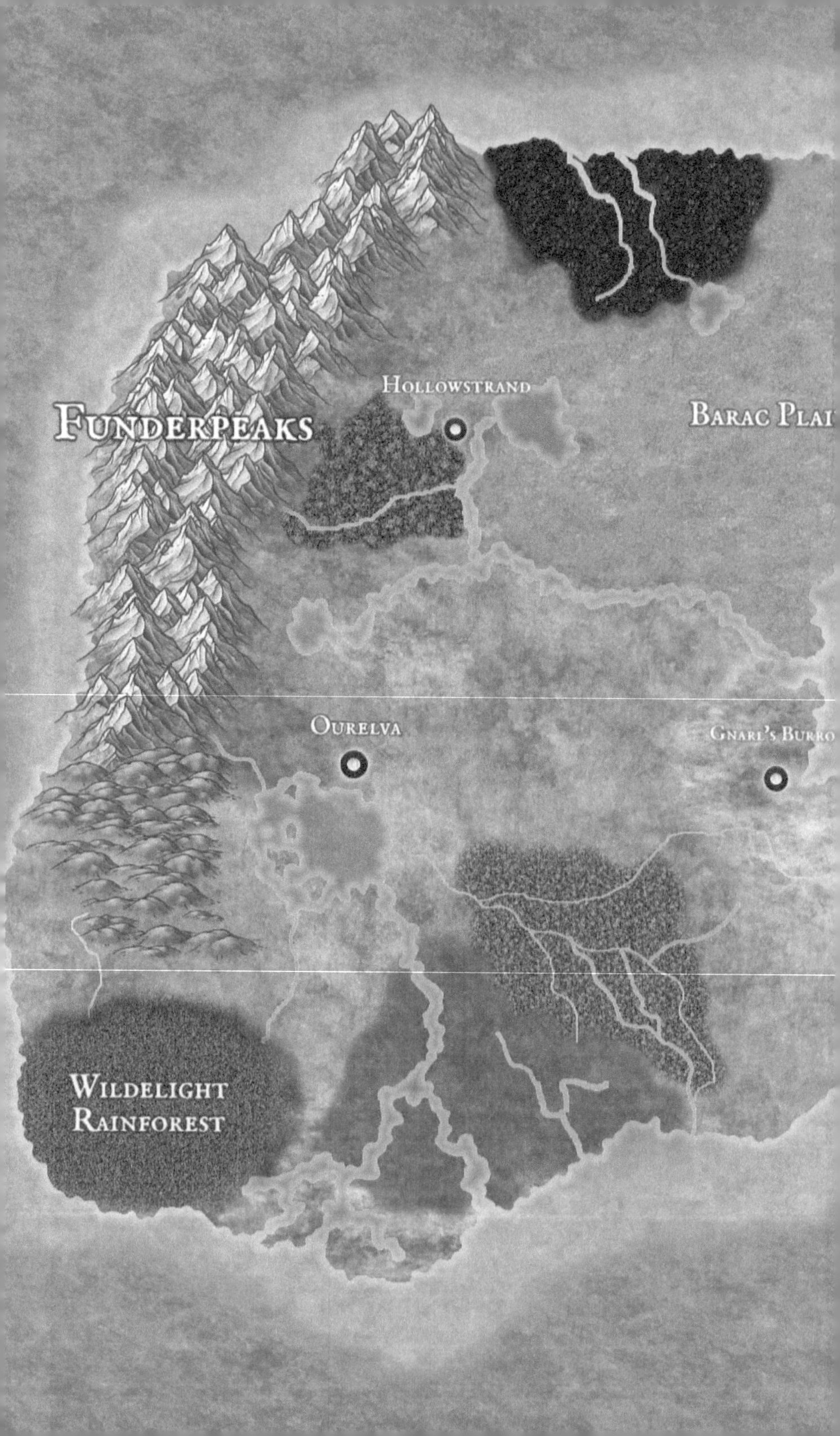

FUNDERPEAKS
HOLLOWSTRAND
BARAC PLAI
OURELVA
GNARL'S BURRO
WILDELIGHT RAINFOREST

Lacorsia
Olunei
Eldergrave Mountains
irit Mountain
Zaros Jungle
Vortheim
N

For everyone who feels like their voice can't make a difference, that you're shouting into the void.
I hear you.

CHAPTER ONE

Isalie's arm and knee impacted with the hard ground, moments before the sword swung overhead. A blur of leather and metal, a roar, and a grunt followed her as she tried to scramble away through the tall dry grass.

Don't lead it toward me! she thought, frantic with fear.

Jentien leaped forward with his shield. He shoved, and the beast backed a few steps from where Isalie lay on the ground. His concerned glance her way made her stomach flutter, though it could have been her terror at seeing the thing looming above her.

It had the body of a bear, antlers sprouting from the sides of its head, and part of its jaw looked like it had been torn off. She could swear one of its legs was a giant cat's leg. It roared, enraged by Jentien's sword jutting from its flank.

"Look out!" Isalie yelled. Jentien wrenched his sword free just as the thing swiped a huge paw in his direction with its dagger-like claws. She grimaced when they left deep gashes in his leather armor, sending Jentien sprawling to the ground with a grunt of pain.

The sight of Jen helpless on his back enraged her, which, combined with her terror, instilled in her an alien sensation of bravery.

"Hey!" she screamed as she grasped a rock from the ground and shot to her feet. Her fingers tingled as she hurled it at the beardeercat. It hit the ground short of the creature and bounced to its foot. "Over here!" She waved her arms in the air, hoping to distract it long enough for Jentien to get up. It was the only thing she could do.

It worked. The thing lumbered toward her, its eyes round and bulbous, its slitted pupils contracting in the afternoon light shining at her back. Slowly at first, and then it picked up speed.

"Shit, fuck, by the Six!" She turned and ran in the opposite direction, Jentien's voice drowned by the pulse of blood in her ears and the roar of the creature.

Isalie ran past the wagon of the nearby caravan as the driver whipped his reins to get the horses moving.

I can't lead it to them! The thought surprised her, so clear and calm as it was in the storm of her fear. But Jentien wanted to help these people, and his wishes took priority over her instinct to flee. She couldn't be responsible for making anything more difficult for him.

She lunged to the right, toward the dried grass in the open plain. She was already out of breath. She'd never had the slim, muscular body that Jen had, and she winced feeling the ample weight on her body bounce with every step. With an arm across her chest to hold her breasts in place, she pushed herself to run faster. Isalie was *not* made for running. She *loathed* running.

She glanced over her shoulder to see the beast had closed on her; she wouldn't get away this time. There was nothing she could do but continue, and she closed her eyes, tensing for the inevitable pain of its claws.

The pain didn't come, but the creature grunted. Jentien's voice rang out above the noise. "Elders curse you!"

Isalie turned, unable to resist the bones-deep need to follow the sound of his voice. One of his arms clutched onto an antler and his legs wrapped around its torso. Jentien stabbed the beardeercat in the back again and again. It flailed its massive paws wildly but couldn't reach him atop his perch. Jentien released the antler and used both hands to plunge the sword deeper, and the thing screeched in pain. It staggered a few steps, its eyes rolling back in its head, and fell to the ground. Jentien rode it down and leapt to the ground at the last moment, landing with one knee braced in the dirt.

Isalie panted, sweat dripping from her hairline, neck, and everywhere she could sweat. She was *really* not made for running. Jentien straightened—sweat glistening off his ruddy, tan skin—panting as he watched the beast take shuddering breaths between them.

Isalie started when the caravan crew bellowed in triumph, breaking the heavy silence after the beast's demise. Jentien was unfazed; nothing could rattle him. He nodded to them with a modest smile their way. Isalie stared at that smile, amazed as she always was that Jentien could take effusive praise with such humility.

Jentien felt her eyes on him and turned a smile in her direction. A flush that had nothing to do with exertion warmed her from her cheeks to her chest and further down. She could walk around the corpse and fling her arms around him. And then he'd wrap his arms around her, hold her close, and whisper how afraid he'd been when she was in danger.

But none of that would happen. It never did, no matter how many times she'd seen it in her dreams. He shook a lock of dark brown hair off his beautiful face, and Isalie sighed. How many times had she fantasized about caressing that face?

In how many dreams had his eyes finally *seen* her? Warm, dark brown with little flecks of gold and grey and green. The kindest eyes-

"Isalie? Can you hear me? Are you all right?" She blinked, and noticed Jentien was standing in front of her. She had been too busy daydreaming about him to see him there.

"What?" Isalie said. She focused on his gorgeous eyes. "Y-yes, I'm fine. Winded. But it didn't touch me. You saved me again."

Jentien smiled, the warmth of it soaking through her like sunshine appearing from behind a cloud.

"Good." His brow furrowed, and she longed to smooth the wrinkled skin, to soothe his worry. "I didn't mean to chase it this way, but I couldn't coax it to follow me. Not like you did." He chuckled, and Isalie laughed too. She loved to hear him laugh.

"I was just trying to help." She shrugged to hide the way her stomach fluttered again when Jen touched her arm. He turned to look at the beast, and she admired the muscles that flexed in his arm when he sheathed his sword.

She longed to tell him how she felt. After so many years of traveling together, she'd hoped he might catch on to how desperately she wanted him, how much she needed to hear him say that he felt the same. But he had bigger concerns. He was going to save the world someday.

He half-turned toward her, staring into the distance as his fingers traced the grooves in his armor. She could have lost him, and suddenly she knew that this was her moment. He could have died, and he would never have known how much she loved him. "Jen?" she said, her voice wavering through the bundle of nerves in her chest.

His head tilted in her direction, but he didn't take his eyes off the horizon. "Hmm?" he asked.

"I've been meaning to talk to you about something."

"What, Iz?" She was grateful that he hadn't turned to look at her. She didn't think she could get this out if their eyes met.

"Jen, we've spent a lot of time together. Almost our whole lives, really, and these past three years have been the best of my life."

"I feel the same way," Jentien replied.

"You do?" Isalie's heart began to pound.

"Of course," Jentien said. "I really feel like this is the path we should be on. And I wouldn't be here without you."

Is this happening? Isalie thought. *Does he mean…?*

"I can't tell you how much that means to me," Isalie whispered. She felt light, exuberant. This was everything she had ever wanted.

Jentien finally turned, walking closer until Isalie's breath caught. She couldn't move, couldn't breathe. She was frozen in anticipation for the words she knew would come next.

"I'm so glad you're here with me," he said. He laid his hand on her shoulder, his thumb resting on her clavicle. She didn't care that it was covered with gore, because he was touching her.

"Jentien..." She trailed off, unable to speak through her joy. *Kiss me,* she thought, pleading for him to see how much she wanted him to.

"Iz, there is no one else I would trust in Vortheim, all of Celuthia even, to be here with me." Isalie waited for him to pull her close. To embrace her. To kiss her with the passion she'd only experienced in her dreams. "I don't know how I would manage the day-to-day without you. I'm much better at slaying beasts than any of the other stuff you do for us."

Isalie's face froze in a wide smile until her cheeks started to ache. "W-What?" she asked.

"All the cooking and everything? The money? I'm terrible with that stuff."

The caravan driver called Jentien. He smiled at Isalie, gave her shoulder a squeeze, and walked around her toward the grey-skinned man. Isalie stood frozen in the same position, crestfallen.

What just happened? she thought. She turned around slowly to watch Jentien walk away. He clasped the driver's forearm in greeting and the driver slapped him on the back a few times to congratulate him before the two men walked toward the wagon. Everyone laughed while Isalie's heart broke.

Isalie's cheeks flushed with embarrassment, but she swallowed it when Jen glanced her way and waved her over. It took everything she had to put one foot in front of the other.

"You saved our lives!" a woman with thick, bark-textured skin yelled as Isalie found a place just behind Jen.

"And our cargo," the driver added. His wide eyes were so green that they seemed to glow. Jentien blushed, and Isalie could see that he felt uncomfortable with praise.

"I'm glad we could help," he mumbled.

"You need a reward for your hard work," the driver announced, more to the crowd than Jen.

Jentien started to shake his head, but Isalie interrupted before he could refuse. She needed to take care of him, no matter her feelings.

"Thank you so much," she said to the driver. "He does need new armor now." The driver looked at her as if he'd forgotten she was there, but she ignored it. Everyone Jentien saved gave her that look.

"There's a bit of gold I can spare," the driver replied, frowning at her before beaming at Jentien. He pulled a pouch from under his seat, and then grabbed something from the back of the wagon. "A bit of fruit as well," he added. He held the bag out to Jentien with a broad smile. "Fresh from the gardens of Wyphea."

"That is very generous," Jentien said as he handed everything to Isalie. She peeked inside the small pouch and smiled to herself. There were quite a few silver and copper coins, and the gleam of a handful of larger gold Malachs.

"Thank you," Isalie said. No one looked at her.

"Would you travel with us?" the driver asked, pointing to the Gloom east of their position. "We're headed southeast, and there is plenty more Gloom and nasty things between here and there. I heard another village was lost in the South, and people are disappearing in the East."

More than one in the crowd shuddered as they followed the line of the driver's pointing finger. Beyond the flat grassland dotted with baobab and acacia trees was a dark cloud looming at ground level like a stagnant fog. Flashes of prismatic light lit the inside, like rainbows shrouded in shadow. When people, animals, or even cities were swallowed by Gloom, most were never seen again. And anything that came stumbling out of those clouds in one piece was never the same.

The Gloom had disrupted life in Vortheim for as long as anyone could remember. It seemed like the world was mad, trying to tear itself apart, and it was getting worse every year. Jentien had made it his life's mission to help in any way he could, and Isalie couldn't let him walk into danger alone, waiting to see him walk back through the door, worrying from afar. If she could keep him fed and distract beasts long enough for him to best them, she'd follow him anywhere, if only to be close to him.

Jentien looked toward the Gloom and frowned. Isalie could see him weighing the idea of plunging into more danger on behalf of these people. It was his way. It was one of the many reasons she loved him.

But they had a contract coming up to guard the twice-yearly Cartographer's Guild expedition to map the northern Glooms. And now he needed new armor.

Isalie put a hand on Jen's arm. "Jentien," she murmured, pulling him aside. "The Cartographer's Guild is waiting, and you know how important it is." She knew he'd let such a lucrative opportunity pass him by, but not such a noble one. The people of Vortheim couldn't trade and travel safely if the maps were inaccurate.

Jentien pulled his troubled gaze from the Gloom and looked at Isalie. He considered her face for a time until his frown softened, and he nodded.

"Okay, Iz," he murmured. He looked at the driver. "I apologize, but I'm needed elsewhere." Jentien pointed to the Gloom in the distance. "On our travels, we saw that most of the charted Gloom is the same as it has been for the past year. You should be safe if you follow the paths. If you'd like, I can look at your maps and make sure they're correct before we leave."

Jentien followed the driver to the wagon, where they opened a large piece of worn vellum and Jentien pointed to different spots, marking one with a piece of charcoal the driver provided.

Isalie watched the driver gesticulate at Jentien, trying to convince him to travel with them. Jentien held his hands out to forestall further attempts, shaking his head with a sympathetic smile. The driver frowned with disappointment when Jentien turned and walked away, but whatever he called after him only elicited a friendly wave as Jen loped toward Isalie.

He looped an arm across her shoulders, steering them northwest toward the capital of Vortheim. Toward home.

CHAPTER TWO

THEY DIDN'T TRAVEL FAR that day along the Founder's Road that cut through the heart of Vortheim, but they put distance between themselves and the Gloom in case it decided to move. Most of the clouds did, eventually, and though they often followed predictable paths, they *could* shift. Every Vorthe traveler knew that to stay in one place for too long was to invite disaster. Only the bravest cartographers volunteered for the biannual call to chart the Glooms, and they lived in riches that could rival the Malachi in their crystal palace at the heart of Lacorsia. If they survived.

That's why any distance between Isalie and Jentien and the static Gloom that sat four days east of Lacorsia was welcome. Isalie didn't want to see any more beasts come running at her from its misty borders.

Isalie sagged with relief when Jentien cut off the road toward one of the many campsites along its length. It was no inn, with a soft bed and a hot meal, but the Vortheim guard patrols and rudimentary walls at least gave them a semblance of shelter and safety.

Isalie nodded to the uniformed Stills stacking firewood in a pile near their fire pit and clearing rubbish left behind by the last visitors, fuming as the word *Still* crossed her mind. She had always loathed the title for people like her. People who weren't Ambient, who couldn't do whatever they wanted with a thought. They could change the world if they wanted to, and labeling everyone else Stills, like they were somehow less capable, had always felt derogatory to Isalie.

But that was the world she lived in. The Ambient Consuls ruled over cities and territories, and the Malachi ruled over them all. The Ambient also healed the sick, fed people in years when their crops didn't provide enough food, and kept the peace. No matter how many times their good work was shoved in Isalie's face in school, though, she couldn't ignore the superiority with which they did them.

Jentien pulled some kindling and logs from a pile nearby. Isalie gathered a few, too, running her fingers over the strangely smooth texture of the grain. All this wood was treated with the Ambience to keep it dry, even in the rain. Anyone could make a fire in all but a downpour. The Ambience had its benefits.

Isalie opened the bag of fruit and pulled some stale dried beef from her pack. Then, she dug her special box of spices and a few carrots that were starting to grow small, thin roots from the bottom where she'd stashed them the night before.

While Jentien started the fire, Isalie went to work on their food. She lost herself in slicing thin strips of carrot and chunks of melon. The beef practically shattered when she cut it, but that wouldn't matter after it was cooked with the moist fruit. She combined everything in a thin metal bowl with some spices and a bit of oil from a carefully wrapped bottle tucked within her spare clothes. When the fire was hot enough, she pulled some coals aside and stuck the bowl on top.

Within minutes, the smell of fruit and spices and meat drifted into the air to tickle their noses with the promise of full bellies. Jentien closed his eyes and sighed when he caught the scent.

"Isalie, I don't know how you can make something so delicious from such strange ingredients. It's a real talent."

Isalie beamed. She lived for compliments like this from Jentien. "It's just something I like to do," she replied. "I'm glad you appreciate it."

Jentien smiled at her, and she felt familiar butterflies in her stomach. There were hardly any moments when they were alone that she didn't feel them, even after her disastrous attempt to talk about her feelings earlier in the day. He shrugged out of his leather chestpiece and threaded a finger through the biggest gash. "I hope your mom can repair this before we leave again."

Isalie wrapped a thick cloth around her hand and shook the hot bowl. "I'm sure my parents have something new set aside for you."

Jentien watched Isalie dish the strange combination of food into a bowl before handing it to him with a small spoon. She smiled and blew her dark blonde hair out of her face. It was always coming out of the low bun she favored and blowing around in the slightest breeze.

When he took a bite, the sweet tang of the fruit and savory spices danced across his palate, and he moaned in surprised pleasure. He would never stop being amazed that she could make something so delicious from food that shouldn't belong in the same dish.

"This is wonderful, Iz," he said through a mouthful.

Isalie smiled again. It was the same shy, pleased smile that always lifted the corners of her mouth after he complimented her.

She has the prettiest smile, he thought.

"Thanks, Jen. I'm happy you like my strange creations."

"They're always so good!" he mumbled as he shoveled more into his mouth. "And they have no right to be, with what you put in them."

Isalie laughed, and the sound made him smile. He didn't know what he would do without her. Starve, most likely.

"I'm looking forward to joining the Cartographers," Jentien said before taking another bite. "I can't believe they chose me, out of all the other Sentinels."

A log popped, and Isalie grabbed a large stick to shove the logs apart. There was no need for more heat since the air was so warm already. The sun fell below the horizon, and still the oppressively humid heat remained.

"You're one of the bravest and strongest men in Lacorsia. Add to that the fact that you don't extort people for more money than they have, and you have a reputation that puts you at the front of the line in the guild." Isalie snorted. "There aren't many people like that in Vortheim."

"I hope so." He sighed, rolling his shoulder as if to dislodge the discomfort that settled under his skin from her praise. "Everyone does the best with what they have. I'm lucky I'm able to help."

"Don't spout Ambient propaganda to me, Jen."

Jentien frowned at the vitriol in her tone. "What do you mean?"

Isalie rolled her eyes, uncharacteristic for her unless someone brought up the Ambient. "That's what they told us in school growing up, that we all had to do what we could to contribute to society. Which is true, but don't you think there should be more to our lives than that? That we shouldn't *only* be defined by what we can do for the Ambient?"

Jentien's frown deepened. He—and Iz—had been taught their whole lives that the Stills served the community the Ambient ruled over because they were responsible for keeping Vortheim safe from the Gloom. If they used their Elder-granted powers to keep the Gloom at bay, it was the least any Still could do to contribute to the everyday tasks that were easier and much less dangerous.

"Iz, most people are happy to do the cooking, cleaning, or whatever else so the Ambient can focus on the bigger issues. The Gloom gets more dangerous every year; can you imagine how bad it would be if they weren't around to protect us?" He shook his head as visions of the entire continent overrun with dark clouds passed through his head. "This is the world we live in. It's not likely to change, and if people are happy and healthy, what does it matter?"

Isalie sighed, and her shoulders slumped. Jentien wasn't sure what the gesture meant, but his heart twisted as he wondered whether he'd disappointed her.

"I know," she sighed. "Sometimes I just wish I had something more to contribute. I don't feel like I'm everything I'm supposed to be."

"You could always take a job in the city," Jentien suggested, surprised by the hollow feeling in his chest as he considered continuing without her. He didn't want her to go, but if that's what she needed to be happy, he would support her. It was dangerous following him around; he'd seen that again today. He would happily dive into dangerous situations the rest of his life, but if he led Iz into something he couldn't get them out of...

Isalie shook her head, seeming to shake off whatever thought had turned her mood dour, because she smiled again. It was infectious, and Jentien couldn't help smiling back.

"No, Jen," she said. "I couldn't leave you." She had that look in her eyes again, like she wanted to say something more.

"Thanks, Iz," Jentien said. A small knot of worry in the pit of his stomach melted away in the warmth of her smile. "I really don't know that I could do this without you."

"Then I guess my contribution to Vortheim is keeping you safe and fed so you can save everyone."

"We're a team, Iz," Jentien said.

She walked around the fire pit to sit next to him. Her hand rubbed gently back and forth between his shoulder blades, a reassuring gesture she'd started when they were kids, when Jentien had spent most nights mourning his parents. Even when they were so young, Isalie had always been his comfort.

"I'm not going anywhere, Jen."

CHAPTER THREE

THE MASSIVE CRYSTALLINE GATES of Lacorsia stood wide to admit the throng of people surging toward the safety it offered. Isalie followed Jentien in, letting him make a path she could follow as she peered south, trying to make out Spirit Mountain in the distance. Someone bumped her shoulder, jarring her before she put her hand on Jen's shoulder to keep him close.

I already miss the quiet, Isalie thought, irritated when someone stepped on her foot, leaving a smear of mud on her boot. A breeze lifted the small hairs from her neck, a relief from the heat of the morning's blazing sun. Unfortunately, it carried the scent of kelp and saltwater, and she wrinkled her nose in disgust.

Lacorsia sat at the northern edge of the isthmus connecting the eastern and western portions of the continent, a gateway between the two, and a bastion of safety from the Spirit Mountain on the southern edge. It was the only way to get from one side of Vortheim to the other, because the mountain was shrouded in a Gloom that killed anyone who strayed too close, and the land between was a treacherous mire at high tide.

That meant that her city was always loud and crowded, something she'd never known she despised until she and Jen left for the first time. Now, the crush of people around them was suffocating. She squinted when the light reflected off the crystal gate before they passed into the outer city's sprawl.

Here, people who couldn't afford the cost of living within the city proper found a haven from the Gloom behind the crystalline walls that towered taller than most trees. Many believed that the Malachi, who ruled over Vortheim, was so powerful that they could keep even the Gloom surrounding the Spirit Mountain at bay, and thus they were safe within the confines of Lacorsia's outer walls. Isalie had her doubts, considering anyone powerful enough to control the Gloom like that *should* be powerful enough to get rid of it entirely, but she knew better than to say it aloud to anyone but Jen. Even he didn't like to hear what she thought about the subject, so it just festered beneath the surface.

She frowned at the collection of squat, hastily constructed homes and the people that huddled around them. Every year more of them crowded here because they had nowhere else to go. A day was coming—soon—when there wouldn't be any room left, and Isalie wondered where the displaced would congregate then.

Isalie took in the dirt-streaked faces of children running through the crowd, and their parents lining up to enter the city through one of the smaller gates to the inner city for work. Every time she saw it, she thanked the Elders for her luck in having the life she lived, while she raged at her inability to do much for the people forced to live like this.

"It's a shame so many people have been displaced by the Gloom," Jentien said, echoing her thoughts. "I wish I could do something to help."

Isalie patted Jentien on the shoulder. "We help as many as we can."

Jentien shook his head in frustration, and Isalie wished the line would move faster. This place always unnerved Jen. He'd been born in a house like these, had lived in this squalor for the first few years of his life, and when his parents had taken work with a trade caravan, they had never returned. It'd been a blessing from the Elders that Isalie's parents had found him in the street and taken him in; there were so many orphans in the Gloom's wake.

"Someone needs to help these people," Jentien muttered. It was as close as he ever came to seeing the inconsistencies in the Ambient rhetoric that Isalie saw. She squeezed his shoulder, and he shuddered before covering her hand with his.

There wasn't much she could say to him on the subject that he wanted to hear. She knew his drive to join the Sentinels came from the grief he would always carry. And though she would have preferred to see him take up a post as a city guard rather than joining the guild paid to safeguard the travelers of Vortheim, she understood and respected his choice. He didn't want some other child like him to watch their parents walk through the crystal gates and never come back.

Jentien nodded and grumbled something Isalie couldn't hear. The crowd thinned as some broke off to navigate the outer city, while Jentien and Isalie continued toward the city wall. Lines of people veered toward one of several large gates meant for visitors and residents of the inner city, and Isalie followed Jen straight ahead toward the largest. Isalie brushed against the wall of a nearby house, the rough wood snagging her sleeve like claws reaching out to grasp her. She had a moment of panic, remembering the beast, and then stifled a nervous laugh when she realized what had touched her.

Her relief was short-lived because when she turned around, the tunnel beyond the open crystal doors came into view. Isalie dreaded this part of returning home. Since she was a little girl, she had imagined that the tunnel was a mouth, waiting to swallow someone who didn't belong. And that the forbidding steel portcullis, currently raised, was a line of teeth that would chop her in half.

She still had nightmares about this tunnel, made worse by the knowledge that she'd never felt like she belonged here, not in the way that her parents and Jentien did. They were all integral members of the community; her parents were the best armorers in Vortheim, and Jentien was a hero who rescued wayward travelers, a Sentinel. They were all attractive and personable and important.

Isalie was not. It baffled her how such naturally athletic, beautiful people had produced a daughter who was nothing like them. She'd been overweight since her teens, regardless of diet and exercise. Her nose was a bit too big for her face, her forehead too large, and her eyes were a bit too far apart. At least, that's what she'd been told by her schoolmates.

Most of the time she told herself she wasn't worried about her looks. In reality, she didn't let herself think about it because she knew that it would only lead to a vortex of self-doubt that made her feel like she didn't belong in her skin, as if it was a shirt that was too tight. But every time she stood facing one of these tunnels, those intrusive thoughts gained ground.

She took a deep breath when they neared the gate. Jentien glanced over his shoulder and flashed her a sympathetic, encouraging smile, anticipating her response. Just as he had since she'd first told him about her fear. He knew everything about her.

Almost everything.

A pair of guards stood at the tunnel entrance, their steel breastplates painted with the Malachi's crest. Isalie distracted herself as her feet moved forward by tracing the lines of tall crystal spire and a silver dragon over a purple background with her eyes, soothing in its familiarity from all her time staring out her bedroom window at the palace grounds.

The closest held her grey-green hand out to stop them. "Names?" she asked in an uninterested monotone.

Jentien answered. "Jentien Themori and Isalie Wylshard."

The woman looked up, boredom replaced by delight in her pale violet eyes. "Welcome home, Jentien," she said. The bald admiration in her tone caught Isalie's attention, just the kind of distraction that could overcome her fear. But Jentien was oblivious to the batting eyelashes and seductive smile. That was Isalie's one consolation for the fact that he didn't understand her affection. He didn't notice that *anyone* was attracted to him.

"Thanks, Korima," he replied, turning to the man next to her as her smile fell. "Everything all right here, Qual?"

"Nothing unusual, Jen," Qual replied. He stretched onto his toes to look at the line behind them. "Maybe a bit more traffic the past few weeks. We've had to place more people inside the walls, which would've ended in a riot if the Consul hadn't stepped in."

Jentien nodded, his lips pursed in anger. "We saw a shift in one of the Glooms last month. It might've moved more since we saw it last; there was a village nearby."

Qual nodded and sighed. "We'll pass that along," he said. He waved them into the tunnel. "Thanks, Jentien."

Isalie hesitated until Jentien grasped her hand and gave her another encouraging smile. She took a deep breath and tried not to imagine the roof coming down on top of them.

Jentien released Isalie's hand near the end of the tunnel when she started to pull ahead of him. She always ran the last ten feet or so, desperate to escape the close confines. After having to walk through the outer city, he jogged beside her, needing his best friend's presence.

The slums were worse every time he walked through, and the smell of sweating bodies and churned mud still tied his stomach in knots as his body remembered the pain of being left alone in that place.

He shook his head to force his thoughts in a different direction, and spotted Iz, red-faced and panting, thin strands of hair plastered to the sweat on her brow. *We're both messes, in our own ways,* he thought. *It's good we have each other.*

He didn't say a word, just held out his hand and waited for her to take it. The corner of her mouth quirked in an embarrassed smirk, and she squeezed his hand in thanks before starting forward with him at her side.

A haphazard collection of stone buildings shaped long ago by the founding Ambient crowded the wide thoroughfare that passed through the city. Wide enough for several small carts or two wagons to roll in tandem, Jentien nevertheless had a hard time navigating through the throng and keeping hold of Iz's hand.

More ragged and weary people clustered here, too, herded through the streets by Ambient Guard, away from the main thoroughfare's bustling normalcy. Jentien watched a throng disappear down an alley in the direction of one of the seedier inns at the edge of the city. He longed to step out of the current of people flowing deeper into Lacorsia, longing to do something, *anything,* to help, but his pack was empty after so long on the road, and he had nothing but empty arms to offer. The crowd moved around them, drawing them further into the city, away from the despondent refugees.

Traders and crafters yelled over the noise of the street, trying to attract tourists and locals alike to browse their wares. Performers juggled, sang, danced, and otherwise entertained; hands reached out expectantly to anyone that stopped to watch them. Foods sweet and savory wafted their scents through the air and mingled into a confused riot in Jentien's flared nostrils.

There was nowhere he'd rather be. After the isolation of travel, his heart swelled at being surrounded by so much life. And the beautiful palace glittered in the sunshine as if to welcome them home.

Jentien waved to a man walking out of a general store and nodded to a group of people standing near a fountain. Everyone waved in response or called his name with a smile. Iz drew in on herself further, catching his attention.

"You all right, Iz?" he asked, stopping to wait while she tried to collect herself. One arm was wrapped around her midsection, the other hand propped on her hip. She closed her eyes and took one deep breath, and then another.

She nodded, though when she opened her eyes, they betrayed her lingering anxiety. "I'm okay, Jen," she said. Her voice was steady, at least. "Let's go home."

The city bustled around them as they strolled down the street, and he marveled at the diversity of the people here. Since he was a child, his favorite pastime had been watching people, trying to guess where their steps would take them. There were humans like Isalie and himself with skin tones ranging from his tan to green, purple, red, or even the color and texture of tree bark. Some had vestiges of gills, some towered above the smaller buildings on the street with legs like tree trunks. And some looked just like humans, but were shorter and wider, or with long, slender bodies and ears.

Jentien waved up at a giant woman with pointed ears and a dark gray complexion. He smiled when he noticed her leather pants and bodice were stamped with Isalie's parents' mark.

"Hi, Jentien!" Her voice boomed down to him, echoing along the wide thoroughfare, ringing in his ears as she passed, each slow step rumbling through the ground.

"Magdalena was wearing some of your parents' work," Jentien told Isalie. She glanced over her shoulder and nodded.

"They were starting on that before we left," Isalie replied, sounding distracted. Her eyes darted between passersby like she was expecting an attack.

"Are you okay, Iz?" Jentien asked. "You seem worried."

Isalie looked at him for a long moment, then took a deep breath and forced her shoulders to relax. "I just have a strange feeling," Isalie replied. She gazed at a notice on the wall, and he followed her gaze to find a scathing call for the expulsion of the refugee population before it further polluted their beautiful city.

"The Gloom is getting worse," Jentien muttered.

Isalie ripped the notice from the board, crumpled the paper, and tossed it into a waste bin near a food stall. "It is," she agreed.

"It's a good thing we're doing what we can to help," he offered.

Isalie hooked her arm through his and pulled tight against his side. Comforted by her proximity, Jentien escorted her up the street.

CHAPTER FOUR

ISALIE BLINKED AS THEY emerged into a circular, crystal-paved marketplace surrounded by the most expensive storefronts in Lacorsia. This was the heart of the city, where the Ambient and the elite spent most of their time, where tourists congregated after visiting the palace grounds through the only gate open to the public.

Here there were no refugees, or any indication of the problems beyond the walls separating the palace district from the rest of the city. All major streets funneled travelers into this area day and night, and Isalie's shoulders tensed as they were surrounded by the near-constant din of voices and footsteps. Jentien sighed, his shoulders relaxing and his stern expression giving way to a wistful smile. Jen truly loved this place, something she would never understand.

A flash of light drew her gaze to the largest store, Ambient Sundries, and the orbs set to each side of the ostentatious sign above their double doors. A man walked out with a wide smile on his face and a cloak in his hands that shimmered in the light when he turned it back and forth. Isalie rolled her eyes. He'd probably spent enough on one piece of clothing to feed a handful of refugee families for a year.

She imagined she could hear her mother's voice as she rolled her eyes again, reminding her that they sold very useful items alongside the frivolous, and that the attraction helped all the businesses in the area. But Isalie couldn't help but compare the smaller Still-run stores to the emporium of Ambience-infused items.

Her parents were like Jen; none of them could see what was so obvious to Isalie. They believed in the supremacy of the Ambient, and the system worked for them. They did what they could to help people in need, and they earned a tidy sum from their specialized trade. Isalie stared at the sign, *Wylshard Leatherworks*, burned into the wood placard above carved, faceless humanoids in leather, and had to smile. No matter her misgivings about the society she lived in, she was home.

She trailed behind Jen, the bell above the door tinkling to announce their arrival, and her father's voice called out to them from behind the counter at the far end of the room.

"Welcome! I'll be just a moment!"

Isalie inhaled the woodsy scent from the leather that surrounded her, with a sweet hint of the citrus oil her parents used to condition their leather. It was a signature of theirs, distilled from a rare fruit that grew on an island near the northern coast. That smell and the sound of her father's baritone grumbling finally let her relax, and she sighed. Jen relaxed at the same time, casting a grateful gaze around the place while heavy footsteps approached.

Her father stood from behind the counter, his thick mane of blonde hair slicked back from tan skin. His clear blue eyes sparkled, and a white smile shone through a gray-blonde beard when he realized who had walked into his store.

"Izzie!" He vaulted over the counter, not bothering to take two steps to the side to walk through the gap. "Ratna! Izzie's home!"

There was a muffled exclamation from the back room, and then she was swept into a bear hug by her tall, muscular father. She gave him the briefest squeeze in return and started to squirm when his arms tightened more.

"Dad, please put me down," she grunted. "You're breaking my ribs."

"Sorry, baby," he said, letting her stand in front of him. She winced inwardly, though she appreciated that even at twenty-eight, he still considered her his baby girl. He stood a head taller than Isalie, making her feel small despite her own impressive stature. While her body was soft, his physique was as burly as any soldier's from years of hard work.

"Hi, Savar," Jentien said.

"Isalie!" Her mother emerged from the back with her long flaxen locks tied back in a bun at her nape. Despite the sweat and brown dye on her flawless ivory skin, she was the picture of statuesque beauty.

She walked around the counter, her lithe muscles and curved body rushing forward as Isalie sighed to herself. How in Celuthia did she have such beautiful parents?

"Oh, my Izzie's home!" Ratna nudged Savar out of the way to squeeze her daughter in an embrace almost as crushing as her husband's.

"Hi, mom," Isalie said. The citrus smell was so strong that her mother smelled like she'd bathed in it. Isalie closed her eyes and let herself feel the comfort her mother's arms and scent provided, and let it chase away her lingering anxiety.

Ratna held Isalie at arm's length and looked her over with a broad smile. "No injuries to report?" She glanced behind Isalie at Jentien, and her eyes narrowed as she scrutinized her scarred work. "What happened?"

"A Gloom beast," Jentien answered. Released from her mother's grasp, Isalie watched Savar shake Jentien's hand as he frowned at the gashes in their handiwork. He embraced Jen as warmly as he had Isalie, and slapped Jen on the back a few times. "It would have killed me if not for Iz. She was amazing."

Ratna turned her narrowed eyes on her daughter. "I thought you said you weren't going to be involved this time," she said. Isalie shriveled at the accusation and disappointment in her mom's voice.

"I couldn't help it," Isalie replied. Her voice sounded small and childish, even to her. "He was in trouble."

"Good for you, Izzie," Savar interjected. "You *should* protect your friends." He slammed his huge hand onto Jen's shoulder, who winced.

Ratna cocked an eyebrow, unimpressed. "Isalie, you don't have the skills Jentien does. He trained with the Sentinels for years." She inhaled deeply and closed her eyes, and then pushed the breath out slowly. When she opened her eyes again, she was calmer. "Please, for me, don't put yourself in danger. If you must galavant through the countryside with Jentien, at least be smart about it." She smiled too brightly, and Isalie knew what was coming next, her irritation rising with every word from her mother's mouth. "It would be so much safer if you let us find you a job in the city. There's this lovely new café –"

Isalie stepped back to cut her off. They would *not* have this discussion again. "Mom, you know I don't want to work here. Any restaurant or café is going to want me to cook what they want, *how* they want, and I can't work that way. I can't just fit into a tidy box like you and dad and Jen."

"So you leave the city to find ways to be killed? What's wrong with a box if you're safe?"

Isalie couldn't help but roll her eyes, her temper getting the better of her. *This* was the argument she'd wanted to avoid, and she'd played right into it.

"I wouldn't be able to do this without her, Missus W." Jen put a hand on Isalie's shoulder, and Isalie scowled to hide the flush in her cheeks. Her mother's direct stare told her she hadn't missed it.

"Jentien, you are perfectly capable of running headlong into danger on your own." Ratna paused, and then touched Jentien on the shoulder, and her face softened as she continued. "Not that we wouldn't be devastated if something happened to you, too. I wish *both* of you would find something less dangerous to do. Settle down in the city so we could see you more often." Isalie didn't miss the significant glance her way when she said, 'settle down.'

"You know this place is yours when you want it," Savar added. "And you'd have something to keep you when we pass."

"Dad, I'm not going to argue with you again." Isalie huffed. She was happy to be home and have a bed to sleep in, but did they have to have this argument every time she walked into a room with either of them?

Savar held his hands up in defeat and shook his head, obviously disappointed. Isalie felt a twinge of regret, but kept her mouth shut. Ratna smiled and clapped her hands together before walking toward the back of the store.

"Well," Ratna said, "I have a couple of things to finish, and I'm sure your father has some work he should be doing. You two should go upstairs, have a wash, and get ready for dinner." She stopped and smiled at Isalie. "Izzie, please, let me make something for you for once!"

"Okay, mom," Isalie said as she followed her parents behind the counter and through the doorway. The workshop was packed with leather panels laid out on tabletops, waiting to become sturdy pants. Many more racks with piles of leather in various sizes and thicknesses lined the large space, ready for her parents to shape them.

"Please, baby," her mom insisted as she sat atop a stool at the table. "I'll be done soon. Let me take care of you."

"Okay," Isalie repeated. She smiled at her mom's back, now bent over the table to resume her work.

The bell rang again to announce a customer, and Savar disappeared in the opposite direction. Isalie heard his booming voice call out to someone before she turned to the side and began ascending the stairs that led to the two upper floors of the home she shared with Jen and her parents.

She emerged into the open space that held the living area, kitchen, and dining room. Light streamed through the walls made of floor-to-ceiling windowpanes, shining off the polished wood floors and countertops. She ran her hand over the closest counter, the smooth surface eliciting fond memories of learning how to combine flavors to make something unexpected. The looks on her parents' faces when a dish didn't work out and the delight on Jen's when it did replayed in her head every time she stepped into this bright space. *Her* space.

She followed Jen to the next set of stairs, stopping when she reached the landing that branched into a hallway where the sound of her bootheels was swallowed by the plush violet rug that ran the length. Jen headed left and Isalie paused to watch him open the door to his bedroom before turning right toward her own.

He smiled when he caught her gaze. The smile lit his face, the corners of his eyes crinkling before he walked inside. When his door clicked closed, Isalie sighed as she turned the handle on the room nearest his. He was so close, and yet there was so much space between them.

She closed the door behind her and leaned against it, staring at the sparse décor of her room. The room itself was open and uncluttered, an intentional contrast to the chaos outside her small sanctuary. The chaos of the city, her parents' chaotic clutter in the workshop, and her messy inner chaos about Jen were all so overwhelming that she craved simplicity, and the only place she could control that was here.

She shut the window to keep the noise at bay before dropping her bag on the table next to the bed. Running her fingers over the stamped crest on the flap, she opened it and began to unpack. This, along with the leather bodice and boots she wore, had been gifts from her parents, given alongside Jen's armor, pack, and boots. Gifts to mark their first adventure when Jen became a Sentinel. It seemed like a lifetime ago; she had changed so much in five years.

And so little.

Jentien stood over the copper bathtub, waiting for the water to fill. His eyes unfocused as he let his mind wander for the first time in months. On the road, he was always alert, always aware of the fact that Isalie's safety was his responsibility. He couldn't afford to let his guard down even for a moment, unless they were safe at home.

He glanced out the window to the water tower between the Wylshards' home and several other businesses. A woman stood on a platform near the top to summon an isolated downpour above the tank so the copper pipes could carry the water within to the tanning vats in the workshop and the tub Jen was standing next to. Jentien had always admired the ingenuity of the Ambient. It was the main reason he always cringed when Isalie mentioned how unhappy she felt about the conditions Stills lived in.

The woman outside was conjuring rain to fill a glorified bucket, and she looked *bored* as she leaned against the building, glancing over her shoulder from time to time to check a gauge on the side of the tower that reflected the level of the water inside. He hadn't meant to stare, but the woman noticed him through the window and waved, a smirk on her lips as she took in his bare chest.

Embarrassment flushed his cheeks, and he quickly crossed to the window and pulled the drapes closed. The tub was almost full now, so he closed the valve and pulled on a thick glove. With his hand protected, he reached inside a stone container as a cloud of steam was released and pulled out an innocuous-looking rock about the size of his fist. Even through the thick leather glove the rock began to burn his hand, so he hastily opened the hatch at the base of the tub and thrust it inside.

In moments heat radiated through the metal of the tub, and then steam rose from the surface of the water. Jentien removed his trousers and stepped in, the temperature rising until it was just shy of scalding.

Jentien heaved a heavy sigh, letting his body relax the rest of the way. Letting the warm water work the tension out of his muscles was the best part of coming home. Slightly more enjoyable was the meal he could smell Isalie cooking despite her mother's request. Every homecoming was accompanied by a feast, as if Iz couldn't help but cook everything in sight after surviving on rations. A pot clanged downstairs, Iz cursed the Elders, and Jentien smiled.

He stayed in the water until his fingers pruned and he heard the Wylshards gather in the kitchen. Isalie's voice rose over her mother's, apologizing for cooking without her. Jentien chuckled to himself and stood, letting the water drip from his body before reaching for a thick towel. It was so soft, and so *clean*, unlike his quick washes on the road. It almost made him want to give in to the Wylshards' request to stay in the city.

He hissed when the towel scrubbed against a sore spot on his side and stomach. A livid bruise had formed where the beast's claws had raked through his armor. A bit more pressure and that beast would have eviscerated him. If Isalie hadn't distracted it, he would be dead. He wondered—not for the first time—how many times he would have died if not for Iz.

CHAPTER FIVE

"I DIDN'T KNOW HOW long you would be," Isalie insisted. Her mother's accusatory stare followed her through the kitchen.

"I asked you to wait!" Ratna scowled. Isalie pulled her shoulders up toward her ears while she chopped some vegetables. The smell of roasting chicken filled the room.

"I know!" Isalie chopped the end off a carrot, the impact of the large knife against a wooden board reverberating up her arm.

Her mom huffed once and then walked away toward the large window overlooking the courtyard below. The sun had started to set, and the sky was a fiery blaze fading from orange to red to violet, her mother a shadow against the glare.

Jen appeared, pulling a linen shirt over his head. Isalie watched the white fabric slide over the defined muscles of his abdomen, forgetting to chop the rest of the carrot as they flexed with his movements. When his face appeared and they locked eyes, she brought the knife down *hard* onto her finger, slicing partly through her nail.

Jen stepped up to the kitchen counter and placed his hands on the smooth, dark wood as he leaned toward her. She tried to smile as she examined her finger. Only the nail had been touched, thank the Elders.

"Something smells good," Jen said, smiling. Isalie heard her mother snort in the corner, and then Jentien grimaced when he noticed Isalie cradling her hand. "You okay, Iz?"

Isalie pulled her eyes away from her finger and smiled at him. "Fine. Almost sliced the tip of my finger off, but it's fine. See?" She held her finger up to Jentien. He grasped it in one hand and peeled the sliced nail the rest of the way off.

He smiled at her, and the warmth of it spread through her like a flame engulfing a piece of kindling. "Everything good downstairs?" Jentien asked Ratna.

Ratna took a deep breath and let it out slowly. Isalie's face grew warmer with every moment that the exhalation continued. When Ratna looked up, she smiled, only at Jentien.

"Savar is closing up. I finished early so I could come up here and cook for you two." She turned a pointed stare at Isalie.

"What have you been working on lately?" Jentien asked, distracting Ratna from her irritation with Isalie. "I saw a lot of new pieces."

Isalie let their conversation fade as she focused on cooking, grateful for Jen's intervention on her behalf. She lost track of the conversation about the intricacies of leatherworking. It had always bored her, which was the biggest reason she couldn't bring herself to accept her parents' offer to join them. The other reason was that when she was bored, she was clumsy. Being clumsy in a place with giant vats of tanning leather was dangerous.

As the vegetables finished roasting in the oven, Savar walked in the door. He beamed around the room, but his smile faltered when he saw the look on Ratna's face. He glanced sidelong at Isalie.

"Jentien, why don't you help me set the table?" Savar beckoned. Jentien leapt to action, flashing a conciliatory smile at Isalie. The tension was nothing new, but that didn't make it any less uncomfortable.

Isalie pulled the food from the oven and turned to find her mother offering a platter for serving. "It smells delicious," Ratna whispered. "I'm happy you're home, Izzie."

Isalie smiled. "Me too, Mom."

Jentien and Isalie walked through the courtyard the next morning to take in the sights of the city and buy supplies before they met the Cartographers the following dawn. At the general store, Jentien spoke with a tall and slender woman with gray skin and long pointed ears, asking for directions to the palace district. Jentien answered her, all the while noticing Isalie watching the interaction with her eyes narrowed at the woman.

"What was that about?" Jentien asked when they walked out of the store with arms full of food.

"What?" Isalie asked. "I wasn't paying him three gold Malachs for this. He was charging us tourist prices!"

Jentien chuckled. "Not that, Iz. You were looking at that woman like she was about to stab me."

"She definitely wanted to do *something* to you," Isalie muttered, rolling her eyes at him.

He frowned, confused. "Ask for directions?"

"No, Jen. You really think she wanted directions to the palace district?" She looked around the street, exasperated. "We're *in* the palace district. The palace is in plain view. I think what she really wanted was to mount you in the middle of the courtyard."

"Women can be friendly without wanting, uh... that." Jentien flushed, embarrassed by Isalie's candor. "Look at us." He gestured back and forth between them. "We've been friends for most of our lives, but that's all it is."

Isalie pursed her lips, clearly upset, but before Jentien could ask her about it, the expression was gone. "Most women aren't lucky enough to know you like I do," Isalie replied.

Jentien watched her closely while they crossed the courtyard toward home, waiting for her to elaborate, but she didn't. She glanced at him out of the corner of her eye, but still didn't say anything. He opened his mouth to reassure her, but Iz rushed away in the direction of the notice board.

It stood in the center of the courtyard, surrounded by a garden of wildflowers and several benches. Pieces of parchment were tacked over one another announcing events for the neighborhood, official edicts from the Malachi, and job postings for Sentinels and common mercenaries alike. Isalie pointed at a fresh parchment at the top of the board, newer than the rest.

"I'm worried about this job," she said. The skin between her brows wrinkled when she frowned, a clear sign of her unease. "One hundred gold Malachs is a *lot* of money, but people go missing on these trips, even in the presence of the Ambient escorts." She looked away from the board at him. "Are you *sure* you want to do this?"

"A few days ago, you were encouraging me not to miss it," he reminded her.

She nodded as she glanced at the notice again. "Only to keep you from running headlong into more danger," she said. "I know how important this is to you, after your parents."

Jentien frowned, and Isalie's eyes softened in that empathizing way she had. It was enough to remind him that he wasn't alone, but not enough to break down the walls he put up to contain his pain. He'd always appreciated that about her.

"No one should run afoul of a Gloom, and if I have a chance to help the people of Vortheim, I'm going to take it."

Isalie sighed, and Jentien felt the tension between them fall away when she smiled. Relief washed over him as she put the disagreement aside.

"I'm just glad they agreed to me joining you. I'm not sure they'd have accepted a cook if you hadn't insisted."

"Don't worry, Iz," Jentien said. "I wouldn't go anywhere without my partner."

CHAPTER SIX

JENTIEN FOLLOWED ISALIE INSIDE the Wylshards' store after their shopping was complete later in the morning, and smiled when Savar touched Isalie's shoulder in passing. Savar turned to face Jentien as soon as Iz disappeared into the back of the shop with a stern expression that halted Jentien in his tracks.

"You're leaving tomorrow," Savar said.

Jentien nodded as his stomach dropped, filling with dread. Savar was a head taller than Jentien, muscular, and fierce when he needed to be, but Jentien had always felt at home here, part of the family. Hearing the harsh tone in Savar's voice directed at him for the first time was more terrifying than facing any Gloom beast.

"I'm proud of you, Jentien," Savar said. "You've found a noble purpose. Isalie shouldn't be out there with you, but I respect her, and I know her well enough to see that she can't be happy here. Not now, not without you."

Jentien remained silent, pinned in place by Savar's intense gaze.

"My girl has a good head on her shoulders. You'll make sure it stays that way, right Jentien?"

"Of course, Mr. W. I would never let anything happen to her."

"Of course not," Savar replied, his voice carefully even. He put a hand on Jentien's shoulder. "You would sacrifice your life for hers. But are you protecting her heart?"

Jentien's brow furrowed. Her heart? "What-"

Ratna's raised voice calling from the workshop interrupted his question. "Jen! Come here so I can fit this armor to you!" Savar let go of his shoulder, dismissing Jentien.

Jentien stared at Savar until Ratna called him again, and Savar nodded toward the workshop without turning around. "You should go before she gets upset. She's worked hard on that armor, and you don't have much time."

"All right," Jentien said, letting his words trail off as he struggled for something to say to Savar after that strange exchange. *Protect Isalie's heart?* he thought. *What does that mean?*

He walked through the door of the workshop and found Ratna standing next to her worktable with an array of new leather pieces. Ratna smiled at him and gestured to the armor.

"It's a good thing I finished this last week," she said. She ran her fingers over the gray-brown surface. The pieces of boiled leather were articulated, layered over one another from top to bottom, with extra pieces riveted over the pectorals. It was laid out with the chest piece tied at one end so the two halves would lie flat. Jentien touched the shoulder plates next to the chest piece as Ratna brought out matching greaves and vambraces.

"These should serve you well," she said, beaming with pride. "I've reinforced parts of the chestpiece, greaves, and vambraces with thin steel plates. Hopefully, that should keep you better protected, but it will be heavier, so you'll need to get used to it."

"Ratna, this is spectacular! How long have you been working on this?" A thrill of excitement coursed through Jentien. This was the finest thing he had ever owned.

"About a year now," she said. "It's taken a while to gather enough material, and I needed some help from the smith in town for the plates." She shrugged. "She owed me a favor for all the times I've sent people her way."

Jentien hugged Ratna, overwhelmed by her generosity and thoughtfulness. "Thank you so much," Jentien said, tears pricking his eyes.

"We love you, Jen," Ratna said as she pulled back and wiped a tear from his cheek. "We want to keep you safe. And if you're safe, Izzie is safe, so, if you think about it, it's really a gift for me."

Jentien laughed. He was so lucky to have a family like this.

"She's been keeping this secret for a while." Isalie's voice called out from behind a screen at the far end of the room. Jentien saw one of her arms pop out from behind the partition before she walked out, looking down at the bodice she was tying. "I'm just glad I don't have to keep it from you anymore."

Isalie looked up, and the blue dye marbling the gray-brown leather made her eyes look like the clearest blue of a cloudless sky. She blew a few strands of blonde hair out of her face and lifted her eyes to Jentien's.

Her cheeks were flushed, probably from the frustration of lacing up a new bodice. It fitted her like a glove, shaping her figure slightly into a wide hourglass to accentuate her small waist.

For the first time, Jentien saw her as a woman, not just his friend Isalie. She wasn't the statuesque beauty that her mother was. Isalie was a woman who took care of herself, a delight to be around, someone who made him laugh, who kept him strong. She was always there for him.

She patted her bosom, and Jentien chuckled as he could practically read the thoughts running through her head, ensuring there wouldn't be too much mobility if she had to run again.

Isalie's cheeks flushed when she noticed him staring, so Jentien looked down at the armor laid out on the table again, trying to hide his own reddening cheeks. "Is that new, Iz?" He pointed in her direction without looking up, even though he couldn't get the sight of her out of his mind.

"Yes, Mom made it from the same Gloom beast hide as your armor."

"I've had a lot from traders lately," Ratna said. "It seems more and more beasts are wandering out of the storms."

"More reason for Jentien and I to get out there and help," Isalie said. Jentien looked up to find her smiling at him, and his chest fluttered with pride. He knew she didn't like how dangerous his work was, but she went out regardless. She was one of the bravest people he knew.

"What do you think, Jen?" Isalie held her arms up to her sides to show off the leather bodice and pants.

"How do they feel?" Ratna asked, walking around Isalie, tugging a lace to straighten the bodice.

"Good," Isalie replied with a smirk. "Like they were made for me."

"Very funny," Ratna said. She tucked a bit of hair behind Isalie's ear. "They were, in fact, made for you."

"You look great, Iz," Jentien replied, his blush spreading to his ears, now.

Isalie's cheeks reddened more, too. She looked away like she was embarrassed, but she had a pleased smile on her face. It was so endearing, and Jentien felt a strange flutter in his stomach. He'd never felt that before, like he couldn't quite catch his breath until he looked away from her.

Ratna cleared her throat. "Well, we should get this fitted." She turned to Jentien. "When and where do you leave?"

Jentien replied. "From the north gate at dawn."

Ratna nodded. "Then we'd better get to work. Hold your arms out."

Ratna released him at dusk, after several alterations. Now, Jentien strode toward the edge of the city, through the glowing streets and the dark tunnel until his boots hit the muddy lanes of the refugee camp outside Lacorsia's main walls. The smell of churned earth, rotting wood, and unwashed bodies hit him like it always did, as if he'd been struck by lightning.

His hands balled into fists and he clenched his jaw as the rest of his body tensed. He couldn't stand being here, but he couldn't stay away. Not when so many were suffering. Not when he had something to give that could help.

He tried not to glance in the open doors that he passed, knowing that he would see people huddled around meager lights, sharing what meals they could scrounge up. Jentien couldn't remember the city he'd been born in, but amongst the scattered memories of his parents were remnants of the stories they told of their life before the Gloom had come. In Lacorsia, they were refugees, but once they'd been wealthy, and comfortable, and safe.

The temple loomed ahead, its stone and crystal walls lit by torch sconces on either side of the wide doors. Jentien strode past the tall statue in the small courtyard and inside to the humid confines lit by hundreds of candles.

A priestess stood near the altar on the west side, her hands clasped before her and her head tilted back and her eyes closed in silent prayer. Jentien didn't say anything when he approached, but waited until she brought her head down and turned her pupilless eyes his way.

Her hair was long and wavy, a pale green with bits of twine braided into it. Her skin was ivory, with a subtle glow, and her canine teeth were elongated into fangs. Jentien bowed when she faced him, his pulse increasing every moment he stood in the still air.

"The Elders have granted you a safe journey, I see," she said in a rasping voice.

Jentien nodded and detached the heavy purse from his belt, holding most of his earnings from the past few months out to her. "They did," he replied. "I've come to make a donation to the refugee fund." He only kept what he needed to contribute to the household, or resupply when it wasn't covered by the Sentinels. The rest of his money, for as long as he'd earned it, had gone to the people living outside the walls of Lacorsia.

He hoped it would help another child like him.

She smiled and took the purse from him. "As always, your efforts on behalf of the people are welcome, and most appreciated. This will feed many."

Jentien bowed again, turned on his heel, and rushed out of the temple. His memories of the pain he'd experienced the day the priestess had told him of his parents' deaths gripped him, leaving him gasping as he raced into the tunnel. It wasn't until he made it back to the dark streets of the Palace District that he could take a deep breath again.

When night fell, Isalie walked out of the shop on her own, heading out of the quiet din of elegant diners at the tables of open-air cafés in the Palace District. By comparison, the rest of the city, the poorer sections, were a hive of life and light. With taller, closer buildings, the lower streets were flooded with bright Ambient lanterns in a variety of colors, bathing the stone façades in rainbows.

Isalie made her way through the crowd of refugees lining the streets with their hands out. More Stills flocked to Lacorsia every day, and while the sight of so many sitting in the filthy street was shocking, she knew that these were the lucky ones. The rest were packed into the squalor outside the city gates, waiting for the possibility of a day when they, too, might have the luxury of being herded like cattle being led to slaughter.

She stopped at a stall and smiled at the woman placing a scarred wooden cup full of fragrant food in front of her. Isalie placed a handful of gold Malachs on the scarred wooden surface.

"Elders Blessings upon young Wylshard," the woman said in a deep graveled voice. "It's been weeks since I've seen you. Tell me, what did you make while you were gone?"

Isalie smiled wider and took a pewter spoon from a basket next to where the coins sat. "Dakai," Isalie said in greeting, and sniffed the cup warming her hand. She caught the scent of mango, cumin, chili, and onion wafting up from between the pomegranate seeds atop the fried chutney and potato pieces. "Nothing as delicious as this smells! Though I did make something with some melon and dried meat..."

Between bites she described the meal she'd prepared, along with a few others from their most recent travels. Dakai made appreciative noises while she cooked.

Isalie finished as a flute and drum started behind her. A singer joined the first two, his melody mingling with the voices all around, drawing a crowd that tapped their feet and nodded along.

"Isalie," Dakai called. She gazed at the street beyond the musicians, to the refugees beginning to gather around the joyful sound that brought a smile to many haggard faces, and then pointedly swept the pile of coins into a basket that she tucked beneath the table. "On behalf of these lost souls, I thank you. The Elders smile upon your generosity."

CHAPTER SEVEN

Isalie yawned, walking behind Jentien through the streets before dawn the next morning. Along the main road there were no signs of the people she knew were sleeping on the cobblestones just around the corner. It was a beautiful façade of a sparkling city hiding the desperate truth so many lived with.

She stumbled over a high cobblestone at the edge of a ring of orb light and caught her footing as she emerged from the darkness into another lit section of the street. Jentien didn't have any trouble with the changing light; he moved with such confidence and grace that Isalie couldn't remember the last time he'd stumbled. She admired the way he moved, rotating his right shoulder beneath his new pauldrons, rolling his shoulders to adjust his pack while stepping over a drain without having to look at his feet. Isalie watched him, and then snagged the toe of her boot in the same drain.

Jentien spared her a glance and a smile as they approached the gate separating them from the dark maw of the tunnel. Orbs lit the way intermittently with Ambient light, but the spaces between were black voids. Jen stepped in front of her, blocking it from view before Isalie could panic. "Just hold my hand and stay close," he told her. "Close your eyes if it's better, and we'll be through before you know it."

Isalie nodded, not trusting her voice as she closed her eyes. The familiar rise of panic churned in her stomach and tightened in her chest. She tried and failed to keep her breathing even. Isalie felt Jen's fingers brush against hers, and she clutched his hand tight to her chest like it was the only thing tethering her to the ground. When his soft lips touched her forehead in a gentle kiss, she froze.

Isalie's eyes popped open, all fear forgotten as Jentien smiled down at her. "I'll keep you safe, Iz, even from your fear. Close your eyes."

Isalie felt a different flutter in her stomach now. *He just kissed me.* It wasn't the first time. It likely wasn't the last, though it wasn't what she longed for every moment of every day. But she was grateful, no matter the context.

She allowed Jentien to pull her forward and shut her eyes before the tunnel's mouth could swallow her whole. She pressed tight to Jentien's back, feeling the hard leather plates on her cheek. It was an uncomfortable, clumsy, and slow walk, but Jentien didn't rush her. He just strode steadily toward the other end of the tunnel.

After what seemed like an eternity, Isalie heard and felt the rumble of Jentien's deep voice. "We're clear, Iz. You can open your eyes."

The Outer City surrounded her, the same small homes and dirt roads, the same pall of desperation and grief hanging like a cloud over everyone they passed. Even this early, Stills lined up at the small gates to enter the inner city for their days of work. In the distance, Isalie spotted the large crystal outer wall, just beginning to grasp the light as the sun rose into the sky.

Their path led them past an old stone and crystal temple as tall as the outer wall and weathered from disuse. No one knew who the temple was originally built for or how long ago it had been built, but it was something of a shrine for the Stills who came to Lacorsia, whether they stayed for a day or the rest of their lives. This was the only temple in Vortheim that was not dedicated to the Malachi or the Six Elders, though the priestess that kept it from falling into disrepair worshipped the Elders.

The reason Isalie loved it caught the sunlight, refracting it into a thousand rainbows. A statue of a woman with her hands raised to the sky, her face up-turned as if watching for the first sign of rain from a dark cloud or the first rays of sunlight to break through the dark night, was so exquisitely detailed that she looked like she might step off her pedestal at any moment.

Every time she passed this way, Isalie stopped for a moment to admire the woman depicted in the statue. Something drew her forward, like the woman was calling her, asking her to brush her fingers over the cool crystal. A shiver passed down her spine when they did.

It felt like something was about to change.

Isalie looked up, past the woman's flowing hair to the clouds above them. They swarmed across the sky, dark and heavy, heralding rain.

"Isalie, I can see them. We're late."

Isalie pulled her hand from the statue and followed Jentien, sparing one last look over her shoulder, wondering what it was trying to tell her.

The uniforms of the Ambient stood out amongst the rest of the group assembled around a large carriage outside the northern gate. The crest of the Malachi was emblazoned on a leather vest of her mother's design, dyed black, with the silver mountain outlining a dragon's wing shaped into the letter 'M.' Leather pants and boots dyed the same black, with silver buckles, gave them an air of severity even the rest of the guard couldn't match.

"Wylshard leather," Isalie said as they came close. The slender Ambient figure with short brown hair, teal skin, and silver irises glanced at her like she was a fly buzzing around their head. Isalie smiled nervously. "I'm glad to see the Ambient are putting it to good use." She waited for a response, but the Ambient looked away.

A brawny woman with cool sepia skin and a short black afro stepped between them, an awkward smile on her face as she held her hand out to Isalie. "Thank you for coming…?"

"Isalie," she replied as she took the proffered hand, relieved after her cool reception from the Ambient. The woman's cloak billowed in a cool breeze that wafted the scent of looming rain. Isalie spotted the crest of the Malachi on her grey cloak outlined by the color of blank parchment. The sigil of the Cartographer's Guild.

"Cerys of the Cartographer's Guild," the woman said, smiling warmly at Isalie. "I'm excited to have a cook with us; otherwise it'd be up to the rest of us." She slid her eyes to the Ambient and the other guards milling around. "Between you and me, we're all pretty terrible at it."

A thrill of pleasant excitement shot through Isalie. *Someone sees me,* she thought. Her grip on Cerys's hand lasted too long, but she was so grateful to be part of the team that she couldn't release her eager grasp.

"Pleasure to meet you," Isalie said. Cerys's smile drooped as Isalie still hung on. Isalie chuckled and dropped her hand before gesturing Jentien forward to introduce himself.

"Jentien Themori and Isalie Wylshard, reporting to the expedition," Jentien said.

"Very formal," Cerys replied with a smirk. "He's going to be a handful, isn't he?" she asked Isalie. Isalie laughed, and the Ambient frowned at her. "Don't mind Yoqua over there," Cerys said, nodding in the Ambient's direction. "They don't want to leave the city. Something about missing the event of the season."

Isalie and Jentien looked at Yoqua, who ignored them and turned back to Cerys.

"We'll try not to bother them," Isalie said.

"You're obviously the muscle," Cerys said, looking Jentien over. "That's wonderful armor, a Wylshard original? I didn't know she worked with metal."

Isalie's heart swelled with pride. "Ratna is my mother," she said. "She made this just for Jentien."

Cerys whistled, impressed. "I hope you don't have cause to break it in on this expedition. We'll be mapping the Northeastern Glooms. If all goes well, it will be a six-month trip. If not, we have you to help, Jentien Themori. Well, shall we be off?" She turned as the rest of the group assembled around them.

Another cartographer stepped forward wearing the same cloak as Cerys, followed by a few armored people sporting the insignia of the Lacorsia guard. Yoqua climbed inside the enclosed carriage without a word and gestured for Cerys and the other cartographer to follow.

Two of the guards climbed onto the top of the carriage. The other guard hopped inside the carriage and closed the door, leaving Isalie standing nearby, wondering where she should board.

Jentien didn't hesitate, just grabbed each of their bags and climbed up the ladder attached to the rear of the carriage and secured them with the others. When he was back on the ground, he plopped down on the bench he'd used to mount the ladder, just wide enough for the two of them to sit if they squeezed together, and patted the open space next to him.

"Join me," Jentien said. He offered a hand to Isalie as she eyed the bronze rails to either side. It seemed such a meager safeguard against being flung off the carriage.

"Thanks," she said as she took his hand and wedged herself as far back as she could manage. Their thighs pressed tight against one another, and Isalie closed her eyes, savoring the feeling as Jen shifted back and forth, trying to get comfortable with his stiff new armor.

"This should be interesting," Jentien said. The carriage lurched forward and Isalie almost fell, but Jentien held an arm out to keep her from tumbling into the dirt.

"Thanks for catching me," Isalie said. She tightened her grip on the rail.

"Always," Jentien replied.

CHAPTER EIGHT

Jentien and Isalie hung onto the back of that carriage every day for two weeks, twisting and turning along the road behind two massive horses. Their arms were sore from constantly clutching the rails as they bumped along the cobbled streets close to the city, and the agonizing rough roads a week later.

The land rose steeply from the delta that Lacorsia occupied to a vast plain of tall grasses, thick bushes, and bare trunks beneath wide canopies of green, tough leaves. The ocean was a sparkling gem in the distance, far below the cliffs they now found themselves traveling along. Each night they stopped in a new town, along a chain of communities clustered within trading distance of the capital, availing themselves of the inns before they traveled away from civilization and were forced to sleep rough.

The luxurious beds weren't enough to ease their pain, no matter how many inns they stayed in. It was exorbitant, in Jentien's opinion, but he supposed it was the normal course when traveling with the Guild, especially with an Ambient in their group. And even if Isalie still provided meals throughout their days of travel, she was being treated to food that could have been served in the palace when they stopped for the night. He couldn't get enough of watching the pure joy on her face whenever she tasted something new.

In each village Isalie bought supplies for the journey ahead, bargaining with the wealthier merchants like she always did for the best deals, using the Malachs provided by the Cartographers. With what she saved, she paid refugees for small trinkets that they offered, to help them arrive at Lacorsia's gates with money to survive. Along with the dried meat, nuts, and fruits that the locals provided, she now had a wood carving of Uonna, the Elder of nature and balance, a tarnished ring from an old man, and a bracelet woven from small strips of bark by a young man. Cerys never questioned the amount she spent, and Isalie was careful to buy things that she could easily carry and hide.

He couldn't help but watch her, the shy woman he'd grown up with comforting people, laughing with them, and pressing gold coins into their hands. Pride swelled in his chest when Iz gave him a wider bracelet with the same pattern as hers, blushing above a shy smile.

After the first two weeks, civilization faded. Outlying cities and small towns along the cliffside rose into a rockier landscape further inland, where hills and plateaus dominated the horizon. They were constantly buffeted by hot, dry winds, and Jentien's armor felt like an oven. Another few days, and the comfort of the inns became a distant memory as they neared the location of the first Gloom.

The carriage halted, and Cerys climbed out after Yoqua. The pair stared at the Gloom in the distance while the carriage drivers cared for the horses and the junior cartographer unfurled the map to take notes. Jentien slid from the bench, and Isalie grumbled as she followed, arching her back.

"The Gloom looks like it's in the same position as was charted on the last expedition," Cerys said. Jentien wandered closer with Isalie in tow. "Can you feel a difference, Yoqua?"

Yoqua closed their eyes as they faced the Gloom, arms aloft, palms forward. The group waited in silence for a long time, until Yoqua spoke, their voice low and rasping. "It is as described. Stable, though I feel quite a few beasts have been caught within recently."

Cerys nodded while her assistant scribbled with a charcoal pencil. "On to the next?"

"I didn't know the Ambient could feel things about the Gloom," Iz whispered to Jentien. She sighed and stretched her back again. "I wish we could take a turn on those comfortable seats inside," she muttered. They watched everyone pile into the carriage and shut the door.

"Me too," Jentien said.

They stopped twice more in the next week to survey smaller Gloom formations, all of which seemed stable and stationary according to Yoqua and Cerys. It was a relief, since Jentien had spent the past few years protecting people from these things. He only wished Yoqua could do more than sense whether they'd changed.

Jentien stared at the looming dark cloud in the distance, Ambient light flashing within, when they stopped to camp a day's travel from the next Gloom on the list. A steaming bowl sat in his hands, and he brought the spoon mechanically to his mouth, not tasting whatever Isalie had given him, brooding over the problem. If the Ambient could feel how the Gloom worked, *why* couldn't they do anything about it?

He hadn't realized he'd spoken his thoughts aloud until Cerys spoke to him. "It's not as simple as that, Master Themori," she said. "Many have tried, and most of those have lost their lives. Those that didn't? They were forever changed. Not even the Malachi himself can do anything about the Gloom, and he is the most powerful Ambient in Vortheim, possibly Celuthia."

"There must be something the Ambient could do," Jentien insisted, looking at Yoqua, who held his gaze with a contemptuous glare. "The Ambient can change the world, can't they?"

Yoqua set their bowl on the ground and sighed heavily. "There is much the Ambient can do, but this problem is beyond even our skill to master. I will put this as plainly as I am able, so that you can understand." Isalie scoffed, but Yoqua ignored her. "Everything is connected through the Ambience, every living thing, every changing season, even death itself. If we somehow were able to just *change* the Gloom, what else would be affected? Would there be a backlash that created a drought for hundreds of years? Or a storm that destroyed the eastern coast, or obliterate every living thing in Vortheim?"

They waited, and Jentien realized that they were waiting for him to answer the question. He glanced around, noticing everyone's eyes on him except Isalie's, because she was scowling at Yoqua. "I don't know," he finally replied.

Yoqua rewarded him with a simpering smile. "Of course you don't," they sneered. "More importantly, *no one* does, not even the Ambient, not even after all our years of study. Which, as Cerys pointed out, has destroyed many minds finer than yours."

"We *Stills* don't know much about the Gloom at all," Isalie interjected, "because we aren't allowed to know more than what the Ambient tell us." She had that glint in her eye that usually meant she was about to say something she shouldn't. "Maybe if the Ambient were more forthcoming about what we all face, we wouldn't understand so little about it."

Yoqua's eyebrows raised as if shocked that she would speak. Jentien's fingers went to the pommel of his sword before he realized it, and a small shock ran through him when he realized that if Yoqua decided to punish Iz for her comments, he wouldn't hesitate to intervene.

Cerys smiled and waited for Yoqua to answer. When they did, there was a small smile on their face, and Jentien thought he detected a note of admiration in their voice, rather than condescension.

"That is a fair point well made. We Ambient get our power from the Ambient Pool, the source of all life in Celuthia. It is the raw creation energy of our world, if you will. And these Glooms," they gestured to the cloud beginning to blend in with the shadows cast as the sun set, "are made of that energy, but somehow changed. Research suggests that an Ambient powerful enough could funnel that energy back into the Pool, but we don't know what that would do to the Ambience as a whole. And we fear that it would alter everything as we know it, perhaps to the point of destroying our world."

"For now," Cerys said, "we watch and wait. And hope that we don't need to intervene."

Jentien released the grip on his sword. "What can an Ambient do, if the Gloom were to encroach on a town?"

Yoqua shook their head. "There isn't much that we *can* do. Evacuate the area, hope that the Gloom moves on so we can get people back to their homes."

"That's why there are so many in Lacorsia's outer city," Cerys said. "People leave their homes with what they can carry, and some never return."

CHAPTER NINE

THE NEXT DAY THEY rolled closer and closer, and Isalie frequently leaned around the side of the carriage to catch a glimpse of the Gloom. She despised having her back toward it; it felt too much like knowing something dangerous stood behind her, and she was just letting it come. This Gloom was larger than the others, stretching higher into the sky like it was trying to join the clouds above. Light flashed inside the darkness as she watched, and to Isalie it seemed more violent than the others she'd seen.

When they stopped, Cerys and Yoqua frowned at it. Isalie had watched them closely over the past few weeks and hadn't seen anything like the concern that was plain on their faces as they observed this cloud, so she sidled closer to hear their conversation.

"...grown?" Cerys asked. "The shape of it is wrong; it doesn't comply with my notes."

Yoqua grumbled, palms out as they probed the Gloom. "It doesn't feel like the others, either. There is something new here, which would account for the increasing number of disappearances reported."

"Disappearances?" Isalie asked.

"Olunei is beyond the Gloom," Cerys said, ignoring her. "It is a large city, but it was cut off from the rest of Vortheim some thirty years ago. My records indicate that a contingent of Ambient was sent to aid the evacuation and were caught in it as well. We have had no contact since they were lost."

"Perhaps they survived, and were able to hold it back somehow?" Yoqua suggested, frowning. "If that is the case, it *could* account for the change. I have a hard time believing that, since it's never been done before."

"I thought you said that was impossible?" Isalie said, unable to contain herself. If someone could do it here, why couldn't they do it all over Vortheim?

"It is more *likely*," Yoqua emphasized the word, "that the nature of the Gloom has changed over time. Olunei had some crystalline construction, yes?"

Cerys nodded as she flipped through her notes. "Minor alterations to the city walls, and a natural supply to work with. One of the Ambient...Zaraia Kiyash is her name..." Cerys looked up, "had a talent for natural materials, and was one of our foremost researchers into protection against the Gloom. She was sent with the others to lead the construction of crystal barriers to aid in the evacuation. Is there anything specific that you can tell me about the change? What is it doing?"

Yoqua furrowed their brows as they concentrated. "There's something strange about the clouds above. They seem to be mingling with the Gloom, but I can't see whether this has any effect on either." They let their arms drop and turned to Cerys. "Kiyash was a force of nature in the academy. We can only hope she and the others were able to find a way to shelter against the effects of the Gloom."

Rain pattered on the dry ground around them as the grey clouds darkened above their heads. Isalie pulled the hood of her cloak up before the rain could make her hair into a frazzled mess.

"It seems the Gloom is beginning to move," Yoqua said. Cerys looked up and started to back toward the carriage with Yoqua.

Isalie followed her gaze to find the grey clouds fading to black, as if the normal cloud was an extension of the Gloom. Cerys gasped, and Isalie wondered whether the Gloom *could* mingle with the weather. If it could, they were already beneath it.

"Everyone back to the carriage!" Cerys shouted, the clear note of panic in her voice sparking Isalie's. The drivers looked toward the Gloom, dropped the buckets of water they offered to the horses, and ran to their seats. Isalie scrambled after Cerys and Yoqua.

"What is it?" Isalie shouted as she ran. Jentien hopped onto the back of the carriage and held out a hand for her.

"The Gloom is moving! We need to go!" Cerys slammed the door shut and someone pounded on the roof of the carriage.

Isalie hopped up next to Jentien and almost fell when the carriage lurched forward. The horses screamed and ran at a full gallop. Jentien clutched Isalie's waist to keep her on the bench with him.

The wind howled as a gale kicked up dirt and flattened the tall grass. The sky was as dark as twilight, but a strange orange glow grew and grew, reminding Isalie of a smoke-filled sky after a wildfire. But this was something different. Many colors refracted through the sky like the prismatic sheen in the Glooms, advancing toward them through the grey clouds like fingers stretching out to snatch them up.

The rain began to pour, and Isalie hissed when a drop hit the back of her hand. Her skin blistered as it burned, and another ate through the cloth of her light linen shirt. A cry of pain from the drivers split the air. "Jen," Isalie said as he turned his face upward. Isalie pushed the top of his head to force his eyes away. "The rain is burning me, cover your eyes!"

"*Ah!*" Jentien cried. A large drop ran down his cheek, leaving a streak of red, blistered skin.

Isalie held her free hand over Jentien's face to shield him from the rain just as the clouds opened, unleashing a downpour over them. Isalie's lungs burned when she inhaled, and everywhere the rain touched cloth, it singed away as if a flame had been held to it.

Lightning shot through the sky and slammed into the ground near the terrified, pained horses. They screamed and kicked into a frantic gallop the next moment when thunder boomed, shaking the ground. Isalie slipped in her seat, but Jentien hauled her backward, half onto his lap. She wrapped her other arm around the back of his neck. Jentien strained to hold his rail as both of their exposed hands sizzled. "Cerys, we need help! Stop the carriage!"

They didn't stop. Isalie's hand was covered in blisters, the burning sensation so intense that it felt like she was holding it in a fire. But she couldn't leave Jentien's head exposed, and she couldn't get his hood up with the carriage tossing them about.

They hit a bump and Isalie felt her body leave the seat. She arced through the air before slamming into the ground, rolling through the mud. She shrieked, her skin coated, but the rain was a deluge that washed the mud from her exposed face. Isalie flipped onto her stomach and tucked her arms beneath her body. She managed to lift her head, searching for Jen, for the carriage, for anyone. She caught sight of the carriage in the distance, canted up at an angle on the right wheels only before it crashed down and the screaming horses pulled it deeper into the dark cloud and out of sight. In the opposite direction, Jentien screamed, writhing on the ground in pain.

"Jen!" she shrieked as she scrambled to her feet. Her ankle buckled, barely capable of holding her upright, but she ran despite the pain. She lunged and spread her body over Jentien's head to protect him from the rain.

"Are you all right?" she asked. Blisters covered Jen's face and neck, and his hands were bloated and raw. He blinked the water out of his reddened eyes, blood mixing with his tears.

"No, Iz. Where's the carriage?"

"It's gone, Jen. I don't know what to do." Isalie sobbed. The open grassland provided no cover, and their only hope of escape was gone.

"We have to get out of here," Jentien grunted. He started to stand, but Isalie pushed him down.

"If we stand up, you'll be exposed again."

"We'll both die if we don't try something," he insisted. "Let's go." He sat up, pulling Isalie with him. They ran.

Isalie searched for tracks the carriage should have left behind, but there were none. They had no choice but to run headlong away from the Gloom. It was too fast, and they were surrounded by searing rain and flashing light. Lightning struck the ground nearby, and the scent of ozone overwhelmed the smell of blood filling her nose.

Another bolt slammed into the ground in front of them, and they skidded to a halt while the air hummed around them. Isalie scrambled to keep Jentien's slick hand in hers, but her ankle gave out and she fell to one knee. Her skin prickled, and another bolt illuminated the cloud around them, just before it lanced through her.

Jentien screamed as Isalie went still. "Iz! No!"

He fell to his knees, pulling her into his lap. Her body was charred, and when he pressed his ear to her steaming chest, he didn't hear a breath or a heartbeat.

"Don't die! Elders, please don't let her die!" He slammed a hand down on her chest above her heart. "Come on, Iz!" he screamed. He hadn't been afraid like this since he was a child, but this was worse than when he realized that his parents weren't coming home. It swelled in his chest, threatening to choke him as his fist slammed into her chest again. And again.

He wouldn't survive if he lost her.

"Iz, don't leave me!" Hot tears ran down his cheeks. His fist came down again, and she gasped in a ragged breath. "Iz!" Sobs of relief tore out of him as he clutched her against his chest. "Iz, thank the Elders. Can you hear me?"

Isalie didn't open her eyes or move anything but her chest as she inhaled. Jentien looked around, trying to find somewhere to take her, but all he saw was the Gloom.

Jentien curled himself around Isalie's unconscious body to shield her from the rain still streaking down his face. He'd take the pain if meant sheltering her from it.

"Iz, I'm sorry," he said. He kissed her head like he had so many times, but this time, it felt different. He'd just brought her back, and he knew they would both lose everything in moments. Their lives flashed before his eyes; Isalie's laugh, the blush in her cheeks, her ferocity and generosity... Every memory was about Iz.

It'd taken him too long to realize what he'd been feeling. What his body had known far longer than his mind. Every blush, every moment when his heart raced in her presence.

He'd be damned if they died before he told her what his heart had been trying to tell him for so long, that he'd been too deaf to hear.

"Iz, I lo–"

A bolt of lightning struck him.

CHAPTER TEN

Am I dead?

Isalie felt weightless, painless. She opened her eyes, expecting nothing but darkness, and was instead greeted by grey. She blinked once, surprised to see a room come into focus. Every surface was grey, even the table next to her bed.

Where am I? Where's Jentien?

She felt so tired. She tried to sit up, but sharp pain stabbed through her temple, and she clutched her head as she laid it back down on the soft pillow.

The door opened, and a man with warm bronze skin and bedraggled shoulder-length white hair stepped inside, his eyes widening for a moment when he noticed her awake.

"How are you feeling?" His voice was monotone as he looked her over.

Isalie's vision blurred when she tried to sit up. "Where is Jentien?"

The man pulled a notebook from a pocket inside the faded gray cloak he wore, leafed through a few pages, and shook his head. "The Ambient found a few bodies in the Gloom, but you were the only survivor."

Isalie tried to calm her breathing, but each deep breath was like a knife to her heart. *Jen's gone. Jen's gone.* The thought repeated, drowning out the sound of the man's voice as he continued to speak. He stopped speaking to stare at her, and she tried to focus on what he was saying again.

"Miss? You need to take a deep breath." He waited, and when Isalie steadied her breathing, he nodded. "Since you're newly arrived to the city, it's my job to ensure you're acclimated."

Isalie blinked. Her head was spinning, trying to reorient around the fact that Jen was gone, and she realized she had no idea where she was.

"Which city?" she asked.

"Olunei."

His answer didn't help her confusion. "That's not possible," she breathed. "It was swallowed by the Gloom."

"You're partially right," the man replied. "Olunei was swallowed, but we survived, thanks to the grace of the Elders and their Ambient." His brow furrowed. "You've fallen victim to the Gloom, and now that you're here..." He trailed off.

"I can't go home?"

"None of us can."

Isalie frowned. No one survived the Gloom. *This must be a nightmare,* she decided. She needed something to shock her awake. "I need to see his body."

The man blew an irritated breath out of his nose. "Any bodies trapped in the Gloom are incinerated to avoid incidents," he looked at his notebook again, "but I can provide a description of them."

Somewhere in her disjointed thoughts, Isalie noted how awful it was that he came with such gruesome information prepared. Rattling off a few descriptions with furtive glances at Isalie, he unknowingly described the guards and the cartographer that had accompanied Cerys. Maybe she and Yoqua had escaped, maybe they'd come back and found Jen...

"...a male body was found with a leather breastplate..."

I need to wake up. She squeezed her eyes shut and pinched her arm, but the room was the same when she opened her eyes. The gray walls seemed to close in on her like the tunnels in Lacorsia. This wasn't a dream, she was trapped. No family and no Jentien, forced to spend the rest of her life in this prison of a city.

"This is your room assignment," he continued, either unaware of Isalie's sorrow or unaffected by it. "Here is a map of the city, and your work assignment. Everyone must earn their keep here, and monitors like me will ensure that if you do, you will be provided with everything you'll need to survive the storm."

He walked away, and Isalie turned her head to see him pause before he left the room. "Welcome to Olunei."

The door closed with a soft click, and Isalie started to cry. She cried until her sobs were dry heaves and she couldn't keep her aching eyes open any longer.

She laid down again, covered her head with the soft blanket, and shook until she fell asleep.

CHAPTER ELEVEN

"Iz!"

Jentien clutched for her body and found nothing but air. The hard ground beneath him was replaced by a soft mattress and cool cotton sheets. The Gloom was nowhere to be seen; he was in a small bedroom with off-white walls, a small table with two chairs atop a lilac rug on the stone floor, and a window with the clear sky beyond.

He surged to his feet, absently noting the lack of pain he'd expected to find over most of his skin as he cast about the room for Isalie. Finding that she wasn't there, he threw himself across the room at the single wooden door and yanked it open hard enough to slam into the wall.

"Iz!" he shouted down the hallway he found outside.

"Elders!" A mousy man in white pants and a loose white shirt trimmed with gold shot to his feet from a small stool a little way down the hall.

Jentien crossed the space between them and clutched the man's shoulder where an unfamiliar gold emblem flashed in the light from a nearby window. "Please, where is Isalie?"

"Wh-who?" the man asked. He swallowed hard, visibly anxious in Jentien's grasp.

Jentien didn't care; he gave the man a small shake. "Isalie Wylshard. Where IS SHE?"

Heavy footsteps preceded a man with black hair appearing at the end of the hall. Jentien locked eyes with him, and read the experience in his assessing gaze, the shift of his feet into a stance ready to charge, and the sword at his hip.

"Ambient Kiyash, do you require assistance?" the man called as he approached.

Jentien froze, but the man in his grasp sucked in a small gasp, and, as if emboldened by the other man's presence, grasped Jentien's hands and sent a jolt of energy through Jentien's arms.

Jentien's body buckled and his heart raced, reminded of the lightning coursing through his body as Isalie slipped away from him. A whimper escaped his lips from the crumpled heap that he became at the Ambient man's feet.

"No, Cortlen, I'm fine," Ambient Kiyash replied shakily. He backed away from Jentien, behind the man named Cortlen.

Jentien's muscles finally stopped tremoring as the other man came to stand over him with a hand on his sword hilt and gazed down with a hard stare, though the corner of his mouth and an eyebrow quirked up in what Jentien thought might be amusement. "I hope you aren't going to assault Suerdis Kiyash again, friend. I'd hate to take you into custody the day after you arrived in our city."

Sitting up carefully, Jentien stared at Cortlen. "Where is Isalie?"

Cortlen's smirk faltered and then disappeared. Some of the light went out of his eyes, as if the mere mention of Isalie had dampened his spirit.

"Were you traveling with someone?" Cortlen asked. He extended his hand.

Jentien took it and allowed Cortlen to help him to his feet. "My friend. Isalie Wylshard. We were caught in the storm..." Desperation and grief choked him as he realized why Cortlen's expression had changed. It was sympathy, and shared grief. Something he'd recognized in the faces of the other refugees surrounding Lacorsia, and in this moment, he couldn't face it.

He shook his head in denial before Cortlen could speak again. *She can't be gone. She was breathing, she was alive...* He sucked in a ragged gasp, which tore like knives through his chest. Any moment he expected them to pierce his heart and kill him. It would be a mercy, if the look on this man's face meant what he thought it did.

"I'm sorry, no one else survived."

Jentien's legs fell out from beneath him. His knees crashed to the stone floor, but the pain was nothing compared to the rending of his spirit.

Iz... no...

Tears streaked down his face, and Cortlen knelt next to him, placing a hand on Jentien's shoulder in support.

"Welcome to Olunei."

Isalie awoke and rolled over, groggy and confused. The blankets tangled around her legs and she kicked, terrified of being trapped for the few seconds it took to free herself.

"Wake up," she called out, surprised that Jen hadn't woken her at dawn. Met with silence, she sighed as she opened her eyes. "Jen, it's time to–" White surrounded her again, and her heart sank as she remembered where she was. She was alone.

The realization hurt more than the first time.

She'd dreamed of him. She'd dreamed he held her in his arms, kissed her forehead, and cried as he told her how much he loved her. It had been a good dream.

But it was just a dream.

She took a deep, shaky breath and pulled herself out of bed. Her muscles ached, her eyes ached from crying, and her heart ached from her loss. *How long have I been here?* she thought. She wandered to the window on the opposite side of the small room and looked out at the city.

Her room was high off the ground—at least four stories from the dour cobbled street below—but the buildings that covered the skyline were taller still. Opaque crystal roofs hung far over the walls, shrouding everything beneath in shadow. Figures darted through the shadows with cloaks over their heads, clustered as far from the open sky as possible.

Isalie looked up, expecting to see the sun, but the light cast throughout the city came from orbs atop crystal towers set at intervals on the perimeter of the buildings. Beyond them, the darkness of the Gloom pushed against the boundary they set.

Rain pattered against the window, and she pulled it open. The moment a drop touched her skin, it burned like the rain outside the Gloom. She hissed as she closed the window the moment before the patter became a pounding downpour.

How can people live this way?

Isalie rubbed at her hand with the sleeve of her white nightgown, which burned through when it soaked up the moisture. She ripped it off, throwing it to the ground before it could burn her again. Looking around the room, she spotted something brown lying atop a white table, and her knees almost buckled. Her leather bodice, pants, and boots were laid out next to a new white shirt, a dark cloak, and an oval piece of leather with crystals affixed to it.

She grabbed the bodice and stroked her mother's mark stamped into the shoulder. *How did this survive?* she wondered. A tear rolled down her cheek, and she swiped it angrily away. She was tired of crying. Instead, she pulled on her clothes and slid her feet into the matching boots. It was a small piece of home, likely the only one she would ever have again.

The thick linen cloak sent a thrill through her fingertips when she ran them over the fabric, just like the things she'd browsed in Ambient Sundries. This cloak was infused with Ambience. *Why would they give me something like this?*

The oval thing was a mystery to her, so she tucked it inside a pocket as the same thrill ran through her fingertips, and swung the cloak over her shoulders.

Striding toward the door, she caught sight of her face in a mirror on the wall and stopped in her tracks. She'd expected to see scars on her face and neck like the mark on her hand, but her skin was clear. Her thin hair stuck up at odd angles, and though she tried to tame it, it wouldn't fall into any semblance of order. So, she tucked it behind her ears and pulled her hood over her head to hide it.

She didn't have anyone to impress, anyway.

I need to get out of here.

Isalie rushed down the narrow hall and staircase and exited the dreary building into the street, unsure of what to do or where to go. She pulled the cloak tight around herself on instinct, but the rain had abated already, as it so often did in Vortheim. She emerged from beneath the overhanging buildings with the map in her hand.

She bumped into someone and started when she looked up into crystalline lenses in a linen hood marred by burn marks. It looked like the same material as the thing in her pocket, though the sheen was gone, as was the sheen on the cloak. Whomever was beneath it stared at her, eyes blinking in open wonder and fear, and then hurried away.

They're hoods, Isalie realized. *The crystal protects their eyes. Clever.* Probably something the Ambient designed to help people live in a place where the sky opened to deliver death every day.

Isalie frowned. *This place is horrible.*

Everyone looked miserable as they rushed through the wet, uneven streets. They all seemed to be running for their lives; was there any room for anything but survival? Isalie wondered how many of these people were like her, forced to live apart from their family because of an incident with the Gloom.

Isalie looked down at the paper in her hands. Written at the bottom in a hasty scrawl was a note about her work assignment, and a line between the building she'd exited and another. When she looked up, she saw an identical edifice to the one behind her.

She wiped a tear from her cheek and kept walking. There was nothing else to do.

CHAPTER TWELVE

Three months.

Three months in Olunei. A bell rang somewhere outside, and Isalie opened her eyes to her dingy room. The only natural light, dim as it usually was, came from the one window that looked out on an alley in constant shadow. The crystal eaves sheltered people from the rain and blocked the light.

Her life was in constant shadow.

Isalie swung her legs out of bed and her feet touched the cold stone floor. She shivered, just like she did every morning. It was always cold here. Her fingers ran through her flyaway hair to gather it into a braid behind her head and tied it with a strip of leather.

She didn't have a mirror, but it didn't matter what she looked like. She was one face in a crowd, just a sad woman among sad people. There had been a few days that her depression had smothered her, keeping her in bed when she should have been working. Those days, the monitors didn't let her eat.

She'd barely managed to get through the next day's shift to earn her ration of gruel and a bit of bread. People disappeared from time to time, and Isalie wondered whether they'd given up to starve in their rooms or given themselves to the rain. Some days, she wondered whether she might become one of them.

Her only comfort was the leather that now slid over her skin. It was a small reminder that she hadn't been alone a few months ago, that someone loved her. The leather was still smooth, untouched by the rain that had eaten through skin and shirts so easily. Isalie pulled on her boots, caressing the maker's mark as she held in her tears. She was so tired of crying.

She pulled a bag over her shoulder that contained her Ambient-made cloak and mask. It rained at some point every day. There was no avoiding the storms.

Her door closed behind her, and she turned the key in the lock before putting it in the bag. There wasn't much to steal; no one earned any gold here because everyone was paid with food and water vouchers, and a place to sleep. Lacorsia had been the same to a certain extent—for the refugees in the outer city, if no one else—but here, shirking responsibilities meant losing the roof over your head, and no new cloak and mask when they inevitably wore out from constant burning rain.

There were other homes here, she knew, for the people who had lived here before the Gloom came, but so many were in disrepair that most people lived in the dormitories now. The crystal roofs meant safety, but they also meant the loss of identity that came with losing your home. In that way, everyone in Olunei was the same. It reminded her of the refugees in Lacorsia, which reminded her of the home she'd lost, and the friend she'd lost.

She stifled more tears, shaking her head in a silent admonishment for the wayward direction of her thoughts. She tried not to think about Jentien if she could help it. His loss was an open wound, and no matter how hard she tried, she couldn't stop tearing it open. She shook her head again, knowing she needed to get something to eat and get to work. If she started crying now, she wouldn't stop, and she'd be late.

Isalie took a deep breath and walked down the dingy, narrow hall to the stairs. Her building housed everyone who had jobs at this time of day, woken by the bells that rang on every story at once. Some of the people packed into the hallway with her chatted, some grumbled, but it was far more subdued than any crowd in Lacorsia.

The foot of the stairs opened onto a long, open room full of tables and benches that served as the meal hall. Many residents were already seated, already shoving gruel into their mouths before starting their workdays.

Isalie could smell the thick liquid already, and almost gagged as she watched congealed masses drop from spoons and mouths. The taste was so disgusting it offended her, no matter that it was nutritional enough to keep people on their feet. It tasted like warm snot, in her opinion. The bread was usually stale, and felt like she was chewing on thick snot when it wasn't.

The line filed past a Still in a gray uniform with a stack of worn rectangles of parchment in their hands. A tall man tried to pass without offering one of the meal vouchers, and the monitor she'd met on her first day put a hand out to stop him.

"Meal voucher," the monitor demanded.

The man glared for a moment before trying to shove past the monitor. The line moved backward, pushing Isalie into the person behind her, making her clutch her own voucher tighter. Another monitor appeared to restrain the man, but he surged forward, sending the people still in line ahead of him tumbling. Food trays clattered to the ground as he launched over the counter and ripped a bowl out of a stunned server's hands.

He gulped as much gruel as he could before three Ambient Guard swarmed him and slammed him to the ground behind the counter. Servers backed away when they lifted him bodily off the floor and hauled him toward the back of the common room.

"Fucking Ambient!" the man screamed. "I just want some food!"

A distant door slammed, leaving the common room in silence until people started to move. Kitchen staff tidied the mess left in the wake of the chaos, and another monitor called out for the line to form again.

Isalie had seen incidents like this before. Amongst the people like her with their heads down, trying to survive, and the people spouting Ambient propaganda, were the people that wouldn't accept Olunei's laws. In darker moments, she imagined fighting against the monitors, too. But it felt like the fire inside her had gone out in her time here. There was nothing to fight for anymore.

When it was her turn, Isalie handed her meal voucher to the monitor, and scowled as she took a plate and followed the line toward where a wide-eyed server plopped gruel onto her plate. She found an empty seat and sank onto it.

There was more chatter than usual, some grumbling about the man's treatment until a monitor neared and they went silent, some loudly wondering why anyone would go against the Ambient's laws. A flash of jade-green eyes caught hers at the next table, the person brushing thick hair away from their cool beige cheek.

They watched her for a moment longer before turning their attention back to the small group grumbling with them. She caught a whispered phrase, "...can't be free without a fight..." before she turned her attention away.

A pair of women whispered to each other as they passed behind Isalie. "...heard he used Prism."

"That's so dangerous! I heard Palea had visions and died after she took it!"

"Poor woman," the first woman sighed. "Some people need to escape reality so badly that they'll risk anything."

Isalie tried to eat as fast as she could to avoid tasting her food. It was a far cry from some of the meals she'd improvised when she and–

No. She wouldn't think about that. The snot-food slid down her throat. She grabbed the cup of water and washed the taste down. It was the only way she wouldn't bring it all back up, and she couldn't afford to skip another meal like she had last night. Her muscles were tired, and her legs and hands shook, sloshing water in the cup.

She put the bread in her bag and brought her plate and spoon to a large bucket for dirty dishes. She walked to the door that led to the street, pulled her cloak out, and slung it over her shoulders. With the hood up and the clasp done, she stepped out the door.

Many cloaked figures rushed ahead of her, huddled against the rain that threatened to fall at any moment. Isalie watched two people detach from the crowd and turn down a corner, and then she heard a muffled shriek. Walking past the narrow alley where she'd seen them disappear, she peered into the dim light between the buildings to find the figures trembling against the wall. A flame bloomed in the dim light, illuminating a trail of smoke. One shrieked again, pushing away from the wall to grasp at empty air. The other coughed, let out a low chuckle, and then Isalie was past them.

She'd heard rumors about Prism before today, a drug that offered users a way to escape their reality as the woman had said, but she'd never seen it first-hand. Judging from the sounds echoing behind her, another shrill laugh that chilled her to her core, it wasn't something she'd like to try.

It was a short walk to the adjacent building where she would spend her day cleaning. She didn't question why she needed to clean an identical building instead of her own. It didn't matter.

She awoke every morning from dreams that were painful reminders of the life she had been ripped away from, or terrifying visions of being consumed by a void. Sometimes the void looked like the inside of the Gloom. More often, it resembled those Elder-cursed tunnels in and out of Lacorsia. Jentien used to hold her hand to give her the strength to brave the darkness like her parents had when she was a child. But there was no one to give her strength here, and hers had run out on the first day.

Isalie snorted as she pulled the cloak from her shoulders and hung it on one of the multitude of hooks on the wall. Even though it wouldn't matter if she swapped with someone else, she still looked at the number above her cloak.

Twenty. Twenty. Twenty. Twenty.

A thin man with wispy brown hair placed his things on a nearby hook beneath the number thirty-two. She watched him pull a small plush deer, faded and worn, from a pocket, kiss it, and stuff it inside his bag. His eyes locked with Isalie's when he turned. She gave him a small smile, trying to let him know that she understood his pain, but he scowled at her before rushing to take his supplies from a shelf near the work monitor and leave the room. Isalie touched the mark on her leather bodice again as she peered at the number above her hook.

Twenty. Twenty. Twenty.

The mantra continued as she walked to the opposite end of the room where another wall of hooks held a multitude of off-white aprons. After donning one that barely reached mid-thigh, she followed the thin man to a rack of metal buckets with long brushes hanging from their handles by leather straps. Warm, soapy water sloshed inside when she picked it up, ready for her day of scrubbing floors. Her knees ached just looking at it, while the monitor noted which apron and bucket she'd taken.

Twenty. Twenty.

"Room twenty thirty-two," she told the monitor. They scribbled her dormitory and room number on the parchment next to her equipment, and then nodded her inside. Isalie arrived in the mess hall as a group headed out the door. She took her assigned spot in the middle of the floor where the tables and benches were bolted down, so she'd need to crawl on hands and knees to accomplish her task. She wasn't looking forward to the number of times she'd smack her head against the hard wood.

She scrubbed for a while; it could have been minutes or hours, but it didn't matter. She cleaned until she was done, or one of the monitors would ensure she didn't receive a meal voucher. Her mind wandered as the brush plunked into the bucket again, bringing soapy water to splash onto the floor. The scrape of the bristles moving back and forth lulled her into semi-consciousness.

Isalie spent most of her time semi-conscious these days.

She looked up and realized that she had scrubbed the last section of floor for far too long while most of the others had moved to clean the floors in the upper reaches of the building.

"Fuck," she muttered to herself. She rose to her feet and stretched her lower back, stooping to pick up her bucket. If she didn't move faster, she would be cleaning floors well past sundown.

The water dried as she walked away, something the Ambient had done to every building in Olunei since the constant rain made it impossible otherwise. It also made cleaning spills that much harder, but Isalie doubted they had taken that into consideration when they enchanted the floors.

Isalie's boots thunked on the wooden steps as she trudged up seven flights of stairs to her next assignment. This time, she strove to keep track of time and hurry through. She didn't want to be caught alone in the streets after sundown.

She heard someone crying behind the door to her right and grimaced. Those sounds of suffering were often the only voice she heard. They surrounded her, and most days, they defined her, as well.

There was no escape from the suffering.

CHAPTER THIRTEEN

Jentien scratched the stubble on his cheek as he peered in the mirror in his room. He'd never grown a beard before, preferring to keep his face clear, but he couldn't summon the energy to shave. He poured everything he had into his duties, because it was the only thing he knew how to do.

He'd never been good at taking care of himself; Iz had done that for him. He'd had something to look forward to, someone to share his life with, even if he'd been too stupid to realize just how deep his affection ran.

His uniform was clean and pressed, and he shrugged into the beige coat, tugging his burgundy cuffs into place. With all the buttons fastened, he raked a hand through his hair and left the room.

After a quick meal—eggs and potatoes atop flatbread—he was out the door, with the familiar heavy footsteps of Cortlen behind him. The sun was bright in the sky overhead, and Jentien pointedly ignored the dark cloud in his peripheral vision.

"Jentien," Cortlen called, and Jentien slowed his pace until the man caught up to him. "Always the first one out the door," Cortlen commented, slightly out of breath after jogging to catch up.

Jentien answered with a grunt.

"I prefer work over the silence of my room, too. I'm told talking to a friend can help ease the grief and loneliness, too."

Jentien took a deep breath and let it out slowly. He knew that he should open up, that he wouldn't survive on his own, but he couldn't allow anyone in again. Not after his parents, not after Isalie. Everyone he'd ever loved was gone, and there was nothing he could do about it.

"I'm going to the census office after my shift," Cortlen offered with a hint of hope in his voice. "You could come with me, see if there's any record of your girl in the past week."

"No," Jentien replied. His tone was harsher than he'd meant, but it was either that or allow himself to feel that grief again after he'd stuffed it behind a wall of apathy. He didn't know when it'd happened, but he found that he was numb, and it was much easier this way.

"At least come eat with us," Cortlen continued. "You've been working every day for months. You're one of the most disciplined people I've ever met, which is saying something, since I've sailed with Ambient-led crews in and out of the capital. If I hadn't tried to move my family to Lacorsia—"

Cortlen cleared his throat at the mention of his family. He'd lost them in the Gloom, like Jentien had lost Iz, so he knew what Jentien was going through. His grief might have been worse, since Jentien had never let himself think of having a life with Iz that included love and children. He'd only taken her to terrifying places and put her in the way of the kind of danger that had taken her away.

Something stirred in Jentien's chest, but it was not as sharp as his pain. He placed a hand on Cortlen's shoulder as they walked and gave it a squeeze. He couldn't tell the man with him that he sympathized, couldn't tell him that it would be all right, or any other platitude that he might have used before Olunei, so he offered silent support instead. It was all he had that wouldn't tear down the wall inside him.

The rest of the walk passed in silence, and they arrived at the barracks near the gate to the Ambient District. Once they'd formed up with the rest of their squad—he spotted Ionna and Wist, who greeted Cortlen warmly—they began their patrol. Every day they followed the same path: along the river that marked the outer edge of the inner city, past the tunnel that connected them to the outer city, and then on a winding path through the buildings.

Most days were quiet, and ended with them running drills in the courtyard outside the barracks. Jentien had begun to wonder why the city had need of so many guards, but Cortlen had told them the first day about Olunei's history of Still uprisings when the Ambient moved into the city. They'd put up the perimeter towers to keep the worst of the wild Ambience away from the city, but since the population had grown so much in those early days of the Gloom's spread, the inner city had quickly become overrun.

After a lottery was announced to decide who would move into the storm, the Stills rioted. Lines were drawn between the instigators and those loyal to the Ambient who had taken charge, and the Ambient Guard had been formed from the ranks of loyalists. Now, they kept the peace throughout the city, and watched for the rare Gloom beast incursion.

The river glittered on their right, even as it reflected the dark clouds overhead. Jentien tried not to look at them, to remind him of the horrific moments that haunted him day and night. Otherwise, he would think of her.

At the rear of the column, Jentien paused when he heard a splash. The river was swift, fed by the constant rain on the far side, leading to the delta that separated Olunei from the ocean. But this wasn't the normal roar he'd grown accustomed to over the past months.

He turned and held his sword before him, watching the tumult of water. The sound of his patrol faded as they moved away, but he didn't call out. Instinct told him that something was moving closer, and if he alerted Cortlen, it would just slink off to find somewhere else to enter the city. His years felling Gloom beasts had taught him that much, at least.

"Themori! Form up!"

A dark shape slithered over the lip of the low wall at the water's edge in a blur. It was on him before he could answer Cortlen, and his sword came up just in time to catch a long, curved claw.

Recruits shouted and rushed forward, giving Jentien a moment to disengage as the thing swung a flat head their way. Its scaled hide flashed in the sunlight, a cross between a fish and a crocodile, and the road sizzled where slobber dripped from its open jaws. Humanoid eyes darted between him and the other recruits, intelligent enough that Jentien read its decision to flee before it slid backward on the slime in its wake.

He lunged, slashing its leg, drawing its attention. "Hey! Here!"

It hissed and writhed in pain, and Jentien lunged again. The beast parried his blade with its long teeth, but he snatched it away before it could clamp down.

"Surround it!" he shouted to the others. "Don't let it escape!"

Cortlen put himself between the beast and the river, and the others followed Jentien's command to surround the thing.

"It's intelligent, so don't underestimate it!" The beast whipped its head his way, and Jentien could swear that anger flashed in its eyes, as if it resented that he'd given away its secret. "That hide is thick, aim for the joints!"

It lunged for Jentien, and he ducked aside while the guards on either side of him thrust sword points into its elbow and armpit. It screeched, setting Jentien's teeth on edge.

"Cort!" Jentien parried a claw. "We need ropes!"

Wist ran toward a nearby building, returning moments later with what looked like a laundry line. Jentien slashed at the thing's foreleg again, trying to keep its attention on him.

"Make a loop and get it to me!" Jentien called. "Distract it!"

Wist shoved the looped rope in Jentien's hands before stabbing at the thick hide. It rolled toward the river, but Cortlen and the others were waiting, their blades flashing in the sunlight when they slashed at the beast again.

With its head turned away, Jentien sheathed his sword and circled to the side of its head. Saying a silent prayer to the Elders, he swung the loop over his head to give it momentum, and let it fly just as the beast opened its mouth to chomp onto Cortlen's outstretched arm.

The rope encircled the top jaw, and Jentien pulled it taut. The beast pulled, but Jentien held it firm. Instead, it rolled, but that only helped to wrap the rope around its head once, twice, until it couldn't open its mouth. It tried to roll the other way, to disentangle itself from the snare, but Jentien threw himself over the thing, pinning it belly-down.

Cortlen and Ionna joined him, and still the beast tried to roll out from under them. Claws slashed at the leg of Jentien's pants, tearing through his calf. He gritted his teeth against the pain and ground out, "Loop its legs!"

Wist and another recruit tied lengths around the legs as they flailed, throwing Jentien and the others off the beast's back. Jentien's forearm was tangled in the line holding its mouth closed, so he pulled as hard as he could. It rolled over him, loosening the bind and knocking the breath from his lungs.

Jentien kicked off its soft belly and pulled his sword. Gasping, he fell forward, driving the point between the scales. It screamed and kicked him away, scoring his hands and making him drop the hilt, the blade still embedded in the beast. It slithered toward the other guards, but Wist and the others with ropes pulled its legs out from under it, onto Jentien's sword.

It screeched before going still, and Jentien finally took a deep breath. His skin was burning where the beast's slime had eaten through his uniform. Blood poured from the deep gash on his calf, but he pulled himself to his feet, closer to the beast's twitching body.

"Jentien," Cortlen called, "you're injured, stand down. That thing is dead."

Jentien shook his head. "We need to be sure. Gloom beasts are more resilient than normal animals. They have to be, to survive in the Gloom. Help me roll it over."

Cortlen waved a few guards forward to help Jentien roll it over and retrieve his sword. Estimating where its heart could be, he stabbed it again, grimacing when the beast arched its back, and then went limp.

Applause erupted in the street, and Jentien looked up to find a crowd of Stills and Ambient Guard cheering for their victory. Cortlen helped Jentien to his feet as a thin Ambient man with long black hair in a violet tunic with opulent golden bangles on his wrists stepped from between the ranks of guards and approached.

"Ambient Rotre," Cortlen said.

"Guard Harra," Ambient Rotre replied. "Your people fought valiantly. Especially Guard…"

"Jentien Themori, sir," Jentien replied.

"Themori." He passed a hand over Jentien's hands, and the wounds healed. He did the same for the wound in Jentien's calf, and the burns marring his chest and arms. "I'm impressed with your prowess against such a creature. Have you fought them before?"

"Yes, sir," Jentien replied. The pain was gone, as if the wounds hadn't happened in the first place. He watched the Ambient heal burns on the other guards who'd come into contact with the creature in awe. "I was a Sentinel."

"How fortunate for us. I'll be sure Mistress Kiyash hears about your exploits."

"Thank you, sir," Jentien said.

Ambient Rotre walked away, and Cortlen ordered the other recruits to shove the corpse into the river and clean the area. He stopped Jentien from joining.

"Looks like the Ambient have a new favorite, our very own golden child. Your trial period is coming to an end, and based on what I saw today, I think I have the perfect job for you."

CHAPTER FOURTEEN

Isalie rubbed her eyes, trying to shake the nightmare she'd been having. She'd gotten lost in the dark, chasing Jen through the tunnel to Lacorsia. She needed to see him, to touch him, to chase that fear away completely.

Where is Jen? she thought. *He was just here.* She'd felt him get out of bed, had heard his feet hit the stone floor and pad across the room toward the basin. Looking in that direction, she saw that he wasn't there, but she'd heard the water splash a minute ago. Had she missed the door closing behind him? She searched for his clothes and boots, but only found hers laid out on the end of the bed.

"He must have gone down for breakfast," she mumbled to herself.

She stood and tried to smooth her hair as she crossed the room and ran her fingers through the cold water. She combed her wet fingers through her untidy mess of hair until it sat flat on her head and rubbed her scalp to ease the headache her hair had caused. She washed her face, neck, armpits, and anywhere else that needed it, her skin prickling wherever the frigid water touched.

When she was dressed in her leather, she wandered into the hall. She didn't remember this inn looking so narrow. Or dark. She rubbed her eyes, wondering how long she'd been asleep. There was no window at the end of the hall, so she couldn't determine what time of day it was. A door opened in front of her, and a person stepped out holding a grey linen bag. She stumbled past them as they turned to lock the door.

"Sorry," she called over her shoulder, but the person didn't acknowledge her.

"Where are you, Jen?" she muttered.

She descended far too many stairs, confused because she didn't remember climbing them the night before. *Was I drinking last night? It feels like my head is full of cotton, and it's still pounding. If the water hadn't been so cold, I'd think this was a dream.* She ran her hands over her sopping wet hair to wring some of the water from it, leaving a pattering trail in her wake.

Isalie wiped the water from her brow before it could get into her eyes. She rubbed them, trying to force her head out of the fog it was in, but she couldn't shake it. She had the nagging sensation that something wasn't right, or that she was forgetting something. But all she wanted was to find Jentien and have some breakfast. Maybe this place had some sweet rolls, or some fruit. She was craving something sweet and juicy, and it felt like an age since she'd had anything like that.

She barely saw the tavern around her, the long room with tables and benches full of dour-looking people, as she wandered toward the door in search of Jen. *Where did he go?* The door was heavy, and seemed to push back when she tried to open it, but she pushed harder and emerged onto the street, almost as dark out here as it'd been inside. Weak sunlight broke through the clouds above, making tiny rainbows dance on the walls around her as it shone through the crystal roofs.

She took a few steps to the left, and then turned and took a few steps in the other direction, trying to pick Jentien out of the crowd of hooded figures. He wasn't here, either.

Maybe he went further into the city, she thought, and turned around again to follow the path he must have taken.

The fog clouding her mind started to lift as she breathed in, an earthy petrichor scent heavy in the air. She felt the rain coming, humidity rising by the second, as a voice in the back of her mind told her that there was something she'd forgotten. Since she didn't know *what* she'd forgotten, she assumed it had something to do with losing Jentien in this warren of buildings. That insistent voice grew louder when the streets echoed with the roar of thunder. A shiver ran up her spine when her mind cleared, and she finally realized the danger she was in.

As if on cue, a drop of rain hit Isalie's hair and seared her skin. She almost looked up at the sky but kept her face down. "Shit, fuck!" Isalie shouted as she ducked back beneath the eaves of the nearest building. She searched for a way out of the rain, but the eave ended directly to her left and right, and there were no doors on this wall. The rain picked up, splashing onto the street to splatter against her boots. She shrieked in fear, anger, and desperation. "Elders curse this place!" She whipped her head around, looking for her building, but she didn't recognize the street name. It all looked the *same.*

Someone in a mask and cloak turned to glance at her, and then hurried away. She raised a hand toward them, unsure whether she meant to beg for help or curse their cowardice, but she froze, caught in a web of her own indecision.

Isalie stood for what seemed like hours, waiting for the rain to let up, pressed against the stone behind her. Each drop splashed into hundreds of smaller droplets that struck her from head to toe. The leather stopped most of it, but the rainwater burned through her shirt to her arms and chest. The biggest danger, though, lurked through the street like a ghost. Heavy fog combined the burning rain with the air she breathed. Soon, breathing became difficult, and she knew it wouldn't be long before she couldn't even do that much.

"Fuck!" she screamed. "I *hate* this place!" She stared at the wall of rain, for the first time considering running out into the downpour to end her misery. Her eyes fell onto the building opposite where she stood, adjacent to a covered alley that provided more shelter at least, and a possible route back to her dormitory, at best. She wouldn't be exposed for long; surely, she could survive that much rain?

Isalie nodded, her decision made.

She straightened and tensed, ready to spring out from under cover, and took a deep breath to steel her nerves. "Elders, protect me for once," she muttered under her breath.

When she leapt into the street, it felt like plunging her entire body into an oven. She stumbled, her foot dropping into a deep puddle that sent a gout of water up her side, eating into the skin on her belly beneath her bodice.

"Aaahh!" Isalie screamed again. Welts formed immediately on her raw skin as she sucked in a deep breath, the mist filling her lungs even faster. She coughed, and tasted blood while her nose, mouth, and eyes burned. She stumbled and slammed hard into the stone edifice of a building, then felt her way around the corner into the alleyway, which was blessedly dry.

She shook her head to rid it of as much excess moisture as possible so that she could see where she was going, flipping her hair back to keep it from burning her face. Picking up her pace, she reached the end of the alley to find more streets with more identical buildings. A pitted stone pillar stood at the corner, the sign long since fallen from its perch.

Isalie hung her head and slumped against the wall behind her. She slid down until she was sitting on the wet cobblestones, struggling to draw each breath. A coughing fit ripped its way out of her lungs, so fierce that she couldn't inhale. Panic overwhelmed her body as she thrashed and slammed her head against the wall.

Each breath was agony, and tears streamed down her face. After another coughing fit she pulled her hand away to find it was spattered with bright red blood, the only color she could see in this terrible place. She chuckled, forcing another coughing fit.

At least I won't have to wake up in this cursed city again.

She took a few more shuddering breaths, and then everything went black.

CHAPTER FIFTEEN

HANDS GRASPED ISALIE'S ARMS. The pain roused her as she was hauled to her feet. Every breath taken was like inhaling molten metal. She opened her eyes, but the darkness around her refused to recede.

Am I blind? Reaching for her eye on instinct, she started when she realized her upper body was covered in thick fabric. She tried to rip it off, but the hands restrained her.

"Don't fight me!" a muffled voice scolded her.

Isalie pushed against their hold and almost fell, but strong arms wrapped around her to keep her on her feet. She was ushered out into the street before she could recover. The rain pattered against whatever was over her face, and she could do nothing but stumble forward or fall into the torrent of rainwater coursing through the street around her feet.

"Almost there," the voice said, deep and smooth, like a distant rumble of thunder.

"W-what are you d-?" Isalie tried to demand, before another fit of coughing choked her words.

"Shallow breaths," the voice urged. "I'm saving your life."

Isalie tried to do as the voice told her, but it was getting harder and harder to breathe. She tripped on a low step and would have fallen if not for the arms around her. Her body trembled in fear as her extremities tingled, starved for air as they came to a stop. She clutched at the fabric covering her face to free it so that she could breathe easier, and this time, the hands didn't stop her.

She looked down at the blanket in her hands and rubbed it between her fingers. The surface was slick with oil, and where it soaked into her skin, the pain eased. She took another shallow breath as she realized her face didn't hurt as much, either. Her gaze swept over wood-paneled walls, snagging on one section replaced by the crystal that covered the buildings.

A person stepped in front of Isalie in a complete bodysuit of patched leather, wearing a matching mask with crystal lenses. They reached over to a metal table, grabbed a mask identical to theirs, and thrust it at Isalie.

"Put this on," they insisted. "Keep taking shallow breaths until you can take a deep one without coughing."

Isalie hesitated, and the person thrust the mask at her again. The blanket fell from her hands as she took the mask and pulled it over her head with an agonized grunt when it scraped over her raw skin. After a few shuddering, shallow breaths, the pain lessened. She took deeper breaths until the urge to cough subsided, realizing that with every inhalation, the pain diminished until it was gone, and she could breathe easily again. In just a few minutes, it felt like she'd never breathed the rain in at all.

The fog of panic left her bit by bit, and she realized that the mask smelled odd. The leather was musky, with a distinct odor of ozone like the sky after a lightning strike. It sent a thrill of fear through her, the scent half-remembered from her nightmares. That fear started to overwhelm her again, and she scrabbled at the mask to remove it.

A gloved hand touched hers. "Leave it on a while longer. It takes some time to filter all the rainwater out."

"How?" Isalie croaked, forcing her arms to her sides. The stranger removed their hand and started to gesticulate while they explained. Their fluttering hands were as expressive as any facial expressions she'd seen, hypnotizing in their effusiveness.

"I granulate the crystal that we use in the mask lenses, roofs, and windows. With the right weight, they filter the acidic properties of the rain and vapor produced by the storm. When you breathe in, it filters all harmful properties out, and when you breathe out, it draws the harmful vapors from your exhalation and trace amounts from your airways."

Isalie blinked inside the mask, sure she was still confused. *What?*

Her savior chuckled. The sound reminded Isalie of a low, resonating note played on a string instrument.

"I'm sorry," they said. "I tend to ramble when I describe something I've made. It's a passion of mine."

They reached up and pulled the hood from their head, and Isalie was surprised to see that deep, rich voice belonged to a woman. Her warm, dark sepia skin peeked out beneath long crochet twisted hair that was black at the roots, but spiraled out into a fan of violet, cerulean, and teal twists. Her eyes were deep brown, almost black in the dim light, and twinkled with passionate excitement. She smiled, revealing a small chip on one of her front teeth.

"My name is Celeste Zynse. What were you doing out in the rain without protection?"

"Dying, apparently," Isalie replied. "I got turned around and couldn't figure out how to get back to my dormitory."

"No one goes out without their cloak and mask," Celeste said. She cocked her head to one side with a grin that pulled the right side of her mouth and dimpled her right cheek. She planted her hands on her leather-clad hips. "You new here?"

Isalie nodded. "I've been here a few weeks." Isalie shook her head. "No, months." The motion pulled the mask against wounds on her face, and she hissed through her teeth at the sting.

Celeste nodded knowingly. "Time runs together when outsiders get here."

She walked away from Isalie, to another table, one of several piled with metal, leather, crystal, and other materials. The far wall had a narrow section that had been replaced with a thick slab of crystal, as if the rain had eaten through and they'd cobbled it back together. A workshop, Isalie realized, so much like her mother's that it made her heart ache. "We haven't had as many outsiders as we did when the Gloom first formed, but there are still more of you than those of us that were born here," Celeste added.

"You'd think outsiders could avoid the massive dark clouds," Isalie grumbled.

Celeste chuckled again, returning to Isalie with a jar in one hand, pointing to the mask with the other. "You can take that off now," she said. "And if it's so easy to see it coming, why did *you* get caught in it?" She quirked an eyebrow as Isalie removed the hood.

Isalie hissed again. Celeste grimaced too, seeing the condition of Isalie's skin.

"Oh, sweetie. That must hurt." She held up the jar. "This is something else I made, but I won't bore you with the details. Just slather it on thick wherever you've got those burns. It'll take care of them." She handed the jar to Isalie, who dug a finger into the oily mixture inside. It smelled a lot like the leather mask. "Go on," Celeste insisted. "Trust me."

It was Isalie's turn to raise an eyebrow. Celeste's demeanor was disarming; her easy smile and earnest authority put Isalie at ease and made her feel seen for the first time in months. She wanted nothing more than to trust this woman, to find a friend in this awful city. A small flicker of life awakened in her chest, but she was afraid that if she nurtured that flame, it would hurt more when it was doused again.

Isalie sighed and dabbed the coated finger onto one of the burns on her left arm. The relief was instant, the searing pain consumed by cooling numbness. Isalie gaped at Celeste in amazement.

"By the Elders," Isalie breathed. She dabbed another burn and sighed when the pain stopped. Before long, she was swiping large amounts across her exposed skin.

Celeste watched with a wide smile on her face, and then turned back to one of her tables. She called to Isalie from over her shoulder. "You should get out of those clothes before the rain eats through that too. You don't want any more burns, trust me."

"Thanks," Isalie said. She unlaced her bodice and boots and pulled everything off until she was left in her long shirt with holes on her arms and shoulders and bosom. "Do you have something I could wear?"

Celeste appeared with a pile of clothes in her hands and looked Isalie up and down, still smiling. Something in her smile made Isalie blush. No one had ever looked at her with such appreciation plain on their face before.

"Here, sweetie, you can change into this." Celeste turned around to give Isalie privacy. "What's your name?"

"Isalie Wylshard."

"Elders light upon you, Isalie."

"And you," Isalie replied. She peeled the shirt over her head, wincing as it pulled some skin free from her shoulders. The fabric dropped to the ground, and she was left shivering in the cold room, trying to apply more salve to her burns.

"I can help with the salve if you need it," Celeste said.

Isalie's teeth chattered. "Th-thank you."

She pulled the new shirt over her head. It was thick, rougher than her ruined shirt, and fell just past her bottom before she tugged her pants over her freezing legs. The sleeves were a bit short and stuck to the salve on her arms. She pulled the fabric away from her injured shoulders and down over her arms as she turned.

"All right," she said. Celeste turned around and stooped to pick up the jar. Even through the cool salve, her callused hands warmed Isalie's skin. She had to stand on tiptoe to reach the top of Isalie's shoulders.

"I think you'll heal without scars," Celeste murmured as she worked. "How does that feel?" The lid clicked onto the jar as Isalie turned around.

"Much better. Thank you."

"My pleasure," Celeste said. "It's not often I get to be a hero."

"Thank you for rescuing me," Isalie said. She smiled, her cheeks stiff like she hadn't used the muscles in years.

"Dying aside, why *were* you out there?" Celeste cocked her head to the side again as she wiped her hands on a cloth tied to her waist. Isalie noticed she'd taken off her suit, and underneath she wore a long tunic tucked into a belt with straps to hold various worn tools. Her legs were covered in patched leather, the same as the body suit. Her bare feet stretched as she reached for a nearby table and replaced something that looked like an awl in a loop on the belt.

"I was looking for a friend," Isalie said. "I was a bit fuddled from a dream and forgot where I was. And of course it started raining, because it's *always* raining here."

"Did you find your friend?" Celeste asked. When Isalie frowned, she continued quickly, her voice too bright. "Honestly, this isn't the first time I've heard that," she said. She shook her head and sighed. "It's a shame, but I get it. This city is a hard place to live in. And when you get stuck with no way home? That's probably one of the worst things a person can go through."

Isalie nodded. Tears pricked the corner of her eyes. "Yeah," she muttered. She didn't elaborate for fear the tears wouldn't stop.

Celeste smiled a sad, sympathetic smile and waved at Isalie to indicate she should follow. "Why don't you come in until the rain stops? I'll get you something warm to drink." She weaved between a maze of tables piled with items that Isalie could only wonder at while following in her wake, her right hip bumping one of the tables.

She wondered what she was getting into now.

CHAPTER SIXTEEN

Another stray, Celeste thought when she glanced over her shoulder at the tall, clumsy creature she'd dragged off the street. One more lost soul stumbling around in the rain. Her city was a mess, and the people being thrown into that mess only made it worse.

She'd lost count of how many she and her friends had saved. The salve had been a pain in the collective asses of the Elders to make, but at least it had been worth it. The cloaks the Ambient provided were wearing out faster and faster, and their visits to the Outers did nothing to alleviate the daily suffering of the people here. Already Celeste was analyzing how quickly this new batch was working on this stray.

The burns healed more quickly; maybe the rain was neutralized faster, or maybe the healing herbs were more efficient. She shook her head. *No, the proportions were the same as the last batch, and we haven't been able to get any more to grow, so I'll have to make do with what we dried. But the rendered fat in the salve was more concentrated.*

Her eyes widened as the pieces of the puzzle clicked into place. *That must be the difference. The creatures' natural resistance to the rain translates so well into other protective equipment, why* wouldn't *that resistance be a systemic property? Perhaps an older creature that has been exposed for longer periods would be even more efficacious.*

Celeste moved automatically through the door to her kitchen and knelt to stoke the slumbering embers in the hearth where her dented copper kettle hung. She lifted the lid to confirm that she'd filled it earlier. There was enough water splashing in the bottom for one cup of tea, but not two.

She frowned, still musing over the effects of the salve when she heard a throat clear behind her. She started and turned, her heart racing. She'd forgotten about her visitor for a moment, even as she prepared tea for two.

"Tea?" Celeste held the teapot up to prove she had one. She plastered a smile on her face to hide her awkwardness. The woman named Isalie smiled, but it didn't reach her eyes. Or her mouth, for that matter.

This one is broken, Celeste thought. *I wonder if she can be put back together.*

Celeste walked to a large water jug on the counter and opened it, twisting her mouth in an irritated grimace when she saw how empty it was. She hefted the ceramic monstrosity with ease and poured some water into the teapot, and then thunked it back onto the counter. When she replaced the teapot over the embers, she bent to put a bit more wood on the fire.

I need to make a trip for supplies soon, she thought.

"I can get something for you to eat," she offered. The poor woman's face was drawn, as if she hadn't eaten enough in a long time, though her curves strained at her borrowed clothes. Even beneath the welts, there was an earnest beauty about her. Something in her shy but direct gaze made Celeste's cheeks warm, and she smiled again so that her obvious admiration wouldn't give her away. *Why does this stray have to be so pretty?*

Celeste turned away from the small gruel pot on her counter and rummaged in a cupboard, only finding a couple of withered apples to offer her guest. She wrinkled her nose in disappointment as she wondered how long they'd been there. When she pulled them out, she ran her fingers over their wrinkled, waxy skin.

"I'm sorry, I don't have much right now, but you can have these if you'd like." She held her hands out to Isalie, who stared at the sad fruit in front of her like she hadn't seen apples before. Celeste waited a few long moments for a response before Isalie reached out and grasped the apples. She brought one to her mouth and bit into it, and tears brimmed her eyelids.

Celeste fumbled for words. "Um, I-I," she stuttered

Isalie clutched the apples to her chest like they were precious jewels. Celeste grimaced, uncomfortable watching the display of desperate emotion, but couldn't look away. This poor woman's grief was so deep.

Without wondering if she was doing the right thing, Celeste bundled Isalie in an embrace. The woman was a head taller than her, broad at the shoulder and hip, but Celeste managed to embrace her like a small child as Isalie melted into Celeste's arms.

"Hush," Celeste murmured softly. "You're safe."

Celeste didn't think about the words that she whispered as Isalie cried into her shoulder. She promised safety that she couldn't offer, she reassured her when there was no way out of this cursed city, but Celeste knew that losing hope was the worst fate a person could suffer. Bodies could weaken like rocks struck repeatedly with a hammer, minds could unravel like a spool of thread, but still, a person could endure and hope to find themselves able to heal when the hardship was through. Losing hope meant that the soul would shrivel like the skin of those apples. Celeste knew that a person with no soul wouldn't last long.

Especially in Olunei. That was why she couldn't turn away a soul in need of comfort.

That was why she was in so much trouble.

Isalie drew back from Celeste's strong, gentle arms. Her face was swollen and her throat and eyes raw from shedding tears held in for so long. The apples were still in her hand. Both looked like they had been sitting in the cupboard for months. But one bite of that near-spoiled fruit had been the most blissful experience Isalie had had since she arrived.

"Th-thank you," she hiccupped as she squinted through puffy eyelids at Celeste. To her credit, Isalie didn't see any pity in her dark eyes, just empathy. Isalie got the feeling that Celeste knew exactly how she felt.

"My pleasure," Celeste said. Her low voice was soothing and calm. She radiated an aura of kindness and patience that infused Isalie's spirit with the same.

After so many months of isolation and grief, Celeste's compassion was a light in the darkness. For the first time in a long time, she needed a way out of that darkness, and Isalie knew she couldn't find it without someone to trust.

"Tell me about that friend you were looking for," Celeste said. She went to the hearth and pivoted the arm holding the teapot away from the flames with a metal rod so that she could add a few pinches of dried leaves from several small jars into a strainer inside the teapot.

Isalie shuddered as she considered sharing her traumatic story after refusing to think about it for months. She'd already let out some of what she'd been feeling; would she be able to stop if she let the full extent of her suffering free?

"I can see how painful it is," Celeste continued. She peered over her shoulder as she grabbed the hot handle with a gloved hand. "If you don't want to tell me, I won't push. It just seemed like it was on your mind."

Isalie steeled herself, watching Celeste pull a surprisingly delicate pair of porcelain teacups from a shelf. Her thumb caressed the floral pattern painted around the rim before she set it down and started pouring hot water into it.

"His name is—was—Jentien." His name was like a pebble in her throat that she had to force out. "We were traveling and got caught in a sudden storm. We were running away, and then we were inside the Gloom, and everything went dark." Celeste nodded and muttered encouragingly. "They told me I was found alone, and it didn't matter how many times I asked about him, the monitors and healers all told me the same thing. We were already burned after being in the rain for so long, so I can't imagine he survived." Isalie took a hitching breath. Drained as she already was, she was grateful that there were no more tears to spill.

"I'm so sorry," Celeste said.

Isalie looked down at the cup warming her hands, such an odd contrast to the dismal city around her. Peering closer, she noticed a web of cracks through the porcelain, as if it'd shattered and been put back together. Watching the liquid slosh as her shoulders quietly shook with the force of the sobs that she held back, she started when Celeste touched her arm.

"You survived, and that's not nothing." She smiled, and Isalie felt the warmth of her sympathy in the way Celeste rubbed her shoulder.

Isalie had done the same for Jentien so many times, trying to give him some comfort in the moments that he grieved for his parents. Another sob bubbled up through her chest, and the effort to keep it in felt like it might rip her apart.

Celeste squeezed her shoulder, drawing Isalie's attention outward again.

"I can show you the city if you'd like?" Isalie's eyes darted to the window and the pouring rain beyond, and Celeste chuckled. "No, I have a map. Come on."

She walked to the dining room and shoved some objects aside on the rough mahogany table that was somewhat less cluttered than any in the workshop. Floor-to-ceiling windows let in as much light as the oppressive clouds allowed, looking out on a dismal city square enclosed by crystal overhangs.

Isalie looked around for the first time, seeing that the rest of the small house that she could see was like the teacup in her hands. Everything was shabby and patched, repaired many times over many years. One table leg was a different shape and shade than the rest, and short enough to need a stack of bricks to make it even with the rest.

Celeste dug out a large parchment from beneath the mess on the table, sliding it toward Isalie when she joined Celeste. It showed an overhead view of Olunei with a sprawling outer city and a circular inner city separated by a river. A single charcoal circle outlined the only point of connection between the two sections of the city. Celeste pointed at a spot in the outer ring.

"This is where we are. The dormitories were built just after they put up the wall." She pointed at a cluster of buildings near the first location. "When the rain started and burned through most of the buildings in the outer city, they were the only place left for our people to go."

"How is this house still here?"

"My father," Celeste replied, looking up at the patched roof. "He used scrap from the construction of the crystal dormitory roofs to cut shingles to cover the existing roof."

Isalie's eyes widened, impressed. "Does your father still live here with you?"

Celeste gave her a sad smile and shook her head. "No. He wanted to save other homes—he helmed the city's plumbing project with the Ambient—but that was in the first weeks of the Gloom, and he didn't have a mask. We didn't know about the long-term effects of breathing in the fog, and even though he was careful not to spend too long outside or expose his face to the rain, it was enough to scar his lungs. He died not long after, and since my mother died in childbirth, my father's friend took me in. But I still have my home, and the workshop where he did so much to help people. I just hope to use it to do half as much in my lifetime."

"You saved *me*," Isalie offered.

Celeste gave her a half-smile. "Then I'm halfway there." She tapped the center of the city. "This is the inner city, where the Ambient live. The storms don't touch it." Celeste said. Her nose wrinkled as her brow furrowed angrily. "The Ambient have made sure that their people are protected while the rest of us huddle like rats."

Her interest and anger sparked, Isalie leaned forward to peer at the map. Segregation between the Ambient and the Stills was not unique to Lacorsia. "How do they do that?" Isalie asked.

"The crystal towers." Celeste pointed out the window at the roof of a nearby building. "They hold a perimeter to repel the other effects of the Gloom, but they can't repel the physical effects of the storm. A second perimeter keeps the storm out of the inner city."

Celeste smirked and Isalie couldn't help but smile back. There was something so infectious about her smile, and it chased away Isalie's grief like nothing else had.

"So," Isalie said, her words a drawl as she thought, "why don't they use the towers to keep the storms out of the entire city?"

Celeste let out a long-suffering sigh and sat in one of the chairs. "The crystal has natural Ambient properties, and no matter how much I've experimented with it, I have no idea what or why. When they constructed them a few decades ago, the Ambient told us that the towers alone won't keep the Gloom at bay, but that they're a necessary part of the puzzle.

"At the time, most of the population was hiding in the inner city, and there were less people to house. Some Stills live there with the Ambient. They held a lottery when they realized we couldn't escape, but most of the winners were the people that came here with them. Unrest became a riot that was put down largely by the same Stills that were chosen. The loyalists that fought became the Ambient Guard, and the rest of the Inners are the few who didn't fight to stay out of the storm.

"They promote people from the outer city occasionally, but the rest of us live here. The plan was that the Ambient would protect the area and we would stay safe there. But," she paused and gestured out the window to the rainy street, "as you can see, we're not exactly safe."

Celeste's brow furrowed, and Isalie could see how frustrated and angry she was. Isalie appreciated that; she'd always been reluctant to accept the propaganda the Ambient perpetuated.

Isalie waited while Celeste fumed and mumbled to herself. Some words were audible, something about inadequate materials and unprotected people. Isalie cleared her throat and Celeste looked up, seemingly surprised to see Isalie again, and Isalie grinned. Celeste seemed to be the type of person who became lost in her thoughts often, to the exclusion of everything else.

"Sorry," Celeste said with a chuckle and shake of her head. "I get so flustered when I think about how much better things could be and how little is being done."

Isalie rolled her eyes and nodded. "Same. I've spent most of my life questioning the rule of law in this country. I'm amazed more people don't."

Celeste smiled, her face lit with the radiance of her surprise and glee. "Finally, someone who understands!" When she laughed, it was almost a song. "And isn't afraid to say it! Most people are." She lifted her cup to her mouth and took a drink.

"That's been my experience," Isalie said. "My family always tried to get me to keep quiet about it." She shrugged and looked down at her empty cup. "It's not as if I could do anything about it anyway."

"After the riot, the Stills have been pretty complacent here. People grumble, but most are too grateful to have any protection at all to question the Ambient again. The cloaks and masks aren't lasting as long, though. Every year the enchantment fades faster."

"Do you think the Ambient are punishing people?"

Celeste huffed. "They say that the Gloom is getting stronger, that their ability to combat it lessens over the years." She placed her cup on the table and slapped her hand down next to it. When she looked up again, her eyes were lit with angry fire. "But I can't believe that. *I* can make something more effective with the meager materials I have here. So *why* couldn't they do more with unlimited power at their disposal?"

Isalie considered the small workshop she'd passed through and knew that there'd be no way Celeste could outfit an entire city, even if she had the materials on hand. "It must take weeks to make one of those suits. And I wouldn't even begin to guess how much work goes into manipulating the crystal for everything else."

Celeste's mouth twitched up into a small smile. "You're right. I don't have the materials to make more than a few pieces of anything per year. Add to that the time it takes to perfect the recipes, and I'm lucky if I can keep myself protected, let alone anyone else."

Celeste rose from her chair and paced the room, her hands gesticulating wildly in front of her. "The only place to get the crystal is deep within the tunnels beneath the outer city. I have friends who work to keep those tunnels clear of Gloom beasts, and when they're able, they pass pieces along to me. The suit I have is made from the skin of the beasts since it seems naturally able to repel the rain. That also means that they can get in and out of the tunnels easier than we can, so we can't predict where they'll show up."

Isalie finished her tea while Celeste ranted.

"Most are small and can be killed so we can harvest what we need, but some are much bigger than we are. And *all* of them are angry. Our people don't always come back, especially considering the crystal is near where the biggest beasts tend to lurk."

"I'm sorry," Isalie said.

Celeste stopped pacing and turned to face her, pursing her lips. "It's hard knowing I can help, but I have no supplies. The real solution would be getting rid of the Gloom. Or extending the barrier the towers put out."

"And that's up to the Ambient," Isalie grumbled. "Which means it's not likely."

Celeste smiled, and Isalie could feel her own smile in response. It was so hard not to smile when Celeste lit up like that. "I think I have enough to help one person, at least." She turned and sauntered toward her workshop, waving for Isalie to follow.

Isalie shivered when she stepped into the stone workshop as Celeste rummaged through a few wooden boxes, muttering to herself again. She pulled something wrapped in cloth from one, and then another. Next, she went to a large wooden cabinet where a suit taller than Celeste hung. She carried it to Isalie and held it up before her.

"I think this will fit," Celeste muttered. She looked up at Isalie with another smile. "Try it on." She thrust the suit into Isalie's arms and turned away, leaving Isalie to catch it when she turned and noisily shoved a pile of metal tools away.

"Uh," Isalie drawled. "Where...?"

Celeste gestured toward the house without looking up. "There's a guest room near the kitchen. First—maybe second—door on the right."

Isalie hesitated, feeling awkward. But Celeste's attention had wandered elsewhere, so she followed instructions and stepped back into the warm room.

CHAPTER SEVENTEEN

THE SUIT FIT WELL beneath her leather bodice and pants as an extra layer of protection from the rain. The cloth-wrapped bundle was a cloak of Celeste's design, made of the same material as the mask and suit, but dyed to match her Ambient-made cloak.

Once she'd dressed, she wandered back into the workshop. She rolled her shoulders awkwardly in the tight material and waited for Celeste to glance up from the worktable she stood behind, blinking as if she'd forgotten about Isalie. Celeste looked her up and down and nodded, and Isalie's stomach fluttered in response.

"Good," Celeste said as she pulled her cloak around her shoulders. "Get your boots on, and we'll go."

Isalie blinked at her. "Where?" she asked. She winced, expecting the stinging wet rainwater that must have pooled inside her boots, but it never came. The inside was cold, but dry.

"To get your things," Celeste told her.

Isalie froze, peering up in confusion as the woman standing above her pulled her numerous locs into a pile on her head so she could pull the mask over them.

"Why?"

"Because," Celeste grunted, finally getting the leather into place before she put her hands on her hips, "you're going to move in here." When Isalie could only stare up in shock, Celeste continued. "I like you, Isalie. You have the same kind of fire about the Ambient that I do. I could use some company here, and I think you could, too. Unless I've misread the situation?"

Isalie shook her head. "No," she said, tears rimming her eyes again. She hadn't expected to feel gratitude again, or anything. But here was this stranger offering her a reason to keep living. Like it was nothing. "I'd love to. Thank you."

Celeste nodded, held the door open, and pulled her hood over her head with her free hand.

"Come on, then."

Isalie didn't spare a glance behind her, just shut the dormitory door and walked away from the cloud of misery she'd been living in. She rushed down-stairs with a spring in her step knowing that even if she was stuck here, maybe it didn't have to be alone. It gave her room to hope for something more.

Lost in this thought, Isalie didn't notice the group gathered at the foot of the stairs, and slammed into Celeste's back. Celeste shot her a wide-eyed stare, then turned back toward the mess hall. Isalie followed her gaze to see a wide space cleared around a central table where a man with long, straight black hair was peering out at the crowd of Stills.

"An orderly line forms here," he said, pointing next to him. "Any sick or injured may seek my attention in the short time that I have allotted for your dormitory. Anyone who isn't in dire need must allow those who are to precede them. Any-one suffering from the effects of the substance known as Prism will be denied healing. If you have any information about the distribution of said substance, please make yourself known to the monitors. As always, credible information about threats to the safety of Olunei and its people will be rewarded with extra meal vouchers."

Stills with livid rain burns, wounds, and terrible, rattling coughs vied for a space in line while the man removed his shimmering cloak to reveal an aqua-marine tunic trimmed in gold. He brushed his hair back from his face, his eyes flashed with bright, prismatic light.

An Ambient.

The monitor that normally collected meal vouchers stepped forward. "Bring your worn cloaks forward for replacement. First come, first served."

Ambient Guard patrolled the lines while monitors kept everyone organized. Celeste nudged Isalie sideways, nodding toward the door.

"We need to leave," she whispered.

Isalie nodded, letting Celeste guide her through the crowd, away from the Ambient. She spared one last glance his way, her height affording her a clearer view than most, and the Ambient happened to look up, locking eyes with Isalie.

It lasted only moments, but it felt like an eternity that she was pinned by that gaze, as if the man could see into her soul, and didn't enjoy what he saw. When he blinked, Isalie quickly turned and ducked after Celeste until she was out on the street again.

"That was a bit terrifying," Celeste said outside. She tucked her locs into her hood to protect from the misty rainfall.

"Why?" Isalie asked.

Celeste chuckled. "I live outside the hierarchy the Ambient have constructed, and I don't relish the idea of attracting their attention. Overseer Cuzao Rotre especially. I can't take the risk that he'll shut down my work; things are bad enough here."

Isalie looked through her thick crystalline lenses at her distorted view of the crystal wall in the distance, and the roiling, flashing Gloom beyond.

"Why doesn't anyone leave?" she asked. "Has anyone tried?"

Celeste stopped and looked in the same direction. "Yes," she said. "I watched one of my friends in a suit I made climb a ladder to the top of that wall. I watched them jump into the Gloom, and I watched the lightning strike them before they even started to fall. There was no scream when they hit the ground. The lightning always finds them."

Isalie made herself at home in Celeste's guest bedroom, placing her only set of spare underclothes and shirt in a neat pile on the bedside table. When she emerged a short time later, Celeste was busily making noise in the workshop, so Isalie walked through the rest of the house to acclimate to her new surroundings. There was a small washroom, another bedroom as messy as the workshop, and a large closet bursting with stacked linens, cleaning supplies, and sealed boxes. The piles shifted forward, threatening to engulf her, so Isalie slammed the closet door shut.

"Isalie?" Celeste called from the workshop. "Everything all right?"

"Yes!" Isalie called. Afraid she'd already overstepped, she walked into the sitting room to peruse the books on the shelf. Several she recognized: fanciful romances of daring adventure and true love. Most of the books had unlabeled worn leather spines, and Isalie chose one at random. Inside was a hasty scrawl amid diagrams and drawings, like her mother's sketchbooks.

Before nostalgia could sweep her down an inevitable path of grief, she replaced the book on the shelf. A slam from the direction of the workshop made her turn.

Low, urgent voices answered her, and she rushed into the workshop to find someone in a mask and cloak turning to the door and rushing outside. The workshop door slammed closed again.

Isalie turned a questioning glance to Celeste, only to find her kicking a rug below the farthest table aside to heft a heavy iron trapdoor in the floor open. Into the black space beyond she began to thrust leather scraps, finished and unfinished cloaks and suits, and a heavy bag that clattered like it was filled with stones.

"What–"

"The overseer is coming," Celeste said with a grunt as the bag disappeared through the trap door and slammed to the ground a moment later. She carefully gathered crystal pieces, placing a small handful at a time into a padded bag that she tied shut, and then lowered into the hole.

"What do they want? Can I help?" Isalie's heart pounded in response to Celeste's frantic rush.

Celeste shook her head, letting Isalie know to keep back. "I don't know what they want, but I don't want them to see everything I have." Celeste placed another padded bag into the hole and stood to frown at the table above. Fine granules and shimmering powder coated the surface. Celeste let out a heavy sigh, pulled the trap door closed, and covered it again. She laid a thick piece of canvas over the granules and shoved another table in the way just as the workshop door opened again.

Masked guards in light brown, burgundy-lined cloaks stepped through, followed by the Ambient Isalie had seen in the dormitory. He flipped the hood of his shining prismatic cloak back, freeing a cascade of black hair. Glancing around the workshop with a casually appraising air, his dark brown eyes settled on Celeste.

"Celeste Zynse?"

"Ambient Rotre," Celeste replied. "I'm honored by your visit, though I'll admit I'm confused by it as well."

Ambient Rotre smiled, though it didn't affect his direct gaze. "The plague of Prism is spreading. It is dangerous and cannot be allowed to continue."

"What does that have to do with me?" Celeste asked.

The Ambient's eyes darted to Isalie and back to Celeste. "I've received a tip that you might be manufacturing the Prism that has recently been distributed through the outer city."

Celeste's eyes widened and her mouth fell open in shock. "I would never—"

Rotre cut off Celeste's protest.

"I have been monitoring your progress, and I've been impressed by your ingenuity in alleviating the suffering of your fellow Stills. While I do not at this time believe that you are supplying Prism willingly, I cannot allow this drug to spread. I must confiscate your entire supply, to stamp out the newest formulation that seems to be circulating."

"None of what I've made has become Prism," Celeste insisted.

"How can you be certain?" Rotre tilted his head to one side. "Is everything you've made accounted for?"

"Yes."

Isalie's anger rose as she watched their conversation. She'd lived with someone with a zealous drive to protect people. Preventing a dangerous substance from spreading through Lacorsia was something Jen would have been passionate about. But what she witnessed now wasn't an altruistic fervor; it was calculating.

"All of it is here, in your presence?" The Ambient peered around the workshop skeptically, pausing on the covered table, waiting for a response.

It came a moment too late. Isalie watched Celeste's nostrils flare, and then she said, "Yes."

Ambient Rotre's eyes narrowed at Celeste, and then he waved a hand, sending the guards with him toward the tables.

"It's too great a risk. All crystal in your possession is being confiscated in the name of the Ambient, and this is your formal notice that you will henceforth be banned from its possession or processing. Failure to adhere to this decree will result in your incarceration."

Isalie stepped between the table and the guards, holding her hands out to halt them. "Celeste is trying to save lives; she saved mine! People will suffer if you do this!"

One of Ambient Rotre's brows quirked up, as if Isalie was a nasty bug that had stumbled across his path. He didn't bother to respond, just waved his hand toward the guards again.

Isalie grabbed the closest guard's hands, trying to keep them from the table, afraid that they might discover the hatch beneath.

"Isalie, don't," Celeste warned.

One guard grasped Isalie's arms and pulled them behind her back hard enough to make her cry out and release her grasp. Celeste surged between the other two guards and wrapped her arms around Isalie.

"Take what you think is necessary. We won't stop you, but the Stills *will* suffer because of it."

The guard released Isalie into Celeste's arms. Isalie watched all four rifle through the debris on each table, including the crystal revealed beneath the canvas Celeste had placed there earlier. She kept her eyes off the floor beneath the table, even when the canvas pooled on top of the shabby rug already in place.

Granules of crystal were scooped with care into a satchel, then the powder was brushed inside as well. Once it was closed, they handed the satchel to Ambient Rotre, who smiled at Celeste and Isalie huddled at the far side of the tables.

The guards and Ambient left without another word, closing the door behind them, leaving the two women in silence save for the pounding of Isalie's heartbeat in her ears. Isalie stared at Celeste, wondering what she was hiding, and just how much worse the Stills would fare without her inventions.

CHAPTER EIGHTEEN

CELESTE FUMED, STARING AT the door. In one swift movement, she scooped a hammer off the table and hurled it to the side, where it slammed against the crystal panel in the wall, her locs falling into her face. Taking a deep breath, she shoved her hair back, and seemed to shrug off her frustration before turning to gather her scattered tools.

Isalie couldn't understand how Celeste was so calm after such an ordeal, why she wasn't still seething like Isalie. She just went to work putting her workshop to rights, replacing what the guards had swept aside. Only when Isalie joined her, listening to Celeste's quiet direction about where to put what, did she start to take deep breaths to let some of the tension out of her muscles.

She continued into the house, clearing clutter from the dining and living rooms by organizing it in the workshop, or replacing it in the kitchen. She spent some time studying the small pot that perpetually produced gruel, wondering how the Ambient had made it—and how Celeste had managed to obtain it—and then experimented with spices that evening to try to make the slimy substance more palatable. The flavor was better, but the texture was a lost cause.

Celeste's friendship over the next few days helped Isalie piece herself together, but the process of healing took time, and was sometimes just as painful as what she'd been through. Celeste was like a ray of sunshine breaking through a long winter of rain and clouds. Whenever Isalie was alone at night, the misery of her first few months in Olunei began to overwhelm her. So, she spent as much time in Celeste's company as she could.

Most of what took place in the workshop—and Celeste's mind—Isalie couldn't fathom. There were pieces of parchment strewn all over the house and workshop that contained complicated designs and formulae for projects not yet started. And *so* much clutter from projects that were in progress that Isalie couldn't understand how Celeste found anything.

Isalie became restless after a day or two of trying to stay out of Celeste's way, so she fell into old habits, cooking with what little Celeste had on hand and keeping the kitchen tidy. Her mother's lessons in leatherworking were helpful in mending clothing, repairing a worn section of the sofa, and even helping craft Cel's suits, but she made sure not to think too hard about her mother.

On the fourth day, Isalie stood in the workshop, watching Celeste mutter to herself and scribble on a piece of parchment with charcoal. She smiled watching her work, smudging something that wasn't right and scribbling again.

She'll push that charcoal through the paper if she writes any harder, Isalie thought.

Isalie cleared her throat to announce her presence. As it always did, the small noise made Celeste startle in surprise to find someone else in the room. Her look of bewilderment was immediately replaced by a radiant smile that crinkled the corners of her eyes.

"Lee," Celeste squeaked. Isalie blushed as she heard her new nickname. The way Celeste said it, like she was the most important thing in the room...

Isalie shook herself. "Celeste, we're almost out of food. We have the gruel," she twisted her mouth into a grimace, "but you had apples, that weird jerky, and real spices. Where did you get that?"

Celeste stood abruptly and walked to the hook where their cloaks hung. She threw one around her shoulders and held the other to Isalie. With a smile and a shake of her head, Isalie walked over and took the cloak from Celeste.

"What?" Celeste asked with a grin that was engulfed by a mask a moment later. The thick crystal lenses distorted her eyes.

"I can't get used to the way you just jump into action without talking about it." Isalie put her cloak around her shoulders and fastened it at her collar.

Celeste's chuckle was muted by the leather of the mask. "There's always so much to do! Why waste time talking about it when it could get done?"

Isalie smiled and pulled her mask on. With the hood of the cloak pulled well over her face, she followed Celeste out into the rain.

Celeste's booted feet splashed in a puddle of water. Most people would step gingerly around it, but Celeste knew that she was protected. She turned to peer at Isalie past her deep hood and watched her skirt the same puddle.

Feeling the patter of rain on her hood, Celeste glanced at the crystal overhangs above that didn't catch enough rain and snorted. There were so many things that could be improved if only the Ambient would care enough to try.

Or provide the materials for someone else to do it.

"It's not much farther," Celeste called over her shoulder after glancing around the street to ensure they weren't overheard. "A few more blocks."

"What is?" Isalie asked.

"You'll see." She couldn't risk talking about it in the open, but after a few days with her, she was certain that she could trust Isalie with her secret. Celeste hadn't stopped thinking about the way Lee had stepped between her work and the Ambient. The fear that Celeste had felt in that moment, the burning pride, lurked at the corner of her whirling thoughts.

What if she can help us? Would she want to?

A sudden downpour hammered against the eaves and roared all around, sending a trio of Ambient Guard hurrying for cover inside a nearby dormitory. Left down another alley, right between two dormitories, straight for two blocks. They were deep in the warren of buildings that hadn't been saved, with only the sections in the shadow of dormitory eaves still standing. These ruins now only provided shelter for Prism addicts, and she spotted more than a few cloaks darting out of sight when she approached.

There were more of them every day, and if Ambient Rotre had been truthful, she had no idea how they'd been able to get ahold of her formula. She hadn't known when she'd started processing the crystal that its healing properties would come with such debilitating side effects. What still bothered her was even if they knew how to process the crystal, they wouldn't have been able to without equipment like hers, and she certainly hadn't been giving it out to anyone but the people she healed, like Isalie. She cursed inwardly for her slip-up days ago. It should have been easier to lie, even though the bulk of what she created had been given to trusted allies.

After two more lefts, Celeste ducked into an alleyway between two buildings that was so narrow the overhang could do its job here. Thick lines of rope hung across the space between the buildings, heavy with drying clothes. A feminine voice called above, and another answered with a wry chuckle. The woman gazed down at Celeste for a moment, took in Isalie behind her, and waited. With her hand close to her chest, Celeste flashed an 'O' at the woman, who nodded and turned back to her conversation.

Ahead loomed the crumbling building that used to be the town hall. It had looked so massive when she was a girl. Now, she crouched next to the wall and pulled aside a slab of stone as Isalie watched.

"What are we doing here, Celeste?"

"Showing you the way," Celeste replied. She ducked into the opening she'd made and emerged inside the dilapidated building. As it did whenever she stood in this place, it called memories of a time when she was very young, watching people gather in this large, square room to discuss the approach of the Gloom and the storm.

There was a huge table at the other end of the hall, she thought. The sound of scuffling boots and a muffled curse caught her attention, and she startled as

Isalie crawled through the opening on hands and knees. As soon as Isalie was through, she grabbed the handle carved into this side of the stone. With one heave, the stone slammed back in place.

Isalie pulled off her hood and mask with gloved hands and looked around. "Wow," she said. Everything was covered in dust and cobwebs, and most of the furniture was shattered, rotted or missing, but the marble columns were still standing with their golden swirling patterns. Celeste pulled off her hood and mask, too.

"This was where the council used to sit," she explained. She pulled her locs out of the neck of her cloak and suit, wincing as she pulled some out of a tangle. "Those swirls were the symbol of Olunei when it was a functional city. Now, they're just a pretty reminder of what we used to have."

"They're beautiful," Isalie whispered. Celeste watched Isalie's long fingers trace one of the patterns, stirring the dust.

Celeste felt a familiar flush of heat. Every time she saw Isalie in a quiet moment, one where the despair wasn't creeping back in, she caught herself staring, struck by how beautiful the woman beneath the pain was. Since she'd stepped between Celeste's life's work and the Ambient Guard, there'd been something behind those dark, sad blue eyes that stirred Celeste's desire. More than a simple physical attraction, it was a desire to make Isalie laugh. To protect her. To help her find a purpose that didn't rely on someone else. It was something she hadn't felt for a long time, and the intensity of it surprised her.

"Come on, Lee." Celeste touched Isalie's arm and watched the skin behind her ears flushed red. *So adorable,* Celeste thought. "This way."

CHAPTER NINETEEN

Isalie took some deep breaths to slow her heart after Celeste walked away. It was strange to feel so drawn to someone that wasn't Jentien. But when she noticed Celeste disappear into a dark doorway, fear chased away everything else.

It's not the tunnel, Isalie assured herself. *Just a dark hallway. I'm not afraid of the dark.* There would be no calming her heart now. She took another deep breath and held it as she stepped beyond the door. The hall was black as a starless night, but Celeste moved aside, revealing a flickering light beyond her as she ducked down a hall to the right.

"Wait!" Isalie called, running forward with her arms out to prevent running into a wall. After a few panicked steps, her hands found something soft and warm. "Celeste?"

Isalie felt Celeste's locs draped over her shoulder and clutched her tight. This was too much like the tunnel. "Come on, Lee. Just a bit further."

Isalie trailed behind Celeste's echoing footfalls, her grip tight. The light grew and grew as they neared what looked like another doorway. When they stepped through, Isalie closed her eyes until they adjusted. Opening them, she found an Ambient light sconce illuminating another large room, but where the floor should have been was a mess of rubble. Isalie looked up to find the remains of a second floor that seemed to have collapsed.

"What is this place?" Isalie asked.

Celeste smiled and led her forward to the edge of the rubble and around to the far side of the massive room. "It used to be the courthouse," Celeste said. "The prison was beneath until an earthquake collapsed the second floor and the one below. We'd hoped to salvage the building, but we found something else."

With hardly enough room to walk between the rocks and the wall, Celeste had to drop Isalie's hand. She moved around a massive boulder and disappeared into the darkness again.

Isalie rushed forward, afraid to be left in the dark alone, and found Celeste's hand reaching back for her, waiting for her. The hand pulled her through the narrow path she hadn't seen, down a slight decline, and into an open cavern.

They stood atop another large boulder at the head of a staircase carved into the tumble of rocks. Light spilled from lanterns set at intervals along the path, winding down into a vast darkness below.

As she followed Celeste down, her fear rose. This wasn't the same as plunging into the maw of the tunnels in Lacorsia, but it felt like being swallowed all the same. Celeste came to a precipice on the edge of the rocks, and Isalie spotted distant glowing pinpoints.

She took one step away from the edge, and then Celeste grasped her hand. A pained whimper burst unbidden from her mouth as she watched a reassuring expression cross her features. She'd seen it on Jen's face every time they went through the tunnels. She clutched Celeste's hand as her heart broke anew at the thought of Jen, until the sound of voices drifted up from below to distract her.

"Welcome to the Undercity," Celeste said.

Like the market square outside her window in Lacorsia on a summer day, the dull roar of distant voices was as familiar as her heartbeat. She hadn't thought she'd ever miss the chaotic cacophony, but compared to the lifeless confines she'd been in, it was as comforting as a hug.

Celeste tugged on her hand and started down the stairs, each step bringing the noise into sharper relief. An echoing din of clicking joined laughter, conversation, even haggling for prices; this was the sound of people living their lives.

How can a city be so dead above the surface and so vibrant beneath?

She was more eager to emerge from the long line of light and stone now. Celeste's brisk pace wasn't fast enough, so she rose onto her toes to see past her.

"Easy, Lee," Celeste chuckled, glancing over her shoulder. "I haven't seen you excited before. It's a good look on you."

Isalie's face flushed again as she sank back onto her feet to match Celeste's pace. The path widened as it flattened. Lanterns now hung from walls and the ceiling much larger than Isalie could have believed. Beneath the flickering light was a city. Not a city of tall buildings and open spaces, but a city enclosed by stone, with a host of tents crammed between the stalagmites, and buildings built into the walls of a cavern larger than the outer city above them.

Towering stalagmites connected to the stalactites above to form massive pillars. Delicate lights illuminated holes bored into these columns, like candles burning in a home's windows.

There were so many people down here, all talking and moving with purpose, laughing, fighting, joking, *living*. They all had passion, ambition, and a vibrance that Isalie had only seen in Celeste.

A barrage of questions fell from Isalie's mouth. "Where did all these people come from? How long have they lived here? Where do they get their lights, or any of this stuff? Do the Ambient know you're here?"

Isalie's eyes darted from person to person, from market stall to stone building. She waited for a response from Celeste that didn't come. When Isalie looked at her, she was beaming.

"You are the most adorable person I've ever met," Celeste said. Her voice was a purr of amusement, making Isalie flush with embarrassed pleasure again. Before she could stammer some awkward reply, Celeste turned to gaze at the cavern.

"All these people lived in Olunei before it fell to the Gloom, along with a small number of refugees. The young, old, and infirm live here with anyone whose outrage was too vocal in the early days. Some adults live here to see to the needs of the residents, but most take turns farming and caring for and protecting the rest. There isn't enough space to house all of them, and if we pack more people in, disease spreads and the Gloom beasts get too curious.

"We saved a lot of our Ambient-made lights, and found out that when they're put together, they make enough light to mimic the sun. We grow most of our food, hunt the beasts for meat, and over the years stole a few of the pots that perpetually make the Ambients' gruel for times when we don't have enough of the rest. We also make a sealant out of the resin from a woody fungus that grows down here, in case you were wondering how we keep the damp out." She frowned. "Very few people know we're here, and those that do guard the secret fiercely."

Isalie took a deep breath of the damp, cold air that brought a riot of scents to her nose. She smelled tanned leather, cooking meat seasoned with cumin, ginger, and—she took another deep breath as she passed the stall where the meat sizzled—cinnamon? Wood and oil smoke wafted from lanterns and braziers, overlying the smell of many bodies packed together in an enclosed space. It was overwhelming.

It was glorious.

Someone shouted at Celeste as she walked between stalls. Celeste made a rude gesture and smiled in reply but didn't break stride. A gaggle of small children ran to Celeste. Two babbled nonsensically at her but the rest were quiet and shy. It was nothing like the glee she'd seen in the children of Lacorsia.

Tears pricked the corners of her eyes, and it took Isalie a few moments to understand why. There had been no children in the dormitory where she'd lived or worked, and no children in the streets.

Isalie didn't have a chance to ponder the reason because Celeste stopped and dug in the pocket of her suit, her mouth twisted in consternation. The children gasped and held their hands out to her. With a look of triumph on her face, Celeste pulled out a handful of small, metallic objects.

As she placed one in each of the upturned palms she said, "I made these a bit tougher this time. But *don't*," she paused and eyed the tallest child with a glare, "throw it against the wall!"

She plopped the last of the objects into the tall boy's hands, something that looked like a turtle with a key sticking out of its back. The two that spoke thanked Celeste and ran off giggling with the others close behind.

"What were those?" Isalie asked.

Celeste smiled. "Some little toys I made. There isn't enough joy in their lives, so I make those when I can't get my head around something I'm working on. It keeps my hands busy and lets my mind go blank. Only way to do it, really."

Isalie smiled wider and followed as Celeste moved deeper into the market.

CHAPTER TWENTY

THE DEEPER THEY PLUNGED into the riot of daily life in the Undercity, the more overwhelmed Isalie became. Aromatic pastries and loaves of bread sat atop a gorgeous blanket dyed with the colors of a sunrise, and her hand trembled as she trailed her fingers across the soft fabric. A woman bumped into her and reached out to touch her shoulder in apology, and Isalie swallowed a sob of gratified surprise.

"What's wrong, Lee?" She stepped forward and grasped Isalie's arms as she tilted her face up to Isalie's.

"I'm fine," Isalie said through a sniffle.

Celeste pursed her lips and narrowed her eyes. "If this is fine, then I'm worried for you."

Isalie chuckled. "It's just... a lot to take in. I haven't seen or felt anything like this," she waved her hand around to gesture at everything, "since I was home. I didn't think I would feel this again. I'm so grateful to be here, so happy to see all of this, but it reminds me of what I lost."

Celeste's smile was full of warmth and empathy. "It may not be where you're from, but that doesn't mean you need to suffer like you would above ground. She paused. "You can stay here in the Undercity if you want. Away from the rain, where you can be part of a community again."

A twinge of melancholy colored Celeste's smile, a twinge that Isalie felt in her chest as she thought about a life underground without her only friend. "No," Isalie said. Celeste practically glowed with happy satisfaction, and Isalie smiled as she basked in it. "I think I'm happier with you. In your house. Not here." Her cheeks flushed with embarrassment, all too aware of how ridiculous she must look. "You know what I mean," she finished.

Celeste laughed. "Wherever you want to be, Lee. I'm happy to have you. With me." She winked and put her arm through Isalie's.

Isalie's flush deepened. Never in her life had anyone flirted with her. She knew what it looked like; she'd seen enough people flirt with Jen.

She turned away from Celeste as the color drained from her face and her thoughts became consumed by his name.

Jen.

When Isalie turned away and her excitement dissolved, Celeste's enthusiasm waned. She already missed that adorable flush to her cheeks, the sparkle in her eyes whenever Celeste flirted with her, the little gasps when Celeste touched her...

"I want to introduce you to someone," Celeste offered. The need to pull Isalie out of the despair gripping her was a visceral thing in the pit of her stomach. "His name is Amalricus. He was the leader of Olunei's council before the storm. People still come to him for advice, and to settle disputes."

"All right," Isalie muttered.

Celeste frowned as they walked to the back of the cavern, to a large arch carved into the back wall between two tunnel openings. Intricate symbols had been carved along the arch, a large circle within a circle prominent at the apex.

"Amal?" Celeste called into the warm light beyond the arch. "You home, old man?"

A dry, raspy chuckle answered her call, and a moment later the sound of slow, shuffling steps. "Come on in, Cellie. You've been gone awhile."

Celeste let go of Isalie's arm and beckoned her inside. "This way, Lee," she said. Celeste inhaled the warm scent of meat, tomatoes, and Amal's signature herb blend. Her eyes watered as she anticipated the slow heat on her tongue. "We might be just in time for one of Amal's famous meals."

A fire crackled happily in the sitting room hearth, illuminating a host of trinkets leftover from their time above ground: a small, broken timepiece that used to ding on the hour and call meetings to order, a teacup lovingly repaired with gold after Amal had knocked it over as he picked her up as a child, the tattered, moth-eaten robe of a councilor whose city had been ravaged by the Gloom, and then stolen by the Ambient that had arrived to help.

She could almost hear her grandmother's voice calling her as her younger self raced over the threshold of the council chamber. Celeste ran her fingers over the deep blue fabric, tracing a long tear at the side seam. Her fingers remembered that silky feeling, clutched as she clung to her grandmother's side, listening to her deep, even voice address Olunei's citizens. First, in the inner city, and then from the crumbling outer city building that marked the entrance to the cavern below. She'd been one of the first casualties after the Stills had been 'evacuated' from the Inners, and her loss still stung like a fresh wound.

Isalie's stammered hello broke her from her thoughts. "Y-you have a lovely home," she said, nodding to Amal. "Thank you for having me."

Amal lifted one of his silver brows as he shuffled into view from the kitchen. His long, silver-white hair was pulled back into a series of braids at his pale, papery neck. One corner of his mouth quirked between his immaculate mustache and beard, where the only spot of color remained and never failed to draw Celeste's attention.

There's fewer of those red whiskers every time I see him, she thought. She looked into his eyes, one clouded and one light blue, as he looked Isalie up and down. He glanced at Celeste, and she could read the question in the slight rise of his eyebrow.

Can we trust her? his look asked.

Celeste nodded, and Amal's wariness disappeared before Isalie seemed to notice.

"Any friend of Celeste is always welcome here," he said, stifling a cough. Celeste frowned as she saw how difficult it was for him to do so. A bit breathless, he continued. "Though *she* could stand to contribute a bit more if she's going to keep coming down here expecting to be fed." He chuckled to himself.

Isalie laughed nervously and turned her beautiful face to Celeste. Celeste gave her a smile that she hoped was reassuring, but she could tell it was a bit too wide, too inviting, and she wasn't sure she would change it if she could. Isalie blushed again. Celeste squirmed, though not from discomfort.

She moaned inwardly. *She has to stop doing that.*

Turning to Amalricus, she said, "Old man, you know you love it when I visit. Stop trying to scare my friend." She held a hand out to Isalie. "Isalie, this is Amalricus Olune. Amal, this is Isalie."

"It's wonderful to meet you, young lady," Amal said. He held out his hand and Isalie took it. She started to shake it, but Amal pulled it to his lips and gave it a chaste kiss.

Isalie's face flashed through several emotions in rapid succession: shock, delight, embarrassment, and delight again. "Thank you," she said. "I'm excited to be here?" She looked at Celeste, who shrugged and rolled her eyes.

"All right, Amal." Celeste pulled Isalie's hand from his grasp. "You old sweetie."

Amal flashed Isalie one more wolfish grin and then smirked at Celeste before turning to shuffle through an arch leading to the kitchen.

Isalie cleared her throat. "Um, Celeste?" she whispered.

Celeste smiled at her as she chewed on her lower lip. *I wonder how soft her lips are.*

"M-my hand?" Isalie squeezed her fingers tighter, and Celeste realized that she hadn't released the hand in hers. In fact, she'd been rubbing the back of it with her thumb.

"Oh," Celeste said, smirking. "Sorry, Lee, I didn't realize."

Isalie's eyes lingered on Celeste's a heartbeat longer. She worried at her bottom lip again, seeming to think something over as Celeste fought the instinct to reach out and run a finger along Isalie's jawline.

Isalie's skin flushed again as she continued to gaze at Celeste, and there was no mistaking the thick tension hanging in the air between them.

Celeste's breath caught in her throat as she pictured touching the pink skin at the back of Isalie's neck, kissing her full lips, pulling that bottom lip out from between her teeth...

"Come in if you're coming," Amalricus called from the kitchen, his intrusion like a cold bucket of water drenching the hot desire growing in Celeste's abdomen. "Food's getting cold."

The tension disappeared as suddenly as it had appeared. Isalie flashed a nervous smile at Celeste and turned to walk into the kitchen.

Celeste took a moment to lean against the wall, brushing a tapestry aside to lean her hot skin against the cold stone. *Be careful, Cel.* Celeste rubbed her hands down her face. *This one could break your heart.*

CHAPTER TWENTY-ONE

Isalie's heart pounded in her chest. She was warm all over.

All over.

She hadn't thought anyone could make her feel this way but Jentien. It had certainly never happened with anyone else. Of course, she hadn't looked at anyone but Jentien since they were kids. And now, Celeste was here with her beautiful, brilliant mind, so easily distracted by the thoughts in her head, so kind and warm.

Isalie waited a few moments for Celeste to appear from the other room, and watched her walk past the kitchen, her locs swinging over her shoulder in a shower of color. Isalie's gaze traveled down to her swaying hips, and then locked onto the swell of her bottom and strong legs as she bounced toward the far wall. She fought to pull her eyes away when she heard Celeste talking to Amalricus.

"What's new down here, Amal? Any new faces? Anything I missed?" Celeste wandered over to a stone hearth with a stone top serving as a cooking surface. A large pot steamed a delicious aroma of meat, tomatoes, and a variety of spices.

Cinnamon, cumin, coriander, ginger, turmeric, cardamom, nutmeg... Isalie rattled off the spices she could guess by their smell rather than focusing on Celeste's curves. Her stomach growled, and she followed her nose forward to the pot. "That smells amazing," Isalie whispered.

Amalricus appeared at Isalie's side. She glanced down to where his head came to her shoulder. "You've been topside for how long?" He peered up through narrowed eyes.

"A few months," she said.

"Nothing but gruel for months." He puffed his lips out in disgust. "I wouldn't wish that on anyone."

"May I?" Isalie pointed at the pot.

Amalricus reached down into an open shelf next to the stove for a bowl and pulled a ladle off a hook on the wall. He handed both to Isalie, who smiled and scooped a bit into her bowl. Heat seeped through the ceramic, and she had to put it down when it started to burn. Amalricus gave her two more bowls, and she filled them as well.

"Table's through here," Amalricus shuffled through another arch that led out of the kitchen, not waiting to see that they would follow.

Isalie scooped up her bowl and scurried after him while Celeste fell in behind her, whispering.

"This is his special recipe. Don't mind the meat; it's a bit chewier than beef, but when all you have are Gloom beasts, you make do. I think it's pretty similar, from what I can recall of the way cows taste."

The dining room was long and narrow, the table taking most of the space with a collection of mismatched wooden chairs pushed in around it. Glass orbs glowed with soft white Ambient light from sconces set high into the walls. Amalricus pulled out his chair and set his bowl down as he sat, gesturing to the other seats.

Isalie didn't wait a moment longer and sat nearby. She took a large spoonful and blew on it, placing the stew in her mouth. It scalded her tongue, but she swallowed and shoved in another heaping spoonful.

"Not the best idea, Lee," Celeste chuckled.

Isalie huffed a breath in and out to cool her mouthful, but she didn't slow down. The stew scalded her chest, and then her stomach, but this was the most delicious food she'd had since the apple several days ago, and she couldn't stop herself. Her body and soul had been starved for real food for so long that she could only act on instinct.

"Let the woman be," Amalricus scolded Celeste. "You know how terrible that gruel tastes!"

Celeste shrugged. "I eat when I need food, and it doesn't much matter to me what it tastes like. Eating takes time away from my projects."

"You need to eat more, and it needs to be real food, prepared in a kitchen. When was the last time you ate a vegetable, Cellie?"

This is amazing. The spices complemented the unique flavor of the meat so well. The three of them shared a few comfortable moments of silence broken by the sound of slurping, chewing, and the scrape of flatware in ceramic bowls. Isalie ate a bit too fast, stopping only for the satisfying and painful distention of a too-full stomach.

When she finished, she leaned back in her chair and closed her eyes. She'd missed how simple and comforting a home-cooked meal could be. She'd missed discovering new combinations of flavors. A belch erupted from her throat, but she was too full to feel embarrassed. "Excuse me," she sighed.

Celeste and Amalricus chuckled. "I haven't had such a compliment in a long while," Amalricus said. "I appreciate that."

Isalie grinned. "The flavor of the meat is interesting. The fennel was a nice touch."

Amalricus's eyebrows rose, wrinkling his forehead. "I'm impressed," he said. "Most people can't pick that kind of detail out of the mix. I think it's the only way to tolerate this meat, but most people are just happy to have something that isn't gruel." He shrugged.

"It's delicious," Isalie said. "Thank you for sharing it with me."

"We need to pick up a few things while we're here," Celeste said. "I'm low on food."

"On everything," Isalie said. "There's not even any salt in her cupboards!"

Celeste held out a hand. "Wait a minute, I have salt!"

"Where?" Isalie asked with a smile. "I haven't seen any in the past few days. Believe me, I looked."

"It's in the workshop." Celeste looked back and forth between Isalie and Amalricus, her brows near her hairline. "What? I needed it for a project!"

"Well, then I would never have found it even if I looked." Isalie smirked. "That whole place is a haphazard mess."

"I have a system!" Celeste insisted. She thrust her lips out in a pout, but only to hide a smile, Isalie thought.

This back and forth felt good, Isalie realized. She hadn't teased anyone but her father before, loath to say something disappointing to her mother and too busy trying to impress Jentien to consider teasing him. With Celeste, it felt natural, and made her feel as though they'd known each other for more than the few days it'd been.

"Your system makes no sense to anyone but you," Isalie said.

Celeste let out a bark of laughter. "That's by design, Lee. I don't know how else to do it." She lowered her head and tilted it to one side, her stare penetrating into Isalie, pinning her in place. The look on her face changed, and Isalie felt a blush creep up her neck again. Her stomach fluttered as the flush continued deeper, *lower*. "But I could teach you," Celeste offered, her voice husky and low.

Isalie stared into those deep brown pools of promise. She couldn't look away, terrified and excited to be pulled into their depths. The space between her legs, that private, sensitive place that only Isalie had touched, pulsed. Her fingers twitched. She wanted to touch the soft skin of Celeste's face and run her finger over her full bottom lip.

"As exciting as this is," Amalricus drawled, "I believe you were here for a reason? Cellie, you know where to get food. Since you have a woman with such a discerning palate with you, why don't you show her?"

Without taking her eyes off Isalie's, Celeste answered. "In a minute, Amal. We have another reason for our visit."

Amalricus waited until Celeste broke her gaze to peer at him. Released from her penetrating, alluring stare, Isalie took a deep breath to steady herself. She blinked, realizing what Celeste had just said, and looked at Amalricus.

He had one brow raised again, and the small smile in the corner of his mouth suggested he hadn't missed any of the exchange that had just occurred between the two women.

"And that is?" he asked.

"I wanted to introduce the two of you because I think she may be just the person that Arru has been looking for."

The swelling of pride and desire rushed out of Isalie, and her brow furrowed into a confused frown. *What?*

Celeste looked at Isalie again, but the smoldering desire was gone. She seemed closed off now.

"Hmm," Amalricus mused, "could be. I'll call her." He stood and collected the bowls and shuffled to the kitchen before disappearing through the arch again.

Isalie waited for a bit, and then rounded on Celeste.

"What do you mean?" Disappointment gripped her as hard as her grief had. Had Celeste taken her in because she needed something? Was that all this was? "Who's Arru? Why would she need *me*?"

"Amal and I are part of a group called the Olugar. We watch over the Stills since the Ambient won't. Amal and Arru, along with a few others, are on the council who govern the rest of us." Celeste hesitated before continuing. "We use every resource available to us so that we can survive... even going so far as to ask people to help us with sensitive missions."

Isalie nodded, her thoughts spiraling inward again until Celeste reached across the table to grasp her wrist.

"I don't want you to think I only helped you because I needed you. But I can't just leave things to chance when I could do something to help."

Isalie looked down at Celeste's hand on her wrist, which looked so pale beneath Celeste's rich dark skin. What she said made sense, and she would have felt the same, but she'd thought that Celeste had genuine feelings for her. This was Jentien all over again.

Withdrawing her hand, Isalie fell into a familiar spiral of disappointment. She didn't have long to stew, because Amalricus's shuffling steps returned a few minutes later. Isalie snatched her hand away from Celeste's, ignoring Celeste's pained grimace.

CHAPTER TWENTY-TWO

AMALRICUS APPEARED, AND BEHIND him, a woman with pale, opalescent skin frowned at Celeste, sparing a glance at Isalie before brushing a strand of golden hair away from her face. She stood a head taller than Amalricus, with large ears and dark eyes with no white around the iris.

"Gracing us with your presence?" Another figure pulled their long, thick hair forward over their shoulder behind the others, and the edges glinted like gold in the flickering light. Their curvaceous body sauntered closer to Celeste. "We haven't seen you down here in a while."

"Nel," Celeste said. The hairs on Isalie's nape stood on end when she heard the growl in Celeste's voice.

Nel walked into the light, the cool beige skin of their hand meeting the deep sepia of Celeste's cheek. Celeste jerked away, and Nel narrowed their striking jade-green eyes. Isalie realized she'd seen them before, in the dormitory, talking to the angry Stills.

"Lee, this is Nel." Nel watched expectantly for Celeste to continue, but she only gestured toward the woman in the room. "And this is Arru Pseka."

"Celeste, I heard you might have a solution for me?" Her voice was deep, and tight with strain.

Now I'm a solution?

"Arru, this is Isalie Wylshard. She's new to Olunei, and I think she might be able to help us, if you could explain what you need." She turned to Isalie, her face carefully blank. "Arru is one of the Silenced, an Ambient who was cut off from her power. More importantly, her daughter is missing."

Isalie blinked, her eyes darting back to Arru, taking note of the worried expression on her face and the constant clenching and unclenching of her jaw while she waited. Now she understood why Celeste thought she would be willing to help; she knew the pain of losing someone abruptly.

"I'm so sorry," she said. "If there's anything I can do..."

Arru took a seat opposite Isalie. "I'm so grateful to meet you, Isalie," she said. "I think you're beginning to understand just how much. My daughter's name is Yesrien Pseka, and she was *promoted* to the inner city three months ago."

The way she emphasized the word 'promoted' made Isalie glance at Celeste. "Celeste told me a bit about that."

"There haven't been many since the lottery," Amalricus said. "The Ambient Guard protects the tunnel to prevent overrunning the inner city, and ferries supplies back and forth. But sometimes, Stills are brought to the inner city as servants who clean and cook and do whatever else the Ambient might need. It's not much different from Lacorsia or anywhere that an Ambient Consul leads."

"Here," Arru interjected, "only the Stills who have proven themselves loyal and hardworking enough have the luxury of moving from the outer city to the inner. It doesn't happen often, illness, injury or death being the main reasons, unless someone is sent here for neglecting their duties."

Isalie frowned. "How do they determine who is loyal enough?"

Nel scoffed. "Elders only know."

Arru continued. "It's near impossible to keep in touch with people on the other side of the river, but Yesrien and I know several tunnel guards well enough to trust them to pass messages twice a month, and they stopped coming. Something is wrong."

Isalie could think of any number of reasons for someone to stop sending letters to their mother. Especially here. Isalie would give almost anything to leave the storm and never look back.

Looking at Arru, with those piercing dark eyes daring to hope for help, Isalie didn't voice any of those reasons. But she still didn't know how any of this related to her.

"You must be so confused," Arru said. She smiled, a sympathetic mother, sending a pang of longing through Isalie. "Celeste thought you might be able to help because we have an opportunity to find out what's going on in the Inners. A woman passed recently who received word of her promotion the day before. Her death hasn't been reported to the Ambient yet, because I've been hoping to find someone to send in her place that might look for Yesrien and send word."

"Everyone who looks anything like her is too well known in the community," Amalricus said. "If they go missing, people will talk, and that would put whomever we sent in danger. But you..."

"I'm new," Isalie offered. "No one knows me, and I've already stopped working. If I disappear completely, no one will bat an eye." She paused, remembering the incident in the workshop. "Except that I got in Ambient Rotre's way in Celeste's house. Wouldn't he or the guards with him recognize me?"

Nel looked surprised, and Arru offered her another sympathetic smile. "It's possible, but unlikely. The position you'd take is with the tailors, and regular staff rarely cross paths with the Ambient from what our sources tell us. I'm asking for so much, I realize, but I don't know anyone who has a better chance of slipping through the cracks. That must sound so callous of me to say."

Isalie grimaced. "You were an Ambient; why can't you go to the inner city yourself?"

Arru sighed. "I couldn't control my Tether, and it was silenced. I am worse than a Still in their eyes. I remind them that any one of us could lose control; they want nothing to do with me. The only reason I'm here is because I have spent my life studying the Gloom's connection to the Ambience, but Zaraia Kiyash banished me to the outer city once she realized that I had no further insights to provide for her." She frowned, and her eyes were rimmed with tears. "I'm just a mother, looking for her daughter."

Isalie looked at each of the people around the table, considering whether she could do what they were asking. It was so overwhelming, and she felt like her head was spinning. Everything had changed so fast, and now it was changing again. But, if there was anyone who could be invisible, it was Isalie. She'd been invisible her whole life.

"I'll think about it," Isalie murmured. "Tell me what I'd need to do."

CHAPTER TWENTY-THREE

Six months in Olunei.

"Your first day training recruits in the Kiyash spire," Cortlen said, nudging Jentien's burgundy-clad arm with his elbow. "Do us proud, golden child."

Jentien glanced down at his chest, to the golden insignia of the Kiyash on his left lapel. It'd taken days to put together a list of important things to remember about Gloom beasts for this assignment, but he'd never been able to resist a call to action. If there was a job for him to do, he'd happily do it.

It was far better than wallowing in grief and resentment for Isalie's loss.

"I'll try," Jentien replied.

"You'll do better than that, since I was the one who recommended you in the first place. It didn't take much convincing after the impression you've made on the commander and the recruits, but all the same, make sure your impression on the Ambient is just as... impressive."

Jentien chuckled, the sensation still strange, and parted ways with Cortlen after a slap on the back. He passed through the open gate to the Ambient District, awash in reflected prismatic light where the sun passed through the tall spire at its heart. It felt so much like home that he choked back the emotion that rose into his throat, took a deep breath, and strode forward a bit faster.

Around the back of the spire was a squat building abutting the crystalline giant, a place he'd been to once before when he'd first been assigned to the Ambient Guard. Commander Silvo Rallac stood with his hands behind his back in his office, and smiled when Jentien entered, standing at attention as a sign of respect.

"Welcome, Guard Themori, to the ranks of the House Guard. I have been monitoring your progress closely after the tumultuous first day you had, and I must say, I wasn't expecting a man who attacked one of our Ambient to become such a model recruit."

Jentien suppressed a wince at the thought of his hands around the small man's throat, and the ghost of lightning coursing through his body. "I'm happy to be of service, sir," Jentien replied.

"After your display during the Gloom beast attack, Guard Harra recommended you for a vacancy here. In addition to standard rotations within the spire, you will utilize your background as a Sentinel to provide training to the Ambient Guard in techniques against creatures altered by the Gloom.

"Now, a few rules. Do not speak to the elder Ambient unless spoken to. Your rotations will be posted daily on the board outside this office, so consult that at the beginning of every shift. Today, we're starting you off with recruits. I hope you've prepared a training regimen?"

"Yes. Sir."

"Follow me."

Jentien followed the older man out of the room and into the spire, where sunlight glowed through the walls, providing natural illumination. Narrow tables lined the halls, with vases, statuettes, and decorative baubles glittering in the ambient light. Tapestries hung between some, with landscapes that reminded him of stories the Wylshards had told him at bedtime. Portraits adorned the main hall that they passed through, including one of the Malachi, the same that had hung in his school and throughout the Palace District in Lacorsia.

They exited a door at the opposite end of the foyer into a wide space of packed dirt between the spire and another building. A massive courtyard with views of the Ambient district, large enough to hold hundreds of people. Currently, about a dozen guards in light brown uniforms stood at attention, until a gesture from the commander set them all at ease.

"Troops, this is Guard Themori. Heed his instruction, and you might just survive a Gloom beast attack as he did." He clapped a hand on Jentien's shoulder before striding inside the spire again.

Nervous with so many eyes on him, Jentien eyed the people arrayed before him. He'd seen a few of them—a tall woman with cool black skin, a lithe man with olive brown skin and a slicked flop of hair and dark brown eyes, and a broad, muscular man with deep brown skin and black hair in braids tied at his nape—but many faces were new. He saw a few guards older than himself, a few younger, even one boy with pale blond hair that looked barely old enough to be considered an adult at the back.

"My name is Jentien Themori," he began, his voice bouncing off the crystal walls of the spire. "I was a Sentinel of Vortheim, traveling the continent, battling beasts that wandered out of the Gloom. Here, I'm an Ambient Guard, imparting my knowledge to you. If you listen, like the commander said, it might just save your life."

Over the next hours he ran them through standard exercises to warm their muscles, and then ran through some of the Sentinel training he'd received. He concentrated his efforts on adaptability, running each one through standard sparring drills Cortlen had taught so that he could change things up, trying to catch them off guard.

When the youngest in the yard stepped into place before Jentien, the veterans stiffened and began to mutter to each other. After a minute, it was clear that the young man opposite him anticipated Jentien's strategies better than any of the guards surrounding them. When Jentien began to sweat—it was all he could do to keep the boy from slamming his practice sword into Jentien's temple—he stepped back and snapped at the group.

"Is there a reason you're interrupting?"

"No, sir," a woman replied. "It's..." She gave a feeble wave toward the young man.

"What?" he demanded.

"The interruption is my fault," the young recruit said. "I'm Baelen. Baelen Kiyash."

Jentien started, understanding. This young man was an Ambient, the heir to Mistress Kiyash, Consul of Olunei. Jentien sketched a stiff bow.

Baelen waved him off. "There's no need for that. I'm just here to train, like the rest of you."

The other guards who'd overheard halted their bows and straightened awkwardly before the murmurs started again. Jentien took a step closer to Baelen to speak in a lowered voice to the boy.

"The Ambient don't usually fraternize with the likes of us. Can I ask, sir, why are you here?"

The young man blushed. "It was my aunt's idea; she believes that I need to hone my body, mind and power. The ideal vessel for Olunei's future, she says. I normally train with the recruits to avoid," he gestured to the crowd of guards, "this. After I heard about what you did, I wanted to train with you."

Jentien considered the continued murmurs and tension in the other guards. If Baelen was determined to be here, Jentien couldn't stop him, but he'd never be able to train the rest with the boy present.

Jentien's mouth quirked in a slight grin. "If that's what you're after, I could offer private sessions. No distractions."

Baelen's face lit in a smile that Jentien couldn't help but return. "Thank you, Guard Themori. That would be amazing."

Jentien turned to the rest. "Take a break, get something to eat. When you return, I expect your *full* attention. Dismissed."

The guards waited for Baelen Kiyash to walk into the spire before they gathered discarded uniform jackets and left, angling around the outside toward the barracks.

"Guard Themori, isn't it?"

Jentien jumped and turned to see a woman with long curled golden tresses. She was close enough for him to see every fleck of gold in her emerald green eyes and the shimmer in her flowing azure gown with a low-cut neckline. She smiled, and a shiver ran down his spine.

"Yes, Ambient," he replied by rote.

"Tulia Kiyash, daughter of the Mistress of Olunei. It's a pleasure to make your acquaintance." She held out a hand palm down in invitation.

Jentien reluctantly took it and gave it a small shake. When he tried to pull his hand away her grip tightened just enough to keep him from withdrawing, and one shaped brow rose expectantly.

He bent forward to brush his lips over her knuckles and retreated a few steps.

She stepped into his eyeline. "I heard about your violent arrival to our city some months ago, and I'm so glad to see that you haven't caused any further trouble, exciting as it was. And now, after such a successful, if brief, tenure with the regular guard, you've earned a position in the Kiyash spire. Well done."

There was satisfaction in her tone, as if her congratulations weren't only meant for him. He kept his gaze trained on the barracks, avoiding her eyes when she turned toward him again.

"I look forward to seeing you around the spire," she purred. A finger trailed along his shoulder as she sauntered out of the courtyard.

Jentien let out a silent sigh of relief. Something about her unsettled him, beyond the unsolicited advance. She seemed to know so much about him, when he'd never so much as seen her. He shrugged his shoulders and put his anxiety aside.

He had a job to do.

Isalie browsed through the market with Celeste at her side some time later. The conversation they'd just left was a blur in her mind. All she'd taken away at the end was that the Olugar would spend a couple of days arranging for her to become one of the tailors in the inner city, and that Celeste would help her to prepare.

She wasn't sure she wanted Celeste to help her with anything else. It might cost too much.

Isalie stopped at a stand with produce, taking her mind off what was waiting for her with a small variety of stunted root vegetables, leafy greens, and even fruit. She touched the skin of an apple, this one much fresher than the last she'd eaten, and wished she had money to buy it.

Celeste appeared at her side and took the apple, stuffing it into a bag on her arm. She gestured to the table for Isalie to do the same.

"I don't have any money," she whispered to Celeste, too embarrassed to let the man behind the table hear her.

"You don't need it," Celeste whispered back with a wink. Isalie blushed. "The food is for everyone."

Isalie tried to hide her grimace with a smile, but Celeste pursed her lips, clearly seeing Isalie's discomfort. She looked away, taking in the rest of the stalls around her. The ingenuity it must take everyone to thrive down here astounded Isalie.

They'd lost so much, been forced to flee an inhospitable home with no way to escape, and still, they'd found a way to live. Beyond the market space, she spied lights at the far end of the cavern, especially surrounding a wide tunnel opening where she spotted a forest of wooden and metal poles and the source of the clicking she'd heard since she'd arrived. Larger versions of the toys Celeste had handed out shook against the poles, creating a chorus of random clicking noises. More of these poles stood sentinel near each of the tunnels she could see.

No matter her confusion, her attention couldn't stray from the produce for long. She eyed a bundle of sweet earthy carrots, a bushel of small apples, even a bundle of sage, rosemary, thyme, and mint to use in a dish that was taking shape in her mind. Celeste joined her, and the eager vendor pushed the carrots into her hands. They encouraged her to take what she needed, and, uneasy as she felt taking something without giving anything in return, she took a small amount of the other ingredients, too.

Celeste was right; when any vendor they passed learned that Isalie was with her, they offered whatever Isalie could carry with a smile and heartfelt thanks. Celeste was a popular figure in the Undercity, and as Isalie watched her new friend hand out salves, powdered crystal, toys, and other such inventions, she understood why. She couldn't pass a single person without being stopped because everyone wanted to know what she was up to, how she was faring above ground, and who her new friend was.

The warmth of their affection for Celeste extended to Isalie, which bolstered her spirit from the depths it'd plummeted to. There was a celebrity about the two women that attracted more attention the longer they stayed. A crowd gathered to hear Celeste talk about the condition of the Outers while a larger crowd assembled to hear about the world beyond Olunei from Isalie.

Never in her life had so many people cared about what she had to say. It was unsettling at first, with so many eyes on her, so much attention being paid to her words.

But she became more comfortable as she realized that these people were genuinely interested in the stories she had to tell. Each person listened with kind attentiveness that Isalie hadn't felt from almost anyone who'd spoken to her in her life. She was surprised how many tales she had to offer. She'd always considered Jen to be the heart of these stories, that she'd only supported *his* journeys, but she'd played a part in them. She'd explored the continent and seen just as many wild things as he had. Isalie was careful not to talk about him. Instead, she painted broad pictures about the adventures she'd had, without the details that would make her dwell on Jen. She didn't think her heart could take it.

Celeste and Isalie eventually extricated themselves from the crowd and waved farewell as they began the long walk up the lit path, arms laden with food and a few gifts they couldn't refuse.

She breathed deeply as they approached the darkness, fixating on the job she'd been asked to do instead of her instinctual fear. She'd been on so many trips, so many missions for someone else, but she'd never known what it was like to feel like *she* had a purpose. Maybe that was why they'd gone out time and time again, to chase the feeling that was building in her chest.

There was something that only *she* could do. To defy the Ambient. To help the Stills. She stood a little taller despite the heavy load in her arms, and strode into the dark, feeling something that she'd never felt before. Importance.

CHAPTER TWENTY-FOUR

CELESTE RECLINED ON HER shabby, comfortable chair, her feet propped on the edge of a small table, cradling a cup of new tea from the Undercity. She sighed and sank deeper into the cushion as the fire popped. Isalie was sprawled on the adjacent sofa with her long legs dangling over the armrest.

She looks adorable, Celeste mused.

Isalie had been silent all the way here, and still hadn't said a word while they put everything away and got settled. She'd promised to think about Arru's—and Celeste's—request. Now, after watching her open and shut her mouth several times over the past few minutes, Celeste willed her to say what was on her mind.

Finally, she sighed and sat up, folding her long legs beneath her as she faced Celeste. "I want to do it," she said without preamble. "I want to make myself useful, and if this is how, I'll go to the inner city."

Celeste smiled as the tension drained out of her body. She hadn't been sure Isalie wouldn't just decide to go back to the dormitory to avoid what they'd asked of her.

"Are you sure?" Celeste asked. "I'd do anything to protect these people, including sacrificing my own life, but I don't expect that from anyone else. If you want to change your mind, I will march down there and tell her myself." She hesitated, but added, "My friendship is not contingent upon you helping the Olugar, Lee."

Isalie nodded. "The thought had occurred to me..." She shook her head before looking into Celeste's eyes again. "I need to do it. For Arru, for you," a flush crept up her cheeks, "and mostly for me."

"Thank you, Lee." Her smile faded as she considered the path before this amazing, shy woman. "It might be dangerous. If the Ambient figure out that you aren't supposed to be there, we don't know what might happen."

"Trust me," Isalie snorted, "being unremarkable is my specialty."

"I have a hard time believing that."

Isalie looked up, her gaze heavy with resentment. "My entire life has been spent in someone else's shadow. I lived with it, but now, after being treated like a person with something to say, I realize that I had no idea how much I *hated* that life."

"What about your Jentien?" Celeste asked, keeping her tone light.

Isalie's shoulders fell, but the fire didn't leave her eyes. "He was the only person who saw me, but even *he* didn't notice me."

"You never talk about him."

"No," Lee replied. "It hurts."

"Because you love him?"

Isalie's face crumpled, like a dam crumbling under the weight of too much water. She dropped her gaze into her lap to watch her fingers slowly rotate the teacup in her hands.

"It's ridiculous, but yes."

"It's not ridiculous, Lee. That kind of love doesn't just disappear. It lingers, even if the relationship doesn't last."

It was Celeste's turn to look down at her hands clasping her teacup. She studied the gold-filled cracks in the porcelain, imagining Nel's long finger tracing the line. She shook off the memory before the pain that accompanied their messy breakup and the awkward Olugar meetings swallowed her again.

When she looked up, Isalie was watching her. Celeste watched her brows lift and come together, a sign of recognition. They'd both experienced heartbreak, and now she knew it.

Isalie tilted her head. "You called him 'my Jentien.' Why?" Isalie's earnest blue eyes bored into Celeste's.

Celeste's heart leapt before she answered. "The way you talk about him. Every time you think about him, you crumble. I have a hard time believing there wasn't something more than friendship between you." Celeste sat up and scooted forward, resting her elbows on her knees, eager for the answer to her next question while also dreading it. "There wasn't something more?"

Isalie's sigh was full of frustration. "He was my friend when we were kids. My *only* friend. The other kids made fun of me when we were young because I was fat and ugly, and when we were older, they just pretended I didn't exist. They all hated that Jentien was more interested in saving the world than playing their games. What they hated *most* was the fact that he was always kind to me."

"I understand," Celeste said, her eyes tracing the lines where her father had repaired the teacup in her hands. "My dad was my only friend when I was young, but then the Gloom rolled in, and we had so much else to worry about. I decided that the people who didn't understand me didn't matter, and when I stopped caring, they saw *me*. But I was already too distracted by my projects to care."

"I wish I hadn't cared so much, and that I didn't care now. But when you hear something said about you your whole life, it becomes part of who you are."

Celeste shook her head. "No, Lee, it's part of the way you see yourself. It's not who you are."

"I'm sorry, I guess that's what I meant," Isalie replied.

A fire burned in Celeste's belly at Isalie's apology. "No."

Isalie frowned in confusion. "What?"

"No. Stop apologizing. Stop agreeing with me when I disagree with you. Stop acting like your opinion doesn't matter, or that it's not worth the fight. What you think, what you *feel*, it matters."

"Experience says otherwise," Isalie said, dejected as she stared into her mug.

"Fuck that," Celeste replied. The thought of anyone telling this woman that she wasn't worth their time was infuriating. "Just because some people didn't realize that you are amazing doesn't mean that you aren't amazing."

Celeste slid off her chair and placed her teacup on the table as she knelt next to Isalie. Isalie watched her, still frowning. Celeste placed a hand on Isalie's cheek and peered into her blue eyes as they widened, surprised.

"Lee, you are beautiful and resilient and strong. You are loyal, loving, and smart. I wish you could see it."

The energy between them hummed with anticipation. Since the moment Isalie had stepped between her work and the Ambient Guard, Celeste had seen that this was a woman who could change the world.

Why couldn't she see it?

Isalie's eyes filled with tears. One rolled down her cheek onto Celeste's hand. "I'm sorry," Celeste said. They'd only known each other a few days, but she already felt that she would go to great lengths to protect her. More than that, there was an allure about her that drew Celeste in. By the look in Lee's eyes, she felt the same.

Celeste left her hand where it was on Isalie's cheek. "I know you've been hurt. That you've been shrouded in misery like the other people here. I just want you to know happiness again. I hope I can help you find that, Lee."

Isalie stared, and her voice came out in a whisper. "You have."

The expression on Isalie's face changed. The insecurity and depression from a moment before were slowly and completely replaced by a confident hunger. Celeste had seen it once, when Isalie talked about Jentien.

Now, all Isalie's focus was on Celeste.

CHAPTER TWENTY-FIVE

Isalie leaned forward, her eyes locked on Celeste's. She didn't want to realize too late that she was mistaking the look in Celeste's eyes like she had with Jen.

I'm tired of being miserable.

Celeste smiled, and Isalie recognized it as an invitation. It was so clear; she'd never seen anything like it on Jentien's face. This was the look that most women gave him. The fact that it was just for her made Isalie breathless with desire.

She closed her eyes as she moved forward and pressed her lips against Celeste's. A litany of anxious thoughts ran through her mind.

Am I pressing too hard? I have no idea what I'm doing! Her lips are so soft. Elders, this feels good.

Celeste's mouth tasted like the sweet herbs in their tea, and her skin smelled like the leather hood she'd removed not long ago. It gave Isalie the comforting feeling of home. Isalie wrapped her arms around Celeste's neck and pulled her closer, deepening the kiss. Celeste gasped against Isalie's mouth.

Celeste crawled onto the couch, her mouth never leaving Isalie's, and ran her hands down Isalie's back, pulling them closer together. Isalie followed Celeste's lead, pressing her body closer, gasping at the feel of Celeste's tongue tracing her bottom lip. She put her hands on Celeste's hips and squeezed, pleasantly surprised when she swung one muscular leg to straddle Isalie's lap.

"I have no idea what I'm doing," Isalie admitted when Celeste pulled back to gaze down at her, her lips swollen. "I've never kissed someone before."

Celeste chuckled. She reached out and tucked a bit of hair behind Isalie's ear. "Then I guess you're a natural, Lee." Her finger continued its journey along Isalie's jawline, sending shivers down Isalie's spine. Celeste shifted in her lap, and Isalie squirmed.

Isalie shook her head. She focused on Celeste's mouth, her pursed lips. She leaned forward for another chance to taste Celeste, but Celeste pulled back further.

"You never found anyone else?" Isalie shook her head again, consternation growing. "Your Jentien was an idiot. And so were you."

Isalie blinked. *This isn't how I thought this would work,* she thought. Confusion tempered her desire as suddenly as it had begun, until Celeste leaned forward and kissed Isalie again. Where the first had been tentative and exciting, the passion in this kiss awakened something in Isalie that she hadn't felt before.

Every piece of her, body and spirit, ached for Celeste. She needed her touch, needed to touch her. She'd never felt anything like this in all the time she'd pined for Jentien. She'd never felt what it was like to have her affections returned, to feel wanted with the same intensity.

Celeste's hands wrapped around Isalie's neck, curling into her hair. As it pulled taut, Isalie groaned, an instinctual part of her relishing the small amount of pain as it heightened her pleasure. It stirred a pulse of desire between her legs again, and her hips rocked forward. She wanted more.

Isalie slid her hands around to Celeste's ass and squeezed. Celeste moaned, and Isalie ran her tongue over Celeste's exposed neck. Another moan, and then her mouth found Isalie's again, their tongues mingling until they were breathless.

"Lee?" Celeste panted against Isalie's mouth. Isalie reluctantly pulled away and saw a question in Celeste's eyes. "How far do you want to take this? I assume if you've never kissed anyone, you've never...?"

Isalie stilled and shook her head. "Not with anyone," she said. "I want you, I want this, but..." she shook her head, "It's so sudden."

Celeste kissed the tip of Isalie's nose and smiled down at her. "Let's take this slow."

So this is what it's like, Isalie thought as Celeste's hands wrapped around her waist from behind. In front of her, an iron pan was heating over the fire, waiting for the couple of eggs sitting on the counter. Her fingers felt sticky after chopping a few pieces of fruit from the pile of food Celeste had acquired.

Such a simple thing, choosing something to eat, but it felt like a victory.

I must be dreaming. Or dead, she thought. Both ideas were disproved by Celeste's hand running down her arm on its way to snatch a piece of fruit from the bowl. She edged around Isalie and popped the tart piece of melon into Isalie's mouth. Isalie smiled as she chewed, and Celeste gave her a peck on the cheek.

When the eggs were sizzling in the pan, Isalie inhaled, savoring the delicious smell. *I will never take that smell for granted again,* she vowed.

Celeste slid a hand around to lay her palm flat against Isalie's abdomen. A delicious tingling heat curled through her belly and up into her chest.

"I'm going to burn myself if you keep distracting me," she murmured over her shoulder.

"I like distracting you," Celeste said, "but I don't want those beautiful fingers to be lost. I have plans for them."

"What plans?" Isalie croaked, excited and terrified all at once. She'd pleasured herself before, but with another person?

Celeste raised on tiptoes to purr in Isalie's ear. "Don't worry, I'll show you."

"I hope I can live up to your expectations," Isalie said, glancing over her shoulder as Celeste moved to the counter and hopped onto it. She wriggled backwards and plucked an orange section from the fruit bowl. She waggled her eyebrows at Isalie and flung her colorful locs over her shoulder.

What did I just say? Isalie wondered. She shook her head. Now that they had some space between them, she felt awkward again.

"You are adorable."

"Sure am," Isalie said. She turned away and grimaced to herself. *Stop!*

Isalie wrapped a thick towel around the handle of the scorching pan and pulled it off the stove. Placing it on a stone trivet, she pulled two plates and forks from their spots and placed them next to the pan.

Her smile was too wide. She could feel it, but she couldn't get rid of it. "Food is ready!"

"Thank you, Lee," Celeste said. She reached over and started dishing some onto a plate. Isalie did the same, and they ate their meal in charged silence.

Arru visited the day after their meeting to hear Isalie's answer and was delighted to find her amenable to their plan. It was simple: join the ranks of the tailors where Yesrien had been assigned, listen and probe for information as safely as possible, and send messages back with Olugar contacts with any updates. If she found Yesrien, they would find a way to get her out, and Isalie could come home.

Celeste kept busy with her many projects, hardly looking up from her designs and tinkering. Isalie helped assemble cloaks, but when the last scraps of leather were gone, she took it upon herself to cook and clean. She knew how to care for someone with a purpose beyond the day-to-day, someone too busy to consider mundane distractions like feeding themselves.

Of course, Isalie was always happy to find herself the object of Cel's ardent attention, especially knowing that Celeste had so much else to do. She couldn't get enough of the feel of Celeste's hands on her skin, her kisses, her smell, even the way that Celeste said her name. Every time she spoke, whispered, purred, or moaned it, Isalie felt like she was the only source of water, and Celeste was dying of thirst. There was no end to the happiness she felt knowing that she could elicit such a reaction from someone.

They received word the second day that it would take several days to arrange Isalie's cover to infiltrate the inner city. It was a relief, since Isalie had no idea how to infiltrate anything. She felt more confident with every passing day, and the hollow feeling in her chest that had haunted her since arriving in Olunei dulled a bit more every time Celeste looked at her.

Another rainy day dawned, gray and depressing, but the warm white walls and glowing candles made her feel safe and content. Isalie gazed through the window next to the dining room at the fog, until her eyes darted toward something moving at the corner of her eye. A person in an Ambient-supplied cloak rushed through the alley. Isalie caught a glint of light from the lens hidden deep within their hood. They ducked their head, showing the worn spot near the top of the hood.

"I wish we could do something more to help them," Isalie muttered to herself.

"Me too," Celeste said. She reached up to kiss Isalie on the cheek, so Isalie stooped a little to make it easier for her. It was becoming a routine between them. "We can make as many cloaks as they give us materials for, but it's nowhere near enough."

"If the Gloom beasts here are anything like the ones I've seen up close, I can't imagine it's easy to harvest more." She shuddered, recalling the beardeercat's claws.

"I want to hear those stories, Lee." Celeste walked into the kitchen and poured some of the tea that Isalie had made.

Isalie bit her lower lip, eager to see if Celeste noticed what she'd added today. Isalie had discovered that she enjoyed experimenting with tea as much as she did with food.

Celeste didn't disappoint her. "Ooh, what did you add?"

"A little bit of mint."

"Very refreshing. I like it."

They ate their scant breakfast at the dining table while Isalie told her about the beardeercat that had almost killed Jentien and her. Celeste laughed as Isalie described how much she hated running, and was appropriately awed by the way Jentien was able to kill it.

"You're the hero of that story, Lee."

Isalie shook her head. "Jentien killed it, Cel."

"It almost killed him until you threw a *rock* at it. You keep saying you can't fight. Seems to me that someone brave enough to take on a Gloom beast with no weapons or skills is a hero."

Isalie paused. This was a perspective she hadn't considered before. At the time, she'd only been focused on saving Jentien's life. "I guess," she drawled, uncertain, "but I just felt terrified at the time. If fear makes someone a hero, I'm the biggest hero in Vortheim."

Celeste stood up with her dishes in hand and walked to Isalie. Leaning forward, she touched her lips to Isalie's and lingered there for a long, slow kiss before standing again.

"You're a hero to me, Lee."

CHAPTER TWENTY-SIX

Isalie walked into the workshop where Cel was bent over a table in the corner with something small in her hands. White dust coated the table, with traces on the teal locs tucked behind Cel's ear. She was muttering when Isalie approached, completely absorbed in her work as usual.

"Stupid, clumsy. And it's *still* not fine enough."

Isalie stomped the last few steps, and then cleared her throat. As expected, Cel jumped; there was no way to prevent startling the woman when she was concentrating.

"Lee, you are so sneaky! Elders, you scared me!" She clutched a gloved hand to her heart, spreading the white dust onto her gray coveralls.

Isalie rolled her eyes, smiling. "It's my favorite game, seeing just how *much* noise I make before you notice."

Celeste laughed so hard her head rolled back on her shoulders. "How is the game going?" she asked.

"I'm undefeated," Isalie replied.

Celeste chuckled. "You can interrupt me anytime, Lee, love."

Isalie's cheeks flushed, and her thoughts turned to the night before, when they'd fallen asleep together in Cel's bed, arms and legs intertwined. With Cel's head tucked beneath her chin, Isalie had fallen asleep feeling like she'd do anything to protect her, and strong enough to do so.

It was a powerful feeling.

"What're you thinking about?" Cel asked.

"Last night," Isalie answered without hesitation. It was so easy to speak her mind with Cel.

"I haven't slept that well before," Cel said.

"Neither have I," Isalie replied. "What are you working on over here?" She walked to the dust-strewn tabletop. "It seems to have you flustered."

Cel heaved a sigh. "Trying to make the granules finer." She waved a hand at the powdery mess on the ground. "And I just spilled the crystal everywhere."

"Finer? Don't they work as they are?"

"They do, but I'm always looking for new ways to refine them. If we can get more use out of less crystal, I can help more people." She sighed again. "But once it's past a certain weight it becomes unstable. Flammable."

"That's odd. You made it into something that can draw the rain out of someone's lungs, but it catches fire when it's finer?"

Celeste frowned and nodded slowly. The look in her eyes told Isalie that her thoughts were turning inward, and though she answered, she was slipping back into her working trance.

"It's strange stuff. It must have Ambient properties, since the rain doesn't burn through it. If I manipulate it too far, it starts to glow and combusts. But it never gets *hot*. It's like it decides to explode if it's broken down too far, or if I heat it for too long when I process it. I just need to find the right weight to get what we need."

"It's time for dinner," Isalie said. Celeste nodded and followed her inside, though Isalie could tell that her thoughts were still elsewhere. The distracted beauty stumbled into the kitchen and rinsed her hands in the basin.

"It smells great," Cel said finally. More powder streaked her face and hairline. Isalie grimaced.

"That's not going to combust, right?" She pointed at the powder.

"No. Why?"

"You have dust smeared everywhere; it looks like you've been grabbing your hair and face."

Celeste's eyes darted up, as if she could see the top of her head and shrugged. "I don't know that I'll ever figure out how that stuff works. But right now, I'm starving."

Isalie served them their vegetable curry and flatbread. They ate in silence, Isalie's mind wandering to thoughts of Jentien. Through all their time together, she didn't know if she had ever felt as comfortable with him as she was with Cel. She'd spent all her time trying to make him happy, to please him enough that he would notice her. There'd been too much anxiety coursing through her to really enjoy their time together.

With Cel, everything was easy. They could talk about anything or sit quietly with their own thoughts. It was everything she had hoped it would be with Jen.

It was better.

After cleaning the dishes and donning her nightshirt, Isalie stood in the doorway to her room with Cel facing her, their hands intertwined. Isalie didn't want to go to bed alone.

"Why the worry, Lee?" Cel asked. She reached up to smooth the wrinkle in Isalie's brow.

Isalie leaned into the touch and still hesitated. The instinctual fear of rejection crept up from her stomach to her throat, choking off the words before she could say them.

"I'm not going anywhere. Take your time and tell me when you're comfortable." Cel's thumbs rubbed circles on the back of Isalie's hands.

Isalie closed her eyes for a moment, letting the contact consume her thoughts. "Would you stay with me?" she whispered.

Cel smiled. "Of course I will."

Isalie shook her head and averted her eyes. She couldn't say what she wanted to say. Her mind screamed the words that wouldn't go past her mouth. *I want you to touch me, and I want to touch you.* Celeste walked past her, pulling Isalie by their linked hands.

"Come on, Lee. I'm tired."

Celeste climbed into the small bed with Isalie in tow and burrowed into the blankets. Isalie slid her arm beneath Cel's head and scooped up her smaller frame, pulling her close as Cel twined her leg around Isalie's. She was too aware of the way Celeste's muscular frame fit against her ample one, and of Celeste's fingers resting on her thick hip as they lay on their sides. Their faces were less than a finger width apart. Isalie leaned forward and kissed Cel's soft lips.

"Goodnight, Cel," she murmured.

"Goodnight, Lee," Cel answered.

Their eyes remained locked, and Isalie's heart hammered so loudly in her chest that the Elders could likely hear it. She was wide awake, and Cel certainly didn't look sleepy. When Cel shifted her leg, it grazed the pulse between Isalie's. Every part of Isalie's body yearned for more than this embrace.

What do I do? Isalie thought. *How do I tell her?*

"Something on your mind, Lee?" Celeste smirked, and Isalie got the impression that Celeste knew exactly what she wanted.

"I..." She couldn't make herself say it. Instead, she traced a finger along Celeste's cheek, under her jaw, and across her collarbone. She traced a light line downward, her eyes locked on Celeste's, willing her to understand.

Cel kissed her, and the fiery passion behind it pulled Isalie in, inviting her to give the same. Every ounce of desire she'd repressed for Jentien, every fantasy she'd ever had, all of it burst out of her at once.

Isalie sucked on Celeste's lip, and when she gasped, Isalie grazed her teeth across Cel's jaw, kissing her way down Cel's neck. Cel arched her back and tangled her fingers through Isalie's hair to gently pull her up to kiss her again.

Cel's tongue flicked out, and Isalie's met it, following its twisting dance inside their mouths. Isalie's hips moved on their own, rubbing the sensitive bundle at the apex of her thighs back and forth along Cel's leg. Cel moved with her, their pace frantic as the pulse between Isalie's thighs intensified, matching her racing heartbeat.

"Lee," Cel gasped between kisses. "I don't... want to do... anything that makes you uncomfortable." She pulled away, leaving Isalie panting. "But I'm having a hard time keeping my hands off you."

"Me too," Isalie panted. She worried briefly what Cel would think when she saw Isalie, how her thick body hadn't changed much, despite the meager fare she'd eaten for months to survive. When she gathered the courage to look into Cel's eyes and saw only desire, and felt the hand grasping her body through her nightshirt, the worry melted away. "I want you to touch me." Isalie's doubts and anxiety were gone. There was nothing but Cel.

Cel cupped a hand around Isalie's breast, caressing and massaging it as they moved their hips back and forth. Isalie moaned and thrust her hips harder against Cel's leg. The feeling was exquisite, an exponentially building pressure that pushed her faster and harder.

"Love, don't you want to take your time?" Cel pulled away and trailed nibbling kisses down Isalie's chin and neck. Isalie grunted, needing more, moving faster, pushing for release. Cel moaned against Isalie's chest while she massaged her breasts again, teasing her nipples. Isalie grumbled, stirred to near madness by Cel's ministrations, before she thrust her hand between Cel's legs.

"Lee...unh." Cel gritted her teeth as Isalie moved her fingers back and forth. Isalie didn't think about what she was doing; she just did to Cel what she'd done to herself. The more Cel moved and groaned, the more Isalie pushed.

Celeste wormed her hand between Isalie's legs. They ground against each other, and Isalie kissed Celeste roughly as Celeste's fingers went deeper.

"Harder, Lee," Celeste whispered, pleading.

Isalie did as she was told, delighting in the evidence of Celeste's arousal on her fingertips, and Celeste grunted as she reached her climax. That sound broke the last thing holding Isalie together. The pressure released, and she felt wave after wave of her orgasm pulsing to the beat of her heart.

After a few moments, Isalie rolled onto her back, pulling Cel closer to lay her head on Isalie's chest. Isalie reached up to tuck a stray loc back from Cel's face. As they fell asleep wrapped in an embrace, one thought repeated over and over in her mind.

I hope this feeling never ends.

CHAPTER TWENTY-SEVEN

Jentien wiped sweat from his brow, thankful that the sun was finally setting. It'd been a long day in the sun already, patrolling the streets near the river and running drills with the Ambient Guard. His sword came up to block a vicious blow from Baelen, parrying the boy's blade to the side.

"At ease," he told the heir. He took a deep breath, chuckling as he exhaled. "Your form is already improving. You're putting some strength behind those swings." He shook out his weary arm muscles to punctuate his point.

Baelen beamed at him. "Thank you, Jentien."

"I'm happy to help, Ambient Kiyash." Jentien slid his sword into his scabbard and smiled to himself. He actually meant it; he hadn't thought it would be possible, but he didn't spend every moment thinking about what he'd lost.

"Please, call me Baelen."

Jentien turned his smile to the young man. "You're still my superior, Ambient Kiyash."

"That doesn't matter to me." Baelen wiped his sleeve across his temple.

"It should," Jentien replied.

"Why?"

Jentien peered at the young man, his expression open, curious. "The rules are in place to maintain order. Stills show respect to the Ambient because they are our leaders."

"I don't lead anyone. And even if I did, I'd rather my friends were able to call me by name, no matter if they're Ambient or not."

Jentien tried to keep his mind on the present, but he couldn't help but hear Iz in his head.

We shouldn't only be defined by what we can do for the Ambient.

He considered Baelen's words and found he had no response. He couldn't see another way for the city to function, but maybe the dichotomy didn't need to be so pronounced between Ambient and Still.

"I'll see you tomorrow," Jentien called, waving at Baelen as he returned to the spire.

Jentien caught a twirl of crimson skirts and curled blonde hair. Tulia Kiyash flashed him another sultry smile before she disappeared.

Most people would likely jump at the chance to be with an Ambient, especially one as beautiful as Tulia, but she wasn't who he wanted. It didn't matter that Iz was gone; he couldn't imagine loving anyone else. Those last moments before the lightning had awoken that truth within him.

He'd always loved Isalie Wylshard. He always would.

Isalie opened her eyes slowly, her eyelids heavy as she woke from a dream. Patchy white walls surrounded her, not the drab stone of the dormitory, or the airy wooden walls of her bedroom in Lacorsia. For a moment, she couldn't remember where she was. Then Cel stirred, and the events from the night before came back to her.

Cel stretched, flexing her leg between Isalie's. Her eyes opened, and she smiled her wide, radiant smile. "Morning, Lee." Cel's voice was grizzled, and she cleared her throat. "How do you feel?" A hint of worry soured her smile.

"I feel wonderful," Isalie smirked, leaning forward for a soft kiss.

"Good," Cel replied, relieved. "So do I."

"Good."

They snuggled in bed for a while longer, and then Isalie made them breakfast, after which Celeste pecked her on the cheek and disappeared into the workshop. Isalie watched her walk away, savoring the sight of her backside swaying, resisting the urge to stop her and lead her back to bed.

Instead, Isalie plopped onto the couch, content to lounge in her robe. She didn't feel the urge to cover herself when she reached for a book and the robe flopped open just a bit. It was a novel concept, feeling comfortable in her own skin.

Celeste hadn't been gone long when she appeared again. "Lee, Amal sent someone."

Isalie's stomach flipped, and she clutched the robe closed as she stood. Cel moved to the door and waved someone in from the workshop.

A young man stepped inside. He wore the uniform of the Ambient Guard; the ensemble was a soft shade of beige, with a long neck on the shirt, and cuffs and neckline trimmed with burgundy. His dark hair was slicked back over his head, exposing a scrubbed pale face and a timid smile that exposed elongated canine teeth. His pupils were slits, like a cat's eyes.

When he spoke, his voice broke. "Hi, Cel."

He's young, Isalie thought.

"Hi, Pelom. What do you have for us?"

"Amal asked me to bring this for you." He pulled a bag over his head and handed it to Isalie. She opened the flap to find a uniform the same colors as Pelom's, but it was the style of the servants. A similar cloak and mask were beneath it, along with a thick parchment that held a seal with the Ambient's starburst symbol.

Isalie looked at Celeste, who was staring at her with a worried frown. Isalie took a deep, steadying breath, trying to calm the flood of anxiety making her hands tremble.

"Thank you," she whispered, her voice trembling as well.

Pelom's eyes darted between the two women, and a blush crept over his neck. "You're expected in an hour." He bobbed his head once and hurried back into the workshop as he pulled his mask out of his cloak pocket.

"I'm going to be okay," Isalie said aloud, more to herself than Celeste.

"I know you will, love," Celeste said. "You'll be back before you know it."

"I will."

Celeste kept her face calm while Isalie stared at her. The fear evident in her wide eyes tore her apart. She'd asked Isalie to put herself at risk, and it was all happening too soon. It took everything she had to stop herself from telling Isalie she shouldn't go.

"I should try this on," Isalie muttered.

Celeste let her hands drop and smiled. "You should. I'll just... wait in the workshop."

Isalie nodded and disappeared into her room before Celeste turned. She waited to hear the door close behind her before she let her shoulders slump and allowed her sadness to wash over her for a moment.

Only one.

She took a deep breath, deciding to leave her worry behind and focus on her formulation of ground crystal. There was too much in fine powder form to let it go to waste. All it was good for right now was as a firestarter; jostled too hard, it would ignite, and with this much of it together, it could destroy the block.

Maybe I can put this to use elsewhere. She separated the dust into smaller piles, then packed it all away in small glass containers, closed each with cork stoppers and gently placed them in a padded box in the compartment below. They would keep until she figured out what else to do.

For now, she had a separate container full of crystal granules to pack into fine netting. The granules tinkled through the neck of the glass jar when she poured a measure into the first packet. *Enough for a few treatments or masks,* she mused, closing the packet with needle and thread. She smiled, thinking of the people that could be saved with this.

Her mind continued to work as she went through the rote task of filling the mesh bags. Fleeting thoughts about the biggest, and most elusive problem to solve: how to change their circumstance. How could they mitigate the threat of the storms? Should they try to get more materials for suits and cloaks? More crystal, to cover every inch of open street in the Outers?

Was Nel right, that the only way to make things better would be to bring the Ambient low and take over the Inners? She shook her head, frustrated. There wasn't much she could do that she wasn't already doing to help people survive this horrible place, so she got back to work.

A noise startled her from her contemplation. She looked around to see Isalie dressed in the beige, burgundy-trimmed outfit of the Inners servants. Her face was clean and bright, her hair swept into a braid that started on the left side of her head and curved around to the right side of her nape.

Celeste looked down at a sketch beneath her fingertips and a pencil in her hand. The crystal packets were gone. It took a few moments for her to remember that she'd finished the packets and had been brainstorming uses for the fine powder.

"You look beautiful, Lee," she said. She put the paper down and dusted off her hands. A smile broke out on her face when Isalie blushed.

"I had to leave my mother's leather in the bedroom, but, thanks, Cel," Isalie whispered as her eyes dropped to the floor.

Celeste put her finger under Isalie's chin to lift it. "Don't do that. You are beautiful and you know it. I've seen it."

"That's something you gave me," she whispered. Her dark blue eyes blazed with fierce desire. And the confidence she usually lacked.

"There you are," Cel murmured. "Hold onto this feeling. You are strong, and you are important. Everyone will see it if you let them."

"Cel, I-I want to tell you something. But I'm afraid it's too soon."

"What, love?"

Her words came out in a rush, like they needed to be released, and she couldn't hold them in any longer. "I'm falling for you."

Celeste's heart swelled, relieved to hear Isalie say the words she'd been wanting to say. She didn't want Isalie to leave without knowing that, but she was afraid. Afraid that Isalie might be lost, and she'd be left broken.

"Lee, I'll be waiting for you. Please, come home to me." Fear bubbled to the surface, trying to push past her carefully composed features. She swallowed it and smiled, trying her best to give off the impression that she was confident of the outcome.

Isalie chewed on her lip. "I'll come home as soon as I can."

"Just make sure you're careful in there."

Isalie nodded and swung her cloak around her shoulders. When they peeked outside, they found dry, gray clouds and a dry street for the first time in days. Isalie pushed her mask into the inner pocket of her cloak and pulled the hood high, just in case.

Celeste saw a bit of sleeve from her suit poke out from beneath her Inners outfit. Celeste smiled and tucked it back in. "You'll fit right in. Remember, don't piss off the Ambient."

Isalie chuckled nervously. "No promises, but I'll do my best."

CHAPTER TWENTY-EIGHT

ONE HAND CLUTCHED THE folded parchment in her pocket while the other grasped the edge of her cloak. Isalie walked down the empty street with her hood pulled forward in case the rain started.

She hadn't been this far north yet and was surprised to see that the city wasn't so compact here. There were fewer buildings and people as she neared the area Cel had shown her on the map. Most of the people were dressed in similar livery as she was, with a few Ambient Guard patrolling the streets. Several guards were posted at the open gate with bars made of crystal, looking bored as they stood outside.

Isalie stopped in the middle of the road and stared, her heart pounding as a wave of fear rolled through her, no matter how she'd tried to prepare for this moment. The tunnel gaped like an open mouth waiting to swallow her.

It looked so much like the tunnel in Lacorsia, without the line of Stills waiting for their turn serving the Ambient. She took an involuntary step back, stepping on someone, and tore her eyes from the tunnel to see Pelom steadying her before she fell.

"Pelom!" Her voice was a bit too loud and shrill, and a guard looked up at them. Pelom smiled at someone behind Isalie and gave her a worried look.

"I'm heading back into the Inners now that I'm done with my assignment. Congratulations on your promotion, Jhera." He widened his eyes, and Isalie realized that he was trying to get her to stop talking so loudly. To calm down and blend in.

I'm Jhera Folci, she reminded herself.

She tried to take a calming breath, but she couldn't slow her heart. She knew the tunnel was behind her, waiting to swallow her.

She leaned forward and whispered. "I can't go through there. I can't, I can't..." She glanced over her shoulder but looked away again.

"What's wrong? Why can't you?"

"I have this thing with tunnels. I j-just, no."

"It's Lee, right?" Pelom tried to put his face in front of her to hold her full attention. "You're looking for Yesrien, and you can do this."

Isalie nodded, frantic. *Yesrien is Arru's daughter. She disappeared, and I'm the only one that can look for her. She needs me.* "I... just give me a minute." She took a deep breath and held it. *One, two, three, four. Out, two, three, four.* She exhaled slowly, clutching Pelom's arm, trying to get ahold of herself and put one foot in front of the other.

"Follow me." Pelom stepped around her and Isalie fell into step behind him, focusing on his back so that she couldn't see the tunnel beyond.

Don't act like the Isalie that followed Jen into that storm. Act like the Isalie who told Cel how she felt, the person Cel believes in. Act like Jhera, because she'd be excited if she was still alive to start a new life.

Pelom moved forward and handed his parchment to the guard. They exchanged a few words, and Pelom started forward, but stopped at the solid crystal door in the gate. Light from the Ambient orbs in the tunnel glittered on the veins of crystal running through the stone walls, ceiling, and floor. Two more guards stood in front of the tunnel, and both glanced at Pelom standing by the doorway.

"Next," the guard called, rolling her shoulders in her beige uniform, jostling the chain around her neck that held a mask. A pearlescent cloak hung from her shoulders; everything she wore looked brand new, more refined than what Cel made.

Body trembling, she approached the guard and presented her parchment. The woman flashed a consoling smile at her. "First time in the Inners?" she asked.

Isalie froze. *What do I say?* she wondered. "Uh, y-yes," she stammered.

The guard peered at her. "It's all right. Nothing to worry about. Less than out here, at least, since the storms can't touch it."

"Yes," Isalie replied awkwardly. "I guess so."

"And besides, you earned your time there. Otherwise, you wouldn't have this." The woman offered the parchment back to Isalie, who stuffed it into her pocket.

"That's true," Isalie said. The guard gazed at her a few moments longer, and Isalie began to worry that her search was over before it could begin.

She knows I'm a fraud, she knows I don't belong. I should just turn around, go home before they can put me in an Ambient prison, or execute me or something.

She slid her foot back a step, tempted to run despite the voice in the back of her head telling her to keep going, to be the woman Cel thought she was instead of the coward she'd always been.

The woman smiled wider. "You look so nervous, dear, but I promise, it's lovely in there. And since you seem to know Pelom," she glanced toward the gate, where Pelom still stood, "let him show you around. He earned his transfer a while back, but not so long that he's forgotten what a big step it is to take a commission in the inner city." She winked. "He'll make sure you don't get lost on your first day."

Isalie nodded, not trusting herself to speak again. Instead, she grasped the hand that Pelom held out and nodded to the woman. Pelom tugged on her hand to urge her forward, and she followed him to the entrance, past the smirking face of one of the guards at the door.

The tunnel glowed from the Ambient orbs, with raised portcullises every fifty feet. Guards stood next to each portcullis, stationed next to levers that Isalie assumed controlled each one, ready to drop them at a moment's notice.

They really don't trust the people in the Outers, do they? Isalie marveled.

It was easier to convince herself that she wouldn't be swallowed with so much light around her, but it was also easier to imagine the walls of the tunnel closing in, collapsing tighter with every step she took. Isalie traded between staring at the expanse ahead of her and glancing over her shoulder for the place she'd entered to reassure herself that the tunnel didn't go on forever.

"You're afraid of tunnels?" Pelom asked.

Isalie grimaced at him, and then tried to focus on his shimmering cloak, rather than her surroundings. Its swaying rhythm was hypnotic, and the distraction helped. "Since I was a little girl," Isalie replied shakily. "They make me feel like I'm being swallowed by some great beast."

"I get it," Pelom responded. "I have the same thing about worms. When I was a kid, one got stuck on my pants in the rain, and its wriggling body burned through to my skin while it died." He shuddered. "Can't stand them now."

Isalie wondered just how old Pelom was; he couldn't be more than seventeen. "Nothing so terrifying happened to me," she said, "I just don't like closed spaces, I think."

Pelom squeezed her hand. "Well, if you need to close your eyes, I can lead you. I'm sorry this is the only way in."

"Thank you, Pelom." Isalie closed her eyes and let the young man lead her, hating that she needed it. She hated that she couldn't maintain her confidence for more than an hour before she almost ruined everything.

The path continued in a straight line, and eventually angled upward to higher ground. Isalie dared to open her eyes when the light changed. Relief washed over her when she saw the sunlight beyond the final gate, as bright and joyous as the clouds covering the Outers were dismal.

She almost ran to the end of the tunnel, like she would have with Jentien, but she felt as afraid of what she might find on the other side of the last portcullis as she was of the close walls. With Pelom tugging her forward they emerged, squinting, into the bright natural light of a clear day. She looked up and gasped.

There were no clouds here, no storm. Just blue sky, and bright sun. She stood still, soaking in her first bit of sunshine in months. It felt so warm and inviting, she wanted to stand here for the rest of her life.

"This way," Pelom beckoned from a few feet away. The square—everything she could see—was open to the sky. No deep eaves, only glittering crystalline towers surrounding the district and a wall of the same material along the river, refracting the sunlight into a prismatic spray that painted the town and the cobblestones in a riot of color. She hadn't seen any of this from the other side; the clouds were so low to the river on the outers side that it'd obscured all view of the inner city.

"You'll need to check in with the census office to get your housing assignment." Pelom led her down the road opposite the tunnel, one of seven that branched out from the octagonal courtyard they were standing in. He lowered his voice and waited for her to come closer before leaning in. "Remember, your name is Jhera. You don't want to slip up. There are steep punishments for Stills."

Isalie's stomach flipped with nervous dread. "What kind of punishment?"

Pelom's open expression closed. "Publicly, banishment to the Outers. But not all the banished are seen again." He shot her a sharp look that made her blood run cold. "Don't get caught."

Isalie shook her head. "Where is the office? I don't want to keep you."

"It's just this way. Things work the same here as in the Outers. You don't work, you don't eat."

Isalie frowned. She knew how the anxiety etched into his features felt. She glanced around at the clean stone buildings, happy gardens and planter boxes with beautiful flowers in almost as many colors as the towers projected. The Stills, marked by their beige uniforms, walked with purpose, but they weren't harried, and seemed... content. A group of children ran screaming from an open door across the street, but they were joyful, playful screams, not screams of terror or pain. This part of Olunei was so happy and calm.

It felt like a slap in the face.

Disgusted, she turned her gaze to the edge of the inner city. Eight towers acted as a barrier against the Gloom in the distance. A wide, fast-moving river was just visible beyond the crystal wall, separating the two sections of the city even further, directly beneath the leading edge of the storm created by the Gloom. The Outers sat shrouded in darkness beneath those roiling clouds, a stark contrast to where she currently stood.

The Gloom itself was massive, and but for this eye of the storm, all was dark. Lightning sparked along the perimeter, like the flash of a predator's eyes stalking its prey. It was always moving, always searching for a weak spot at which to pounce. A shiver passed down Isalie's spine.

The wide street branched off into three smaller lanes and Pelom veered right, away from the edge of the Inners and the Gloom. Sweat dripped down Isalie's neck, plastering her hair to her damp skin.

I'd almost forgotten how oppressive the heat was, she thought. It'd been early spring when they'd fallen to the Gloom, but she could feel the approach of autumn by the weight of the humidity in the air.

Pelom stopped in front of a brick building with an open door. "This is it," he said, pointing inside. "Good luck."

"Thank you for your help, Pelom." Isalie clutched his hand and shook it. "I really appreciate everything you've done for me."

He ducked his head, embarrassed. "You're welcome." Pelom turned and hustled back the way they had come.

Isalie took a deep breath and walked inside. She found a bright space with light, polished wood floors and tall windows to let in the sunshine. A line of people in burgundy and beige stood waiting their turns in front of her.

In no time, she had a piece of paper with her assignments, both housing and work, and she stepped out into the light again. After taking a moment to bask, she looked left and right, and followed a sign that pointed her in the right direction.

CHAPTER TWENTY-NINE

ISALIE COULDN'T BELIEVE HOW much *space* they had here. Tall stone, brick, and shingled buildings stretched from the ground in a grid pattern that was easier to navigate than Lacorsia, but even in the capital they hadn't had so many gardens, lawns, and parks. Patches of green manicured lawns sat between each store and dormitory she passed, and an entire block was dedicated to a sweeping flower garden and small stand of trees.

She frowned, not recognizing any of the plants and trees she saw, wondering how the grass stayed so green in this heat.

Is this *what the Ambient spend their energy on?* she wondered, growing increasingly infuriated. *There are people dying in the Outers, and they have room to* sunbathe*?!*

Her tentative footsteps became angry stomps as she followed the trail the attendant had hastily scribbled for her. It wound around to the left and ended in a tall, crystalline wall. Beyond it, tall spires like the spires of the Malachi's palace twined gracefully toward the sky.

I must be getting close, she thought. She skirted along the edge of the wall, looking at the uniform buildings across the street, arranged like a wall to block sight of the Ambient district from the rest of the Inners. Isalie snorted in derision. *Typical Ambient, keeping even the view of what they have from the rest of us.*

She shook off the frustration, taking note of the building numbers instead of what they represented. *Two more,* she thought, passing a dormitory building on the left. Next to the building number was a bulletin board with several papers tacked to it. *Next one. Here.*

A woman in guard's uniform stepped through the door Isalie was facing and glanced up at her with a nod as she passed by. Isalie nodded back and walked to the door of the building. Her hand hung just above the knob as she took several steadying breaths, taking a moment to scan the bulletins, seeing an arrest report with a name she didn't recognize. *Banishment-outer city,* the sentence read. Shuddering as she considered what might happen to *her* if she was caught, she opened the door and stepped inside.

The interior was so like the dormitory she'd lived in, its layout almost identical. The décor was different; rather than the drab, gray, sparse look that inspired despair, this space was designed to evoke comfort. The wooden floor was light, reminding her of home, and there were comfortable chairs along the wall, arranged so that people could stop and have a conversation next to large windows that looked out on the street, filtering the sunlight to illuminate the room.

"Your first time in the inner city?" Isalie blinked at a man peering at her from the midst of a group seated next to the window. She looked over her shoulder for the person he must be addressing, and he chuckled, pointing directly at her. "I'm talking to you, ma'am."

He, like the rest, wore a burgundy uniform trimmed with beige, and all their jackets were open as they relaxed. He had jet black hair and piercing blue eyes, with warm olive skin beneath a neat beard and mustache.

Remember what Cel said. Be confident. Isalie cleared her throat and smiled. "Yes." She tried to smile. "I guess it's obvious."

The man with the raven hair smiled. "It is, but there's nothing wrong with that. What's your name?"

"I–" she cut herself off before she gave her real name. "Jhera."

"Well, Jhera, my name is Cortlen, and these are Wist," he pointed out a blonde, muscular man, "Ionna," the woman with ringlets of bright red hair, "and Lor." He pointed at the last man in their group, who was short and stockier than the rest, with a thick head of dark brown hair and a ruddy complexion. "Welcome to your new home."

"Thank you," Isalie replied. She glanced over her shoulder in the direction of the stairs, her body tensing to run. She wanted nothing more than to find her room and hide for as long as she could. But she had a job to do, and she couldn't do it unless she started talking to people. If this group was inclined to be friendly with her, maybe she could use that to her advantage.

"Do you see many like me?" she asked. "From the outer city, I mean."

Ionna nodded. "A few. Everyone who's promoted tends to stay, though, so new faces are rare."

Cortlen looked past Isalie, and his smile grew. "Finally, golden child. We've been waiting to have our breakfast until you came back from your run. We just had the pleasure of making a new friend. Jhera, meet our golden child."

Isalie turned around as a figure walked past the end of the wall into view. Chin-length brown hair was tucked behind a familiar ear, and his chin was dark with stubble. Her knees felt weak, but her body went rigid at the same time.

"Cort," Jentien said. His voice was like a balm to Isalie's nerves, and she inhaled sharply.

Jen's eyes went wide with disbelief when he heard her gasp. His whole body stilled, and Isalie felt a tear trickle down her cheek. He looked so tired, deep bruises beneath his eyes like he hadn't been sleeping. They'd had a few harrowing journeys on the road that had lent him this hollow, haunted look, and her heart broke seeing him in such a state.

"Iz," he whispered. His tone was wary and suspicious, but hopeful. A prayer, rather than a confirmation.

"Hi," she whispered. He reached forward and touched her cheek with two fingers. She placed a hand on his cheek, the stiff whiskers rasping against her palm.

His face crumpled when he felt her touch, as if he hadn't believed she was real until then. His eyes bored into hers—pained, relieved, broken—and then he pulled her into a crushing hug.

⁂

She's here, she's real. My Iz.

Jentien clutched her, not ready to let go. He dreamed most nights about her; the warmth of her smile, her sense of humor, their deep bond. She'd tortured him in his waking moments since she'd been ripped away from him.

He'd held himself together for all this time, pouring himself into his assignments with a fervor that matched his pain, and now that she was in his arms, that hold slipped. Tears fell down his cheeks before he knew he was crying, and he knew that there would be no stopping this outpouring of his pent-up emotions. This was everything he had ever wanted. She was alive.

"Jen," Iz's voice was muffled against his shoulder. "Can't breathe."

"Sorry," he said, his voice thick with tears. He pulled away and held her face between his hands so that he could search her face, to convince himself that this wasn't another dream. Her eyes were the same, but her hair was longer, and less frazzled than usual. She looked healthy, without the scars that most people got from the rain.

"I didn't know anyone could cry this much," Wist said from behind them.

"Jentien?" Cortlen asked.

Jentien pulled Isalie away from the others without a word, heading for the stairs. He heard them call out, but he ignored them.

"Jen, where are we going?" Isalie's breathing sounded a bit labored, but they were almost on the right floor, so Jentien didn't stop.

"To my room," he said. He wiped a hand across his cheek to mop up the tears and smiled over his shoulder. Tears sparkled in her eyes as well, but Jentien was rewarded with a wide smile. Despite his shock, he felt comforted. He felt whole for the first time in these seemingly endless months.

"Okay," she murmured, a blush growing in her cheeks.

She's more beautiful than I remembered, he thought as he rushed up the stairs.

They stepped out of the stairwell and down the hall to his dormitory. He fumbled the key in the lock until the door sprang open, revealing his tidy room. He shut and locked the door, not trusting that the others wouldn't come by later to see how they were getting on. He wanted Iz all to himself.

He rested his head against the door, suddenly uncertain about what he should say or do. He was half sure when he turned around, she would be gone. He'd had those nightmares, too, and he didn't know if he could stand that right now.

Iz put a tentative hand flat between his shoulder blades to let him know she was there, just as she had when they were children and she'd sought him out in his dark room to help him through his nightmares. He shuddered, and she rubbed her hand back and forth.

Jentien let out a choked sob. *Of course she's trying to comfort me right now,* he thought.

He glanced over his shoulder to see her standing so close that the heat of her body warmed his back, waiting for him to speak as she always had. He just let her hand move back and forth, back and forth, soothing him. He felt like a little boy again, with his best friend sitting near him while he wondered where his parents had gone.

But Isalie was here. She had come back from the dead.

He turned, but she didn't remove her hand. It slid to his shoulder, and he placed his hand over hers. He couldn't stand her touch to leave him now that he'd found it again.

"I can't believe you're alive," he whispered. His voice was rough to his ears.

She smiled, sad and happy at the same time. With his free hand, he reached up to wipe a tear from her cheek. "Same," she said.

"I'm so sorry I led you here," he said. "I didn't mean for this to happen. I thought you were dead, and then you weren't, and then I woke up here and you were gone. They told me you were dead." He couldn't stop the words from falling out of his mouth. "I'm sorry I didn't find you."

Isalie just smiled at him. *How does she do that?* he wondered. *How can that sad smile make me feel so seen?* He was a mess, and she was standing there, calm and patient.

"I didn't find you, either."

Jentien nodded. "I guess not," he said, but then he frowned. He'd checked with the census office every day since he'd arrived with no sign of her. "Where were you?"

"The outer city."

"Then, why couldn't they find you? They said they had a record of everyone in the outer city, too!"

Isalie shook her head. "I don't know, Jen."

He pulled her into a hug again, needing to feel her in his arms. He buried his face in her hair, inhaling her scent.

"I missed you," Isalie said.

"You have no *idea* how much I've missed you," Jentien replied.

They stood there, just holding each other. Jentien felt like everything was how it should be. His whole life with her by his side had been a waste. It should have been so much more.

Through all these months without her, he had replayed so many conversations in his mind. He thought about when she'd finally told him how she felt, and cringed at how stupid and oblivious he'd been in the face of such a declaration. But Isalie had been his heart since they were kids. It took losing her to admit it to himself.

Jentien pulled back so he could look at her and brushed a lock of hair off her face.

I can do it right this time, he thought. *We're together, and I can give her the life she's always wanted.*

Iz smiled ruefully at him. "I need to report to my assignment. I wish I could stay longer..."

Jentien nodded, only now realizing that he was still soaked in sweat and would be late for his shift if he didn't clean up immediately. "So do I, but..." He glanced at his uniform hanging from a hook on the wall and back at her with a pained grimace. "I'm so afraid that this is just another dream, and as soon as I let you out of my sight, you'll disappear."

Isalie's face crumpled, and more tears spilled down her cheeks. He didn't resist the urge to wipe them away, and relished the blush that crept across her skin.

"It's not a dream," she whispered, her voice hoarse. "I'll come back. We have more time."

He followed another impulse to take one of her hands and brush a kiss across her knuckles. This felt right, and didn't leave him uneasy, as it had with Tulia Kiyash. Iz blushed harder as she closed her eyes and inhaled sharply.

Before she could open her eyes, or he could consider what he was doing, he leaned forward and kissed her lips. She inhaled again, then leaned into him as if she'd been waiting for this moment her entire life. He ran his fingers through her hair, and then released her.

Her sapphire eyes opened, and she smiled at him with a mixture of surprise and longing before quickly turning away. In that moment, he decided that he would spend the rest of his life trying to make her smile like that. He would spend his life letting her know just how important she was, and how much he loved her.

CHAPTER THIRTY

Jen is alive. Jen is alive. The words had repeated in her mind as he insisted that he would stay with her, that his assignment didn't matter. But *she* had a job to do, which she reminded herself as she resisted the urge to turn and run back to him after he'd escorted her to the tailor's building. It was long and low, a few streets away from the tunnel to the Outers.

Several Stills passed her, and she turned to follow them inside to find several tables that ran the length of the building. A heap of brown fabric and spools of sparkling thread sat before each chair. The air hummed with Ambient energy that set her teeth on edge, just like Ambient Sundries at home.

A door on the far end of the wide space stood open, and a petite woman with a chin-length bob of green hair that twined together like seaweed approached. Her large gray eyes peered up at Isalie with her hand out.

"Jhera Folci?" she asked.

Isalie fumbled the parchment with her assignment from her tunic pocket and held it out, trying to keep her hand from trembling. Her anxiety roared to life, the stupor that finding Jen had put her in evaporating as she snapped her focus back to the job she needed to do. It ebbed a bit when the woman handed her the parchment and crooked a long indigo finger at her to follow.

"Your workstation," she said, gesturing to an open seat at the first table, about halfway down. "You have a quota to fill each day, which you will present to me at day's close. No meal vouchers are required, but I report to the monitors daily, and the rules here are the same as in the outer city. I assume you can sew?"

"Y-yes," Isalie stammered.

"Good, then follow the pattern and don't make mistakes. The thread is a precious commodity; the enchantment in it is what makes the cloaks rain resistant. Each cloak that we make is sent directly to the outer city, and you will be expected to accompany deliveries on a rotating schedule. New promotions are required to attend on the next delivery date, which is in about two weeks." She put her hands on her hips as her shoulders rolled back. "We take pride in the good that we're doing here, and I expect all of my people to reflect that."

"Yes, ma'am," Isalie said.

The woman nodded and strode away, leaving Isalie to take her seat and stare at the pattern on the table. It was simple enough, and she'd had some practice lately, thanks to Cel's designs. A pang of longing and guilt ran through her, but she put it aside as she pulled some fabric close and got to work.

Jentien was waiting for her when she walked inside the dormitory after dusk. He ushered her toward the stairs, away from the curious glances of the other Stills. "What's your room number?" he asked.

Isalie pulled the map out of her pocket. "Four-twelve."

"The floor above mine. I'll show you."

She followed him up, trying to reconcile his presence with the turn her life had taken in such a short time. She felt like a different person, someone who had just begun to realize her self-worth, someone who had a part to play in a game much larger than herself.

Now, here was the man she'd pined after for as long as she could remember, but she'd started to move on with someone else. Could she tell him about her mission here? He was an Ambient Guard, part of the highest Ambient house, judging by the insignia on his uniform. But he was *Jen*, and she'd always been able to trust him.

Could she put him in the kind of danger she'd willingly stepped into?

Isalie was panting by the time they reached the fourth floor, and she had to force herself to keep moving down the bright hallway until Jentien stopped at her door.

It was unlocked, and opened to reveal a room with a similar floor plan as her dormitory in the Outers, though with less dingy furniture and a bit more room. On the table across from the door was a bronze key that matched the doorknob and a spare uniform and set of underclothes.

She turned to see Jen step inside and close the door, separating them from the outside world again. Isalie wasn't prepared for this moment, as she'd spent the day focusing on her work and eyeing the people around her, wondering who she might talk to for more information. Now that she was here, she had no idea what to say, or how to explain the past few months, or how to explain Cel.

Jen's kiss still lingered on her lips, both everything she'd dreamed of and more than she'd hoped for. She'd felt his love in that kiss; that moment had cemented something between them, and there was no going back to the way they'd been. It was deeper than the blazing attraction she felt for Cel, borne of friendship and respect and companionship, and it called to her spirit profoundly.

But Cel was waiting for her, and she couldn't betray that any more than she already had. She had to tell Jen about her, before anything happened that they'd both regret.

Jen stood awkwardly across the room, which was something Isalie had never seen before. "How was your first day?" he asked.

She almost laughed; the question seemed so absurdly normal compared to the war taking place inside her. "It was fine. I'm a tailor; my parents would be so proud if they knew I'd finally settled into the life they always wanted for me." Eager to change the subject before bitter grief could creep in, she asked, "How long have you been working in an Ambient House?"

Jentien looked up, and she could almost see the calculations in his mind. "Not long, maybe... a week? Why did Cort call you Jhera?"

She grimaced, and Jen's eyes narrowed as he took a few steps closer. The way he was peering at her was intent and discerning. Before Cel and the Olugar, she would have delighted in him paying this much attention to her. Now, all she could do was stare, unable to lie to him, and reluctant to tell him the truth.

"Iz? What's wrong?"

Isalie pulled her lips between her teeth, and Jen took another step, closing the gap between them. "Jen, I... Nothing is wrong."

Jen frowned and grasped her shoulders. "You're nervous, Iz. You only do that thing with your lips when you're nervous." His eyes traveled to watch her lips, and the muscles in his cheek tensed when she untucked them.

She bit her lip again, watching Jen catch the movement, and groaned inwardly.

It felt like his heart had stopped beating while she was gone, and only the sight of her could have started it again. Jentien couldn't keep his eyes away from her mouth, even while his intuition screamed at him that something was wrong. Why was she so nervous? Why did she introduce herself to his friends as someone else?

She sighed and drooped in his arms. "Jen, I... I have so much to tell you. Can we sit down?"

"Sure, Iz." He let her go and took a seat, watching her hands fidget in her lap. She bit her bottom lip again, and Jentien couldn't help the fleeting impulse to run his finger over the spot.

"I spent months feeling like I'd died out there. You were gone, and the outer city feels like the underworld, with all of us like spirits damned by the Elders to live in torment for eternity. Every day is filled with gray clouds and burning rain."

Jentien furrowed his brow. He'd spend all his time here absorbed in his own grief, and he hadn't thought about the people on the other side of the river. He'd never taken the time to ask the other Stills, even those that had been promoted, about the outer city.

"People live in fear of being killed by the Elders-cursed *rain* every day. They eat gruel." She pointed out the window. "In here, it's as if the people in the Outers don't exist! People are starving, people are burning, or coughing up blood because they dared to *breathe outside*. And the protection the Ambient provide is falling apart."

Anxiety that he'd fought so hard to suppress became a living thing, making his hands tremble and sweat bead his brow. He despised this feeling. He'd felt it when his parents disappeared, when the Gloom beast had almost killed Isalie, and he'd never felt it so strongly as when he'd awoken to learn that Iz was gone. The realization that he'd ignored something so egregious as the outer city's suffering brought it all crashing down on him.

Iz put her hand over his, her steady, understanding gaze as comforting as it had been in the darkest moments of his life. She was his tether, and he lifted their joined hands to his lips to kiss hers.

She frowned, and the pain in her eyes made him go still. "I had to learn how to live without you. I had to pick myself up when I didn't have you to help me. And I almost didn't." She looked at their hands and swallowed hard. When she looked back at Jentien, her eyes were wet with tears. "I met someone who helped me pull myself together, and I... I'm falling in love with her."

His mind went blank, and his hands dropped to the table and fell open. Iz pulled her hands away, and it felt like he was losing her all over again. Tears rimmed his eyes, and the same emptiness that he'd only just begun to claw his way out of threatened to swallow him whole.

I was too late.

Jentien didn't know what to say, and even if he did, he couldn't form words around the lump in his throat. Isalie's shoulders shook, and tears rolled down her face. He could only imagine what she was going through, what she'd already *been* through, and how she'd survived. Her eyes met his again, and all he could see was the girl that had held him while he cried, the woman that could make a meal out of anything, and he was grateful she was here. His best friend was here, and she was in pain.

A lifetime of instinct kicked in, and he put aside his own pain, pulling his need to protect her around him like armor. Leaning across the table, he grasped her hands again and gave them a reassuring squeeze. She needed his help, and if he'd missed his chance to love her the way she'd always wanted, then he'd make sure she knew that he would always be her friend.

"What's her name?" Jentien asked.

Isalie looked up, and he watched a tear roll down her cheek. "Celeste," Isalie hiccupped.

"She's lucky to have you. Does she know that?" He looked up at her, his eyes blazing through his tears.

Her face crumpled and she sobbed harder. Jentien crouched by her chair and wrapped his arms around her shoulders. "Yes," she whispered.

"Good. You deserve someone who knows how amazing you are."

"Jen." Isalie threw her arms around his neck. "I'm so sorry."

"Me too, Iz. But I'm proud of you."

He kept a tight rein on his heartbreak. He couldn't stand the thought of making Iz feel like she'd done something wrong. He'd been too oblivious to realize how wonderful his life could have been, and he knew he should be glad she was here, that she was safe. But he couldn't stop his heart from breaking; all he could do was hold her, and push the pain down.

CHAPTER THIRTY-ONE

Isalie sobbed into Jen's shoulder. Everything was wrong; she was supposed to be invisible while she searched for information so that she could go back to Cel. She was so grateful to have Jen back, but his reaction to her had put her in the public eye, and then she'd broken his heart. She'd watched it happen, and she'd watched him put that pain aside. She'd seen him suffer after losing his parents, but he'd never hidden it from her.

He pulled away and used the end of his sleeve to wipe a tear from her cheek. "Why *are* you here?" His brow furrowed in confusion, highlighting the frown he'd been fighting to keep off his face. "I'm so grateful that you are, that I know you're alive, but... you left her behind. Why?"

Isalie grimaced, trying to figure out what to say, before Jen continued.

"You still haven't told me why Cortlen called you Jhera, Iz."

She racked her brain for something to tell him. Finally, after a few long moments of him staring at her, she sighed, and let the story unfold. Jen listened in silence, concern making his brows furrow deeper, until she was finished.

"I've always hated the way Stills were treated," she said, needing to explain when he still didn't say anything, "and I've never been able to do much. Giving money to the refugees never seemed like enough." He blinked, surprise replacing concern. "Here, I've made cloaks that work better than what the Ambient provide, and now I have a chance to help a worried mother. I know it's nothing like what you've always done, but at least being nobody is finally worth something."

"You're not."

"What?" She'd expected him to argue against what she'd chosen to do, to tell her that it was too dangerous, or that the Ambient weren't villains. The passion in his eyes as he clenched his jaw took her aback.

"You're not a nobody. You never have been. Not to me."

"Jen–"

"I want to help," he interrupted, cutting off her protest. He'd known it was coming; he knew her so well. "I'm in the Kiyash spire every day. If anyone knows what happened to the woman who went missing, it's Mistress Kiyash."

Isalie shook her head. "Absolutely not. It's too dangerous."

"Which is why *you* shouldn't risk it, Iz."

"I'm already here, Jen. I'm not going back until I have something to report, or until it's my turn to make a delivery."

"I'll go with you," Jentien asserted. She started to shake her head again, to insist that it wasn't necessary, and it would attract too much attention, but he kept talking. "I want to see it for myself. Recruits are supposed to have an outer city rotation, but I never did. Maybe if I had, I would have found you sooner."

She wanted so badly to stay by his side like she had before the Gloom had swallowed them. She needed to keep him close so that she wouldn't fear losing him again. But that was selfish, and it was dangerous. She needed to steer clear of the Ambient, and being with one of their guards would only increase the chances of meeting one.

"I don't want to lose you again, Iz." His voice broke on her name, and she could see how much effort it took to keep his tears at bay. "I know it's selfish, but I can't let you go. You're my best friend. I was lost without you."

Isalie smoothed a lock of hair behind his ear and cupped his cheek. He leaned into her touch, and even though she knew that this was all it could be, she relished the feeling. Comforting him had always felt like the most important job she'd ever have. That wasn't the case now, but it was still important, and it made her feel like this one piece of her life could be repaired.

They brought their meals up to Isalie's room, and Jentien watched her eat her sauteed taro root and roasted Gloom beast with occasional huffs of displeasure. He still couldn't believe that Isalie had become a sort of spy for the Stills, nor that the Ambient would abduct people. Cortlen had trained them about the procedure for anyone who committed crimes: apprehend them and any evidence, then bring them to the barracks until an Ambient and their Guard arrived to process them. From there, the Ambient would hold a trial, and decide the punishment.

Jentien hadn't witnessed any crimes like he'd heard about in Lacorsia. There was no need for theft as long as you worked, and squabbles that could lead to physical violence were almost unheard of, with the literal cloud hanging over the city. Crimes committed seemed limited to dereliction of duty, and the more serious crime of speaking out against the Ambient and their laws, no different than the rest of Vortheim.

Jentien hadn't seen any arrests, but he imagined the Ambient would have a prison, where Stills would wait until they were banished to the outer city or released. If this Yesrien had been a spy like Iz, maybe she was still imprisoned. But if she'd only just been promoted here, why would they want her?

"I want to meet her," he said without preamble. He smiled as he winced inwardly.

"Who?" Iz asked, her brows drawing together. They shot toward her hairline a moment later. "Celeste?"

Jentien nodded. He'd made this decision as they stood in the food line downstairs, that if Iz had given her heart to someone, he needed to look that person in the eyes and make sure they wouldn't hurt her. It reminded him of the way Savar had looked at *him* all those months ago, and asked if Jentien would protect her heart.

"I-I'm supposed to go on a delivery in two weeks," she offered.

"I'll see if I can get assigned to that run. They always take a few guards, and they have the rest of the day as leave. We should have enough time. If you think it's a good idea."

Iz took a bite of taro and chewed, her eyes distant as she thought. When her eyes locked onto his again, there was a glint of hope and excitement there.

"I'd love to introduce you to Cel," she said. A blush started in her cheeks, and she smiled that shy smile that he'd spent his nights dreaming of.

Brushing off the thought, he smiled back. "Good." He stood and took her empty plate, turning toward the door. As much as he didn't want to leave her, he needed some space to sort out his feelings, and if he didn't leave now, he might just end up sleeping on her floor.

Walking into the hallway was one of the hardest things he'd done, but he put a smile on his face when he bid her goodnight. She looked at him like she wanted to say something, but he turned his back and headed for the stairs.

He spent the night staring at the ceiling, imagining her sleeping above him. He longed to rush back to her room and beg her to let him in, but he couldn't do that to her. He'd seen how much it hurt her to tell him that she'd moved on, and he wouldn't force her to do it over and over again.

When the sky lightened from inky black to a dull gray, heralding dawn, he got out of bed, pulled on his recruit jacket, and went for a run. Focusing on the pounding of his feet over the cobblestones, his beating heart, and his steady breathing helped him sort through the disappointment and heartbreak of the last day.

He'd been numb for months, and Iz coming back was so much. The joy of seeing her again, the fear of losing her, the pain of knowing that her return wouldn't be what he wanted, at least he could *feel* it. Now that she was here, he wanted to feel again. When the pain threatened to choke him, he took another breath and reminded himself that she was here. She might not love him the way he loved her, but his best friend was alive, and she was happy and whole.

Sweat dripped down the back of his neck when he returned to the dormitory, just as the sun broke over the horizon and flooded the inner city with golden light. The world had been so dull before, but now he could see its beauty again, because Iz had brought it back to him. He looked up at the building with his hands on his hips, taking deep breaths to calm his racing heart, and smiled to himself.

Isalie was up there, and she was safe. He would do anything to ensure she stayed that way.

Isalie coaxed a large needle through the hem of the thick fabric cloak. After a restless night worrying about Jen, worrying about Cel, and worrying that she'd end up hurting both, she'd been glad to get dressed and find her breakfast. Jen had been pleasant as they ate, though his eyes were filled with pain despite his smile.

She glanced at the other Stills around the table, all sewing. The thread in her hands thrummed with Ambient energy, and she took care not to waste it.

No one met her glance, all studiously focused on their work. She could pick out the Stills that had been here the longest by the quick efficiency of their work and in their more relaxed postures. The more recent promotions were stiff, as if afraid that they'd be removed any moment, sent back to the Outers to suffer again.

She watched for a time, hoping to catch someone looking, and was rewarded by the person sitting across the table meeting her gaze. They were about a decade older than her, with long white hair pulled back from their pale green face. Their ears were shaped like leaves, and embarrassment or fear made them blush, which crept up their ears, changing from green to yellow to red, like leaves in autumn.

Isalie smiled, and they looked away. When they nervously looked up again, she leaned forward to whisper to them.

"Your work is so neat; I hope I can be as good someday."

They smiled, their ears darkening to red. "Thank you."

"Have you been here long?" Isalie suspected she knew the answer, since their shoulders hunched around their ears and they whipped their head toward the supervisor's office nervously.

"A few months." They looked down at their work, clearly finished with the conversation.

A few months. That *could* be around the time that Yesrien was promoted. Was it possible that this person knew her? Could they know what had happened to her?

Isalie glanced at them, studiously ignoring her, and decided that she needed to be patient. They wouldn't appreciate her badgering information out of them. Perhaps she could try to speak to them again while they ate lunch, away from the workstations, where they could talk more freely.

Not today, but soon. She had two weeks before she'd be in the Outers again, and perhaps she would have something to tell Cel.

CHAPTER THIRTY-TWO

Just ask for an assignment no one wants, Jentien coached himself. *There's nothing wrong with that.*

Jentien opened the door and stepped inside the Kiyash spire guard entrance to find the foyer empty and quiet. The deep blue runner absorbed the sound of his feet as he walked past countless House Kiyash sigils adorning tapestries and banners. He gazed up at all the sunbursts over gray and blue, something he'd associated with bringing light to the darkness of Olunei, in the rare moments that he'd thought anything of them at all.

Now, they seemed to mock his ignorance as he strode to the end of the wide hall, toward the commander's office. Gazing at the paintings of landscapes surrounding Olunei between tapestries, Jentien wondered what it must have been like before the Gloom rolled in. This peninsula had been beautiful once, a jewel of modern construction surrounded by sparkling aquamarine waters. When he neared the door to the commander's office, he put his musing aside and rearranged his face into a blank expression to mask his anxiety.

Jentien knocked on the door, and his commander's voice answered, muffled by the closed door. "Come in," he called. Jentien opened the door, blinking at the bright light shining through the window directly behind the wide oak desk.

Commander Rallac ran his finger over his black mustache, peppered with grey, that matched his short-cut hair and bushy eyebrows. Those brows rose with happy expectation when he saw who had opened his door, and then his gaze flicked back to the paper poised on his desk.

"Jentien! I was just wondering how things are with young Master Kiyash."

"Surprising. I hadn't expected to train an Ambient, but he's sharp, and is excelling. Sir, I wonder if I might request one of the outer city assignments."

The commander looked up from his desk in surprise. "No one *requests* those assignments." He sat back in his wooden chair, clasping his hands together on his desk as he studied Jentien's face. "In a short time, you've earned a prestigious assignment, safe within the inner city. Why would you jeopardize that safety to run an errand?"

Jentien's direct gaze didn't waver, because he couldn't let the truth slip free. He couldn't put Iz at risk. "Most of my squad did rotations in the outer city, braving the storm. I just want to earn my way like they did."

His commander studied him a moment longer with a slight smile, and then he pulled a drawer in his desk open, removing a logbook. He rifled through the pages as if looking for something specific and stopped to scan a page. "That selfless attitude will take you far."

Nodding to himself, he replaced the book and pushed away from his desk to walk around it and clap a hand on Jentien's shoulder. "The next equipment run is in two weeks," he reached to the right, pulling a paper from the stack.

Leaning sideways, he used an inked quill to carefully scratch the location of his assignment on a blank line, and, with wide sweeps, signed his initials at the bottom next to the Ambient seal. "The assignment is to accompany the delivery, ensure the safety of the Stills in your care, and see that they return to the inner city. Don't stray far in the outer city; it's dangerous. Equip yourself appropriately; you'll find everything you need in the storage locker." He handed the paper to Jentien.

"Thank you, sir," Jentien replied.

"Thank *you*, Themori. I have a good feeling about you, son. One day, you could become commander, if you continue to put the well-being of others above yourself. I'll make sure the Ambient know your name."

He fell into a routine with Isalie over the next few days. They ate breakfast in her room, talking about Jentien's training and her work from the previous day before they went to their duties. They took their evening meals in his room, and then he spent his nights sleeping fitfully, wishing she would lay next to him like she had so many times on the road.

He was grateful for the workout he was putting Cortlen's new recruits through a week after Isalie's reappearance, and even more grateful that Cort had joined them; he was so tired that he might be able to sleep that night.

The sun dropped behind the Kiyash spire, bathing the courtyard in a prismatic glow, when he called for them to get some water. Cortlen joined him at the barrel where he scooped it into cups for the recruits. Together they handed out the water and watched Kiale join a group a short distance away as they commiserated about the heat.

"You know," Cort said, "you don't *need* to involve me in every workout. I'd be just as happy watching."

Jentien laughed, something that would have been much harder a week ago. "And let you go soft?" He pushed his hair off his face. "We can't have that."

Cortlen watched Jentien hand over the last of the cups with a smile on his face. He didn't stop when Jentien took several for himself, letting the last drop over his head to wash some of the sweat away. After smoothing his hair back again, thankful when a gentle breeze wicked away some of the moisture from his skin to cool him, he turned a curious look at his friend.

"What, Cort?"

"You're different."

Jentien didn't answer him, choosing to retrieve the lid of the barrel and push it firmly in place.

"Who is she?"

Jentien felt his face heat and stooped to pick up his discarded uniform coat to avoid looking at Cortlen. He hadn't been subtle, he knew that, but he'd hoped that the others wouldn't care that Isalie had affected him so strongly. He'd been avoiding Cortlen, specifically, since his friend was so observant, but he hadn't been able to avoid this moment.

"Who?" Jentien asked.

Cortlen scoffed. "Jhera."

Jentien searched for the right words, something that would appease Cortlen without giving anything away. This was the one person he'd shared some of his story with, so he had to be careful.

"She's... I don't know, she makes me happy."

He finally looked at Cortlen, and he could see that his vague answer hadn't been enough. Cortlen knew there was more to this story.

"She does," Cortlen replied. "And I guess that's all that matters." Cort clapped him on the shoulder and turned toward his recruits. But he paused and leaned close to whisper in Jentien's ear. "Whatever is really going on, please be careful, golden child."

Isalie rubbed her fingers, which were raw at the end of every day from forcing the heavy needle through thick fabric. She'd spent the past twelve days buried in her work, listening intently to the Stills at their midday meals, catching snippets of gossip from those that had been here longest. Nothing that pointed her in Yesrien's direction. The strongest hope she had was in the person she'd briefly spoken to on her first day. She'd cast shy but friendly glances their way at meal-times, but was careful not to push too hard and scare them away.

Twelve days into her new job, she was surprised to see the pale green skinned person sitting near her usual space in the adjacent room for meals, and smiled to herself as she sat down. Placing her linen napkin in her lap, she picked up her fork and speared a piece of mango. Her eyes closed as she savored the sweetness of it; whatever the Ambient did to grow the fruit here, their mangoes were always perfectly sweet.

"My name is Creno," her companion said, surprising her again. "What is yours?"

"Jhera," Isalie lied. She kept her eyes on her plate, knowing that her face could give her deception away.

"I am pleased to meet you, Jhera," Creno replied with a shy smile. "You are new here?"

"Almost two weeks now. I still can't believe there's no storm here."

"I am grateful for every day."

Isalie smiled at them and then looked down at her plate again, trying to decide what to say next.

"Were you in the outer city long?" Creno shuddered instead of answering. Isalie cursed inwardly. "Apologies," she said. "I'm still adjusting, and I sometimes forget how to talk to people." She shrugged, seeing Creno peering at her out of the corner of their eye. "You know what it's like out there."

Creno nodded. "I do. No apology necessary."

"Thank you."

They ate in silence for a few minutes, until Creno spoke again.

"I have also found trouble speaking to others, even after so much time here. It is nice to talk." Isalie smiled again, and this time Creno smiled back. "Were you born here?"

Isalie shook her head. "I came from Lacorsia. I got too close to the Gloom and was swallowed by it."

Creno nodded sadly. "I hailed from the mountains to the east, until I suffered the same fate."

"I'm so sorry," Isalie replied. "My home was so noisy, I always wished I could find some peace. But it's so strange to live in a place that is so silent."

"At least the inner city is alive," Creno said. "The plants and animals can sing here. Out there, there is nothing but the drone of the Gloom."

"Do you know many people here?" Isalie tried to make the question casual and took another bite of food.

Creno shook their head. "I knew no one in the outer city. Here, I recognize only the faces of the few that were promoted with me."

"Are the others you recognize working here?"

"Not all. One was..." They trailed off.

Isalie fought the urge to lean forward and force herself into their line of sight when they looked away.

"Assigned somewhere else?"

"I cannot speak of it."

"Is something wrong?" Isalie asked. "I hope I haven't offended you."

"There is no offense." Creno leaned closer, lowering their voice. "You must not ask questions when Stills disappear, or you might be next."

Isalie's eyes widened. She didn't need to pretend to be nervous. "Disappear? Did they do something wrong?" When Creno nodded, Isalie continued. "I thought Stills would be banished back to the outer city as punishment?"

Creno shook their head. "We will speak no more of this."

They picked up their tray and stood, walking briskly toward the door to the workroom. Isalie turned back to her lunch, mulling over Creno's words. They knew more about Yesrien, Isalie was sure, but she recognized the desperate terror in their eyes. They'd already said more than they were comfortable with, and it would take time to coax those secrets out, if she could at all.

Her assignment to the Outers was days away, and she had nothing to report. She longed to see Celeste, but didn't want to disappoint her. And it wasn't just this task; Jen would be with her, and she wasn't sure she could handle the introduction that loomed.

Isalie waited in Jentien's room, watching for him through the window with a plate in her lap on his bed. He'd given her permission to come and go as she pleased, and while she hadn't used it before, something in her yearned to be close to him tonight.

Maybe it was the pressure of having nothing to contribute yet, or the constant nagging feeling that she was betraying two people she loved by being too selfish to let Jen go, but she needed his solid presence.

Eventually, as sunset crept closer, she spotted Jen's face when he looked up before ducking inside the building. Standing when she heard the door handle turn, their eyes locked. The love—and pain—in his took her breath away, because it was the same look she'd seen in her own after he'd been taken from her.

He carried his meal to the bed to join her. "Hi, Iz," he said, his voice hoarse, as if choked by the emotion he was struggling not to show her. "Did you learn anything today?"

She grasped the distraction from the aching hole in her chest like the lifeline that it was. "The person I talked to in my first days?" Jen nodded to let her know he remembered. "Their name is Creno, and they remember Yesrien. They *were* promoted at the same time, and her disappearance—their word—scared them. They wouldn't talk about it."

Jen leaned forward. "That's odd." When she shot him a questioning look, he explained. "They post arrest notices outside the dormitories, but they always list the offense. Mostly dereliction of duty, but Cortlen told me there were a few people charged with hoarding resources about a year back. Even a Prism user.

It doesn't happen often, and the Ambient always let the rest of us know what happened as a deterrent."

Isalie nodded, distractedly chewing on a piece of flatbread. She hadn't seen any signs of Prism here; not like she had in the Outers. Perhaps people were better at hiding it here. Or, they weren't as desperate to escape as the people on the other side of the river.

"My point is," Jen said, "if she'd been arrested, why wouldn't Creno be able to talk about it? And why would they call it a disappearance?"

"I don't know," Isalie said. "Hopefully I can find out soon." She sighed. "Not before we go to the Outers, though." Isalie eyed Jentien, watching his throat bob as he drank the last of his water from a ceramic cup. "You don't have to go with me, you know."

His eyes shot to hers, determined. "I'm coming, Iz."

"I'll be safe, I promise."

He shook his head. "I want to see things for myself. I want to meet Celeste. Mostly..." Fear and loss haunted his features. "I need to see you through this."

"Jen—"

He cut her off by putting a hand over hers and giving it a gentle squeeze. "I've spent all my energy protecting people because I needed to. I couldn't protect my parents, but I'll save as many others as I can, even if I need to go against orders to do it. And I'll protect you," he said, his eyes flashing with ferocity that made her swallow any protest she might have made, "because you are the most important person in the world. To Celeste, to Yesrien... And me."

CHAPTER THIRTY-THREE

"It's a bit disconcerting, walking toward the thing that we've been taught to avoid all our lives." The Gloom roiled and shifted beyond the towers glinting in the early-morning sunlight. Isalie looked away from the Gloom to find Jentien staring at it, and a shudder passed over him.

"It is," she agreed. "It's even worse knowing you're surrounded by it day and night." Isalie took a deep breath and looked at the tunnel, feeling Jentien's eyes on her. She hadn't noticed on her way in, but there were booths to either side of the tunnel with guards seated behind each counter. Nearby, a trio of guards stood scrutinizing the shipment Isalie had loaded the afternoon before.

The task was simple: accompany the crates to the Outers, help offload and inventory them in the warehouse near the tunnel, and head back to the Inners. They weren't required to report to their inner city duties until tomorrow, and Isalie hoped they could slip away from the rest of the detail without incident.

Isalie and Jentien joined the guards, one of whom perked up as he recognized Jentien.

"Jentien, you headed to the Outers?"

"Lawgra, good to see you. I'm on delivery escort today."

"Finally pulled the short straw? Well, be careful out there." The man barely glanced at Isalie, only checked the paper that she offered with her assignment written on it.

"Thanks," Jentien said. He joined Isalie behind the heavy cart floating in the air, and followed when it hovered forward in the wake of the leading guards.

They approached the gaping maw of the tunnel, and Isalie's anxiety spiked. The darkness seemed to swallow them when they passed the booths and the open gate. Without a word, Jentien reached over and clasped her hand.

"I've got you," Jen whispered low enough that the other guards wouldn't hear. She smiled, the familiar words comforting. She had already survived the worst thing that had ever happened to her, so she could survive another trip through this accursed place.

It was so much easier with him holding her hand, and she tried not to think about what Celeste would think about how much Isalie needed him. Jentien let go before they stopped at the guard post on the Outers side. There was a man stationed here this time, and he hardly looked up as he waved them through.

Jen pulled his mask over his face as Isalie did the same. Jentien stepped forward, taking in his first glimpse of the Outers from this side of the division.

While he took in the dismal sight, Isalie got to work. First, they offloaded crates, and then began the painstaking task of reconciling the inventory with the warehouse monitor. They counted every mask, cloak, and pair of boots before Stills sorted them into the allotted spaces on their shelves.

It took most of the morning, and the guards with them cast impatient looks her way, eager to head back. Finally finished, they gathered the cart and started for the tunnel.

When she and Jen didn't immediately follow, one of the guards turned to Jen with a hint of warning in their voice.

"Guard Themori, we must return to the inner city."

Isalie had hoped this wouldn't come up, that they could just quietly disappear without notice. Jen took a moment to answer, and only she saw his slight movement, squaring his shoulders before he rounded on the guard.

"I have another assignment, and Ms. Folci and I will return as soon as that allows." Muffled as his voice was, there was an air of command in it that Isalie hadn't heard before. It sent a shiver down her spine, and she was glad that it wasn't meant for her.

The guard hesitated. Isalie couldn't see their eyes, but she imagined that they were looking at the insignia on Jen's chest. A drizzle started, and the guard ducked their head.

"We typically don't—"

"I am a member of the Kiyash House guard," Jen interrupted. "There is nothing *typical* about my rank." He didn't explain further, just waited for a response as he seemed to tower over this guard.

They held their hands up in deference and nodded. It seemed they didn't have anything more to say, so they returned to the others. Isalie watched them retreat to the Inners until Jen let out a sigh of relief.

"We're going to hear about that when we get back," she warned him.

"I'll take the blame, Iz," he replied gruffly. "Let's go see your girl."

Isalie had always rushed through the streets of the Outers, but this time, it wasn't fear that pushed her forward. She glanced over her shoulder every time she rounded a corner to ensure Jen was still following. He was quiet, not that she could have heard him over the din of the rain.

Isalie paused to wait for him with her hand extended. "It's all right, Jen. It's not much further." He took her hand and squeezed it hard, and she felt his anxiety through the rigidity of his arm and the slight tremble of his gloved hand. He took a deep breath, hunched his shoulders, and then let them fall.

Isalie rounded another corner and spotted the familiar outline of Celeste's home ahead. She pulled Jen toward the workshop door and pushed it open. With Jen safely inside, she shut it again and carefully removed her cloak and mask. Jen did the same, and Isalie pointed to a rack set over a drain in the floor.

"Hang your cloak and gloves on here," she said. "There's a shelf for your mask," she placed her mask on said shelf, "and you can put your boots here."

"And then you can be introduced," Celeste said from behind them.

Isalie beamed as she turned. "Cel!"

Celeste pulled her goggles atop her locs as she stepped away from one of the tables. Dust streaked her brow, cheeks, and jaw, and she held her arms open as Isalie darted across the room to embrace her. Their lips met, and it felt like coming home.

Celeste smiled with her bottom lip between her teeth, and then looked over Isalie's shoulder. "Who is this?" she asked. Her eyes snagged on his uniform and its golden insignia.

"Cel, this is Jentien. Jen, this is Celeste."

Celeste's eyes widened and her nostrils flared. She took a step forward, almost involuntarily, and touched his arm. When she looked at Isalie again, her eyes were still wide with disbelief.

"*Your* Jentien?"

Isalie nodded, the tears welling in her eyes mirrored in Celeste's. She bit her lip to hold them in and turned to Jen, wondering what he thought of this display.

Celeste took his hand and held it between hers. Her voice thick with emotion, she said, "I'm... I don't know what to– There isn't a word for how wonderful it is to meet you!"

"Thank you. Iz has told me so much about you." He glanced at Isalie, and despite the flicker of sadness she saw there, his smile was wide and genuine.

Celeste released Jen's hand and wrapped her arms around his waist. He was taller than Isalie by a few inches, and Celeste looked tiny as he returned the embrace. He smiled down at her colorful locs, and then turned the smile to Isalie.

"I've heard almost everything about you, Jentien." Celeste stepped back, leaving her hands on Jen's waist. He put his hands on her shoulders and smiled down at her. "Everything," Cel repeated. She winked at him, and he chuckled.

"Should I be worried?" he asked her.

"Yes," Cel replied. She stretched to touch his cheek, and his eyes widened in surprise. Cel released him, walked back to Isalie, and kissed her cheek as she whispered in Isalie's ear. "I'm so happy for you." She wiped a tear from her eye and seemed to collect herself, giving Isalie an approving wink. "He's even more handsome than you made him sound. You have excellent taste in men *and* women."

Cel wrapped her arm around Isalie's waist while Jen watched with an eyebrow quirked. Isalie shrugged, nervous.

"Well, invite the man in so we can have a drink! We can celebrate him coming back from the dead, and you can tell me all about your time in the Inners." Celeste pulled Isalie's waist, and they led Jentien inside the house.

CHAPTER THIRTY-FOUR

I can see what Isalie likes about her, Jentien thought. He hesitated, feeling strangely apprehensive to walk in after them. Celeste was so open and inviting, and he could see the ardent desire she felt for Iz on her face. After everything that Iz had told him, his instincts told him that he—and Iz—were safe with her. Now that he'd met her, he *wished* he'd found a reason to mistrust her.

Iz laughed, happy and confident in a way that he'd never seen, even before they came here.

I never made her feel that way. He didn't know if he could handle being in the same room as the two of them, knowing that all he wanted was the one person he couldn't have.

Celeste called his name, so he shook his head to clear it of the depressing thought and walked through the door. The interior looked like it'd been held together with scraps and the determination of its resident, but he found comfort in the familiarity of Iz's influence. The kitchen, sparse as supplies were, was organized in the same way as her kitchen in Lacorsia. Because this was her home.

"Sorry, Lee," Cel was saying as she pulled a few glasses from a cupboard. "I know you don't like the clutter, but I can't keep things as neat as you."

Jentien looked to Celeste in surprise. *Lee?*

"I'll take care of it later, Cel, don't worry about it." She leaned against the counter at Celeste's side. "We only have the day, and then we need to get back. I haven't learned much..."

Celeste stooped beneath the counter to pull out a bottle of amber liquid while Isalie filled her in. She rolled her eyes at the description of the inner city's splendor, just like Iz would, and nodded as Iz told her the suspicions she and Jen had discussed.

"It sounds like you're making progress, even if it's slow." Her shoulders slumped in relief. "I'm just glad you made it out, even for a little while. Of course, if you don't need to report back until tomorrow morning, maybe I can convince you to stay the night?" She glanced at Jentien again, letting out a disbelieving chuckle. "I still can't believe you're *alive.* You two must have the Elders' own luck.

To found friends, and loves that come back," she said as she raised her glass, winking at Isalie.

Jentien blushed and swallowed the contents of his glass. It tasted like smoke and citrus and burned all the way to his stomach.

She gave Jentien an appraising look that lingered on the golden accent to his burgundy uniform. "Since you want to see the Outers in all its glory, you'll need to change before we go anywhere. I don't think it would be wise to advertise that you're Ambient Guard. Ambient Rotre and Ambient Kova aren't due for about a week, but it would be unwise to have you looking like their advanced scout."

"Whatever you think is best," he replied.

"What will you do when you see how awful it is here?" Celeste asked. She swirled the amber liquid around in her glass, her expression carefully neutral. "What *can* you do?"

Jentien shrugged. "I don't know. If I can do something about it, I will."

Celeste narrowed her eyes at him, her stare so penetrating that he imagined she could read his thoughts. A flush crept up his neck, so he tried to cover his discomfort by finishing off his drink.

"I think I like your Jentien," Celeste said to Iz after a long moment. She pursed her lips in a smirk. "He's so earnest."

"Always earnest," Iz replied. She gave him a warm smile, and Jentien's stomach fluttered. He couldn't tell whether it was the way she was looking at him, or if it was the knowledge that she wasn't his any longer.

After dressing in the thick white shirt and grey trousers Celeste gave him, Jentien walked quietly through the streets of outer Olunei beside Isalie. It was dry for once, and a bit of light peeked through the cloud cover and pervasive Gloom. Jentien walked without a hood and mask for now, the better to see what Isalie had described.

"Most days don't look like this," Iz was saying. Every building was tall and covered with a roof of the same crystal the towers were made of. Some of the inner city's buildings closest to the Gloom had them, but here the overhangs blocked sight of the sky and cast the streets in perpetual darkness.

Every building was the same dreary stone, the streets were riddled with puddles of the Gloom-touched rainwater, and every window was closed. The air was still and quiet, like the hush around a funeral pyre. The one person they passed had their mask on and their hood pulled low despite the clear sky. Their cloak was shabby and threadbare, with small holes eaten through the fabric.

They turned down a narrow street, and muffled voices echoed ahead. Celeste stopped in her tracks, holding her arm out to stop them, too.

"What is *he* doing here?" Celeste whispered.

Iz cocked her head toward the voices, and then she went still, too. Jentien leaned closer to her, about to ask what they'd heard, but closed his mouth when a cloak shifted, catching a bit of Ambient light from a nearby sconce. It shimmered like a prism.

What is an Ambient doing in a back alley in the Outers? He looked around, noticing no burgundy uniforms. *Where is his guard?* He spotted a flash of brown in the darkness, and the Ambient reached out to a pale hand that grasped whatever had been offered.

Celeste swept her hand backward, motioning for them to leave the way they'd come. Jentien did, but he kept his eyes on the Ambient until they were around the corner again.

"I thought you said he was due in a week?" Isalie asked after they'd put some distance between themselves and the Ambient. "What was he doing *here?*"

"I don't know, Lee." Celeste cast another glance over her shoulder, and Jentien did the same. "But someone was with him, and it wasn't another Ambient or their guards."

"Does Ambient Rotre usually visit with people individually?" Jentien asked. Iz had told him about the one visit she'd witnessed, and it hadn't sounded like the overseer was likely to take special interest in anyone.

"Not that I'm aware of. Though, that part of the city has a lot of ruined buildings that Prism users frequent. Maybe he's tracking them down?"

"He gave something to someone," Iz said. "If he intended to arrest them, wouldn't he have done it?"

A few drops of rain fell, and Iz and Celeste donned their masks while Jentien struggled to pull his over his head. He finished a moment before the downpour began.

How can anyone live this way? he thought.

A scream rose above the patter of rain somewhere in an alley nearby. Jentien turned toward the sound, his muscles tensed to run in that direction before a strong hand clamped down on his arm to stop him short.

"Don't run off on your own," Celeste warned.

Jentien pulled his arm free and left despite her warning. He heard her curse and call for Iz, but he was already rounding the corner, running and splashing through the puddles.

CHAPTER THIRTY-FIVE

ANOTHER SCREAM SOUNDED CLOSE by, around the next corner. Jentien rounded it at full speed, his gloved hand gripping the edge of the building to steady himself, and found a narrow alley with several people pressing themselves against the stone wall beneath the eaves.

An old man stood over a couple of children, trying to shield them with a tattered cloak. The two younger children had no cloaks of their own, and a teen boy was doing his best to use his too-small cloak to help the rest. Jentien spotted scars and fresh burns through the holes in the cloak, covering the old man's arms, neck, and face.

He glanced up to see that the eaves here were barely enough to cover the base of their own buildings. He skidded to a halt next to the group amid a chorus of children's screams and pained grunts from the teen and the man. The wind lifted the cloak from the teen's back, and his shirt instantly soaked through with rain. Bleeding welts rose beneath them, and his cries joined the children's.

"Hold on!" Jentien yelled. He whipped the cloak off his back and draped it over the teen and part of the older man, but it wasn't enough. He heard the splash of running feet behind him and turned to see Iz and Celeste sprint into the alley.

"Fucking rain," Celeste muttered.

She took the cloak from her shoulders and flung it over the old man, covering anything still exposed. The rain picked up, slamming onto the street in a steady roar. Lightning flashed again, and thunder rolled through a second later.

"We need to get them inside!" Celeste shouted.

Jentien couldn't see any doors in the alley, but remembered a few the way he'd come. He cursed, knowing they'd be exposed the whole way.

"How many kids?" Iz asked.

"Two, plus a teenager," Jentien replied.

She looked up at the open sky, to one end of the street, and then the other. "I can take one of the kids under my cloak," Iz said. "I'll come back for the other. Then the other two can use your cloaks."

Celeste nodded. "We'll wait here, Lee. Hurry."

Isalie ducked under the cloak. Jentien couldn't make out what she said, but soon she straightened with a bulge under her cloak. She waddled, hunched, to the mouth of the alley, and Jentien's heart swelled with admiration. Searing pain distracted him from his thoughts, and he glanced at his shoulder to find the rain had soaked through his thick shirt, melting it to his skin.

Jentien waited, watching for Isalie to come back. The skin on his shoulders stung where the rain soaked through, as Isalie darted back into the alley with her arms free.

"She's inside! Give me the next one!"

A hand reached from within the cloak and Isalie spread hers wide to catch the small boy that ran to her and huddled close as she pulled the cloak tight around them. She darted away again toward the alley's mouth.

Jentien helped Celeste arrange their cloaks around the other two, and then the four of them followed Isalie's path. The closest door on the right side of the street was ajar, so they ushered the others forward. It opened further when they arrived, and their group crashed inside as the door slammed shut behind them. The interior was dim, with only a few candles providing meager light. Hushed voices and whimpering replaced the din of pounding rain.

Celeste's voice rang out above the others when she'd pulled her mask from her head, her locs tumbling out around her shoulders. "Sir," she said to the old man, "we need to put this mask on you."

He nodded, his answer more wheeze than word. "All right."

Celeste put the mask over his head with the care of a mother dressing her newborn. "Take a few shallow breaths to start. The mask is going to pull the rain out of your lungs." She glanced at Isalie "Lee, I need yours, too."

Isalie started to take off her mask, but Jentien beat her to it.

"Take mine," he said, thrusting it toward the teen. The young man nodded, black dreads bouncing on his dark skin. Even in the dim light, Jentien could see oozing sores covering his chest and arms.

Isalie pulled the mask over her head, too. Her hair spilled in a wild halo around her face, illuminated by the flickering glow of the candles. She looked stunning with the blush high on her cheeks and her eyes bright, especially when she turned a gentle smile to the children in front of her.

"This has special crystals that take the rain out of you." She pulled the mask over the small girl's head and smiled at her. "I used one of these once when I was very hurt, and it saved my life." Isalie turned her smile to Celeste, who beamed and winked before she pulled a jar from another pocket.

How many things has she hidden in that suit? Jentien wondered.

"Jentien, I need you." Celeste gestured for him to take the jar from her hand. "Help him rub this over his burns. Start with the head so that you can put the mask on him. Then, help him get out of his clothes so he can do the rest."

"Got it," Jentien said. Celeste smiled at him, and he felt a swell of warm pride in his chest. He followed her instructions, helping the young man apply the thick, creamy substance to any place he couldn't reach. Once they were done, the mask slid easily over his head. A woman appeared at Jentien's elbow while he was trying to figure out how to remove the young man's shirt. It had stuck to the skin where the rain burned through.

"You can use the bedroom for that, sir," the woman said. She was older, about the same age as Isalie's parents, with graying brown hair and kind blue eyes.

"Thank you, ma'am," Jentien replied. He led the way for the young man wincing and hissing in pain. "I think your clothes are ruined," Jentien told him. "Do you think you can get them off?"

The young man nodded and started to peel them off. The damage wasn't too bad on his lower half; the rain had splattered against the bottom of his pants and his boots, and most of it was still intact, though the pants were worn nearly through. The skin beneath was just swollen, not broken. His upper body was a different story. His shirt was still burning, adding new welts to what was already exposed. Jentien grasped the edges of a hole near the hem.

"I'm going to have to rip this open. Brace yourself."

The young man tensed and Jentien wrenched the shirt apart, the flimsy fabric practically falling apart in his grasp. The skin peeled away with the fabric beneath, and the young man screamed and writhed away from him.

"Cel!" Jentien shouted. "I need some help!"

She arrived a moment later with another jar in hand and whistled when she saw the state of the skin on the young man's shoulders. With a glob of the stuff in her hand she slathered it on the exposed skin, and the young man sighed the moment it met his burns. He resolved into a trembling mass as Jentien slowly peeled the rest of the shirt away with Celeste applying salve just behind the wounds. As soon as everything was removed, Jentien dropped it to the floor and backed away to give Celeste more room, realizing he was shaking as much as the boy.

"I've got this. You get your shirt off," Celeste barked.

"I'm fine," Jentien protested.

"Now, Jentien."

He grabbed the hem of his shirt and started to pull it over his head, but stopped short when his skin started to pull, stuck to the thick fabric. He pulled a bit harder, hissing through his teeth as his skin peeled away. Celeste put a hand out to stop him.

"Elders-cursed rain," she muttered. "Lee, your Jentien needs you!"

Jentien bumped into the single bed nearby, the movement jarring the shirt in his hands to rip more of his skin away. He gasped in pain as Isalie walked in, her eyes wide with worry.

"Get his shirt off before his entire chest is burned," Celeste ordered.

Isalie looked at Jentien's chest and hissed. "It's going to hurt."

"It already does," Jentien groaned. His chest, arms, and lower legs were burning where the sodden fabric clung to him.

"Okay, I'm going to pull. One, two—"

She pulled, and Jentien screamed. It felt like all the skin on his torso was rent from him with his shirt. More than that, he had flashes of being caught in the storm, with Isalie dying in his arms, and then his body hurtling away from her as lightning struck him. A sob of pain—mental and physical—tore out of his throat, and his eyes locked on the bloody fabric as it fell to the floor from Isalie's hands, his body cold and bleeding.

His mind turned inward, fixating on the shame, regret, and grief of burning in the storm, unable to protect Isalie, waiting to die. Tears flowed from his cheeks, and somewhere outside his pain he felt Isalie's hands hastily spreading salve over his chest.

"I have to take your pants off before they burn you, too," she whispered, her voice muffled and distant to his ears. He nodded, incapable of speech as his body shook. Isalie unbuckled the belt at his waist and pulled the pants down.

Unable to keep his trembling legs under him, Jentien sat down hard and shivered. Isalie's face appeared before his eyes, saying something he couldn't hear over the roaring in his ears as his trauma transformed her concerned frown into the still, charred image of her near-lifeless face that haunted him. His head jerked upward and the spell broke. Isalie had forced him to look at her stern expression.

"Stay with me, Jen," she demanded. "Don't leave me again."

Tears continued to stream down his face as he inhaled, taking her challenge to heart. Jentien nodded at Iz to let her know he'd heard her, and she continued her ministrations as he stared at her face to keep himself grounded in the moment. Everywhere the salve touched the relief was instant, like a cool breeze on a hot day. Jentien watched the small wrinkle between her brows persist while she worked, transfixed by her focused, deep blue eyes.

"Are you all right, Jen?" Isalie asked when she looked up. She sat back on her haunches in front of him and ran a hand down his cheek, searching his eyes.

He touched her hand and tried to smile, but his face felt stiff. "I'm fine," he whispered. "How are the others?"

She gazed at him without speaking, and then she answered with a glance through the door. "The children are fine; I don't think they had much exposure. The old man breathed in a lot, but I think he's improving." She lowered her voice with a glance at the teenager behind Jentien. "I'd feel much more comfortable if I could take them with us." She and Celeste exchanged significant looks.

Celeste squatted next to them and inspected Jentien's wounds. "I think you're going to heal well, which is lucky. Most people don't make it out of the rain when they're caught like that."

She stood and strode into the other room, and Jentien took Isalie's help to stand so they could follow. They found Celeste standing before the old man with her arms crossed in front of her chest, scowling. "What were you doing without protection?" she demanded.

"Haven't had any for a few weeks, now," he replied. He let out a muffled cough and took a deep breath. "Cloaks and masks wore straight through, and there haven't been any new ones for those that don't earn them."

"None of you are working? What about your families?"

The old man shook his masked face, and the light reflected off the crystal lenses. "The little ones' parents died a few months back. I haven't been able to work since I came here; the rain scarred my lungs, and I can't breathe well enough to work. My grandson in there," he pointed to the bedroom, "was due to start this week."

Jentien looked around the room at the rest of the people. The children looked terrified, the adults weary and depressed. The woman who lived here had a young woman behind her with a baby in her arms, who was softly cooing as its naked gums chewed on its fingers.

Isalie touched his hand and he looked at her, unable to keep the grief and anger from his face. This was so much worse than the slums outside Lacorsia. People dealt with this every day, and the Ambient, safe in their towers, knew. There was a fire blazing behind Iz's eyes. It was the same fire that had blazed whenever she argued about the Ambient at home.

Jentien felt it catch in his heart.

CHAPTER THIRTY-SIX

"Tʜᴀᴛ ᴡᴀs ʀᴇᴄᴋʟᴇss," Cᴇʟ growled at Jentien as he crawled inside the hole marking the entrance to the building that held the Undercity. It'd been a slow journey with four extra people in tow, but Celeste had marked a path with the most coverage between the house where they'd taken refuge and the old city hall building, and they'd made it without crossing any guards' paths.

She shoved past Jentien and grabbed the handle on the stone to heft it into place. She was glaring at Jen with her hands clenched into fists, and Isalie worried she might punch him in the face. "You risked all our lives, throwing yourself at something you don't understand."

Jen pulled off his hood and mask and stood still, looking down at the angry woman whose head only came to his collarbone. He was silent, but Isalie knew the thin line of his lips and the muscle tensing in his jaw meant that he was just as angry. He kept his mouth shut and stared back at Cel, refusing to apologize. Isalie ushered the others along the path to the Undercity, lingering long enough to watch the two people she loved face off.

Just as suddenly as she'd berated him, the tension fell out of Cel's shoulders, and she smirked. "I'm glad you did." Jentien's eyes flew wide, and Isalie stifled a laugh as the enmity between the two evaporated. "These people would have died without help, and even if they'd survived the rain, they might have died without our salve and masks." Cel placed her hand on Jentien's chest, and his jaw dropped as a blush crept up his neck.

"I had to help," he murmured.

"I can see that," Cel said. She stretched onto tiptoes to kiss his cheek, and the blush moved to his face. "You're every bit the hero our Lee said you were. Now, let's introduce you to the Undercity. These people need a hero."

She took his hand and led him further into the building, and Isalie took the lead for the group. "I think you'll like it down here," Cel said.

They followed the same path down, through a path of lights, and over the carved stairs. When it opened into the large main cavern, Isalie sent the children and old man toward Amal's house. Jentien stopped next to her, his mouth open in astonishment.

"This is... wonderful." His eyes roamed the cavern, flitting from the stalls to the doors carved out of columns to the tent city lit by lanterns.

"It is," Cel replied. "If you can stand the occasional Gloom beast attack and the smoke lingering from the cookfires."

Cel proceeded to explain the structure of the Undercity as she had to Isalie, who trailed behind them. She felt content here, even in the damp darkness, despite the echoing noise of voices all around. A few people noticed her and stopped to chat; the most common question was about her travels outside Olunei, the second most common was to ask who Jentien was.

She answered their questions as best she could, telling them that Jen was a new arrival. It was gratifying to just talk to these people, who were so kind and attentive. She felt seen every time she came down here.

"I want you to talk to Amal," Cel said. "You seem like you need to help, so let's see how we can put you to use."

Jentien followed her inside with Isalie at their heels. She inhaled and was rewarded with a new combination of delicious smells; melons enhanced by the tang of mint, basil, and cured, salted meat.

Amalricus smiled when she entered the kitchen. "Isalie Wylshard, you are a sight for sore eyes." He peered at Jentien. "Who is this?"

Isalie filled Amalricus in on everything between bites of the refreshing salad he'd made with the ingredients she'd smelled. When she finished, Amal and Cel told Jen about the Olugar as they'd explained it to Isalie. Jentien listened intently with a frown that deepened the more they described the situation they were in.

"Have you had any trouble with Ambient Rotre?" Isalie asked.

"No," Amal replied. "Nel spotted him just this morning, but we've been a bit distracted. We've had a rash of Prism users that had extreme reactions: fevers, hallucinations, and seizures."

Celeste shot him a surprised, angry look. "When?"

"Just the past week."

"Why didn't anyone tell me?"

"We had our hands full, Cellie."

"You should have told me! I could have helped!"

Amal hesitated, but kept a direct gaze fixed on Cel. "I didn't want you involved, Celeste. Not after Rotre confiscated your crystal. Not with him so close. I couldn't risk having you going back and forth in case he was watching you."

Celeste's anger deflated, though there was still a hard glint in her eyes. "I'll take a look at them after I take care of the people we brought with us. They're stable, but they aren't earning topside. They need protection."

Amal nodded. "They'll have it."

Cel took a deep breath. When she spoke, her tone was controlled, but Isalie could hear the anger behind it.

"Every year the protection the Ambient provide is less effective. What used to last years is now only months. How long before the Ambient leave us with nothing?"

"You think it's intentional?" Jentien asked.

"It's possible that the Gloom could be changing, but why wouldn't the Ambient adapt to it, too? I think it's more likely to be neglect, or sabotage. Either they don't care as much about keeping us alive as they claim to, or they want to make sure we don't have the strength to change our circumstance."

Jen put his hands on his hips and paced a few steps away. "You don't have enough supplies to make more of your suits and masks, do you?" Jentien asked.

Celeste shook her head. "Especially the crystal. It's a naturally occurring resource, but everything on the surface was used to construct the towers and the roofs. We've found pockets in the tunnels, but the beasts roam freely back there. It's too dangerous. And now, I have an Ambient watching me, so I'm sure it'll be even harder to source."

"What if we formed hunting parties to thin the beasts in the tunnels you need? It would provide you with more supplies for cloaks and suits and give you better access to the crystal."

Celeste was already shaking her head before Jen finished. "We've tried that. We have spears, clubs, and bows, but their hides are too tough for us to kill them head-on. Our hunters have traps in the tunnels, but we mostly catch smaller beasts."

Jentien nodded. "You need shields and swords."

"They're restricted to the Ambient Guard," Celeste said. "And they're so closely monitored that someone would notice if they went missing."

Hurried footsteps preceded Arru's entrance. Isalie winced inwardly when the older woman caught her eye and crossed the kitchen to grasp her hands.

"Any news of Yesrien?" she asked. Desperation and hope warred for dominance on her face. "I came right away once I heard you'd come back."

Isalie's stomach dropped. She'd been dreading this moment beneath all her other worries. "No, Arru," she murmured. "I know she was working with the tailors, and then she disappeared. The person I spoke to was terrified of the Ambient being involved."

"Why?" Arru asked. "Yesrien is smart; she wouldn't have stirred up trouble."

Isalie shrugged, wishing she had more to tell Arru. "I don't know what happened, but I'll keep asking."

"As long as you stay out of trouble," Arru said. She dropped Isalie's hands and backed against a counter. "I don't want you to be lost, either."

Isalie frowned. "It will take time for them to trust me enough to talk about it, but even then, they might not know where Yesrien would be."

"I understand," Arru said.

"I'll ask around, too," Jentien offered. "If the Ambient are behind it, the servants in the Kiyash spire might have heard something."

Arru noticed him for the first time, blinked once in confusion, and then another round of introductions gave Isalie space to hide in the corner. She knew that she couldn't force the information Arru wanted out of people, but it didn't stop her from feeling like she wasn't doing enough. She got to live in luxury while everyone here suffered. She'd found Jentien, but Arru might never find her daughter. It wasn't fair.

"I appreciate the offer, Jentien," Arru said. "I just want to know what happened to my Yesrien."

"How are the servants chosen for the Kiyash spire?" Isalie asked. All eyes turned her way. "I'll keep talking to my contact, but if nothing comes of that, maybe I could find more information if I worked there. The servants hear so much, and they might know more. Even if Yesrien isn't with them, even if..." She let the end of the sentence hang unspoken in the air. She didn't want to tempt the Elders to make Yesrien's death true.

"They're promoted from the other servants already in the inner city," Jentien said. "I don't know how they're chosen any more than we understand how Stills are chosen from the outer city."

"Do the Ambient Guard ever make recommendations?" Celeste asked.

Jentien nodded slowly, his eyes never leaving Isalie's. She could read the thoughts flashing across them; concern for putting Isalie in danger, disgust at the situation, and resolve to make a difference.

"They do," he said finally. "Occasionally, when a position opens, the commander has mentioned it to guards who have loved ones with lesser positions. I could mention that I know someone who would be a good fit." He blushed. "He thinks highly of me, so as long as he doesn't hold this detour against me, if I tell him I have someone in my life that I wanted to put forward, he might not question it."

Isalie blushed, too, and ducked her head to hide it from Celeste. When she looked up, however, Celeste flashed her a knowing smile. She hadn't missed the exchange.

"I like this plan," Amalricus said. "Get as close as you can to the Ambient and keep your ears open. Don't take any risks, of course, but whatever information you can get to us would be appreciated. You can use Pelom to let us know what you can learn of Yesrien's fate."

Losing track of the conversation, Isalie was surprised when Celeste touched her arm. Jentien was the only other person in the room, though Isalie could hear Arru and Amalricus talking in another room.

"I'm going to check on the people we brought down, and then the Prism users. I'm hoping if I infuse a bit of it into the salve, that we can use *that* to wean them off the inhaled stuff. I'll be done soon; I was hoping we could spend some time at home before you head back."

"That would be nice," Isalie said. Glancing at Jentien, he offered her a tight-lipped smile, still lost in thought. She followed Jen outside to give Cel time to work, stopping when they crossed the path of a woman a bit shorter than her with a child holding each of her hands.

"Oh, excuse me, Isalie!" she said with a flustered laugh. "I didn't see you there!"

Her name was Maretha, Isalie remembered when she laughed, a very pretty woman with pale blonde hair tied at the back of her neck. The older child was a boy with strikingly dark hair, and the girl couldn't have been more than five, with curly brown pigtail braids.

Isalie smiled. "That's my fault, I wasn't looking where I was going. Maretha, right?"

"Yes," Maretha beamed. "We were just going to see if Amal has any of Celeste's salve. Cort was a bit impatient for breakfast this morning and touched a hot pan."

"Oh, I think I have some!" Isalie rummaged in her bag and found a mostly empty jar. "There's not much, but it should help."

Maretha sighed, looking relieved. "Thank you, you're a life saver! Thank the Elders for you and Celeste, and that salve."

Jentien went still on Isalie's other side. Isalie quirked a brow at him in question.

"Cort?" he whispered. He was staring at the boy, and then the woman, as if he couldn't believe what he was seeing.

Maretha glanced at Jentien, bid them farewell, and then pulled her children along with her. Isalie nudged Jen, who was staring after them with his mouth hanging open.

"What is it?" she asked again. "Why are you staring at them like that?"

"Cortlen."

Isalie frowned in confusion. "Your friend from the Inners?"

Jentien nodded. "He came to Olunei five years ago. He was traveling with his son and his pregnant wife."

Shock ran through Isalie's veins like ice. She tried to find them in the crowd now, but they'd been swallowed in the bustle. "They were separated?"

"He thought they were dead. He doesn't know he has a daughter."

"We need to tell him," Isalie said.

"What if there are more people like us?" Jentien asked. "I thought it was a coincidence, that we'd been separated by accident. But, if the Ambient are making Stills disappear, what if they're ripping families apart, too?" He ran his hands through his hair, grasping it by the root. "Why would they do that? What do they stand to gain by making us miserable?"

"I'm not sure," Isalie replied, her dark blue eyes full of rage and compassion that matched the storm raging in his heart, "but maybe misery is the point. If we're focused on survival, we don't have the energy to question anything. Stills have accepted that the Ambient can live in comfort while we live in fear; that's how it's always been, even if the contrast isn't so stark everywhere else." She leveled a glare at Jentien. "I think it's time we start asking questions."

CHAPTER THIRTY-SEVEN

Celeste called Isalie to a small tent nearby to help with the Prism users, but Jentien couldn't follow her. He needed to move, to work out some of this angry energy. He balled his hands into fists hard enough that his nails bit into his palms, and then strode toward the back of the cavern.

The glow of hundreds of lanterns and globes illuminated the stalagmites, tents, and stalls, but it only held the darkness at bay. He couldn't see the ceiling above, just the tips of huge stalactites that seemed to float in the air before being swallowed by that impenetrable shadow.

There had to be something he could do to help. He'd never been good at sitting still; it was the reason he'd never found work in Lacorsia, why he and Isalie had wandered around, looking for trouble. Now, Isalie was the one in trouble, and all he could do was wait.

A light drew him forward, until he found an Ambient orb affixed next to the mouth of a smaller tunnel surrounded by posts with clever mechanical devices affixed to them. They clicked and chattered, the sound he'd been hearing over the noise of the city much louder here. He hesitated, wondering whether he should be here, but curiosity won out. It was wide enough for two people to walk astride, but it felt much smaller after the vast expanse of the Undercity behind him.

After walking a short way, Jentien realized that he could see tool marks in the stone walls. There was light somewhere ahead, and Jentien moved faster, eager to see where it was coming from.

The tunnel opened onto a smaller cavern, and he found a mass of orbs affixed to the ceiling to shine down on a dirt plot on the ground. From the dirt sprouted a bounty of green.

The farm plot Celeste had mentioned, Jentien realized, spotting corn, peppers, grains, yams, and more that he couldn't name. The clicks were louder here, as the sound from the barrier of poles near an exit on the far wall echoed from closer walls and seemed to ricochet around the room. A few people were hauling buckets to water the crops as Jentien walked toward them. They gave him questioning looks when he approached.

"Can I help?" he asked.

"Sure," a man replied, waving a spindly, scale-covered arm in the direction of a water barrel at the far end of the cavern. "We'll never turn down a helping hand."

Jentien carried water buckets, watered crops, and refilled the water barrel from a nearby spring until the day's work was done. Exercise helped him relax. Knowing he was doing something useful helped more.

Sweating, he gratefully accepted a ladle full of water from the man who'd welcomed him, then paused with his hands on his hips. He'd tuned out the noise from the deterrents while he worked, but there was a new sound beneath that. He straightened and faced the far exit when he realized what it reminded him of: the sniffing of some large beast just out of sight.

His fingers closed around the worn wooden handle of a garden hoe, and he cautiously stepped closer to the tunnel. The farmers stopped and looked at him, so he held a finger to his lips to urge them to be quiet, and held the hoe before him, ready to strike.

Down the tunnel, he spotted the shine of two large eyes at waist height, and his heart started to pound. Whatever it was, it didn't advance, just seemed to study him when he moved between the posts. He tensed for a fight, and then a riot of sound rose in the small cavern.

Everyone brandished a tool, slamming them against the stone walls of the cavern as they shouted toward the tunnel. Jentien watched the beast's eyes dart around, and it backed away until the shine was gone. After a minute or two of watching for it to return, Jentien replaced the hoe and got back to work, keeping an eye on the tunnel until they'd finished.

Followed by a chorus of thanks from the farmers, he walked back to Amalricus's house. He found Celeste alone in the kitchen with a cup in her hand. She looked him up and down, and smirked.

"You look like you've been busy," she said. The amusement was plain in her voice, but he thought it was masking something else. He didn't know her well enough to know what.

"I couldn't sit still," he replied. "Water?"

Celeste pulled a tall wooden mug out of the cupboard behind her and filled it from a carafe on the counter. He accepted it with a smile and drank deeply while he watched her.

She was beautiful, but he didn't think that was what drew Iz to her. She was so forthright, so intelligent, and so playful. He'd never met anyone like her.

"I want you to know that I appreciate your willingness to help," she said. Jentien put the mug on the counter. He could feel a 'but' coming.

"But," she said, looking down at her cup, "I don't want you to put yourself in danger. The Ambient won't spare you if you're caught."

"I'm not concerned about myself," Jentien began.

Celeste interrupted, her voice a harsh whisper. "You should be," she insisted. "Thinking you were dead broke her." Celeste didn't need to tell him who she meant. "Did she tell you how we met?"

Jentien thought for a moment. "She said you saved her when she got caught in the rain."

"Did she tell you that she stumbled into the street looking for you? Driven by a nightmare that still makes her scream in her sleep?"

Jentien stilled as grief crept through him. The kind of grief that had kept him awake most nights for months.

"If anything happens to you, Jentien, I don't think she'll survive it."

"I can't do nothing," he said, his voice thick with tears held at bay. "People are suffering, and I was ignorant of it for too long already."

"They've suffered for a long time, Jentien. No matter what we do, the Gloom will persist, and the storm will continue. I'm doing my best to change things, but sacrificing your life will only lead to the person we love suffering."

Jentien stared at her. Celeste didn't break her gaze.

"What do you want me to do?" he asked.

Celeste sighed. "For now, I would feel better if I knew you were keeping Lee from hurting herself. She's more stubborn than you are, and I'm afraid she'll push too hard for information."

Jentien nodded. Iz had *always* been eager to point out the inequities between Stills and Ambient, but she'd never had a chance to effect change. Here, now, she just might. But only if she wasn't caught before that happened.

Celeste walked up to him, so close that he could smell the sweet herbs in her tea. She reached up and placed her hands on his cheek. "She loves you, Jentien. That means that I love you. For us, please don't do anything stupid. I promise the time will come when you can help us. I will make it happen."

Jentien stood still, unsure of what to say or do. Celeste's hands were rough and warm, and he leaned into them without thinking. He'd been craving Isalie's touch so much, and now, here was this alluring woman who'd stolen her heart from him with her hands on his face.

She gently slapped his cheek and walked past him, breaking the trance he'd been in. Isalie called her name in the next room.

What was that? he thought.

Jentien watched Isalie pull her cloak over her shoulders. His eyes lingered on the blue shirt above the leather bodice her mother had made for her, and the swell of her breasts when she inhaled. Realizing he was staring, he looked away before she caught him.

"Make sure you have that cloak pulled tight," he told her. "I wouldn't want you to get wet."

"Thanks, Jen," Isalie said, but the roll of her eyes was evident in the tone of her voice.

Jentien lowered his head to hide a smile. It felt good to talk to Iz like this, like the past few months hadn't changed them as much as he'd feared. Like he hadn't lost her after all.

Down the hall, Celeste and Amalricus were talking. She clasped the old man's hands in her own and kissed his cheek, and he gave her a peck on the forehead. Celeste smiled at Amalricus like he was her beloved grandfather.

In a hushed voice that he hoped wouldn't carry, he said, "Are you sure you want to do this, Iz? The Ambient aren't easily fooled. If you make one mistake, you could disappear like Arru's daughter."

She gazed into his eyes, calm and confident. Imagining her walking around the halls of the spire made him anything but.

"I'll be fine, Jen. It's the perfect job for me, no one sees me."

"*I* see you, Iz." He held her gaze, trying to convey everything he felt for her in his words since he couldn't express it any other way. "You aren't invisible."

"I am to most people," she insisted. "Especially the Ambient. I can use that against them. Finally, feeling like I don't exist will be useful."

Jentien saw the pain that flashed across her face before it disappeared. He took her hand in his. "You have always been the most important person in my life. I won't let anything happen to you."

"You'd better not," Celeste said. Jentien dropped Isalie's hand and smiled when Celeste slipped an arm around her waist. "Because if you come back without her, I will leave you in the rain."

"That's fair," he said. "I would do the same to you."

Isalie rolled her eyes at them, and then blushed when Cel kissed her cheek. For a moment, he was content, bantering with Celeste and teasing Isalie. It felt comfortable and natural, like Celeste had been with them for years, instead of hours.

Then his intrusive thoughts pushed to the surface. *I wish I could hold her like that,* he thought. Guilt rose like bile in his throat, and he pushed it down, focusing on the warmth in his chest from seeing Iz so happy.

"You two ready to go home?" Celeste asked.

He smiled when they passed people who waved in greeting. They strolled through the market, up the stone stairway and into the dilapidated building that marked the entrance to the Undercity.

It was a shock to step out of the warm embrace of the Undercity into the harsh, cold, deadly rain, even with their masks and cloaks covering them. He knew he was protected, but the memory of the burning pain hours prior settled over him like a shroud. He flinched when lightning flashed overhead, and the downpour became a flood.

They managed to push through the stream of rainwater two inches deep along the streets until they reached Celeste's house. Inside the workshop, Jentien started to remove everything soaked with water.

Isalie stripped out of her outerwear, too, and Jentien grabbed a blanket from a hook inside a cupboard to wrap it around her shoulders. She smiled at him and looked over his shoulder, then her eyes went wide at the same time a flush crept up her cheeks.

When he turned around, he saw Celeste pulling her suit off, exposing the smooth skin of her back and everything else. He turned away, and Isalie smiled, embarrassed, before brushing past him in Celeste's direction.

"Cel, Jen is right here!" Her voice was almost a shriek, and Jentien sputtered a laugh.

"He knows what a naked woman looks like," Celeste scoffed. "Don't you, Jentien?"

"Uh, um, y-yes," he stuttered. He wasn't sure whether he wanted to laugh or run away. In truth, he hadn't seen many naked women in his life. He always thought he'd have time for it later.

"See, Lee? He's fine."

Jentien heard the heavy leather suit slump to the floor, and then the soft sound of bare feet slapping on stone as Celeste walked to the cupboard to his right. He caught a glimpse of the deep sepia skin along her side and turned in a different direction.

"Lee, do you want me to make dinner tonight? Amal sent me some food the other day, so the cupboards are as stocked as they'll ever be."

"Why don't you get dressed?" Isalie asked. Her voice was still high-pitched and flustered. "I'll cook."

"I can help," Jentien added, waving back over his shoulder.

Celeste chuckled. "All right, you two. I'll get dressed." She laughed under her breath, and her voice carried when she walked toward the door to the house. "So fussy."

Jentien peeked over his shoulder a few moments after he heard Celeste's footsteps recede. Isalie was watching her go with her mouth open.

"I can't believe she just did that," Isalie said.

"She doesn't seem like she's bothered by much," Jentien said.

"She's not," Iz said. She turned an apologetic grin to him. "Sorry, that was probably a bit uncomfortable for you. I think she likes to make us uncomfortable."

"I think so, too," Jentien said. They walked inside, and he watched Iz sort through the cupboard's contents. "Tell me how to help, Iz."

CHAPTER THIRTY-EIGHT

ISALIE SNIFFED THE POT, savoring the scent of the meal she had thrown together. Jentien was slicing some slightly stale bread when Celeste walked out of her room and sauntered to the counter.

She put a hand on Jen's shoulder and smiled at him. Isalie grinned when she noticed Jentien peek at Cel out of the corner of his eye before turning to face her.

"Don't worry, Jen, I'm decent again," Celeste teased, making Isalie raise an eyebrow. Her voice was low and rough, and Isalie suppressed a shiver of desire. That was the voice she used when she was trying to get Isalie excited.

It was working.

Cel didn't miss Isalie's reaction. Her smile sent a thrill of desire through Isalie's body. There was no suppressing the next shiver.

"That smells delicious, Lee."

"Thank you. Now, we just need to wait while it cooks for a bit."

"Perfect," Cel said. "I'll pour us a few drinks. I'm going to run through the last of my dad's collection at this rate!"

"Just a small one for me," Isalie said.

"Same for me," Jen replied.

Isalie watched Cel pour some drinks into glasses and stirred the contents of the pot once more before she put the lid on. She followed to the couch and sat with her side against Cel. Jentien relaxed into the armchair with a sigh.

"You two are amazing," Cel said. "We've had people come through our ranks over the years, but none have been so eager to help, or so willing to throw themselves into the fire to do it."

"They didn't have the opportunity," Isalie said. She sipped at the amber liquid in her glass. The smell scorched the inside of her nostrils, and she coughed against the burn in her throat.

"They're like Nel," Cel said. "Full of ideals and drive, and no common sense."

"The person I met with Arru?" Isalie asked, incredulous. "The one that looked like they wanted to eat me?"

Cel nodded. "Beneath that intimidating exterior is a person who feels the pain of the people around them, and that makes them angry. It makes them volatile, too, but that's what Amal's voice of reason is for."

Jentien chuckled to himself. "That reminds me of that kid in the swamp. Iz, do you remember that village? What was it called? Tree Hollow?"

Isalie shook her head. "Gnarl's Burrow. It was so hard to get to, but you made us tromp through the muck with that caravan."

"That's right," Jen replied. "This kid was barely eighteen, and he wanted to see the world. He was so..." Jentien trailed off, squinting while he searched for the word.

"Reckless?" Cel asked.

Jentien laughed and sipped his drink, and Cel smiled at him. Warmth spread through Isalie's chest watching the two of them talk to each other like old friends.

"You could say that. He almost ran off into the Gloom chasing a beast, and I had to grab him by the scruff of the neck to stop him."

Celeste lifted her glass. "Well, here's to you, Jentien, for saving people too stupid to keep themselves out of trouble. And you, Lee, for making sure he doesn't do the same thing."

They drank, listening to the kitchen fire pop and the rain hammer the roof. Isalie didn't know what to do with herself; she crossed her legs, uncrossed them and tucked them under her on the couch, and twirled the glass in her hands. She was nervous about returning to the Inners, and humming with tension with Celeste so close.

Isalie couldn't touch her, though. Not with Jen watching them.

"So, Jentien," Celeste said, "tell me what our Isalie was like before all this." She gestured to the room around them.

"No," Isalie said with a firm shake of her head. Her cheeks instantly flushed a lovely pink color. "No stories about what I was like as a child. We are *not* doing that."

Jentien smirked, grateful for the reprieve from treasonous talk and ignoring his inner turmoil. "I have a lot of stories," he replied.

Isalie flushed with embarrassment. "No."

"Lee, let the man speak." Celeste leaned close and kissed Iz on the cheek.

Isalie glared at Jentien, a clear threat in her eyes even as she hid a smile in her glass. "It's my favorite subject," he teased.

Isalie rolled her eyes at them and left them to talk while she cooked. He caught a pleased, if still embarrassed, smile on her face, but she caught him looking and turned away again.

"She's most comfortable when she cooks," Jentien added after a particularly loud snort from Iz. "I've never eaten as well as I did when we were on the road, and she had nothing but scraps to put together.

"She used to buy produce from the refugee camp," he continued. "They didn't have much, but she paid double—sometimes triple—what it was worth, and she would come home with the smallest, wilted carrots, taro, and potatoes. Whenever she did, she made the most delicious soups! We got sick once, but it was the *best* stew I've ever had, and Isalie always washed the produce after that."

"Dinner is on the table," Isalie grumbled.

Celeste snorted. Jentien let out a bark of laughter, surprising himself. He didn't know when it'd happened, but he felt light and unburdened. A gargantuan task awaited them, surrounded by Ambient with the power to rip them apart and the inclination to punish anyone who got in their way. But right now, with Isalie flustered and Cel laughing as she leaned over to squeeze his arm, he felt content.

"Why does she look like she's about to run away?" Cel asked. Isalie stiffened in surprise. "Like that!"

"She hasn't heard enough nice things said about her. I think it makes her shy."

"Ah. Well, she's shy about a *lot* of things. It's one of her more endearing qualities," Cel said. She turned back to Jentien with one eyebrow cocked over a wider smirk. "What do you find endearing about our Lee?"

Jentien's stomach fluttered with nerves or excitement; he wasn't sure. He watched the spoon in his hand pushing the soup around and around his bowl to avoid Celeste's expectant gaze.

"Well, she's my oldest friend," he said, hedging around the question. He could feel Celeste and Isalie staring at him. "She's the kindest, smartest person I know. The world would be a dark place without her." He finally looked up, matching Celeste's intent gaze with his own.

Celeste opened her mouth to say something, but Isalie huffed and dropped her spoon into her bowl with a loud clink.

"All right," she said, loud enough to drown out whatever Cel might say next. "Enough conversation. Your soup is getting cold!"

Jentien chuckled into his bowl, and they ate while Cel chattered about crystal granule weight and its applications. It was so far above his head that he couldn't begin to understand. He admired her passion and couldn't stop staring at her hands. They were flying everywhere between bites, almost as expressive as her face.

When the bowls were empty, Celeste collected them before Iz could get up. "I've got this, and then I'm headed into my shop for a bit. All this talk has the gears in my head turning, and I've got to make some notes."

She kissed the nape of Isalie's neck before she dumped the bowls in the kitchen and disappeared. Jen watched Isalie watch Cel, smiling at her lingering gaze. It was a look he'd seen directed toward him more times than he could count.

"She's... amazing, Iz. I can see why you like her."

Isalie blushed hard and didn't say anything. Instead, she looked down at her hands to hide her face.

"Thank you," he said, and she finally looked at him.

"For what?" she asked.

"For bringing me here." He shrugged, feeling as self-conscious as she was. "It just feels... right."

"You're welcome," Isalie said. "I'm so happy you two are getting along." She winced, making Jentien smile a bit wider.

"It's easy," he said. It wasn't exactly what he meant, but he was a jumble of conflicting emotions that he couldn't express. "There's something about her that makes me smile."

Isalie's smile lit her entire face. For a moment, Jentien was transported to their last day in Lacorsia, when their biggest worry was the next adventure. When her eyes met his, he basked in the warmth of her affection, refusing to feel anything but joy.

"Me too."

Celeste returned from the shop and gave them another round of drinks while they settled in the living room. Isalie joined her on the couch, and Jen took a seat in the blue armchair nearby. Celeste traced circles on Isalie's leg with the tip of her finger, teasing and delightful. Isalie saw Jen notice, and his gaze followed Cel's suggestive path a few times. He smiled to himself before he looked away.

Cel's lips spread into a suggestive smile that made Isalie shift in her seat with the memory of it above her. Cel flashed it in Jen's direction, and Isalie felt a pang of jealousy to have Cel's attention divided between them. It was quickly overcome by curiosity about what it would feel like to have both of them touching her.

Isalie heard Jen shift in his seat as well and wondered whether he had the same thought.

"There's a spark between you two," Cel said. She glanced between Isalie and Jen as she said this. A thrill of unease shot through Isalie.

Did I say that out loud?

Jentien cleared his throat, clearly as taken aback as Isalie felt. "What?"

"Lee told me there was nothing more than friendship between you, but it's easy to see the torch she carries."

Isalie choked on her spit and turned wide, shocked eyes to Jen. His stare reminded her of a prey animal trying to decide whether it should flee.

"What I *didn't* know," Cel continued, "was that you are in love with her, too, Jen."

"Celeste," Jentien managed to say while Isalie gaped, "you don't need to worry about me. Iz made it very clear that she wants you."

Isalie looked back and forth between them, her cheeks so hot they could have been ablaze.

"I have no doubt," Cel responded. "But you didn't deny it."

"Cel," Isalie said, "why are you talking about this?"

"Lee, love, I'm not trying to make you uncomfortable. Since he came home with you, I've been able to feel what it is between you. I don't want to stand in the way."

"Cel–"

"No, Celeste," Jentien said at the same time.

Celeste held a hand up to stop their denial. They fell quiet, and Isalie's stomach dropped. *I'm going to lose her,* she thought. Tears welled in her eyes.

"I don't want to lose Lee, but something needs to change. You're pining for her, Jen. I don't want you to live like that." She locked eyes with Isalie. "And I don't want to see you deny yourself the chance to finally feel Jentien love you the way you've loved him for so long."

She paused, and it felt like Isalie's heart stopped beating until she continued.

"I think we might work together. *All* of us." She paused again, as if waiting for one of them to say something. Isalie's mind was blank, and all she could do was blink at Celeste.

"We would have to all agree and set boundaries that everyone is comfortable with. I've known some people who had their relationships fall apart because everyone wasn't completely honest about what they wanted. Things that go unsaid tend to fester." She leaned forward, holding each of their gazes in turn.

Shock wouldn't let Isalie form a thought. From the corner of her eye, she saw Jen stir.

"I don't know what to say," Jen admitted.

Celeste smirked. "I can see that." She took a deep breath and cocked her head to one side. "Finding you was a shock, but it didn't take more than a few minutes for me to see how special you are, Jentien. At first, I worried that you might come between Lee and me; now, I think you might just be the piece that was missing in my life. In *our* life together."

Mumbling into his hands, Jentien said, "It's too late." He looked up then, directly at Isalie. It wasn't the longing look he'd been giving her since she'd rebuffed him. It was the look Celeste gave her, and it called to the slow pulse building between her legs.

"Lee, you're quiet," Celeste said. She took Isalie's hand in hers and squeezed. "What do you think about this?"

"I don't, I have no..." Her mind started working again, conjuring images of limbs tangled in a bed.

Celeste took Isalie's face in her hands and kissed her. It was gentle but insistent, and Isalie leaned into it, letting her body react how it would. The kiss wasn't enough; she wanted more.

Jen inhaled deeply through his nose and let the breath out in a snort. Cel pulled away and smiled at him.

"We don't know how long it will take you to find what you're looking for," she said, glancing in the direction of the inner city. "While you're there, I want you to explore what it is between the two of you, then decide what you want." She stood and kissed Isalie's cheek, and then sauntered to her bedroom door. Her eyes bored into Isalie's. "I'll be here when you do."

CHAPTER THIRTY-NINE

Jentien didn't know what to say when Celeste closed her bedroom door behind her, so he poured more burning alcohol into his glass and drank it too fast. Here was an offer to be with Isalie in a way that he had been too stupid to take when he had the chance. Something that'd been snatched away from him when he found her again.

It looked like Isalie was struggling as well. He knew she still felt something for him; it was plain on her face whenever he caught her staring.

"Iz," he murmured. Isalie pulled her gaze from where Celeste had shut her door behind her. "Are you all right?"

"I don't know," she whispered. "I don't know what to say."

Jentien shook his head. "Neither do I."

Iz was *everything* to him. He'd never desired anyone else, but he had to admit, Celeste's intelligence and passion was alluring in a different way than Isalie was. His face was burning like Isalie's, whether from the situation or the alcohol, and he felt a surge of confidence that he hadn't felt before.

Jentien caught Isalie's eye, and tried to convey everything he felt—hope, desire, fear—into the look they shared. "No matter what happens, it won't change how I feel about you, Iz." The flush in her cheeks deepened, and her eyes flicked down to his mouth. He waited for her to look up again before he told her what he needed her to hear.

"I'm going to think about it."

Jentien realized that he'd had too much to drink when he tried to stand. Iz pointed out the guest room, but he only succeeded in bumping into every chair and table on the way until she rescued him.

With one arm draped over Isalie's shoulder, the two of them wobbled and stumbled toward the doorway. "Iz, this is why I don't drink this stuff," Jentien said. He blinked, his eyelids closing so slowly that he almost couldn't open them again.

"You are so heavy," she grunted, heaving his arm higher onto her shoulder as she glanced back to Celeste's closed door.

"You are so wonderful," he slurred. "You know that, don't you?"

"Let's get you to bed, Jen," she replied.

"How are you so walking?" he asked. *That didn't make sense.*

"I didn't drink as much as you and Celeste."

They made it into the bedroom, and Isalie turned them around so she could flop him onto the bed. He forgot to let go of her arm, though, and brought her with him.

"Jen!" she shouted. They landed on the soft mattress with her head on his chest.

"That feels nice. Don't leave."

"Jen..." Her eyes were dark in the low light, but he could see her forehead wrinkled with concern. A look that let him know that she was afraid of disappointing him.

He cupped her face in his hand and rubbed his thumb on her cheek. "You don't have to worry, Iz. It's okay. You don't need to choose, and I won't lose you again." *Shut up, Jentien,* he scolded himself.

She smiled as she sat up and leaned on her side next to him. Her hair fell over her shoulder, and he reached up to run his fingers through it.

Soft.

"How about I get you comfortable, and then I'll stay with you until you fall asleep?"

He nodded and tried to shove himself farther up onto the bed, but his feet slipped on the comforter, and Isalie shook her head. "Come on, Jen." She rolled him onto one side and moved the blanket out from under him so she could roll him back and cover him. She climbed onto the bed next to him and pulled a spare blanket over herself.

She seemed so comfortable here, after living in this house for such a short time. "You're happy here," Jentien said.

Isalie ran her fingers through his hair slowly, and tucked a loose lock behind his ear. He groaned, content, and let his heavy eyelids close.

"I am," she replied. "But I'm much happier to have you here, too."

He felt her lips kiss his forehead and grabbed her free hand. He pulled it close to his chest, just over his heart.

"I love you, Iz."

Isalie reached out, trying to cover Jen to protect him from the burning rain as darkness swarmed around them and light shot through the sky. Each droplet singed her skin, the burn worsening the longer it sat. Her clothes clung to her skin as the water began to burn her back, her chest, and her arms. She couldn't move; something was holding her down.

She screamed as her eyes fluttered open. "Jen!"

Her arm was outstretched, though there was no rain, and Jentien was sleeping peacefully next to her. He'd fallen asleep facing her with his head nestled against her chest. She blinked the sleep out of her eyes as she realized that she'd fallen asleep with him.

The skin on her arm stippled when the cool air touched her sweaty skin. Jen's arm was draped over her waist; she tried to extricate herself from him, but his arm was too heavy. When she tried to move her leg, she found that it was trapped, too.

Isalie craned her neck to look behind her and let out a squeak of surprise. Celeste was lying on her other side, her arm draped over Isalie and Jentien. She was stirring, sending teal locs tumbling when she lifted her head.

"Lee?" she mumbled, still half-asleep. "You all right?"

"I'm fine, Cel," Isalie whispered.

Cel opened her eyes, smiled up at Isalie, and then shut her eyes tight, her face pinched in pain. "Oh, that hurts." She laid her head back on the pillow with a groan, and then pressed her fingertips into her eyebrows. "Too much to drink. How's Jentien?"

"Asleep."

"That's probably for the best. I saw you were asleep in here and I decided to join you. I missed you too much to sleep alone."

"I missed you too, Cel," Isalie said. *She's not angry?* she thought.

Cel rolled over, away from Isalie and Jentien, and slid her arm over her eyes to keep the small amount of light from the hall sconce at bay. Isalie took the opportunity to move Jen's arm off her so she could scoot to the end of the bed.

"I'll make us all some tea," Isalie whispered, and winced when her feet touched the cold floor.

Cel groaned.

Isalie darted to the kitchen and pulled some peppermint tea from the cupboard, hoping it would help with both the headache and the sour stomach after drinking so much. With the iron poker from the rack nearby, she stoked the embers still sleeping beneath the pile of charcoal in the kitchen hearth.

She marched to the washroom and splashed cold water on her face, using her hands to scrub away the last of her drowsiness. She rubbed her hand on the back of her neck, ran wet fingers through her hair to comb it, and then she stripped out of her crumpled outfit and pulled a worn but soft robe from a hook on the wall.

The teapot started to whistle, quiet at first but getting louder every moment. She didn't want to wake the others just yet, so she padded back to the kitchen, clutching her robe closed to finish preparing the tea. The sky was still dark, just beginning its slow transition to dawn.

We need to gather our things soon. Where is my uniform? Distracted, she turned around and bumped into Jen.

He stood bleary-eyed and squinting in the bright kitchen, his body swaying forward so much that Isalie had to grasp his shoulders to steady him. One of his hands wrapped around the small of her back, and the other rested on her hip.

"Sorry, Iz," he muttered. "You making tea?"

"Yes," she answered. "Is Cel awake?"

Jen started to nod, but stopped and grabbed his head. "She's cursing the Elders for inventing alcohol." He looked toward the door, then turned back to Isalie with a confused look on his face. "Did you both sleep in there with me?"

"I must have fallen asleep, and Cel came in later. She seemed fine with it?" Isalie shrugged.

"She *is* fine," Celeste said, brushing against Isalie when she reached for her teacup. "Relax those shoulders, Lee. They're up around your ears."

Isalie let her shoulders fall, but the awkward tension remained.

"How's your head?" Celeste asked Jen. Isalie took her cup and retreated out of the kitchen to watch the two interact.

Celeste seemed as relaxed as she ever was. There was still a hint of pain behind her bright eyes, but she watched attentively as Jentien took his own cup and blew across the top. He grinned at her, his dark brown eyes half-lidded and his hair ruffled atop his head. His borrowed pants and stretched white shirt made him look even more disheveled. It was a strange look for him; he'd always had a hard time relaxing, as if letting the tension and duty he carried go was letting go of the armor he wore to keep his worries at bay.

Celeste drained her cup, and then she started moving throughout the house, gathering supplies into a bag. "It's almost dawn; you need to get back before they send someone for you." She handed the bag to Jentien.

"There's some salve, tea, and charcoal with parchment. Don't forget to send word." She paused, and then cupped a hand on his stubbled cheek. "Keep her safe. Don't let your impatience for justice make you reckless. Lee, don't let him do anything stupid. I can't shake the feeling that you two are the blessing from the Elders that the Olugar has been looking for."

She took Isalie and Jentien's hands. "The Stills' eyes are closed, and it will take more to open them than we've been able to do. You two are the first people we could trust in such an advantageous position. Be careful, please, and come back to me."

CHAPTER FORTY

After hastily dressing and lingering in Celeste's shower of kisses and embraces, Isalie and Jentien rushed through the lightening streets beneath dark grey clouds heavy with rain.

The streets were empty at this hour, and after a quick check of their papers, they passed through the tunnel hand in hand. The thrill of fear at entering the tunnel ran beneath the others: the fear of being found out by the Ambient, the fear of failing to find Arru's daughter, and the fear of letting Celeste and every other Still down, all fought for dominance long enough to distract her. That didn't stop her from closing her eyes when they passed the first portcullis, but the rest of the trip was easier.

Especially with Jen's hand in hers.

On the other side, they stepped into the light of an early day where thin clouds streaked the pale blue sky. Vendors were setting up stalls and calling greetings to passersby. An air of contentment covered the open space.

Isalie glanced over her shoulder at the other world they were leaving behind. Taking a deep breath, she steadied her resolve. She could help more people from here. Jen squeezed her hand, and she smiled up at him. His presence was a balm to her spirits. He would help her do what she needed to do; he would keep her safe.

Jentien walked her to her work assignment and led her around the corner, out of the main thoroughfare and away from prying eyes. Pulling her close, he kissed her forehead, letting the contact linger.

Isalie closed her eyes to savor the soft feel of his lips on her skin. Celeste's proposition rang through her mind again, and she wondered what it would be like to have Jen. She'd spent so long dreaming about it, but after being with Cel, she didn't know if it would feel the same. Celeste had a way of making her feel powerful and beautiful; could she be the same person with Jen? Or would she worry that she wasn't pretty enough, or thin enough, or *good* enough?

She slipped her hand around his waist and hugged him tight, her stomach fluttering and her heart pounding in her chest. She wished they could go back to his room and talk, but there was no time.

Creno walked toward the front door, pausing long enough to glance at Isalie and smile before they were blocked by the corner. Isalie pulled away with a rueful smile.

"I have to go."

Jentien tucked a stray lock of hair behind her ear and smiled. "I'll be counting the moments until I see you."

Isalie chewed on her lower lip, trying to figure out what to say. Instead, she kissed him, and it was better than every dream she'd had. It was passionate, and hopeful, with no guilt holding her back. She gave herself to this kiss, letting all the pent-up yearning from their life together flow through their connection.

Jentien clutched her and snaked his fingers through her hair. He groaned against her mouth, and his hand slid down her back. Isalie pulled away, her eyes on his lips, and took a deep breath, trying to douse the desire coursing through her.

"I need to go." She tore her gaze from his lips to find that he was staring at her mouth, too.

"So do I," he said.

⁂

"Themori!"

Jentien winced when his commander's voice boomed across the barracks, but when he rose, he made sure none of the trepidation he felt showed on his face.

Protect Iz, he told himself.

He could feel suspicion in the air when he closed the office door behind him and stood at attention. His commander was sitting at his desk, his hands clasped atop it. His scowl deepened the lines between his eyebrows.

"Where were you?"

"The outer city, sir."

"You were expected on this side of the tunnel after your assignment. Was I unclear?"

"No, sir."

"And your reason for disobeying orders?"

"I…" he dropped his gaze and let some of the pain he'd felt these past months show before he looked up again. "I lost someone when I came here. I had to know if she was alive."

The commander sat back in his chair, and his stare became less intense. "Did you find her?"

Jentien shook his head. He took a deep breath and shoved his feelings aside again.

"A woman was with you," he lifted his hands to glance at the paper beneath them, "a Jhera Folci from the tailors. What was her involvement?"

Here, Jentien had to be careful. His reunion with Iz had been public, and word was sure to have gone around that they'd been together most of the time since she'd come to the inner city.

"She was promoted recently, and I thought she'd be the best person to help me. I didn't want to wander aimlessly. I told her it was an assignment from the Ambient so she wouldn't question going against orders."

The commander closed his eyes and shook his head. "I expected more from you, Themori." He took a deep breath, and the stern gaze was back when he opened his eyes again. "You defied a direct order and gave false instructions in the name of the Ambient we serve. These are serious charges. However," he paused with a look of consternation, as if he resented his next words, "your position was requested by a member of House Kiyash, the Kiyash heir has spoken highly of your training, and your service has been exemplary until this point. There will be no demotion at this time, nor will there be charges brought against you. But I will be watching you closely, Themori, and if you defy me again, I'll see you stripped of your rank at least, and thrown in prison at the worst."

"Understood, commander," Jentien replied. His tense muscles relaxed a fraction.

The commander nodded and waved him toward the door. Before he could leave, the man spoke again.

"I understand the need for closure, Jentien. Make sure it doesn't lead you astray again."

"It won't. She's not out there."

It'd been a long day, and all Isalie could think about was Jentien's lips and his hands in her hair. When they were finally released from their work, she rushed through the streets, ignoring the beautiful sunset, and ran upstairs to find Jentien opening the door to his room.

He smiled at her and pushed the door wide enough to let her inside first. Isalie brushed past him, suddenly shy now that the moment was here.

Jen shrugged his coat off his shoulders and hung it on a hook by the door. Using his toes, he kicked off his boots and shoved them beneath the coat with his foot while she tried to find her voice. Finding the right words was terrifying; what if she said the wrong thing?

She opened her mouth and closed it again, and Jen wrung his hands together when he turned around. He was waiting for her to start, she realized.

"I want to talk about what Cel said, but I don't know how to start," Isalie blurted.

"Me too," Jen said. His knuckles were white.

She closed the distance between them and grasped his hands, smiling when his fingers relaxed and intertwined with hers. They looked at each other, and Isalie could see the anxiety on his face. His brow was wrinkled with worry, and his eyes darted across her face while he chewed on his lip.

Chuckling, Isalie said, "I don't know why this is so hard."

Jentien shook his head with a smirk. "Neither do I."

"I'm still trying to decide whether that conversation with Cel really happened," she sighed. "It seems too good to be true."

Jentien didn't reply, but his restless gaze settled on Isalie's eyes, boring into them. His wrinkled brow smoothed, and he asked, "It does?"

Isalie nodded. Her heart raced as she stepped closer, bringing their hands up against her chest between them. Her face and neck flushed, and she could feel her pulse in her ears, in her stomach, and between her legs. Her body flooded with desire, half-expecting him to turn away like he would have before Olunei.

Instead, he held her gaze. "I never thought I wanted this," he murmured, brushing his lips against hers. "When I realized I did, you were gone, and all I had left was wondering what would have made you proud of me. Now, you're here, and all I can think is that whether you still love me or not, I'll do anything to protect you, and to make you happy."

"I love you, Jen. Death didn't change that. Loving Celeste didn't change that."

Jentien's smile was as radiant as the sun. He kissed her, so gentle and filled with longing that Isalie moaned.

When they pulled away, Isalie's breaths were quick and shallow. "What about Celeste?

Jentien nodded with a smirk. "I'm looking forward to proving her right."

Isalie wrapped her arms around his shoulders, pulling him closer with one arm and snaking her fingers into his hair with the other. He held her just as tight while his hands roamed over her body before he lifted her and swung her legs around him.

He backed away from the door, and Isalie gasped when he fell backward and he ended up flat on the bed with Isalie straddling his hips. She rubbed against the hard bulge beneath his waistband, making Jen groan.

"Iz," he grumbled, his eyes blazing as he stared at her. "Please don't do that if you don't mean it."

She rubbed again, slower this time. He growled and sat up, flipping her onto the bed beneath him. He paused, searching her eyes.

"Are you sure this is what you want?" he asked. "If we do this, nothing will take me away from you again."

"I love you, Jen. *Please.*" She punctuated her request by pushing her hips up against his.

Isalie felt him tremble as he lowered himself slowly and ran his hands up her sides, pushing her shirt up to expose her skin. She squirmed when he peeled her tunic up, arching her body to help him. He threw it across the room, and she grasped his shirt and did the same for him. She touched his warm chest, the dark brown hairs rough against his ruddy, tan skin.

Jentien slid down the bed, pulling her pants off and leaving her in only her corset and shirt. He ran his warm hand, as rough as Cel's, up her leg, sending shivers of anticipation through her.

Thinking of Celeste excited her more, and she reached to unlace her corset, but Jen grasped her hands to stop her. With gentle pressure, he pushed her onto her back and slowly pulled each lace free. His eyes held hers in place while she waited, the pulse between her legs intensifying beneath him.

The lace came free, and he peeled the corset away. Isalie took a deep breath, as she always did when relieved of the confinement from a corset, and Jen watched her chest move.

He reached down to slide his hands up the sides of her body, pulling the shirt with it. It bunched up around her shoulders, so she sat up and let him pull it free. Jen perched on his knees between her legs where his hungry gaze raked over every inch of her exposed skin. The longer she lay there, the more she wondered if she was good enough. Self-consciousness crept over her, making her want to cover herself, to prevent his inspection in case he found it too flawed. But the feeling fled when his eyes found hers.

She gasped as she saw the naked desire in his eyes. The depth of emotion she had only glanced when they found each other again. It was like a pool with no bottom, and she might never find the surface.

His hands explored her skin, sending ripples of tingling gooseflesh across her body. For all the years she had dreamed of this moment, her dreams had never come close to this. The tips of his fingers traced down her abdomen. They went further, until they were brushing the space between her legs. Jen raised an eyebrow at her, asking for permission. She responded by lifting her pelvis toward his hand.

He was tentative, unsure of himself as his finger entered her. She moaned and arched her back as he went a bit deeper, and pushed slowly against him. Jen matched her movement, pushing deep in time with her rhythm.

I need more, she thought. The sensation of his finger inside her wasn't enough. She reached down and touched the hem of his pants.

"Off," she whispered.

Jen's eyes widened and he pulled his finger out to obey. Isalie chuckled as she watched him fumble with the belt, his hands moving too quickly in his anticipation to undo the clasp. His pants fell away, and Isalie writhed on the bed as the echoes of his touch reverberated through her.

His undergarments fell too, and she had a momentary glimpse of his erection before he climbed back onto the bed. He hovered over her, his hands on either side of her shoulders.

She touched the tip of him with her finger, and he rocked his hips forward. Her hand grasped the length firmly and angled it toward its destination.

Jen couldn't help himself; he pushed his hips forward again and Isalie felt the pressure of him filling her for the first time. He pushed in deep and gasped while she moaned, and she rose up to kiss him.

"Iz," he whispered. "Iz."

"Go slow, Jen," she said, breathless.

Jentien pulled back and slowly filled her again. They moved together, unsure at first, but soon the pace increased. They stared at each other like they couldn't believe this was happening, like they couldn't believe it had taken so long to get here, and Isalie felt herself coming to a climax. Just as she reached that peak, Jen grunted and flexed, shoving deeper.

Jen took several shuddering breaths before he pulled away and flopped onto his side next to Isalie. Her body relaxed as her pleasure throbbed with the beat of her heart, and she rolled toward him, lifting her head to let him slide his arm beneath it before nestling into his embrace.

He took another shuddering breath and kissed her forehead. She felt boneless and replete with his arm heavily draped over her and their legs entwined.

"I love you, Iz," he mumbled.

"I love you, too, Jen."

CHAPTER FORTY-ONE

I DIDN'T KNOW ANYTHING *could feel this good,* Jentien thought as Isalie wriggled closer. He wrapped the arm beneath her around her shoulders, his other arm too heavy to move from where it rested over her belly. Her legs wrapped around his, the slickness between them making him wish he wasn't so spent.

From the moment she told him she loved him, the cold feeling in the pit of his stomach that marked his time in Olunei had melted. Now, with her in his arms, it felt like his chest was filled with a blazing fire.

I wasted so many years, he thought. *We could have been together for so long.*

One of his feet snaked under the quilt at the end of the bed. He pulled it up with his toes, unable to let her go for even that long, and then draped it over the two of them to keep the chill of the stone room at bay.

He dozed off, only waking when Isalie tried to move away. He clutched her tighter, not wanting to let her go. She grunted and tried to roll away.

"Jen, wake up," she said.

His eyes cracked open. The light was gone, the sunset swallowed by the dark night that had fallen while he slept.

"What is it?" he mumbled. He stretched, loosening his arms enough for Isalie to escape. Her feet hit the floor, and she grabbed a blanket from the foot of the bed to wrap around herself. Her pale blonde hair was a mess, but her eyes were bright when she turned to him.

"I'm just..." She sighed and rolled her shoulders. "Happy."

"You are so beautiful," he said. She blushed, and he wanted nothing more than to pull her back into bed with him. She sat on the edge, so he reached out to pull her on top of him. She kissed him and squeaked against his mouth when he grasped her backside and pulled her flat against him. His erection pushed against her belly, and she moaned again.

That was all the encouragement he needed, so he unwrapped her like the gift she was. Before he could prop himself up, she put a hand flat against his chest and pushed him onto his back.

"I need you, Iz," he growled.

She smiled at him, the same inviting smile Celeste had given them. He was almost finished by the seductive promise in her eyes.

Iz swung her leg over him and settled down onto him. They gasped, and Iz wiggled her hips back and forth, pulling him with her. He wrapped his hands around her bottom and gripped hard.

Her voice was wild with desire. "I need you too, Jen."

Isalie winced when she pulled her undergarments on the next morning.

Pain should always feel this good, she thought.

Jen slid his arms around her from behind and pulled her against him. At least he had his pants back on. His chest was warm, and she felt his heartbeat pick up as he nuzzled against the side of her neck.

"I think we should bring our food back here instead of eating with everyone," Jen said. He nipped the skin at the base of her neck, and she rubbed against him, smiling when she felt him twitch against her backside. One hand pulled her closer while the other grasped her breast.

"I'm not that hungry," Isalie said, but her stomach gurgled, betraying how hungry she was.

Jen chuckled and let her go. She let out a disappointed sigh and turned toward him, basking in the eager look in his eyes roaming her body. When his stomach gurgled, he closed his eyes and pouted.

"We both are, Iz. And you promised to keep me from being stupid, remember?"

"I did," she said. A pang of longing gripped her when she thought of Cel.

I wish she was here with us.

The dark sky was lightening with every passing moment; she knew that dawn would come soon, and they'd both need to report for their duties. Jen moved around the room to bring order to the mess their night had made of his room, then dressed in his uniform pants and a plain white shirt.

Isalie forced herself to gather her clothes, too. Pulling on her pants, she caught Jen watching her, and smiled every time their eyes met.

Isalie clutched his arm when they walked downstairs, refusing to let him go when they emerged into the dining hall. Jen put his other hand over hers, and she knew he felt the same.

The smell of roasted meat made her realize how hungry she was, and when they lined up behind the other people waiting for their meals, she tried to make the line move faster by staring at it.

Jen stiffened, and Isalie followed his gaze to see Cortlen and Ionna walk into the room from a staircase opposite to theirs.

"Do you want to tell him now?" she asked. She pictured the faces of his children in the crowd of the Undercity.

Jen shook his head once. "Not just now. And not here. The others told me that Cort has struggled more than I did. We've had to pull him out of his room more than once, and he spends most of his nights awake, grieving them."

"Let's invite him up after we eat," she said. Jen's concerned gaze softened at the hopeful smile on her face. "He shouldn't have to wait any longer."

They moved through the line and found a table nearby where they could watch Cortlen's progress. Isalie devoured her meat—it tasted a lot like Amal's preparation of the beast the night she'd met him—and started in on some fresh greens when Jen waved. She looked up to see Cortlen headed their way with Ionna in tow.

Cortlen smiled, genuine happiness dispelling the sadness in his eyes when he took a seat across from her. Jen's leg touched Isalie's beneath the table and she tilted her head toward him with a brief, private smile.

"Golden child, you're back," Cortlen said. He reached across the table and Jen shook his hand. "With the lovely Jhera. I'm happy to see you."

"Me as well," she replied. "Ionna, you look well."

"Thank you." Ionna looked at her elbow touching Jen's. "You never told us how you two met, Jentien. If I didn't know better, I'd think you and Jhera knew each other before the storm. But you said that you lost your friend to the Gloom. Now you're taking assignments to the outer city to be with her?"

Isalie froze, not sure what she could say. Thankfully, Cortlen shoved Ionna and rolled his eyes.

"Leave them alone, Ionna. They're happy, and so few are."

Ionna shot him a pained look, opened her mouth, and shut it again before saying anything.

"I *was* surprised to see you'd taken an assignment in the outer city," Cortlen said. "But if spending more time with Jhera is your reason, I understand it."

Jen nodded and took another bite, color high in his cheeks. He turned the conversation to the affairs of city guards: rotations, schedules, new recruits, and the prospect of promotion within the ranks. Jentien was at ease with them, talking about things that Isalie had no context for. She enjoyed watching him talk, though, and her mind drifted to the events of the hours before.

When the meal was finished and the sunlight pierced the windows, Ionna and Cortlen stood with their trays. Isalie caught Jentien's eye and tilted her head toward Cortlen.

"Cort," Jen said. The other man stopped with his tray in his hand. "I'll walk with you." Jen stood and grabbed his and Isalie's tray. Isalie smiled up at him, and he winked before following Cortlen to where they could drop their dishes.

Ionna smiled at Isalie, but there was something about it that made the hair on the back of her neck stand on end. "I need to get ready for my shift," Ionna said. She rose from the table, swinging her leg over the bench. "I'm happy you're going to spend more time here with us. I'm looking forward to getting to know you."

Isalie watched Ionna leave, jumping when Jentien put a hand on her shoulder.

"Let's go upstairs," he said, offering a hand to help her rise.

She took it and followed Jen to his room with Cortlen behind. Cortlen sat and leaned back in the chair.

He looked up expectantly at Jentien with a smile. "All right, golden child, what did you want to tell me?"

CHAPTER FORTY-TWO

Cortlen shook his head and backed to the door. "Don't do this, Jentien," he said, his voice full of warning. His shoulders were hunched, his mouth curled in a grimace, and his breath came out in a sob. "If it's not true—"

"It is," Isalie insisted. She took a step forward but stopped, forestalled by Cortlen raising his hands as if to ward off the hope that they offered.

"I spoke to your wife, Cort. I saw Maretha." Cortlen's arms fell to his sides as tears streamed down his cheeks. "Your son, Cort, is the image of you. So is your little girl." Cortlen fell apart; he slid down the door to the floor, sobbing silently behind his hands.

Jentien crouched near his friend and put a hand on the man's shaking shoulder. "She has your eyes, Cort."

Cortlen clutched Jen's hand, and Jen pulled him into a hug. Isalie waited, hearing Jen murmur to Cortlen without understanding his words in the tone he always used to soothe her anxiety.

Isalie grabbed a handkerchief and poured a glass of water, placing them next to Jen. Cortlen took the handkerchief and rubbed it hard against his red-rimmed eyes.

"I have to go to them."

Jen let him stand but stood between him and the door. "Of course you do," Jen replied. "But if you aren't careful, things will get a lot worse for them. For everyone."

"I was never assigned out there, so I had to rely on the census office. They told me they had a record of everyone in the entire city, and Maretha wasn't on it. They *showed me* the census. Why would they lie?"

"They did it to me, too." Reaching behind him, he took Isalie's hand and pulled her forward. "This is Isalie, Cort. They told me she was gone, but she was out there, too."

Cortlen frowned and his brows rose in shock. He and Jentien shared a look of grief and amazement that Isalie felt deep in her chest.

Cortlen took a deep breath, squaring his shoulders. "Some of the tunnel guards owe me favors. After my shift, I'll go to the outer city and disappear. Everyone will assume I was lost to the rain."

"That seems like a stretch," Jen said. "And what happens to the people who let you through without leave? They'll lose their jobs at best."

"I'll figure it out, Jentien," Cortlen replied. "It's my problem."

"You should take extra cloaks and masks if you have them," Isalie said. "And food, if you can manage it. All of it is scarce down there."

"Thank you. I might get my family back because of you."

"Be careful, Cort," Jen said, shaking Cortlen's hand. "Good luck."

Creno set their food tray on the table next to Isalie and smiled at her, their ears blushing like they always did. Isalie had been picking at her midday meal, her stomach in knots as she wondered what Cortlen would do.

"Hello, Creno," she said. "How are you?"

"I am well, Jhera. Elders' blessings upon you. I heard that you had an adventure on your first trip back to the outer city." They blushed harder and ducked their head to hide a conspiratorial smile.

"I did," she replied. "I was asked to help one of the Ambient Guard find someone." She hadn't had any repercussions thus far, but she kept her voice low, just in case.

"Did they?"

"No."

"It is so sad when people disappear. I had no one, and I can't imagine the pain of losing a friend."

"It's hard. I had a friend named Yesrien before," she paused, watching Creno's skin darken from green to russet, "but I lost track of her after her promotion. Are you well?" she asked after Creno slumped back in their chair.

"I-I am sorry." They shoved their chair back and rushed out of the room.

Isalie followed close behind, finding them striding to the far end of the building. When they turned to face her, they were wringing their hands. She hadn't seen Creno so agitated, even on the first day when they'd warned her against asking questions.

"I knew your friend, Jhera. One day, we were speaking after our shift. We said farewell, and I was around the corner, admiring a flowering vine when I heard voices and went back to listen. A woman invited her to the Kiyash spire, and I didn't see her the next day. I watched for the arrest notice, but it never came."

"Did you see who invited her?" Isalie asked.

"No, but the way she spoke made me think she was a Guard." They pulled away, their eyes pleading. "If I had known she was your friend, I would have told you sooner. But I was afraid that if I spoke out of turn, I would disappear, too."

Isalie touched their hand. "I appreciate you telling me now, Creno. You are a good friend."

Creno let out a sob of relief, and their color faded back to dark green. "I think not," they replied with a wince, "but I am glad to know that you consider me a friend."

"I do," she said. "We should finish our meal before we lose it entirely. You may have steady hands, but mine shake when I haven't eaten."

Creno chuckled, and seemed surprised by the sound. It was light and airy, like a breeze rustling leaves. Isalie's smile widened as she followed them inside, but her mind was already working.

Yesrien went to the spire. I need to get in there.

The next day, they woke to find a thick folded parchment leaning against Jentien's door. Inside were two words: *Thank you.*

Two crisp pieces of parchment were tucked within, blank assignment papers with Commander Rallac's seal. Somehow, Cortlen had managed to abscond with these, and Jentien suspected that he'd forged his own assignment to get access to the Outers.

News of his disappearance spread over the next week. The Guard was abuzz with speculation for the first couple of days, and those posted at the inner city tunnel entrance were demoted to servant status. When a body was found in the outer city too marred by the rain to be recognizable, the only clue to their identity was the ruined uniform of an Ambient Guard, and most of the guards accepted that Cortlen had been another victim of the Gloom.

Ionna was more skeptical; the first day she questioned Jentien about their conversation, and every day following she became more insistent. After the body was found, she went silent, and her suspicious glare followed Jentien and Isalie whenever they were unfortunate enough to be in the same room.

Jentien was certain that Cortlen had found his family, that it wasn't his body, but he would have felt better if he could know for sure. The storm was dangerous, and Cortlen hadn't been in it before. Isalie sent a message at the end of the first week to Celeste via Pelom, but they hadn't received a reply yet.

Despite their daunting task and his worry about Cortlen, that first week and the one after it were the best of his life. He counted the moments that he was away from Iz and savored every one that they spent together. Their relationship was better than he could have imagined, and he'd never felt so alive. Her touch was like a fire, igniting his body, his mind, and his soul.

Jentien spent the next weeks gossiping with the guards in the Kiyash spire. He couldn't ask any direct questions for fear of suspicion, especially with Commander Rallac in the other room. He was still being watched closely after his trip to the Outers.

Jentien had tried to speak with the servants, as well, but they stiffened whenever he was around, like they expected him to report anything they said to the Ambient.

Unable to sleep after a nightmare, one morning Jentien woke early to go for a run and recognized two servants from the spire on a walk before sunrise. He slowed to match their pace, straining to listen to their gossip while staying as silent as possible.

"She's far enough along to show now," one of them said. "Since it's an Ambient's child, they're removing her from her duties to ensure the baby isn't compromised."

The other woman sighed. "I wish I could live in luxury like that."

"You'd have one of their children for a year or two of luxury?" the first asked, incredulous.

"Of course I would! When I lived in Bajaala, the Ambient held a ball whenever their children came of age, looking for Stills with enough Ambient potential to bear the next generation. It's a great honor to bring more Ambient into the world."

The first woman wrinkled her nose in disgust. "The Malachi doesn't hold any such balls in the capital."

"That's because they only breed in Ambient lines," the second retorted.

Jentien listened, both intrigued and horrified that Stills would be treated like breeding stock. Here, he'd only counted a dozen or so Ambient adults, so it made sense that they'd need to find partners outside their ranks. The thought didn't ease the wave of nausea in his stomach, especially when he considered Tulia Kiyash's attentiveness.

"How do they know who has potential?" the woman from Lacorsia asked.

"The Consul could see the Ambience in everyone, so I suppose that's how they chose Stills. I wonder who will fill her position."

"I'm sure they'll fill it soon. They don't like a mess, especially under the Consul's nose."

They tittered at each other and Jentien slowed his pace to let them move away. Disappointment settled into his gut. After the stunt he'd pulled and his commander's warning, he knew he couldn't put Iz forward for the job. There was already too much suspicion around him that he couldn't pass to her, if he hadn't already.

They'd need to find another way to get her in the spire.

CHAPTER FORTY-THREE

Ambient Rotre's been spending more time here, and he's searched my workshop twice more. Ambient Kova was with him the last time with the excuse that since he's in charge of enchantment, he's more sensitive to the crystal's resonance, but I saw him eyeing my suits. Had to hide everything else, which means I can't help the people that need it. What's worse is that the Prism use is out of control, and when we finally tracked down some of it, it was mine. Not the stuff that I've given out, because that's all accounted for.

That leaves Ambient Rotre. He's the only other person who had access to what I made. All I wanted was to help people, and what I've made is making it easier for people to lose their minds. I'm starting to wonder if everything that's wrong with the Outers isn't just a sick game for Rotre. Become overseer and see how hard you can push the poor Stills until they break.

Amal thinks I'm reaching, but it would explain so much. Their cloaks are failing faster, people are dying of substance abuse, and are finding out that they've been separated from their families. Cortlen found his family, by the way. Tell our Jen that I approve of his recklessness again.

I don't know what Rotre or any of the Ambient stand to gain, but if you find a way to stop it, we're ready to move. Nel is convinced that it's only a matter of time, so they're organizing able bodies into a sort of militia. I don't think it's a good idea, but Amal is letting it happen. Says it's going to keep people busy, since Maretha's reunion has them riled up.

Be careful, Lee. I hope you and Jentien are taking care of each other. I can't wait to see you again.

Love, Your Cel

Isalie folded the letter and wedged it into the seam on the underside of a dresser drawer, next to the blank orders. She wished she could be there to help, but there wasn't much she could do from the Outers. There wasn't much more she could do here, either, since their excursion to visit Cel. She'd agreed with Jen that it was too risky for him to suggest her for the open spot now, but there was nothing more to learn where she was.

If she didn't do something soon, she might never find Yesrien.

"If we can't get you into the spire, then I'll have to get it done." Jen was pacing after reading the letter Pelom had passed him. "We need to know if all of this is the work of one man, or if it goes all the way to the Consul."

"The servants won't talk to you. Short of rifling through their chambers, I don't think there's much more you can do." She shook her head to stop him from latching onto that course of action. "I'm not suggesting you rifle through their chambers; it's too dangerous. We may not be able to take advantage of this opportunity, but I can talk to more people. Something may come up."

"I hate this kind of thing," Jentien grumbled. "I wish there was something I could do."

"We'll figure it out, Jen." Isalie reached toward him. He took her hand, kissed it, and then kissed her cheek. "I'm not giving up."

The streets were quiet the next morning when Isalie made her way to the tailor. Her thoughts revolved around Yesrien, and a pit in her stomach told her that her time was running out.

She was so absorbed by her inner turmoil that she bumped into someone when she rounded a corner, and grasped their arm to keep both of them upright.

"I'm sorry," she said, but froze when she noticed the long black hair and shimmering cloak on the man's shoulders.

He peered at her like she was an interesting insect, his dark brown eyes narrowed above a smirk. "No harm done."

Isalie released him and tried to move past, but he blocked her way. When she darted the other direction, he waved a hand in the air and her legs stopped moving. She almost toppled from the waist, but he caught her shoulder and helped her upright.

"I know you," he drawled. Isalie opened her mouth to protest, but his astonished laugh stopped her. "You tried to stop my lawful seizure of Prism. What is your name?"

"J-Jhera Folci," Isalie replied. Her heart pounded and her body flushed with fear as he studied her.

"How did a friend of Celeste Zynse find herself in the inner city? It seems like quite a leap from obstructing Ambient law."

Isalie glanced around, searching for help, but the street was empty save for the two of them. She had no idea what to say, and whether this man might be able to extract the truth from her if he chose.

"Judging by your silence and the look of terror on your face, I'd say that you aren't supposed to be here. Given your association with the defiant Ms. Zynse, I'd wager you gained entry through nefarious means. What is your intention here? To spy for the Olugar?"

Isalie's mouth dropped open. How did he know about the Olugar? Did he know about the Undercity and all the people living outside the Ambient-mandated living conditions? Were they in danger?

He chuckled again and circled her like a vulture. "Interesting. It seems I've hit the mark, which means that you are in quite a lot of trouble."

Isalie pictured Yesrien, alone and afraid in some Ambient dungeon, and shivered. That was the fate awaiting her, and Jen and Cel would never know what happened to her. She expected to be swallowed by fear and panic, but the thought of being taken away from them ignited the rage that had been simmering beneath the surface of all her insecurities her entire life.

This Ambient piece of shit was threatening her family, and they'd already suffered enough. "How much trouble will you be in when the other Ambient find out that you've been supplying Prism to the Stills?"

She was surprised by her boldness, but not as surprised as Ambient Rotre seemed to be. He paled, and his eyes went wide. She felt a sick satisfaction at seeing him taken aback, so she continued.

"The Ambient are supposed to care for the citizens, but you've been treating the Outers like your personal playground. Would the Consul approve of your actions? If I went straight to the Kiyash spire and requested an audience, do you think she'd be more interested in a nobody Still who happened to be promoted despite her association, or in the fact that the work that she's doing is being undone by one of the Ambient under her purview?"

Rotre glanced around as if making sure they hadn't been overheard, his entire demeanor having shifted from arrogance to genuine fear. She'd never imagined she would see an Ambient so worried, but a dark part of her loved seeing it.

"You won't have a chance to tell her. I can destroy you with a thought."

"You think I'm the only one who knows? That I was able to come here under false pretenses without friends? There are more of us here than you think, and unless you help me, your life as you know it will be over."

He scowled at her, but the fear didn't leave his eyes. It took a few moments for him to consider what she'd said, and then the hold on her legs relaxed. Letting out an angry huff of breath, he asked, "What help?"

"You can buy my silence with yours, and you can tell me what happened to Yesrien Pseka after she went to the spire."

He furrowed his brows. "Who?"

"A Still recently promoted from the outer city. She went missing a few months ago after she was called to the spire. Where could she have gone?"

He lifted his chin slightly. "The prison, most likely. But if she's there, there's no way to get to her."

There was something guarded in his expression that told Isalie that there was more to it than that. She couldn't go to Arru with an assumption of imprisonment and nothing more; they'd already considered the possibility, and she'd been sent here to learn the truth.

"Find the information for me," she demanded.

His face fell, and fear washed over him again. "I won't poke into the Consul's business."

Isalie scowled at him, wondering how someone so powerful could be such a coward. "If you won't help directly, then ensure I'm promoted to the opening in the Kiyash spire staff."

Ambient Rotre scoffed. "I don't have control over staffing, what do you expect me to do?"

"Lord your Ambient superiority over the supervisor." She smirked at him. "You've certainly had enough practice at it."

He stared at her for a long time, and she held his gaze. In the back of her mind, a voice told her to run, that she'd pushed too hard, that she wasn't built for this.

But the edification she felt at finally venting some of the frustration about the Ambient to Rotre's face, to call him out on their bullshit, was more powerful.

"Fine," he finally said. "I'll put your name in today, and you'll be in the spire tomorrow. But if anything happens to me, I'll take you down with me."

She smiled, showing too much of her teeth for it to be friendly. "And if anything happens to me, Mistress Kiyash will hear about your exploits. Since you're so concerned about that, maybe you should avoid Prism for a while. And leave Celeste alone."

He gave her a slow shake of his head. "Elders help you if the Consul finds out what you're up to."

Isalie remained silent and watched him spin on his heel and storm away from her. Minutes after he was out of sight, the sheer will holding her upright rushed out of her, leaving her shaking against the wall of the nearest building.

She'd threatened an Ambient. Replaying the conversation in her head, she couldn't believe the things she'd said, almost as if she'd been a different person for those fleeting minutes. The sound of footsteps on the cobblestones shook her out of her flustered disbelief, and she ran her hands over her face, pushed away from the wall, and walked to work.

CHAPTER FORTY-FOUR

THE SUN WAS BRIGHT through the early morning fog two days later as Isalie walked with Jen to the Ambient District. The tall, crystalline Kiyash spire loomed ahead, a centerpiece for the city. The wide street that led from the gate was unobstructed, with lesser Ambient spires flanking the street. It felt like marching between rows of vigilant soldiers that eyed her from above as she approached their queen.

Burgundy outfits with gold trim surrounded them, the golden symbols of the house they served emblazoned on their chests. Some wore cloaks that shimmered like the crystal surrounding them; the cloaks belonged to House Kiyash's personal guard, like the one around Jentien's shoulders.

A woman strode in their direction, her dress flowing around her as she moved. It was soft and light, deep red like the rubies dangling from her ears and neck, and hugged the slight curves on her statuesque form. Her golden-blonde hair streamed behind her, wavy and thick.

Every servant moved out of her path, bowing at the waist until they were parallel with the street. Jentien pulled Isalie aside and did the same by tugging her hand down. She obeyed, though she couldn't help peeking at the woman who walked past without a glance in their direction.

Once the woman was out of sight—she swept through the gates amid a flurry of bowing Stills—Isalie stood. All the Stills in the courtyard did the same, and Isalie's sigh of relief joined the collective of sighs around her.

"Mistress Kiyash?" Isalie whispered.

Jen straightened his tunic as he stood. "Yes," Jen replied.

"Now I know who to avoid," Isalie grumbled. Rotre's terrified face came to mind, and she understood now how he could be so afraid of someone.

Jen offered Isalie his arm. She took it with a smile, and they continued toward the spire in the center, curving around the small path at its base to the rear of the structure.

"I'll see you at the end of the shift," Jen whispered, and kissed her forehead. "You'll be amazing. I love you."

"I love you too, Jen," Isalie whispered. She gazed up at him for a moment, and then turned to walk through the door.

The interior was as light as the exterior. The crystal acted like a thick pane of glass, but it colored the gray, cloudy illumination through its prismatic interior to wash everything in a riot of glowing color.

Hooks lined the wall to her right, and large cubbies crowded the rest of the walls. Isalie moved to one side, unsure of where she should head next until a tall man sidled up to her. She noticed his hair first, a long, intricate brown braid slung over his shoulder to his chest. He gave her a warm smile behind his thick beard.

"Are you our new recruit?" he asked. "Jhera Folci?" His voice was low enough to rumble in her chest.

"Yes," Isalie replied.

"Follow me." Isalie followed him into a small office where a narrow desk flanked by two chairs sat in the center. Against the far wall was a rack full of papers, scrolls, and books. "Congratulations on the promotion," the man said.

Isalie waited while the man sat before doing the same. "Thank you," she replied.

He smiled wide, his eyes crinkling in the corners. "Well," he said, placing his hands on the desk, "this is much like what you no doubt were used to in the Outers. Cleaning the spire in your designated areas, unless otherwise informed by myself at the start of your shift or are requested by the Ambient. There is a rotating schedule, so you'll have to check the board each morning." He pointed to the wall just outside his office.

"We're only here during the day for general cleaning, and the house staff takes care of everything during the night. There are times when we require more staff to be on hand, but you will have ample warning of those dates." He squinted at the board behind her. "I'm pairing you with...Elarna. She'll be your guide."

Isalie nodded along with her instructions. It was a relief to see that she would be given full range of the spire over time; maybe she'd be able to do more than ask questions of the staff.

"I understand," she replied when he finished. "I won't let you down."

"Good," he said. "My name is Fyron. If you need anything, let me know."

"Thank you," Isalie said.

"Elarna!" Fyron shouted. A woman about as tall as Isalie with short blonde hair walked into the office. She smiled, accentuating the spattering of freckles across her cheeks and nose. "This is Jhera. She's going to be your trainee."

"Wonderful," Elarna said. "Happy to meet you, Jhera." She shook Isalie's hand vigorously.

"Nice to meet you," Isalie replied.

"Let's get to work. The Ambient require our silence unless we are directly spoken to, so keep quiet."

Isalie fell into step behind Elarna, who proved to be very chatty while they were inside the servant's passages. She lamented their assignment to the entryway for her first day, gossiped about the other servants and guards, and went in depth about her plans for the night after her shift. Isalie's head was spinning by the time they reached the door to the spire proper.

Elarna shut the door behind them, and when Isalie turned around, she couldn't tell where it'd been. The other woman was silent now, and put a finger to her lips to let Isalie know that she should be quiet, too.

Isalie followed Elarna as she dusted fragile, valuable items with barely any dust on them. There were small sculptures made from crystal and gold, ceramic vases, and a plethora of plants—some that Isalie recognized from across Vortheim, some that she had never seen before—throughout the enormous entryway.

They spent hours cleaning, stopping only to take a small meal, until the light in the spire dimmed, marking the approaching dusk. They'd worked around the base of the spire, avoiding the closed, guarded doors leading to the center. Once the door was closed behind them, Elarna let out a sigh and stretched her back.

"It's so hard to be quiet for that long." Elarna said as she took Isalie's bucket and placed it with her own. "You did well today."

"Thank you," Isalie replied with a smile as Elarna's chatter picked up again. Isalie hoped it wouldn't take much to steer her in the direction she needed.

After a few sentences the topic of the pregnant servant came up, and Isalie smiled to herself before she took her cue.

"Do people leave often? I hope to be here a while, so I hope I won't lose it."

Elarna hesitated mid-step but kept walking and smiled over her shoulder at Isalie. "Don't worry, hon, you'll be fine."

CHAPTER FORTY-FIVE

THE SUN ROSE EVERY day with Jen's arms around her, reached its zenith to shine through the windows she cleaned, and set as she followed the same route through the bright and beautiful streets. Being a Kiyash spire servant had one benefit: their midday meal was prepared by the spire kitchen staff, and while it wasn't as extravagant as what Jen told her the Ambient ate, it was still a step above what she ate in her dormitory. And a far cry from the gruel she'd had in the Outers.

Her strength had returned since she'd come to the Inners. She hadn't lost the weight that had been with her since adolescence, but she felt as healthy as she had when she and Jen had walked the length of Vortheim for his Sentinel missions.

A few weeks after her promotion passed, and Isalie hadn't been able to coax any information out of her fellow servants. She overheard some conversations between the Ambient, and she kept out of sight to avoid their attention. But when she heard Ambient Rotre's voice in the foyer while she was dusting the adjacent sitting room, she moved closer to the entrance.

"Elders blessings, Master Kiyash," he said.

A young voice answered. "Hi, Cuzao. Dad said you two were in the outer city yesterday."

"Indeed," Rotre answered.

"What can you tell me about Prism?"

Isalie strained to hear a response, and it was a few moments before it came.

"Why do you ask?" Rotre's voice was wary.

"I heard people are getting sick, and I want to know if I can do anything. Since I'm a Conduit, maybe I could go with you and dad next time, and... I don't know, heal them?"

"That is very noble of you, Baelen. The outer city is a bit too dangerous for someone so young, no matter how powerful you are."

"I can wear one of the cloaks my dad makes," the young man insisted. "Or, you could take me on one of the trips you take *without* my dad."

Rotre's next words were lower, conspiratorial. "Ardaf Kova is brilliant, and his cloaks have made a tremendous difference to the poor souls in the outer city, but I think he would have my head if he knew I took his son out there. The Prism problem is under control. Regarding the trips I take alone, I've been trying something new, something that will help far more people than your father's artifice has. The only reason I'm testing it on my own is that I'm worried that since it doesn't fit their plan, they'll stop me. I could change the lives of every Still in Olunei, maybe Vortheim. Since you want to help, I hope you can keep this between us, at least until I have more information."

"All right, but promise me that you'll tell me if you need help. I don't want people to suffer if I can help it, and Dad told me to stop bothering the Mistress about bringing more Stills to the inner city."

"Your compassion does you credit. I'm eager to see what kind of Consul you'll make one day. Should the need arise, I won't hesitate to call on you for assistance."

"Whatever you're doing," Baelen continued, "it won't hurt anyone, right?"

"If it does, I will gladly submit myself to the Ambient Guard, and they can march me down to the prison to await the Mistress's judgement."

The conversation ended, and Isalie ducked behind a chair when footsteps echoed past the sitting room, only straightening when they faded in the distance. She thought of the guarded doors at the center of the spire, leading to the personal quarters of the Ambient. There were tunnels beneath the Outers, why not the Inners?

She'd need to find a way to confirm whether the prison entrance was somewhere deeper in the spire. Isalie doubted she would be able to force Ambient Rotre to take her there, but maybe she would overhear something that would confirm her suspicions.

Despite her frustration, every day she showed up to work, going out of her way to be friendly to everyone and keeping her eyes on the floor if an Ambient came anywhere near her. Making herself invaluable to the staff was the best plan she had, and it seemed to be working. Fyron seemed impressed by how hard she worked, and Elarna was grateful to have a partner that made her job easier.

So, when several of the senior servants were called to attend Ambients Erre, Tsia, and Jusan Kiyash on a perimeter inspection of the crystal towers throughout the city, Elarna and Isalie were told they'd be cleaning the Ambients' chambers. Isalie's heart raced as she followed Elarna deeper into the spire than she'd been before. Her heart beat faster the farther she walked, both from the exertion of carrying her heavy bucket so far, and the anticipation of finally getting past the first barrier between her and possible clues to the prison's whereabouts.

Elarna pushed open a door on the right side of the hall to reveal a suite of rooms. A crystal chandelier hung from the ceiling, and in place of candles were orbs that could fit in Isalie's palm, catching and refracting the light to cast dancing rainbows on the walls. Plush chairs and sofas, all deep violet, were arranged around a circular rug that reminded Isalie of a still pool of clear blue water. The floors were polished wood, the walls painted to resemble a view of the ocean, and atop every shelf were gilt vases, bowls, and frames holding family portraits.

"Wow," Elarna whispered, taking everything in as Isalie was. "I couldn't imagine living this way, surrounded by so many precious things." She chuckled, then glanced around nervously. "If I had anything like this in my home, I'd be too afraid of breaking it to enjoy it. Let's start in the bedroom and work our way out."

Isalie followed to the bedroom, where they changed the sheets, dusted all the surfaces, and tidied the few odds and ends left out. Isalie placed a heavy, leather-bound book on a tall shelf next to a wide mahogany table that served as a desk, her eyes straying to the papers scattered atop it. Most had creases—missives that had been opened and read—and had been left in a haphazard pile.

With a glance over her shoulder to assure herself that Elarna had moved to the sitting room, Isalie pulled the top paper closer and began to read.

Research Update

Tsia Kiyash, lead Gloom researcher

The salve has proven most effective in our testing, easing the pain of the subjects and healing the burns left by the rain. More elusive is a treatment for the inhalation of rain, but I truly believe that we are close to a breakthrough, and the healers assure me that their efforts on behalf of their subjects have shown some benefit.

I hope that you will allow our studies more time...

Isalie started when she heard Elarna's voice softly calling her from the bedroom doorway. She hastily replaced the papers, hoping they were in the same place she'd plucked them from, and rushed back to the bed to smooth the duvet as Elarna popped her head back into the room.

"Everything all right in here?" she asked, furrowing her brow in confusion when she noticed Isalie smoothing the bed clothes again.

Isalie flushed, and her heart was pounding so hard she was surprised that Elarna didn't hear it. "I bumped into the bed when I was putting a book on the shelf," she lied. "I didn't want it to look a mess." She walked quickly past Elarna, her stomach churning.

Her mind buzzed as they finished cleaning the suite, moved on to a nursery, and then two other suites. She'd seen Ambient Rotre heal severe burns in the Outers, but he'd *never* used salve or masks like Cel did. If the note wasn't talking about those people, who were their test subjects? Where were these tests being done?

CHAPTER FORTY-SIX

Isalie's body arched beneath him as he found his release, the muscles low in his abdomen clenching as he groaned in her ear. Tremors wracked her body, and he relished how powerful he felt, knowing that he'd been able to give her that kind of pleasure. He rolled to the side, his muscles relaxing while Iz breathed deeply at his side.

The smile on her face was so blissful that his heart ached. He would never get used to seeing her like this. For all the time he'd wasted before, he was determined to make up for it every day of the rest of their lives, as long as she'd have him.

She rolled toward him, groping for the blanket that had been shoved to the foot of the bed. Jentien reached down and pulled it over them, smiling as she snuggled close with her head propped on his outstretched arm. She hummed, the sound vibrating in his chest. Iz's legs intertwined with his, and she hummed to herself again.

He started to nod off, but Isalie stirred, bringing him back from the edge of unconsciousness as she started to speak. "I need to find that prison. What if any-one they arrest is being used, somehow? What if Yesrien is being experimented upon?"

They'd been talking in circles about this since they'd gotten back to his room. "They could be talking about people they'd healed in the Outers," he murmured into her hair. "Ambient Rotre knows who Cel is, maybe he told Tsia Kiyash about the salve she's given out, and they've replicated it to treat anyone who sustains burns on patrol."

"It *must* be below the Kiyash spire. I just need to find it."

He eased a lock of hair off her forehead, and she gave him a half-hearted smile. "You'll find it," he assured her. "Just... be careful."

He could feel change in the air, like the change in pressure before a storm. There was more to Yesrien's disappearance than they'd realized, and Iz was on the cusp of discovering something that could be a catalyst for something big. The

Stills were angry, and, at least in the Undercity, they were starting to realize just how deep the inequity ran between the Ambient and themselves.

They fell silent, and the sound of Isalie's quiet snores brought a smile to his lips. As long as they were together, they could do anything.

Celeste peered out at the downpour, her thoughts on Isalie and Jentien. She hoped they were safe, hoped even more that they were happy together, despite everything on their shoulders.

She rubbed her arms to ease the ache to hold Isalie, to feel her body moving against her own. She ran a fingertip over her bottom lip, wondering what Jentien's tasted like, and whether she would get the chance to find out.

Shaking her head, she moved away from the window, through the kitchen, and into the shop. She untied the sleeves of her coveralls from her waist and slid her bare arms inside. She had work to do and couldn't stand around pining for the rest of the day. There were people who needed help, and she had a fresh batch of crystals to grind, sachets to make for the masks.

Ambient Rotre hadn't harassed her in weeks, but she was still wary. She worked on small batches of crystal that could be easily hidden. It tested her patience, but she couldn't afford to be arrested. No one here could afford that.

She grasped the ends of her locs and wound them into a bun at the back of her head before tucking them inside her full mask, pulling the smooth fabric over her face. Its leathery smell had faded over the past few weeks, leaving the mineral and petrichor scent of the ground crystal in the sachet alone. She was thankful for that; the Gloom beast musk was potent and unpleasant, and the smell of freshly tanned hide still made her gag after all this time. She didn't think she'd ever get used to it.

The crystal sparked when she brought her hammer down on the formation. Again and again, with a ring more metallic than any organic material she'd worked with, until it fractured into several smaller pieces. Celeste repeated the process with each piece, until it was small enough to use the mortar and pestle. But first, she had to heat them briefly so that they were more pliable and easier to grind into fine dust. She placed them in a metal basket, stoked the flames in her enclosed stove, and shoved the basket inside.

Her mind drifted as she waited for the crystals to heat. Isalie's smile, reports of Ambient activity in the Inners, the way Jentien's mouth twitched as he watched Isalie flush with embarrassment. Something popped inside the stove, and she cursed.

"Elders' dimpled asses." She lifted the latch to open the door, thrusting her thick glove inside to pull the basket out. Slamming the door closed, she lifted the basket to peer inside. "You all look intact," she muttered. "Focus, Cel," she scolded herself. "Don't have enough of these to work with in the first place, and you start daydreaming."

She pulled the lever to open a small door in the bottom of the basket, and the crystals fell into her large ceramic mortar. Before they could cool, she slammed the pestle down onto them, over and over again, the muscles in her arm burning as they finally began to break apart. She switched hands and kept going, ignoring the door slamming and the sound of someone removing their drenched clothes in favor of completing her sensitive task.

"Cel?" a voice called. She grunted in response as she switched to a swirling motion to make the crystals finer. Footsteps approached her, but she didn't look up. "I've got some news about your girl."

That got her attention, though she only glanced up while she switched the pestle to her other hand again, continuing to swirl it against the mortar. Nel stood a few feet away, watching Celeste with a look that she knew all too well. They had always loved to watch her work. Her traitorous body responded with a throb of lust between her legs, so she clenched her thighs. There was no way she would go down that path again.

"What about Isalie?" Celeste snapped, satisfied by the sudden frown on Nel's face.

"The Olugar sent me to let you know she's been promoted to the Kiyash spire staff." Celeste hesitated, and then kept grinding. "Pelom had a note from her, but since one of their own went missing, he hasn't been able to get away like he did before." They set a folded parchment on her worktable, knowing well enough that she couldn't stop what she was doing to take it.

They sighed behind her, and she heard the irritation in that exhale. "We're paving the way for her to have higher access. Hopefully we'll start to see returns soon, for all the trouble we went to to get her in there. I still don't see why we couldn't use the assets we have there."

Celeste felt a flood of relief. It had been too long without word of Lee and Jen, and she'd been worried that they'd gone the way of Yesrien. She didn't want Nel to see what she was feeling, so she rolled her eyes before returning them to her work. "Because they don't have that kind of access to the places where we need eyes," Celeste replied. "Not without supervision by the guard or the Ambient. The last servant we sent was Yesrien, and the other is working in a dormitory. Lee fit the description we needed, and her man is part of the Inner guard."

"What's to stop them from giving us up?" Nel asked.

"You saw the look in Jentien's eyes, so you shouldn't have a doubt in your mind that he'll follow through for the Olugar and all the Stills in the Outers. Jentien was born to protect the weak and uphold justice. And Isalie," Celeste paused, thinking about the fire in Isalie's eyes, "I don't know if *she* knows it, but there's a righteous wrath inside her." Celeste glanced at Nel, who pursed their lips like they'd tasted something sour. "Something tells me those two are going to be the key to everything."

Nel smirked. "I hope they're enjoying their time alone."

Celeste snorted and knocked the pestle against the side of the mortar to loosen the ground crystal. "I certainly hope so. I told them to."

Nel frowned. "I thought you and Isalie had a thing going."

"We do." Celeste quirked an eyebrow, considering whether to have this conversation with her ex-lover. The temptation to open up to them like she had in the past was strong, but she sighed, realizing that Nel was still as hurt about their split as she was and didn't want to hear the details of her new relationship. "Is there anything you need while you're here?" she asked, her voice even.

"If you have any more of those crystals ground up, we could use a bit. The last rain caught a few people unawares, and nothing else helps."

"Of course," Celeste replied. She pulled a few sachets out of the hatch in the floor and handed them to Nel. "Thank you for the update."

"Yeah," they replied. They opened their mouth but closed it again and turned away.

Celeste turned away, too. She had so much more to do.

CHAPTER FORTY-SEVEN

A VICE-LIKE GRIP SLAMMED onto Isalie's arm as she walked into the servant's quarters the next morning. Elarna was staring at her with wide eyes as she clutched Isalie's arm, pulling her to the side of the room.

"Ow," Isalie began, but Elarna interrupted her.

"Did you hear what happened?" she hissed. Isalie could barely hear her over the shouting behind Fyron's locked door. "One of the senior staff was found with sensitive information in her room. She was arrested! Fyron has her partner in his office *right now* to see if she knew about it."

Isalie frowned in confusion. That was supposed to be *her* job. Just how many spies did the Olugar have here? "That's awful," Isalie whispered. "What's going to happen to her partner?"

Elarna shook her head, equal parts horrified and excited about this dramatic occurrence. "Demoted, to start. If they find out she's a traitor too, she'll be arrested, as well."

Isalie watched the door open, and Elarna released her grip as she spun around to watch. The woman that preceded Fyron was slight, blonde, and very pretty, and Isalie was shocked to see Eilyn so terrified. She and her partner Siera had been here since the Ambient came, their servants from home. Isalie had thought those two, the highest in rank among the servants, were the most loyal Stills in Olunei.

"Elarna, Jhera," Fyron barked. He waved them over impatiently, and Isalie hurried after Elarna into the office. Fyron huffed as he plopped into his chair, rubbing a hand over his face before looking up at the two women. "I apologize that you had to see that, but it left us with an opening to fill. Elarna, you are the next in line for promotion to the inner palace, and as her partner, Jhera, you'll be joining her."

Elarna was the picture of demure acceptance, and Isalie nodded. She couldn't help but wonder at the turn of events. She'd only been here for a few weeks, and already she was going to be positioned to find more information for the Olugar? They had to be behind it. If they'd framed Siera to get her out of Isalie's way…

"I don't have to tell you that this is a big step up, in responsibility as well as station. Here," he handed each a circular gold pin with a stylized 'K' in the center, "these will mark you as senior servants, so you can pass freely in and out of the private rooms of the Kiyash family without exception, as was the case yesterday. Elarna, take some time to accustom Jhera with the rules."

He dismissed them with a wave of his hand, and Isalie followed Elarna out of the office. Elarna fastened her pin on the collar of her shirt, below the right corner of her jaw. Isalie mimicked her, listening intently as Elarna listed off a litany of dos and don'ts for the senior servants cleaning the Kiyash wing.

"Just don't look them in the eye and you'll be fine," she said. Isalie nodded. "You must bring the luck of the Elders," she said with a grin. "Most of us *never* get promoted to the senior staff. After just a few weeks' service, here you are. I can't wait to see what you'll do next."

Isalie tried to smile, but she was already wondering what she might find in the most secure parts of the spire. She spared one last glance at Eilyn before Elarna led her into the hall. As she watched her partner's curly hair bounce above her shoulders, she pictured Elarna's face if she discovered what Isalie had been sent to do, and what the Ambient might do to her for Isalie's crimes.

The day was ending as Isalie finished scrubbing the floor in a large study lined with bookshelves, the light of crystal chandeliers overhead glistening off the wet floor. She flexed her back, her spine popping after being hunched for so long, and plopped her wet brush in her bucket. Wiping sweat from her brow, she turned when she heard light, quick footsteps in the doorway. Always alert for sounds of approach, she recognized Elarna's gait, so she lifted her gaze from her work.

Elarna flashed her a smile as she glanced around the room. Seeing it empty, she risked a whisper. "Good, you're almost done. You remember where to empty your bucket?"

"Yes," Isalie replied.

"Meet me in the hall in a few minutes. I heard the family heading to dinner, so keep your head down if you hear anyone come through."

She moved away, and Isalie listened to her receding footfalls until silence surrounded her. She waited for a few moments more, senses alert to any sound or movement. When she decided she was truly alone, she rose to her feet and crossed the room as silently as possible to a large desk of some dark wood with gold inlay around the edges.

A stack of papers sat in the center, and with one eye on the doorway, she picked up the first pages. Her hands trembled, her fear of being caught rising with every moment she stood there, eyes darting across the lines scribbled across the paper.

She found personal correspondence with other Ambient, reporting on the situation in the Outers: deaths, injuries, and new arrivals. Another page detailed the flaws in the protective equipment, stating that they weren't meeting expectations and their construction would need to be adjusted.

She paused when she found another familiar name listed.

Celeste Zynse continues to improve her designs and formulas. Without the Ambience, she has been able to make strides that we have not, and bears watching. Until recently, the Prism use in the city hasn't correlated with her efforts, though Ambient Rotre reports seizing some of her finished product to be sure it doesn't hit circulation. This lack of crystal for medicinal use will alter the living conditions of the Stills, and we will monitor for change, intervening if necessary.

Isalie's hands shook when she turned the page to see a comprehensive list of everything Isalie knew Cel had been working on. Rotre certainly *had* been watching her, unless there were others out there informing on her. Nothing here was worth taking, though, even if it made her blood boil. Hoping she'd put everything else back the way it had been, she picked up her bucket and rushed out of the room.

She heard footsteps again, but it wasn't Elarna this time. These were long strides, steady and confident. Someone who didn't feel the need to creep around the halls like most of the servants. She opened the door and let the water slide down the open chute in the center. The smell turned her stomach, but an impulse made her shut the door behind her, hiding from whomever might be approaching.

Darkness swallowed her and she held her breath, both to keep from making too much noise, and to keep the stench out of her nose. The steps were right next to her, and then they moved into the study. Another set followed close behind, rushing after the first, and for a moment she worried that Elarna was looking for her. But she didn't recognize the reedy voice that echoed in the room across from her hiding place.

"Mistress Kiyash," the woman said.

Isalie froze. The most powerful Ambient in Olunei was right across the hall. "I have the latest test data and resulting projections for the storm's growth, and several new reports from the outer city."

"Place them on the desk, Erre," Mistress Kiyash replied. Her voice was deep, resonant, and commanding, her words slow and deliberate. "I will peruse them when I have a moment. Has the leak been addressed?"

"Y-yes, Mistress," he stammered. "Ardaf—pardon, Ambient Kova—assured me that there will be no further issues once the replacement of the crystal is finished. The laboratory will be secure. Ambient Kova is overseeing the project personally."

Laboratory? Is that where the test subjects are?

"Did they say what caused the damage?"

"The saturation of the rain bore through the crystal, and the affected auxiliary tunnels were sealed. The main staircase here is now the only reliable entrance. With regular maintenance, it shouldn't reoccur. The observations of the woman from the outer city have been invaluable in the repairs."

"It seems that she has made more strides with fewer resources than Ardaf or even Tsia." The Consul's words dripped with disdain. "Her recent breakthroughs with the crystal make her cooperation necessary, though I fear she may need some persuading to give up her crusade for the Stills. I need a full assessment of her connections and avenues of approaching her."

"Of course, Mistress," he replied.

Isalie couldn't catch her breath while she listened to Celeste's fate being decided on the other side of the door. There was no way she'd consent to working with the Ambient; they'd have to take her by force.

"Is there anything else you require before I adjourn for the evening?"

There was a long pause, and Isalie's lungs screamed for a breath that she dared not take. If they heard her, Cel would never know that they were coming.

"That will be all," Mistress Kiyash replied. Footsteps scurried away, and Isalie heard a long-suffering sigh. She took the opportunity to draw a quiet breath, too. Isalie waited, straining her ears to hear the woman leave the study, but heard the scrape of chair legs, and then the creak of wood as the Consul sat down.

Knowing that Elarna would be wondering where she was, she held her breath and turned the handle to open the door. She blinked as the light from the orbs set in the wall penetrated the darkness, and slipped out as silently as she was able. Scratches of quill on parchment drifted from the office and Isalie gritted her teeth, inching the door closed. The click of the door shutting may as well have been an avalanche of stones as it echoed down the otherwise silent hallway, and the scratching stopped.

Isalie winced when she heard the chair move again, and then the click of Mistress Kiyash's steps approaching her. She considered running, but didn't have the time to do more than take one step toward the servant hall before she saw a shadow in the study doorway. She dropped her eyes to the floor and dropped into a curtsy with her hands clenching the bucket in front of her.

"Ah," Mistress Kiyash said with a hint of boredom. All Isalie could see was the hem of a golden gown at the edge of the hall. "You must be one of the new servants. Go about your business."

Isalie curtsied again and fled without lifting her gaze. Her heart pounding, she managed to find the door and slip inside before her body succumbed to her fear, and tears fell from her eyes. The bucket fell from her grip and clunked on the floor, but the close stone walls absorbed the sound, unlike the grand hallway she'd left behind.

She shook her head and leaned against the wall.

Cel needs to know. Her hands trembled. *They can't take her. I'll tear this spire down with my bare hands before I let them.*

Isalie took a few deep breaths, thinking of Jen, and the staircase Erre Kiyash had mentioned. She'd been right; there was an entrance to whatever was underground—prison, laboratory, or both—somewhere nearby. "I'm all right," she said. "I'm all right. I'm all right." She wiped her eyes on her sleeves and stooped to pick up her bucket just as Elarna rounded a corner and spotted her.

"Isalie, where have you been?" she asked, frowning. Isalie arranged her face into an apologetic smile. "I've been waiting for you." Elarna's frown disappeared when she came close enough to see Isalie clearly. "What happened?"

"Mistress Kiyash came to the study when I was emptying the bucket," Isalie replied. "I-I panicked and hid in the closet, but she saw me when I came out, and I was just so scared," she said.

Elarna's mouth dropped open and her eyes widened. "I don't blame you," she murmured. "I think you could use some rest and food after the fright you've had. Your first day, and already you've bumped into the Mistress." She shook her head and whistled, slinging an arm behind Isalie to shepherd her back to the servant quarters. "At least you're still in one piece!" she laughed, but Isalie didn't.

Isalie knew better than to laugh at the fortune the Elders had shown her. Perhaps they *were* watching over her, and they might not be so charitable next time.

CHAPTER FORTY-EIGHT

SAFE IN THEIR ROOM after dinner, Isalie still couldn't shake the feeling that she'd escaped death or worse. Ambient Rotre's vague threat about the Consul finding her echoed through her head, and she had to wonder how much more damage the woman who terrified him could do.

"We need to talk to Celeste," Jentien said while he held her hands. She'd given him a thorough account of what she'd overheard, and she'd never seen him so angry. "They'll have to go through us if they want to get to her."

"We need more information," she said to change the subject. "Celeste is monitoring the equipment and monitoring the Ambients' movements in the Outers. I need to find that staircase and uncover whatever they're doing underground."

"You're right, we need more." He cast her a worried glance. "But I don't like the idea of you poking around under the Consul's nose."

"What else can I do?" she asked. "I need to find a way below the spire. I need damning evidence, or I need to bring Yesrien home. Anything less won't be enough."

"I can rifle around in the study," he insisted. "If they find me somewhere I'm not supposed to be, I'm more likely to be able to talk my way out of it."

Isalie was already shaking her head. "People know you, Jen. The *Ambient* know you. The entire reason I'm here is because people don't notice me. I've resented it my entire life, but now, it's a skill I can use."

"That's not true," Jentien said. "People notice you."

"Not like they notice you," she replied. She took a deep breath and set her face into a determined mask that hid the depth of her fear from him. "I can do this. I'll be careful. And if I find something the Olugar can use, we bring it to them and don't come back."

Jentien took a deep breath, nodded, and leaned forward to kiss Isalie's forehead. "All right," he said, "we'll try to send a warning to Celeste for now." He sat back, his eyes boring into hers. "Promise me that you'll be careful, Iz. I need to know that you won't get into trouble when I'm not there to help you."

"Trust me," she replied, "I don't want to get caught. I'll be careful."

Jentien watched Isalie disappear into the servant's quarters, his heart pounding in his chest. Even after another week of returning to him every night, he couldn't shake the feeling that it might be the last time he saw her. He walked away, trying not to dwell on his worry.

He filed in at the head of his squad, strapping his sword belt around his waist as they marched out of the barracks.

Leading them through the servant quarters, they soon exited into the clean, bright, and opulent foyer. A sight that he'd once seen as a symbol of hope and the benevolent power that guarded Vortheim from the Gloom. Now, he couldn't help but wonder how many of the people suffering in the Outers could live comfortably in even one of the empty rooms around them.

A few minutes passed before he heard the thunder of small feet rushing in his direction. He suppressed a smile when two young boys careened into the door frame and fell into a heap. A girl the same age walked past them, holding the hands of two toddlers on either side, scolding the boys. Jentien nodded at Baelen Kiyash, who nodded back.

The children were followed by a large contingent of adults, all dressed in flowing silk gowns, tunics, and shirts, and each of them sparkling with sapphires and rubies and diamonds. Jentien kept his eyes forward and his face neutral, despite the contempt with which he now viewed these excesses.

His squad took positions around the family and escorted them outside, to a shaded dining table in a private garden off the foyer. The children assembled at the far end of the garden while the adults stood near their chairs, leaving the head of the table empty. They waited until Mistress Kiyash walked into the sunshine, and everyone fell silent. She passed in front of Jentien, her long golden hair in gentle waves down her back, in a pale gown that mimicked the color of the crystal spire hugging her curvy, statuesque frame. She nodded to the others as Jentien took a few steps forward to pull the chair out for Mistress Kiyash, sliding it forward beneath her. He stepped back into place as the rest of the Ambient, adult and children, took their seats and looked to the head of the table.

"Good morning," Mistress Kiyash said. "Please, eat."

Gloved servants appeared with trays of tangy fruits, baskets of steamed buns with spiced pork, and a plate of flat, flaky bread slathered with honey. A riot of sound began, and Jentien kept his gaze moving around the garden, catching the eye of each of the other guards occasionally to ensure they were at attention.

Tulia Kiyash caught his eye, flashing him a flirtatious smile, and Jentien winced inwardly. "Good morning, Mistress," she said, fluttering her lashes at him. He'd had the good fortune to avoid her of late, but it seemed her interest hadn't waned.

Mistress Kiyash looked at her daughter, noticing the direction of her gaze. She glanced at Jentien from the corner of her eye, and the corner of her mouth twitched. "Guard Themori," she said, a grin forming on her lips when her daughter's smile faltered, "how long have you been with us now?"

Jentien felt pinned in place as Mistress Kiyash turned her full attention on him. "Close to six months," he replied.

"Such a short time, and already honored with our protection. There must be something... special... about you." He struggled to think of a response, but she looked at her daughter, who blushed and looked away from Jentien.

He wanted nothing more than to take Iz and escape whatever game these people were playing with him. He would give anything to be home in Lacorsia, to settle down with Iz in her parents' leatherworks and make a family with her.

Instead, he remained stock-still with his gaze on a flowering bush away from the table. He waited for the Ambient to finish their meal and leave the garden before he let out a heavy breath and followed.

Isalie moved to the side of the bedroom she was cleaning when she heard hurried footsteps approaching, and cast her eyes downward, clutching her dust rag. It was something she'd become accustomed to in the Ambients' sanctuary; they came and went as they pleased and expected her to pretend she didn't exist long enough for them to leave, then continue her work.

Today was no exception. She spotted the black and silver hem of Ardaf Kova's robes pass close by before he rummaged in his desk, then rushed out of the room again. Isalie made to move away from the wall she'd tucked against when his footsteps halted in the hall, so she stayed put in case he came back.

"Kova, I need you to do a final inspection on the repairs."

"Tsia," Ambient Kova replied, "I'm free in an hour or so. Will you be here?"

"Yes," she replied. "Find me in my quarters, and I will accompany you. I'd like to discuss the latest projections as well."

They bid each other farewell while Isalie's mind raced.

They were repairing their laboratory. Maybe I can find it tonight! Or at least hear more about it if I can get close enough.

Jentien didn't see the Mistress or Tulia Kiyash for the rest of the day, and he was glad of it. He focused on archery with the guards today, and continued the lesson for Baelen when the rest had finished. The young man surprised Jentien again, picking up the knack for a bow quickly.

"I've used one before," Baelen admitted when Jentien complimented him after their lesson. "I just haven't had anyone to show me how to do it right."

"You could've fooled me," Jentien chuckled.

"Can I ask you something?"

"Of course," Jentien replied.

"What's it like out there?"

Jentien followed Baelen's gaze to the Gloom beyond the towers. "Awful. I've only been there once, but it was enough to see that people shouldn't be living like that."

Baelen frowned. "I wish they would let me help. I'm the Mistress's heir; I should be able to do something."

Jentien studied Baelen, noting the frustrated set of his shoulders, and wondered if Baelen might be able to help them.

"It would be nice if the Stills had protection that lasted longer," Jentien said. "Too many cloaks are wearing thin."

"My dad is always trying to improve them," Baelen said. "He goes to the outer city every month to check on what he made for the Stills, and I know he keeps notes about how everything works. Maybe if the Stills know how hard he's working, it would help them understand."

Jentien smiled, hating that Baelen had inadvertently given him information that Isalie could use. But what she was doing was so much more important than his feelings, or even this young man who seemed to genuinely care.

"Maybe," he replied. "Because it certainly feels like the Stills are on their own."

"I'll ask him tomorrow after the Tethering ceremony."

Jentien nodded and took his leave, heading back to the dormitory where Isalie would be waiting. Tomorrow, he and Isalie could rest. He didn't know what a Tethering ceremony was, only that Stills couldn't be within the spire while it happened.

On the long walk back to the barracks, his thoughts revolved around what would happen if Iz found something that would incite the Olugar to act against the Ambient. They'd been taught about failed uprisings in their history classes, tales of villainous Stills who sought to topple the peaceful empire the Malachis of old had built to bring order to chaos. He'd never imagined he might someday side with those rebellious Stills, but he couldn't shake the feeling that he was in the middle of a revolution in the making.

He wondered how many of his friends in the Guard might rally behind him if he asked. He would need an army to do what was right, no matter which side he served.

CHAPTER FORTY-NINE

"…BEHIND SCHEDULE. WE NEED to adjust the enchantment, Kova."

Isalie willed her footfalls to be silent as she tiptoed toward Tsia Kiyash's room. Her shift was almost over, and she'd slipped away from Elarna so that she wouldn't miss this conversation. She glanced back to make sure she wouldn't be spotted before she tucked behind the open door in the hallway, her heart pounding so hard that she worried it might give her away.

"It's already done. Mistress Kiyash made me aware of the coming change."

Isalie didn't move, even though her skin felt like it was on fire. *What change?*

"Ensure that you do. If the intervals do not match the proposed schedule, the data will be useless. And Suerdis has enough to do without being dispatched to the outer city."

Ambient Kova lowered his voice conspiratorially. "What of Cuzao?"

"He will be dealt with. The Consul was not pleased when the correlation between her overseer and Prism was noted by the Guard. Can you believe he tried to pass it off as *their* fault?" Tsia Kiyash scoffed.

Shit, Isalie thought. *If Ambient Rotre was exposed, he could give me up. I need to get proof, get Yesrien, and get out of here. Now.*

Hearing footsteps approaching her hiding place, she tucked as far against the wall as she could and held her breath. The two Ambient passed her hiding space without a glance in her direction and continued further into the spire, away from the common areas.

Shit! Isalie rushed behind them on tiptoes as silently as possible. This was her chance to find the staircase, but she could lose them in the winding passages if she wasn't fast enough. She'd have to come back to Ambient Kova's chambers later, and hope there was something there she could take to the Olugar.

They followed the curve of the spire's outer wall, and then turned into a warren of spiraling halls that wound toward the center. They passed Tulia Kiyash's room, the private library, and other rooms that she only glanced at to ensure no one was watching her. Isalie waited at the opening of the spiral, and heard their voices muffled by the wall in front of her.

She inched forward, pausing when the voices became louder, and moving again when they quieted. Eventually they echoed back to her, and she came to a staircase that disappeared into the dark. A light below bobbed as it dimmed.

Cold air from the darkness chilled her. *I have to get back,* she told herself. *Elarna will be looking for me soon if she isn't already. It would be stupid to follow them.*

She hesitated, though, as the impulse to look for Yesrien fought against reason. Tsia laughed, reminding her that she shouldn't be here, so she turned around and retraced her steps.

The halls were quiet, but she couldn't help but feel like she'd be caught at any moment. She slowed every time she approached a door, then sped up again to put distance between herself and the possibility of discovery.

The door of Ambient Kova's chambers was still open, and her bucket with supplies was still tucked behind it. Elarna was at the other end of the hall, and looked up when Isalie straightened, casting a questioning frown her way.

Isalie touched the open door and lifted her bucket, breathing heavily. Elarna waved her on with a narrowed gaze. Isalie flashed a smile she knew was too wide and ducked into the room.

She hastily straightened the bedclothes and collected a wine glass and pewter mug from the bedside table. There were scraps of crumpled paper there, too, and she opened one to find a sketch of a horizontal cylinder atop a table. Part of the cylinder was lifted away like an open door, arrows pointing to the hinge, release mechanism, and an infuser at one end. There were notes in the margins about concentrations that she couldn't decipher.

Not knowing what it was, she crumpled it again and stuffed it into one of her skirt pockets. If anyone noticed she'd taken it, she could claim she'd forgotten to dispose of it when she tidied the room. She moved to the desk near the window, which was as much a mess as any of Celeste's work spaces. After a glance over her shoulder again, she filed through the scattered papers.

More vague notes and technical drawings were here, but nothing damning. The drawers beneath had scraps of fabric and several spools of enchanted thread, but no missive or notes there. She touched a few of the spools, but the familiar thrum of Ambience seemed different between the first and the last. She picked up the closest spool, replaced it, and then picked up the farthest.

There was a definite difference between the two. She'd spent enough time with the thread in her hands that the thrum of energy was palpably less in the second spool. Knowing it was dangerous, she stuffed the two samples in her pocket next to the note, shut the drawer, and knelt beneath the desk.

If I were like Celeste, like Ambient Kova seems to be, then I would hide sensitive information in case someone decided to do exactly what I'm doing. She ran her fingers over the floor, but found no seam. She craned her neck to look at the underside, but there was nothing there. *If they have something, it's probably hidden with Ambience,* she thought.

Isalie sat back and felt a shift. Something pressed against her backside, and when she scooted away from it, she saw a part of the floor displaced. It was small enough that she might not have noticed it if she'd stepped on it, but she'd certainly felt it touch her ass.

Inside was a cubby the length of her forearm, wide enough to fit a thick leather-bound book. She hefted it onto her lap and let it fall open to a random page to reveal a meticulous log of dates, batch numbers, projected dates, and actual dates.

A chill ran down her spine as she took a spool out of her pocket and compared the number on the bottom to the numbers in the book. It was the same format, which meant that this was a log of the enchantment on the thread, including the times that they were *expected* to fail.

"Fuck," she muttered. "Cel was right." She flipped to an older page and pressed the seam to remove it with as little trace as possible. If Ambient Kova realized that the log had been tampered with, they'd start searching for the culprit before she could get away.

Isalie crumpled the proof like the other garbage she'd pilfered and stuffed it into her other pocket. She needed to tell Jen. And soon, she'd go back to that staircase and find Yesrien.

Somehow, she made it through the last hour of her shift and out of the spire. The dormitory came into sight, and it was all she could do to stop herself from running inside. Jen always waited for her before he ate his evening meal, and seeing his face light up with delight was the best part of every day.

He didn't disappoint her, rising from an armchair facing the door where he'd been sitting near some of the other guards. His entire body radiated joy as he swung her into his arms, and she wrapped hers around his neck to hold herself up. The paper rustled between them, and he peered down at her with a questioning look.

"Upstairs," she whispered. Jen set her on her feet and took her hand to lead her to their room. She pushed him to move faster, propelled by her success, which might just change everything.

Jen closed the door and locked it while she fumbled to take everything out of her pockets. She watched his eyes flit across the log page, his expression growing darker as he read.

"Elders," he whispered. "This is…" He blew out a forceful breath. "So much worse than I'd imagined. Cel was right; the cloaks, the masks, they knew it would fail. They have it *scheduled* to fail." He unfolded the other page and looked at it. "I have no idea what this is, but I'm sure Cel would love to take a look."

"I think I've found the entrance to the laboratory," she said, and recounted what she'd heard, too. "I'll need to find a time to go down there and see what I can find."

Jen snarled. "How can they do this?" His angry stare tore away from the paper in his hands and landed on Isalie. She grasped his face between her hands to return his stare.

"We're going to stop them," she whispered. "No one can argue with us; the evidence is right here. The Undercity is only the beginning; there are more of us than there are of them. If we all rise up, they can't stop us."

Jentien held the stare a bit longer before his gaze dropped to her lips and he leaned closer. Isalie ran her thumb over his lower lip, desire sparking in her core, and then his mouth was on hers, angry and insistent. Isalie was just as angry, just as desperate to feel something good, something *real*, when they were surrounded by so much deceit. Their hands fumbled at clothes until everything had been tossed aside and they slammed into the wall. Jen wrapped her legs around his waist, lifting her bodily from the floor.

"I knew you could do it," he said against her lips. "My Iz." She arched her back against the wall, and his teeth grazed her chin, and then her neck.

"Say it again," she moaned.

"Mine."

With one thrust, he was inside her, slamming into her over and over, anything but gentle. She raked her nails across the skin of his back, leaned forward to bite his shoulder, and relished in the steady thrum of their bodies hitting the wall. Pleasure built inside her until she gasped, her climax crashing through her even as Jen grunted and thrust once more, deep and hard, and then went still. She panted against his neck, still pinned against the wall, until he carried her to the bed. Gently, this time, he laid her down on the blanket and rolled behind her, brushing her hair away to kiss the spot where her shoulder met her neck.

"Sorry, Iz," he breathed, sending shivers down her spine.

"What for?" she asked, equally breathless. Aftershocks of her orgasm tore through her, making her shiver harder and arch her back toward Jen. He extricated the blanket from beneath them to drape over her.

"That was... rough, like I was some wild beast that just–"

"You're allowed to be angry, Jen." She rolled toward him, and her brow narrowed seeing the embarrassed flush in his cheeks. "Don't you dare apologize for what just happened, because it was..." she inhaled, looking for the word, "...satisfying." She puffed out the breath she'd held, ruffling the hair falling over his face.

He laughed, the sultry sound making her insides clench expectantly. "Satisfying?" He skimmed his nose over her cheek. "Just satisfying?"

"Glorious?" she purred. "Delicious?"

"Hmmm." He grazed his teeth over that spot he'd kissed at the base of her neck, and her hips rolled forward into his. "If you're happy, then I'm happy." He sighed, and she pulled away. His expression was serious now. "We need to get this to the Olugar before the Ambient figure out it's missing. It won't take long for them to put together that their newest servant could be stealing information."

"Elarna told me we aren't allowed in the spire tomorrow. Why don't we use the orders Cortlen left us?"

"I can get you a recruit uniform and walk us through."

"Let's go early," Isalie said. "Less people will be in the streets, with less of a chance for us to be recognized."

CHAPTER FIFTY

JEN LEFT BEFORE DAWN for a run, and Isalie pulled the orders from their hiding place. They'd been a bit rough with the edges, but that just made it look like they'd been handled, which seemed like a more realistic option. Now, she just had to try to copy the commander's handwriting well enough to fool the tunnel guards.

She set an old assignment of Jen's on the table and picked up the quill Jen had begged from one of his neighbors. She dipped it in the inkwell it came with, touched the nib to the lip of the well to remove excess ink, and started writing.

Her fingers remembered the long hours she'd spent writing in school with these temperamental things, and spent a while just trying to write without splotching the blank paper she'd decided to practice on. Once she found a rhythm, she tried to emulate the commander's sweeping script.

It looked closer the longer she kept at it, but she couldn't make her wrist move the right way to get a good curve on the initials. No matter how many times she tried it, she couldn't stop herself from hesitating on that final arc.

Jen came back with a pile of fabric slung over his arm just when she was deciding whether to break the quill in half or not.

"I can't get this signature right," she grumbled.

"Do you want me to try?" Jen asked.

"No," she replied. "I've got it." She scowled at him as he passed in front of the lamp on the table. The light shone through the damp fabric of his white shirt, and Isalie gasped, holding the orders up in front of it.

"Ha!" she shouted, seeing the dark ink clearly through the parchment. "Jen, hold this," she called.

Jen obeyed, and his face split with a big grin when he watched Isalie trace the lines of the commander's handwriting from the old page to the new. When she finished, she blew on the ink to dry it while Jen beamed.

"Well done, Iz. If I didn't know any better, I'd say you'd been a spy your entire life!"

"Thank the Elders I wasn't," she replied. "Otherwise, you would have starved on the road."

They donned their uniforms and left the dormitory just as the sun poked through the clouds. The streets were almost empty, but they took a circuitous route near the river to avoid any unwanted eyes.

Jen led her to the tunnel guard, and she hesitated when she recognized Lawgra. He'd checked her papers before; would he recognize her and know that her papers had been forged?

Isalie offered her orders, and Lawgra started to look her way, but Jen stepped forward and pushed his paper into the man's hands, grabbing his attention.

"Jentien, I didn't know you'd been cleared for the outer city again. Last I heard, you took a walk against orders." He looked down at the papers in his hands, and Jen shifted in front of Isalie to block her from Lawgra's line of sight.

"I have clearance this time," Jen said. "Just a routine patrol." He leaned forward to clap Lawgra's shoulder. "Trying to take a shift to worm my way back into the commander's good graces."

Lawgra glanced Isalie's way, only glancing at the uniform before he smirked at Jentien. "Seems like the smart thing to do." He handed the documents to Isalie, pausing when he finally looked at her face.

She took the paper, ducking her head to fold it and tuck it into an inner cloak pocket. Jentien cleared his throat and she saw him motion for his orders.

"I'm looking forward to seeing you in training this week," Jentien told him. "Most of the Guard have no idea how to hold a bow, but I heard you're an expert."

Lawgra chuckled, finally turning away from Isalie to smile at his friend. "You heard right, Themori. I'll make sure I teach *you* something for a change. Be back by sundown. Anyone who isn't is facing disciplinary action, thanks to you."

"Right," Jen replied. "I'll do that."

Jentien held her hand through the tunnel, distracting Isalie from her fear by running his finger over her skin, reminding her of the night before. Dawn was swallowed by the storm overhead when they made it to the outer city. She hadn't missed the mask that she pulled on before she breathed in the fog hanging low in the streets. Before she knew it, they were removing their soaking cloaks, gloves, boots, and masks in Celeste's workshop. It was the same messy space that smelled like leather, stone, and metal, and the same diminutive figure with a wild mass of vibrant locs tied at the base of her neck was bent over a table with no idea that they'd arrived.

Isalie strode across the room with Jentien close behind and circled her arms around Celeste's waist. Celeste started, screamed, and lurched sideways, her hip grazing the worktable. She stumbled into Jentien, who flung his arms around both women to keep them from tumbling. Isalie let out a peal of surprised laughter when Cel took a deep breath, her eyes wide.

"Elders, you scared me!" She turned toward the table and let out a relieved sigh. "The powder isn't glowing, so I don't think it'll explode." She brightened and threw her arms around them, squeezing so hard Jentien thought his neck might break. She kissed each on the cheek, and Jentien fought the hard blush creeping up his neck. "You're back! I missed you!"

Isalie kissed her, long and slow, and though Jentien tried to remove himself from such an intimate moment, neither of them would let go. When they finally pulled away, Celeste gave Jentien a quick kiss on the lips, too. His eyes went wide when she finally took her arm off his neck.

"So," Celeste drawled, her eyes darting between the two of them. "How did it go?"

Isalie started rummaging in her pockets, which was hard, since both Celeste and Jentien were pressed too close to her. "We got it," she said, eyes bright and cheeks flushed. "Proof the Olugar can use."

Celeste's brows rose almost to her hairline. "You did?" Isalie nodded, finally pulling the parchment and spools from her pants pockets.

"It's almost too awful to believe," Isalie said. "But there's power in that. We're too busy fighting to survive to look around and notice that we could change things. There are enough of us to overthrow them if we band together."

"You sound like Nel," Celeste grumbled as she looked through the papers. "This is amazing," she whispered. "I'm amazed you were able to get close enough to steal this." She peered at the crumpled schematics, the distant look on her face telling Isalie that she was puzzling something out in her head.

"It was all Iz," Jen said. "*She's* amazing."

Celeste flashed him a knowing smile, then turned it on Iz. "You two have done the impossible, and I'm so grateful." She set the papers aside. "But that's not *really* what I was asking." Jentien felt like his heart had dropped out of his chest, and there was no stopping the burning sensation that shot all the way to his ears.

Celeste took note of it, and the way Iz's mouth gaped open, her eyes darting from Jentien to Celeste and back again as Celeste went on. "This," she waved her hand between the two of them, "feels different. Easier. I assume things went well?" A knowing smile spread over her lips, sensual and expectant.

Jentien sputtered. "I... we..."

"Cel..."

"Lee, I told you what I wanted before you left. It hasn't changed. I'm *happy* you two finally got the chance to feel what you've been missing all these years. Now,

I'm wondering... if that's something that both of you would like to share with me?"

Jentien still wasn't thinking when he blurted, "Yes." He trailed his gaze over Isalie's hair, her wide eyes, her beautiful mouth, then to Celeste's. Those plump lips, that easy smile, her sharp wit... He couldn't help that his dreams had become a playground for him to explore her suggestion. It was all tangled limbs and passion, so much so that he'd woken several times to find his hands all over Iz before she'd helped him ease the tension.

He was surprised to see that there was no doubt in Iz's eyes. Just hungry desire.

"Yes," she said. His answering hunger was a ravenous beast, snarling like it had when he'd taken her against the wall.

Cel trailed a finger across her lips and leaned forward to kiss him.

CHAPTER FIFTY-ONE

THIS IS WHAT IT feels like to combust, Isalie thought, watching Celeste and Jen kiss with Cel's finger caressing her lip and Jen's hand clutching her waist. Jen pulled away, panting, his hazel eyes locking onto Cel's as if he'd come awake after a long sleep. It'd been that way for Isalie, too.

"Later," Cel said with a sultry smile, "we are going to discuss what to do about the Ambient." She pursed her lips. "But now..." She trailed off and leaned forward to kiss Isalie again, and the fire inside her blazed. Every inch of her skin tingled with anticipation, and when Cel's hands ran down her arms, her back, her legs, she would have sworn they left trails of fire. Jen's fingers dug into the small of her back, and there was no hiding his arousal.

Cel pulled away, leaving Isalie panting with desire, and then pushed Jen toward her with a smile. His lips met hers; she could almost feel the wall at her back, and her insides quivered with the echo of those powerful thrusts. He pulled her close against his body and snaked his hand into the hair at the nape of her neck to hold her close.

Isalie couldn't remember moving through the house, couldn't remember shucking her clothes. She only felt the urgency of Jen's hands and lips, and Cel's soft, teasing nibbles and caresses. She popped her eyes open when she was tipped onto Cel's bed with Jen beside her and Cel on top of them.

"What–" Jen began, tensing. Cel silenced him with a rough kiss, and Isalie squirmed against Jen's leg as Cel explored his mouth with her tongue.

"Just follow my lead, Jen," Cel told him. She rolled onto Isalie's other side, leaving her lying between them, looking at each of them with her body on fire. That fire burned in Jen's eyes, and Isalie felt a faint tremor throughout his body. It was the same tremor she'd felt when she'd found him again, as if he could hardly contain whatever emotion he was keeping beneath the surface.

Isalie closed her eyes when Cel kissed her shoulder, and her fingers danced up Isalie's bare stomach. She gasped when Jen's larger hand clutched her hip and his lips passed over her breast. Cel teased one nipple just as Jen sucked on the other, driving a groan of wanton desire from her throat.

Jen's hand moved between her legs, and then Cel's joined it, guiding Jen to stroke the center of her desire while Isalie squirmed and groaned against them. She could barely make out Cel's voice gently urging Jentien to push a finger inside, and then she was on her side, guided against Jen by Cel.

Cel lifted Isalie's leg, and Jentien gently entered her. Every hip thrust drove her against Cel's hand as it continued to stroke between Isalie's legs. Jen's arm snaked beneath her to hold her close, and Cel took his other arm, guiding it between her own legs, letting Jentien make use of what she'd just shown him. To Isalie, nothing existed but this mass of writhing bodies and limbs, the panting moans of both of her partners, and the mounting pressure inside her.

Jen thrust forward and grunted. It sent Isalie over the edge, her orgasm ripping through her like the firestorm she'd been working toward, obliterating everything in its wake. Celeste traced a finger over Isalie's lip, smiling as she watched Isalie come apart and then lie panting on the bed.

"That was worth the wait."

Celeste didn't let them languish long, and too soon, they were out of the house along familiar streets. Clad in Celeste's leather cloaks, they skirted several guard patrols, ducking into a ruined building to avoid them before darting into the alley leading to the old courthouse. There had been so many more Guards here after Cortlen's disappearance. The Undercity was bustling as they wound through stalls and stalagmites toward Amal's central pillar home. Cel didn't bother knocking, just burst inside, shouting Amalricus's name as she went. Isalie hurried behind her, and only Jentien paused long enough to shut the door.

"Amal!" Cel shouted again. His voice called out from the dining room, and Cel changed direction, striding through the dim house until she emerged into the light, where they found more than Amal seated around the table. "Oh," Cel said, stopping short.

Nel was there, elbows planted on the table, their head cocked to one side to watch the trio arrive. Arru looked expectantly at Isalie. Amal stood, the eyes of his guests following him. He darted an admonishing glance at Cel before smiling at Jen and Isalie.

"Jentien, Isalie, welcome. Celeste," he said, admonishment in his tone, too, "perhaps you could show our friends out until we can finish–"

"No, Amal, I think what they have to say is important for the Council to hear."

Isalie didn't wait for an invitation but extracted the papers and thread from her pocket. She set it all on the table and smoothed the parchment for them.

Amal sat slowly as he read, his eyes going wider and wider. "This..." he said, trailing off. Arru handed her paper to Nel. Their blank expression was instantly replaced with angry triumph.

"Is *exactly* what we needed," Nel finished. Their eyes were alight, and Isalie didn't like the darkness she found there. "With this," Nel waved a different paper before their face, at the others, "we can rally people to push back against the Ambient!"

Amal flipped the page over. "This is genuine?"

Nel waved their paper again, the wax seal flapping. "The Kiyash seal! How can anyone refute this?"

"Where did you get these?" Amal asked.

With her stomach squirming, Isalie said, "In Ambient Kova's chambers, hidden in the floor. The thread holds the enchantment for everything they provide, and I can feel the difference between what's being used now and what is prepared for months or years from now. I didn't have time to decipher everything in the log, but what I saw detailed a long timeline of failure." Everyone's eyebrows shot up in surprise. Isalie told them all that she'd heard and seen, and when she'd finished, everyone started speaking at once.

"You can't honestly think the people will believe this!"

"How can they deny what we have here?"

"What are we to do, parade around the Undercity and the Outers waving these around?"

"The Ambient won't let us get away with it–"

"Then we'll take the fight to the Inners and tear their spires to the ground!"

Amal stood and slapped his palms onto the table. "Enough," he said, not bothering to raise his voice as everyone fell silent. "What we have here is a start. I agree that the people need to know, that we should begin to gather support for a more... direct intervention in the way this city is run. But," a glance at Nel, "if we shout it through the streets, the Ambient *will* retaliate."

"We don't have the numbers to go up against their power," Arru added. "Without the support of the Stills in the Inners..."

"Iz and I will speak to them," Jentien volunteered, and Isalie's blood ran cold. "There are so many people here that would be grateful to hear that they may still have family left. The guards might enjoy the sunshine, but they're Stills. They *must* see how unfairly the rest of us are treated by comparison."

Nel scoffed. "That kind of idealism is going to get us all killed." They turned back to their fellow Olugar. "We can't count on anyone from the Inners. There's no way they'll give up what they have to help us."

"Cortlen did," Jentien insisted.

"Yes," Nel replied with a dismissive wave, "and that's a story that we can use to our advantage. Our best chance is to bolster our ranks from the Outers. *These* people have been suffering, and it's *these* people that have the most to gain.

We have the anger to use in the coming fight. That's what we need, not empty promises and false hope."

Jentien opened his mouth to argue, but Amal silenced him with a gesture. "Without Jentien and Isalie, we wouldn't have even the slim chance we see before us now. If they believe they can help without putting themselves in more danger, I think we owe it to the people to try. Jentien, are there other guards who might be open to hearing what we've learned, and would keep it to themselves? If even a whisper of dissent gets back to the Ambient, at best we can expect to go without new protective equipment. I don't want to think of the worst-case scenario."

Jentien was already nodding. "I can think of a few that would be willing to listen."

"Use the utmost caution, or Nel's predictions will prove correct." Nel started to protest, but the others silenced them. "Nel is right about getting our people involved. They need to know what has happened—what is *still* happening—so that they can prepare themselves, if nothing else. But perhaps, we can start to sway people toward the Olugar's aims as well."

"People need to know their cloaks and masks will fail," Jentien said.

Nel heaved an angry sigh. "I'll spread the word, and we can move people down here if they have nothing else to protect them. It will strain our resources, but I can't let people suffer." They began to run through a list of supplies they had, to determine how many they could take on. Isalie waited, not knowing what to say, or whether she should say anything more.

Arru left the conversation behind to join her. "Isalie," she sighed. "Thank you." Her voice wavered. "Thank you so much for what you've risked, for bringing this to us."

"I haven't found Yesrien, but I may know where she's being held."

Arru gave her a sad smile. "I'm so grateful for what you've done, and grateful that you've come out the other side of it." Isalie's eyes darted to Jentien, making plans to subvert the Ambient's hold on the Stills in the Inners. "I won't give up hope of finding her, but at least we have this." She squeezed Isalie's hand. "But, if you *do* find her, at least tell her that I love her."

Isalie watched Arru walk away, and knew that whatever was decided here, she needed to go back. She would find Yesrien if it was the last thing she did.

CHAPTER FIFTY-TWO

They didn't linger in the Undercity, and just as the clouds began to darken overhead, heralding the sunset hidden beyond them, Celeste led Isalie and Jentien above ground.

She felt empty inside, knowing that they would leave before long, but she couldn't let them without having her say. Not after seeing the fear in Isalie's eyes mirrored in Jentien's. She hoped Jen's steely determination would be enough to shelter them from harm, but Cel had lived here long enough to know how much danger they were in. She grabbed each of their hands; Jentien squeezed her hand in reply, and Lee clutched it in a way that told Celeste she felt the same emptiness.

"You'll be missed if you don't leave soon," she murmured. Jentien placed a gloved hand on her shoulder. "I want you both to know that I have every confidence that you'll come back to me, likely with an army in tow, if I know our Jentien half as well as I think I do."

"We *will* be back," Jentien assured her. Isalie closed the distance and wrapped her arm around Cel's back. "I'll keep Isalie safe, and I'll bring her back to you. For us."

The empty feeling abated, just a bit, from the conviction in his voice. "I know," she told him, cupping his cheek. "I wish we had more time to talk about us. For now, know that I care deeply for both of you, and I want you to be happy, to take comfort and pleasure in each other whenever you can." She pulled Isalie tight against her. "Most of all, I need you to take care in the company you keep. Assume everyone there will sell you out, and don't take chances with your lives, because I don't know what I would do if I lost either of you."

She'd spent every day that they were away thinking about them, fantasizing about them, and worrying about them. She'd built up this idea of what their relationship could be, and now that she had it, they had to leave again. That emptiness grew until she felt like she was standing at the edge of a precipice, and one strong breeze would send her tumbling.

They had enough of that to contend with and she wouldn't add to it. So, she pulled each of them into a crushing hug, wishing their masks weren't between them, and watched the pair disappear into the rain. Long after they were out of sight, her gaze stayed fixed on the spot she'd last seen them, praying to the Elders that they *would* come back.

Jentien couldn't help but glance over his shoulder to get one last look at Cel through the rain. Neither could Iz, and when they turned back, they clutched each other's arms, terrified to let go of each other as they'd just let go of Cel.

He still couldn't quite believe he'd said yes, that he'd allowed himself to say that one word. Celeste had given Iz what he couldn't, had cared for her when he couldn't, and was so brilliant and selfless and confident that there wasn't anything to do but fall for her. The fact that both of the women he desired wanted him, and wanted each other, still seemed too good to be true.

Jentien wished he could hold Isalie when they walked through the tunnel, after presenting their papers to Pelom at the tunnel's mouth, but she walked with her back straight all the way through. On the other side, the sunset lit the sky in a riot of pink and orange, the air warm and balmy in contrast to the cold damp of the Outers.

Their room was dark when they finally reached it, another stark contrast to the warmth of the Undercity and Celeste's house. There, he'd felt welcome. Wanted. Here, his skin crawled with the invisible threat the Ambient posed.

All Jentien knew was he'd do whatever it took to convince these people to help the Olugar if it didn't put Iz in danger. And as they climbed into bed, nestled in each other's arms, Jen held her close, repeating his vow to Celeste silently to himself.

Jentien shoved his soaking wet hair out of his face after washing himself the next morning, letting the water run down his body. He'd woken too early and watched Iz sleep while the world brightened by degrees, terrified to let her out of his sight. He didn't fear his part in the possible uprising but knowing that she was walking back into the lion's den was almost too much to bear.

Iz watched him warily from the bed, and he forced himself to take a deep breath and let some of the tension out of his shoulders as he exhaled. He'd been clutching his hair so tight that he was surprised he hadn't ripped it out by the root.

"I'm going to be fine, Jen," Isalie said. "You're going to talk to the people you trust, and I'm going to get down those stairs. If Yesrien's alive, maybe she's with the test subjects they've mentioned." Isalie shuddered, and Jentien sympathized. It was difficult to consider people like them being experimented upon.

"Ambient Kova could discover the missing page any time," he argued. "I don't want you anywhere near the spire if that happens." Stalking to the window, he looked down at the street where several guards were coming back from their night patrol with tired smiles on their faces.

He didn't know their names, but they looked like they didn't have a care in the world. It reminded him how difficult his task would be. Too many Stills didn't want to ruin what small joy they'd found in such a horrible situation. That's what a life without the threat of rain was: joyful, at least in comparison to what they'd left behind, or what they'd been lucky enough to avoid in the first place. He'd never felt such righteous fury in his life as when he considered just how well the tactic was working.

His angry gaze landed on Isalie, whose dark blue eyes were still fixed on him, waiting for him to come out of his reverie. "Is this how you've always felt?"

Her brows drew together, forming a wrinkle that made her confusion so adorable that it almost wiped out the fury that had been simmering in his soul since he'd arrived here. Almost.

"Like you're burning from the inside out, and you want to scream at everyone you see that they're slaves, that they need to wake up and fight. But you also know that the only thing that will come from it is your own punishment, so you keep quiet and watch everyone around you feed the system that's slowly killing us."

Isalie's cheeks flushed, and her brows drew up—in relief, pity, or understanding, Jentien couldn't tell—while her eyes stayed hard like sapphires. She didn't need to answer the question; he could see it, that fire, deep and hot. It'd been burning a long time, and he still couldn't understand how he'd dismissed it for so long.

"I'm sorry we're in the middle of this, Jen," she said.

"I'm sorry for every time I told you to keep quiet," he muttered, and shoved his wet hair out of his face just to have it flop back again.

He reached up to yank it out of the way, but Isalie's soft hands caught his. She put a finger under his chin, and gently, insistently, lifted his face until he was trapped by the steel in her gaze.

"You're here now, and that's what matters. Whatever happens to us, we've given the Stills a reason to fight."

With her back to the window and the dawn limning her flaxen hair with golden light and that inner fire glowing through her eyes, she looked like an Elder come to life. There was no trace of the nervous, unconfident girl she'd been months ago. She was a goddess, an avenging spirit that could burn the world with the inferno that had blazed inside her for as long as Jentien could remember.

He just gazed at her, full of pride and love, and let his own inferno blaze with hers.

Every day was the same again in the days following their visit to the Outers. Wake up, go to work, clean the Kiyash spire while looking for some opening to break away from Elarna and the Ambient, come home. The opportunity to retrace her steps to the staircase hadn't come, as Elarna had been more suspicious since the day Isalie had followed Tsia and Ardaf. She hovered over Isalie, watching her movements as closely as she could without neglecting her duties. Isalie just went to work as normal, careful to assuage Elarna's fears so that when the moment came, she had the ability to take it.

Where she'd been numb during her first days in Olunei, Isalie was a bundle of raw nerves from the moment she woke to the moment her head hit her pillow. The only time the anxiety loosened its grip on her heart were the moments that Jentien overwhelmed her with other, more pleasant sensations. And then the fear came crashing back as soon as his breathing slowed and he fell into a blissfully dreamless sleep.

Isalie, however, had nothing but nightmares.

She awoke in a cold sweat every morning, and every morning she pictured the moment when Jentien had finally, fully recognized what Isalie was made of. Cel had helped her awaken it, and Jentien had given voice to it. But she was learning to embrace it, giving her the conviction to keep moving forward.

The fifth day began the same way, and when Jen split off to the barracks, she entered the servant's quarters, readying herself to spend the day in deference to Elarna and the Ambient. The practice was wearing on her nerves, taking more effort to play the demure nobody that she'd always been.

Elarna seemed distracted today, but Isalie kept her head down and kept working, cleaning every bed chamber from top to bottom before moving to the next. Ambient Kova appeared in the afternoon, just as they neared his room on their rounds. He ignored them, and Elarna waved them onward until the Ambient's voice rang in the hall.

"Elders' eyes," he cursed. "I need a servant here."

Isalie looked to Elarna as the senior servant in their partnership, who gestured down the hall and pivoted to attend the Ambient.

"This glass spilled, and it's everywhere," he complained.

Isalie heard the thump of Elarna's bucket as she walked away, stopping at Tsia Kiyash's room to peek inside before she entered. She caught a glimpse of the Ambient she'd barely spied before, seeing the same golden hair as the Consul, though it was cropped short. This woman's body was more angular than the Mistress, as well, her sharp jawline clear in the sunlight streaming through her window to shine on the desk where she was seated.

Isalie pushed toward another chamber, but stopped short before she reached it. Elarna was busy, the Ambient were busy, and the hall was empty. She only hesitated for a moment longer, then, as silently as possible, she ran.

The hall felt longer than it had before. She wound through the spiral to the center and paused at the top of the steps. Her heavy breaths were loud, and she willed herself to calm so she could listen for anyone approaching. After a few long moments, she took a deep breath to steady herself and took a step into the darkness below.

CHAPTER FIFTY-THREE

Celeste hated waiting. Waiting for more materials, and worst of all, waiting for news from Lee and Jen. Every morning, she awoke to the sound of rain and an empty bed, reliving that brief, glorious meeting of their bodies. Every morning, she rushed to the Undercity to find that they hadn't heard anything, that they had no more leather or crystal to give her, and she had nothing to do for another day but wait.

Days passed, and she was starting to lose sleep. She'd been awake most of the night before, unable to sleep for her anxiety. She was already dressed in her leather suit, ready to leave as soon as it was reasonable, comparing the schematics Lee had recovered with a design it'd inspired. Not that she had the materials to construct something like this, but she had to admit that Ambient Kova was onto something here.

Her charcoal pencil snapped. "Elders," she cursed, reaching without looking for another, but sending one of her vials over the edge of the table. It shattered on the stone floor, and she snapped. The anxiety and frustration she'd been sublimating boiled over, filling her with rage.

"Shit!"

She hurled the nearest tool toward the wall and swept the rest onto the ground to clatter amongst the glass shards. Her elbows hit the empty table and she slammed her face onto her upturned palms.

It took a few moments and deliberate breaths to calm herself, and then she lifted her head to survey her workshop. Her tools were everywhere, and the shards reflected the light from her lantern in a dazzling array. Celeste hung her head with a sigh, and looked around for the tool she'd thrown first.

Her eyes snagged on the crystal section of the outer wall and a dark spot she hadn't seen before. "Oh, shit," she groaned as she approached. It was a crack, indented from the tool she'd hurled this way. "That shouldn't happen," she mumbled, and looked down to find the pestle she used for grinding crystal. She groaned again. Of course she'd thrown the one tool on her table that could break the panel. *Of course* she'd thrown it in exactly the wrong spot.

Celeste huffed and bent to pick the pestle up, and a piece of crystal tore through the sleeve of her suit like it was nothing, scratching her arm.

"Fuck!" She recoiled, staring at her torn sleeve. Her anger resurfaced as she stomped over to snatch her spare suit from its rack. She'd clean the shop later; she couldn't stand her empty house any longer.

The Undercity was abuzz with news of what Isalie had uncovered. The Olugar had made an announcement shortly after Lee and Jen left, and many of them had flocked to Nel's growing militia ranks. Celeste was glad to see Cortlen with them when she arrived; The older man had spent years training recruits, and seemed much more sensible than Nel ever would be. Hopefully Cortlen's steady presence would bring a perspective that they'd lacked so far.

She was personally eager to move the uprising Nel was planning along, so she could storm into the Inners herself and get Lee and Jen back. Nel spotted her and followed to Amal's house, where they gathered around the dining table.

"I can't sit around any longer," she told them.

"Celeste," Nel huffed, rubbing the bridge of their nose, "we can't force change in a matter of days. The people want to help, they're preparing as best they can, but we still don't have the numbers to storm the Inners. The Ambient aside, we're outmatched by the Guard, and we won't have a chance of winning a battle, let alone a siege, without more people fighting for us."

"There must be something I can do," Celeste insisted. "Give me Isalie's evidence and I'll go person-to-person topside to convince them. I'll tell them they might have families on the other side of the river, and your army will grow."

"What then?" Nel asked. "We'd have more angry people stuffed into the tunnels, demanding to know what we're doing to reunite them. Or worse, they try to storm the Inners and alert the Ambient to what we're doing! They would destroy us!"

She touched her arm, remembering how easily the sharpened crystal had cut through her thick leather. "Then get me more crystal, and I'll make spear tips, arrowheads, *something* to make fighting the beasts easier! I'll make more cloaks, and we can amass more of a force to storm the tunnel."

Nel sighed. "Cel..."

"I can't sit here and do nothing," she insisted.

"We're trying to change our entire city," Nel replied. "It's not just the Ambient, it's the Gloom, and the broken spirits of everyone who lives in it. It takes *time*."

"And what about Jen and Lee? They're supposed to just stay there, putting themselves at risk indefinitely?"

"If that's what it takes," Nel said, their lips in a thin line.

"If anything happens to them because we didn't act fast enough..." Cel shook her head.

"You aren't the only one with something to lose," Nel said quietly.

"No," Cel agreed, "we all have *everything* to lose. Get the rest of them to make something happen, Nel. Or we *will* lose everything."

Jentien's trainees sagged in the heat of the late afternoon as he led them through drills, sweat pouring down his neck and back. They would stop for water soon, but he couldn't let them quit yet. He had more than their training to drill into their thick skulls today.

"Block low," he called, and their training swords swung down to clack against one another. Almost in sync, Jentien noticed, giving a short nod of approval. "Block left." Another resounding clack. "Block right." One sharp sound this time. He let just a hint of a satisfied smile crack his stern countenance. "Block high."

He made them keep that block up for a full minute, watching their arms shake before he called for them to relax.

"Water," he barked, and they dragged themselves to the side of the training yard to fill wooden cups from the bucket. Jentien watched them drink, and then took a slow lap around the yard, checking every window, door, and arch for movement or listening ears. When he found none, he stepped to the middle of the training yard—as far from the possibility of being overheard as he could—and called them over.

They obeyed the order immediately, and Jentien swallowed another satisfied smile. After Cortlen's disappearance, there'd been a class of recruits with no one to train them. Increased patrols in the outer city meant Jentien was the only person who could take them on, and he'd put them through the same regimen that he'd instituted for the veterans he'd trained. He was proud of the progress they'd made, from an unruly mess to a cohesive unit

"Well done," he said, keeping his voice low to force them all closer to hear him. "You should all be proud of yourselves." He eyed his recruits, a mix of people from all over the continent. He could see the devotion in their eyes, even the fresh recruits added to Cortlen's last class. It was time to test the waters; if there were any guards that he could influence, it would be them.

"You're some of the best I've trained. You would have made excellent Sentinels outside." There were smiles all around, a glow of pride on their faces at the compliment. "I wish we could make such a difference here." He shut his mouth, turning away with a grimace as if he'd said something he shouldn't. He wasn't sure he could pull the ruse off, but he'd practiced it in the mirror over and over last night, hoping to make himself more comfortable with the act.

Confused frowns replaced their smiles. One of them asked, "What do you mean? I thought serving in the Ambient Guard *was* making a difference."

Jentien winced and gave a quick shake of his head. "Apologies, I shouldn't have said anything."

"Sir," a woman with cool black skin, standing a head taller than the rest said. Kiale had come from the Outers, and long scars ran down her left arm from the rainwater. "If you had your choice of assignments, where would it be?"

He gave her a long look, as if gauging her worth. "The Outers," he said, and several of their jaws dropped. "If I had a post there, I'd be able to help those poor souls. They live in the Gloom every day," he gave Kiale a long look, noticing the haunted look that crossed her face. "After devoting my life to keeping people away from the Gloom, it's hard to live so close and not be able to do anything."

"The Ambient keep them safe," said another. A broad, muscular man with deep brown skin and black hair tied behind the nape of his neck. Tsunal was one of the younger recruits, and he'd come straight to the Inners, avoiding the rain in his time here.

Jentien gave him a wan smile. "They do their best," he said. "I just wish their power could stop the rain, or make stronger cloaks, or food that the people could enjoy, rather than the gruel I've seen them eat. Sometimes it feels like they forget people are suffering when they are behind these walls, living in the sunshine."

He saw what he'd hoped to see in Kiale and a few other's eyes, that spark of anger that he could fan into a flame. The rest seemed confused, but he'd take that over a staunch defense of the Ambient. The more people that doubted the intentions of the Ambient, or even thought about the people in the Outers, the better.

It wasn't enough, but it was a start.

CHAPTER FIFTY-FOUR

It was as cold as the Outers down here, Isalie decided. The air was filled with the same smell of rain-soaked earth with a hint of something acrid that made her instinctively pull her tunic over her mouth and nose to protect them. Why would the Ambient have that smell in the depths of the spire?

She'd been walking for long enough that she knew she'd be missed above, but she hadn't found anything but a maze of stone halls with crystalline veins. She wouldn't leave until she had some idea of what this place was, whether Yesrien was here, or she was caught.

Spying a light ahead, she picked up the pace, her footsteps almost as loud as her unsteady breaths. This was the culmination of her nightmares, being stuck in the bowels of the earth as if she'd been swallowed by the beasts she'd imagined every tunnel to be. She couldn't contain the shudder that ran through her, and she let out a relieved sigh when she finally emerged into a large chamber full of light.

Isalie found an open space of bright crystal, with light from Ambient orbs refracting all around the room. A network of opalescent halls opened from this point, leading to Elders-knew-where. A glance over her shoulder to the dark maw she'd left behind convinced her to move forward across the open space to the opposite hall.

She didn't pass any doors, but every ten feet or so the crystal walls thinned enough to see through them like a window into smaller chambers made of the same crystal. They were barely tall enough for someone to stand upright, and not long enough to lie down. Each was empty save for crystal cylinders crisscrossed along the ceiling, and as she continued, she couldn't imagine what their use could be. When she'd passed about a dozen of them, she looked inside the next and stopped in her tracks.

It wasn't empty; inside was a pile of rags, and a smear of red brown on the floor. The cylinders were leaking, a steady drip of water that coated the floor in a puddle that trickled through a small drain in the far corner.

The rags shifted. Heat flooded her body and her limbs tensed, telling her to run even as her mind scrambled to figure out what she was looking at. A flash of pale white, and then a dull brown eye peered up at her from the floor beneath the rags.

"No," Isalie whispered, placing her hand on the crystal window. A voice that sounded like Celeste screamed at her from the back of her mind, telling her to obey the fear coursing through her body and run. But she stood rooted to the spot, staring at the red, blistered face that resolved beneath the disintegrating hood of the cloak, a single word forming on their lips.

"*Help.*"

Isalie ignored the voice in her head that screamed again and searched the wall for a door, a latch, something that would free the person inside. They tucked back inside the threadbare cloak, hiding from the droplets. Isalie slammed her hands against the wall, the window, and the floor.

There was nothing, not even a sign that a door had ever existed.

"Fuck!" she shouted, and then she moved, continuing down the hall the way she'd been headed. Her head swiveled left and right, up and down, searching for some mechanism that would open the non-existent doors.

She passed another window, where mist coated a poor soul inside with bloody tan skin. They didn't look up when she slammed against the window. She started jogging, past another and another of these rooms with people huddled away from the rain, hiding beneath broken-down protective equipment.

A sob tore from her throat when she passed an elderly woman standing in a foot of water, shaking as it ate through her patched boots. Isalie didn't look inside any more. She just ran, as fast as her legs could carry her.

The hall opened into another wide chamber, where a small table was stationed at each of the four branching hallways. She came to a halt, panting next to one of the tables where orbs the size of her palm showed her the people she'd passed in the hall as if she'd been standing in the room with them.

She didn't notice the echoing click of footsteps on the crystal floor until it was too late to hide, and she recognized the man that stepped into the chamber across from her. She'd seen Ambient Suerdis Kiyash in the spire, and knew that this diminutive member of the house was their resident healer. He was staring at a notebook in his hands so intently that he didn't notice her. She stood still, not daring to make a noise as he walked straight toward her, so engrossed in whatever he was reading that he didn't stop until Isalie was close enough to lunge at him.

Her arm wrapped around his neck to choke off shouts for help, and she looped her arm through his, wrenching them behind his back, letting her burning hatred guide her without stopping to think about what she was doing. The man was so stunned that he did nothing but let out a strangled squeak of protest when Isalie growled in his ear.

"How do you open the rooms?" He tried to shake his head, and she squeezed tighter. "Point with your chin, show me where the release is!"

He jutted his chin in the direction of the table, and she shoved him forward. He jerked his arm as if to reach out, and Isalie hissed in his ear. "If you do *anything* but let these people out, I will break your neck." It didn't matter that Isalie didn't have a clue how she would do it, or whether she had the strength. The man believed her and let out another strangled noise in the affirmative.

She released one of his arms, tightening her grip on his neck and the other arm, and let him lean forward enough for his hand to hover over the blank space between the orbs. It lit up, brighter than the room around it, and he pressed his palm flat onto the glowing space.

The ground rumbled, and a sound like stone scraping against stone echoed through the halls. Gasps and cries rang out, and Isalie dragged the man to the hall opening to watch the people stumble out and crumple to the cold floor.

"Are there more?" Isalie demanded, swinging him around to face the chamber and the other hallways. Her arms burned, and she knew that she wouldn't be able to hang on for long. The man gurgled a reply, nodding his head as far as he could. "Open them."

She marched him to the other three tables, the crystal sliding open to release more and more captives, and soon, Isalie stood in the middle of more than thirty bleeding, scarred people, holding this man so tightly that she could feel every wheezing breath.

And she had no idea how to get them all out of this maze.

CHAPTER FIFTY-FIVE

"Which way," Isalie growled, pulling harder on the arm in her grasp. A new, vicious part of her was gratified to feel an Ambient twitch in pain. He whimpered and gestured with his chin toward the tunnel opposite where she had come in, and Isalie looked at the people assembled around her. "Follow me," she said, trying to sound as gentle as she could through gritted teeth.

They moved slowly, as he struggled and stumbled and the mutilated people shuffled along behind. She had no idea how long it would take for someone to notice these people were missing, and she didn't dare allow the Ambient to take a deep breath and regain his faculties. It didn't matter that her muscles were screaming, ready to give out.

She marched past so many cells with the solid slab of crystal wall slid to the side, revealing the gore left behind and the gentle patter of rain falling within. Isalie kept to the center of the hall, as far from the splashing and runoff as possible.

One cell to her right was still closed, a plate on the wall like the one Suerdis had used to open the other cells, and Isalie started when she recognized Cuzao Rotre pacing inside. He had no visible wounds, but his normally immaculate clothing was rumpled and dirty, his long raven hair tangled into knots, and his eyes were wild when he noticed Isalie staring at him.

He slammed his hands against the solid crystal, his mouth contorted with rage when he shouted something she couldn't hear. Isalie smirked and turned her back on him.

Suerdis Kiyash whimpered and tilted his head to the left, toward an opening Isalie had assumed was another cell. She stopped and peered around his shoulder, finding a dark hall that sloped upward.

"Does this lead outside?" Isalie asked. He nodded, choking against her grip. "Do I need you to open it?" His bloodshot eyes widened, wet with tears, as his face drained of color. One slow nod, and Isalie swung him around and proceeded into the hall.

She ignored her old fear, overwhelmed by the fear of being found, the fear that these people would fall behind, or that her grip would loosen enough for this man to unleash the Ambience on them. Beneath all of that, waiting for a moment of respite to rear its ugly head, was the fear that she'd doomed Jentien to a fate like the one she was trying to save these people from.

The hall evened out, and still they continued, the tunnel growing colder, the walls exuding an earthy scent now that she recognized from the depths of the Undercity. Light flared behind them, and Isalie froze, watching it bob up and down as it moved toward them. She ushered the rest of the group ahead of her and then spurred her captive forward, hissing in his ear.

"Is it close?" A small nod. He gasped for air, and she loosened her grip enough for him to take a shallow breath before she clamped down again. "Move."

After a tense moment, Suerdis swung his head to the right and thrust his shoulder forward. Isalie let go of the arm to let him slap his palm against a spot on the rough wall that looked like a carved handprint, visible now as the light grew behind them. The stone slid to the side; a perfect, rectangular doorway opened onto a rough stone tunnel lit with Ambient orbs.

The prisoners noticed the light and gave it a nervous glance. Isalie urged them to go into the tunnel and called out to the last before she disappeared. Her large eyes were wide and dark, with lank hair pasted to her raw face. Isalie leaned close to whisper in the woman's ear.

"I don't know where you'll come out, but get to the Undercity, and tell them Isalie Wylshard sent you. Find Celeste, and Amalricus." The woman's eyes widened even further, and then she was gone.

"Close it," Isalie growled, and slammed Suerdis against the wall next to the plate. The wall slid closed and she whirled around, hands cramping, to face the light that resolved into multiple Ambient orbs floating above the heads of the Ambient rushing toward them.

At the head of the group was Mistress Kiyash, her beautiful face contorted with rage, her arm outstretched. Isalie held her head high, a single obstacle between the group fleeing behind the wall and the tempest of Ambient power descending upon her.

⁓⇌◊⇋⁓

Where is she? Jentien wondered in his room. Iz should have been back already, and he had a nagging feeling that something wasn't right. *I went too far*, he thought. *If I put Iz in danger, if something happened to her because I was reckless...*

A knock on the door interrupted his thoughts, but it didn't ease his concern. Iz wouldn't knock.

He opened the door, surprised to find Kiale and a handful of his recruits in the hall.

"Sir," Kiale said.

"Yes?"

Kiale looked at the rest, who shrugged or nodded, and then back at Jentien. "Sir, we were hoping we could talk to you about some concerns we have." Jentien raised an eyebrow in question, waiting for her to elaborate. She swallowed hard, glanced around to ensure no one was watching, and leaned forward to whisper, "About the Ambient."

Jentien waved them inside and shut the door before anyone could overhear them. "What about them?" he asked carefully.

"We've been hearing things," Kiale said. "My friends in the tunnel guards have heard rumors about the Ambient intentionally separating newcomers from their families, about cloaks made to fail." She glanced around the room. "Please, tell us what's happening."

"What I say doesn't leave this room," Jentien warned them. He sat on the edge of his bed. "If it does, we'll all be at the Ambients' mercy."

Tsunal spoke up. "Agreed, sir."

Jentien began to explain what he'd seen in the Outers, and his suspicion that the rumors were true, though he didn't cite his reasons for fear that he would put Iz in more danger. When he finished, he stared at the door, willing Iz to come home while the guards talked.

Tsunal furrowed his brow as he took in the tense set of Jentien's shoulders and his preoccupied stare. "Everything all right, sir? You've been staring at the door."

"My—" he stopped, unsure of what to call her. "My partner hasn't come home."

"Should we look for her?" Kiale asked.

Jentien considered the offer. It would be a relief to have help, but knowing what they were here for, and what Isalie had already done to subvert the Ambient's hold on Olunei, he didn't want to implicate them, too.

"No," he said, trying to shrug off his worry and put a smile on his face. "I'm sure she's held up; she's a servant in the Kiyash spire."

They exchanged concerned looks. "After all we've said, you aren't worried about her?" Kiale arched a dark brow.

"I don't want any of you involved," Jentien replied with the same hard edge to his voice that he used during training. Most of them nodded, conditioned to follow his orders, but Kiale held his gaze.

"We're already involved. Just by talking to you, with all that I suspect you're doing, we're involved. So, let us help."

Jentien shook his head, picturing them running amok in the Kiyash spire, rousing suspicion. "None of you would have access, so asking questions would be too conspicuous. But if you're looking for a way to help, I have a few ideas."

It felt like hours before the Ambient closed with her, and Isalie hoped it was at least enough time to make a difference. She spared a nervous thought to the fact that she had no idea where they might end up, but kept her eyes on the imposing figure of Mistress Kiyash.

"Well, this is an interesting development," she said. Though her voice was soft, there was no mistaking the menace dripping from every syllable. "Drop him."

"No," Isalie said, surprised by the lack of quaver in her own words.

"I wasn't aware you had this much of a spine," the Mistress sneered. "I'm impressed."

Confused, Isalie replied, "You know who I am?"

Her hand dropped to her side, and a small, mocking smile lifted the corners of her blood-red lips. "My daughter took an interest when you seemed to steal the heart of one of our rising stars."

Isalie's stomach dropped.

Mistress Kiyash continued. "Guard Themori had such a promising future, but now..." She trailed off, the smile disappearing behind that deadly stare. "Perhaps he can still serve a purpose; we seem to have lost a great deal of test subjects. Though perhaps I will still allow Tulia to take him as her plaything."

Isalie tensed, and Suerdis choked. "Don't *touch him*," she spat, rage sweeping her fear aside like wildfire tearing through her soul.

"You aren't in a position to make demands." Mistress Kiyash transferred her disdainful gaze to Suerdis. "And you, why have you allowed this woman to capture you? You are a Tether, are you not? Release yourself."

He sagged in Isalie's grip but couldn't respond. She rolled her eyes and exhaled a long, exasperated breath.

"Why we put such weak Ambient in charge of anything, I'll never know. Well," she glanced at the man, and his neck whipped to the side. The resounding crack of his spine severing reverberated through Isalie's body. His body went limp and slid out of Isalie'sgrasp. "Dump him in the river. But this one," her eyes locked onto Isalie's, and sharp pain shot through her head, like a knife being inserted behind her eyes. "This one we keep."

Isalie gritted her teeth against the pain, clutching the sides of her head as if she could force it out if she just pushed hard enough. Mistress Kiyash's triumphant smile flashed through her head, and Isalie screamed, shaking her head violently to wrest the woman from her mind. The pain remained, and when Isalie opened her eyes, the Mistress was frowning down at her. Isalie didn't know when she'd fallen to the ground.

Mistress Kiyash narrowed her eyes and waved a hand toward Isalie. Several Ambient surged forward to lift Isalie from the cold ground. As they carried her in the direction of the cells, she heard the Mistress mutter one word through the splitting agony.

"Interesting."

The crystal preferred being made into weapons, Celeste decided. Cel had accompanied Nel and their mining group into the tunnels to extract as much as they could before they attracted any beasts with the noise, then spent the afternoon and night carving the slabs into useable chunks.

The spear tip and arrowheads assembled on her workbench had been so simple to construct, and the scraps she could use in her sachets. She only had a few of each, but hopefully it would be enough to fend off the Gloom beasts near the crystal deposits.

If they could assemble enough weapons, Celeste would be able to outfit a fighting force to break through the tunnel's defenses, to secure the Outers and hopefully move more people to the Inners.

Arru approached her, peering at the scraps and the mortar and pestle Celeste had set aside to produce more granules for her sachets.

"Would you like help?" Arru asked.

"Sure," Celeste said absently while she sharpened the edge of an arrowhead. It sparked against the whetstone when the tiny particles came free. "Just be careful not to make it too fine or it'll combust."

"Such an interesting substance," Arru mused. "It repels the effects of the Gloom, but seems to have its own latent Ambience. Perhaps if it's fine enough, we could manufacture other catalysts for that explosive force."

"You're right," Celeste mused, staring at the glittering dust on her table. "It's so difficult to work with, but maybe that's something we can use against the Ambient."

They worked to skirt the line between the healing benefits of the ground crystal and the destructive capability that lay within. All of Celeste's experimentation made quick work of it, and by morning, she and Arru were confident that they could destroy the gates to the Inners. With a bit more time, maybe she could find a way through without bringing the tunnel down around them.

Arru helped her make as many arrowheads as they could from the crystal before taking her leave. Celeste wrapped the crystal in thick linen and stashed it in the bag slung over her shoulder, beneath her cloak. With her mask over her head and her cloak secured, she headed into the street, toward the heart of the Outers.

A roar of voices caught her ear over the sound of rain pattering on the street, and she whipped her head in the direction of the tunnel. Their distress propelled her faster, the rain splashing around her feet until she rounded the corner, and the tunnel came into view.

A horde of people rushed out of the tunnel past stunned guards. Celeste wove between people in ragged clothes, their skin raw and bleeding, and grabbed a guard's shoulder.

"What's happening?" she demanded. Beyond the guard, she saw more ragged people, some supporting others too weak to run, rushing from an opening in the solid wall. The last one came through, and the wall slid closed, leaving no trace of the doorway that had been there moments before.

Celeste pulled the guard around, finding Pelom staring at her beneath his hood. "We don't know where they came from," he said.

The other guards were starting to move, to reach for the slowest of the group as if to detain them, while another reached for the lever to drop the portcullis.

"We have to get those people out!" Celeste told Pelom.

Pelom rushed into the tunnel, taking advantage of the chaos to slam the guard away from the portcullis lever. Celeste pushed between the guards and their quarry.

"What's happening?" she shrieked, clutching their uniform to give the wounded group time to escape.

"Out of the way!" the guard ordered.

She shoved Celeste backward, out of the tunnel. Metal creaked, and the portcullis slammed down in front of Celeste, locking the rest of the guards inside and the ragged people out. Pelom cast Celeste a significant look before she turned away.

Two people were moving slowly, a tall woman supporting a man as he limped, and Celeste draped the man's other arm over her shoulder. The woman craned her neck to glance at Celeste, her eyes fierce despite the bloody tracks left by rivulets of water. Celeste staggered, recognizing her large gray-green eyes and sharp cheekbones, and collected herself enough to lean forward to be heard over the commotion.

"Yesrien! We need to get these people inside. *Now.*"

Yesrien blinked. "Celeste??"

She nodded. "They're going to get that portcullis open. We need to get these people to safety, and your mother needs to know you're alive. *Move!*"

CHAPTER FIFTY-SIX

Jentien clenched his fists and his jaw, glaring at his commander. The man was infuriatingly calm; his face hadn't changed from a neutral expression, and his hands were still clasped together atop his desk, even after the accusations Jentien had thrown his way. When he spoke, his tone was neutral, calming.

There wasn't anything the man could do to calm Jentien. Isalie hadn't come home the night before, and he'd found no sign of her in the servant's halls.

"Think about what you're saying," he told Jentien. "Stills have been imprisoned for much less."

"My partner is *missing!*" he bellowed, slamming his hands onto the desk. "I've searched the spire, the servant's halls, and I've questioned everyone. Something happened to her, and the Ambient," he gestured toward the spire beyond the barracks, "know everything that happens inside these walls. If you won't get me an audience with Mistress Kiyash, I'll find her myself!"

He shoved away from the desk and whirled around to stride out of the room. The chair screeched behind him, and the commander's hand wrapped around Jentien's upper arm, pulling him to a halt.

"I'm giving you one last chance to stand down, otherwise I will throw you in a cell myself."

"Maybe I'll find her in the prison, then," Jentien growled, and shrugged the commander's hand off his arm. He threw the door wide, startling the other guards when it slammed against the wall. Seeing all their eyes on him, he said, "The Ambient are experimenting on Stills, separating us from our families, and knowingly giving cloaks and masks designed to fail to the outer city."

He heard the impact before he felt it, and then he was lying on the floor, staring up at his commander's blood-smeared pommel.

"Jentien Themori is hereby charged with sedition, and if any of you want to avoid his fate, you will disregard what you just heard." He looked down at Jentien and heaved a heavy sigh, his face warring between guilt and disappointment. "You should have left it alone."

A soft voice broke through the unending agony. "Why don't you just tell me what we need to know so this can stop?"

Isalie clutched her head when pain tore through her like lightning—a familiar kick to the chest, an unending roaring in her ears—ignoring the words. She'd heard them already.

"Tell us what the Stills are planning, and this will stop. Tell us who your contacts are, and you'll be free of me. They must have *some* organization in place, if they're tracking their people."

Isalie shook her head and screeched when the pain intensified. Her tears were long spent, and her throat was raw from screaming. She couldn't give them anything. She *wouldn't*.

"You confound me," Mistress Kiyash sighed, and the pain subsided. Isalie gasped and went limp. She'd been wrong; now that the pain was gone, she found she still had tears of relief to shed. "Most break long before now, but for some reason, you resist my control of your mind. Not resistant to my power, not powerful yourself, but your resolve is well beyond any I've encountered before." She sighed. "Interesting as you are, even *I* am growing tired of this."

So was Isalie, but she glared as she opened her eyes, knowing there was nothing she could say to save herself. She didn't want to give this awful woman any more satisfaction in seeing her try. Mistress Kiyash threw her long hair over her shoulder and leaned forward to gaze down at Isalie.

"Three days, and you've given us nothing. When I say that I'm growing tired of interrogating you, you should know that when I decide I'm done with you, your life will become so much worse. But," she sat up, stretching her back and rolling her shoulders, "if you cooperate, I can ensure that your time here is brief. You will not be subjected to the same experiments as the others."

"You *are* experimenting on people," Isalie croaked. "What could you possibly learn from watching people suffer like this?"

The Mistress crossed her arms over her chest. "How else will we understand what will happen to you Stills when the Gloom finally overtakes us? Everyone in this prison is providing us—and future generations of Stills—with valuable data. We *must* prepare for the inevitable."

"So, you let them suffer until they die? Just to find out what will happen?" Isalie rolled onto her side, every movement an extreme effort. *Keep her talking,* she thought. *Keep her distracted, so she doesn't give the pain back. Get information the Olugar can use.*

"Oh, no, my dear. What a waste that would be!" She shook her head with a small smile. "Our subjects are monitored closely by Ambient who have an affinity for healing. When our subjects' bodies fail, we bring them back to health so that they can serve their fellow Stills."

She leaned forward, her voice dropping to a conspiratorial whisper. "I'm quite proud of the work we're doing here. And the towers have allowed us to control the strength of the rain, so that we can test Kova's inventions and entertain variables in the strength of the Gloom. We haven't let the full brunt of the Gloom hit the outer city, but soon, we will see the full effects. I've been quite delighted by the inventiveness of one of the Stills, and I do hope that her cloaks hold up; she's been the greatest success from this endeavor."

Disgust turned Isalie's stomach. If she'd had anything to eat recently—how long had she been here?—it would've come back out. She hoped it masked the fear that coursed through her at the reference to Celeste.

"You're controlling the storm?" Isalie asked, planting her hands on the ground to raise herself to a sitting position on shaking arms.

The Mistress laughed. "If you've told me nothing else, at least I've learned that you don't know much. No, we don't *control* the Gloom or its storm, we manipulate it."

"Why don't you stop it?"

Mistress Kiyash smiled, but this one was predatory, a showing of teeth. "I adore your tenacity. It won't do you any good in the end, but I'll humor you. The towers bring us the power we need, and I don't have permission to draw enough to stop it, *if* it could be done at all."

She rose to her feet and strode to the doorway, but paused before she passed over the threshold. "I really do admire your courage and fortitude. I anticipate many fruitful years of your service to our operation." She glanced over her shoulder with a wicked smile. "Perhaps Guard Themori will be more forthcoming."

Terror gripped Isalie harder than the pain. She crawled toward the opening, dragging her body along behind her since her legs were too weak to do anything but scrabble at the slick crystal floor. Her hand crossed the threshold just as the crystal slab started to slide, and she was forced to pull her hand back before it was crushed.

She put her head down on the cold floor. And when the rain began to pour out of the tubes in the ceiling, she screamed.

Jentien's scream echoed through the tall chamber, his fists bloody from pounding on the crystal walls. He had no way to accurately track the passage of time apart from the three meals they'd served him, and he'd spent every waking moment pounding against the walls, the floor, and the place the door had been, looking for weaknesses.

There were none.

He slid down the wall, exhausted and defeated, his fists leaving bloody trails behind. "Iz," he whispered, tucking his legs against his chest, "I'm sorry."

CHAPTER FIFTY-SEVEN

Isalie had been captured.

Celeste knew it; she'd felt dread sitting in the pit of her stomach for days now. It stayed with her no matter how she tried to ignore it, even as she wound through the makeshift hospital they'd set up to help the people Isalie had freed. They hadn't seen what became of her, but she'd put herself between the Ambient and them, and Celeste knew she hadn't gotten out.

It'd been too long since she'd heard from Jentien, too. She hadn't slept in days, and since the miners had been hard at work, she'd put her extra time and the slabs of crystal to good use. The injuries the captives had sustained were horrific, and too extensive for her normal methods of treatment. Ambient Kova's schematics were invaluable, a way to pull the corrosive moisture from them on a larger scale, which she hadn't expected to see from the Ambient.

Her dread was so overwhelming that she didn't feel any satisfaction in unveiling and utilizing the chamber. Panels of crystal were assembled in a rectangle long enough for an adult to lie down, then fungus resin mixed with oil rendered from Gloom beast fat sealed it shut. Prism was the crucial part, though. Burning the fine crystal granules made a smoke that dehydrated anyone inside, and as long as they weren't inside for too long, the deadly side effects couldn't manifest.

She looked down through the crystal exterior at Yesrien's sleeping face, taking note of the healing wounds turning to scars before her eyes and the way her breathing had settled over the last few hours.

Arru settled beside her, her golden hair pulled into a tight bun at the crown of her head, though many strands had fallen loose. Her pale skin was drawn tight by the intense frown on her face as she gazed down at her daughter, tears swimming in her large eyes.

"I thought she'd gone to the Elders," she whispered, more to herself than to Celeste. "And now she's here. I can't fathom what she's been through all these months." She looked up at Celeste, and her face crumpled. "I am so sorry that Isalie didn't make it out. If there's anything I can do..."

Celeste gave her a tight smile and shook her head. She didn't trust herself to speak through the grief that choked her. After a time, Arru moved away, wiping her eyes as she straightened and moved to the bedside of another escapee to offer aid.

As Celeste watched her go, she caught a bit of movement from the corner of her eye and turned to find Cortlen winding toward her between the cots. Maretha trailed behind him, as well as a tall woman with cool black skin, a head taller than either of them. When Maretha spotted Celeste, she directed the two toward her.

"Celeste," Maretha said as the man held his hand out in greeting. Celeste took it, feeling the calluses on his firm grip. "This is Kiale," she said, gesturing to the tall woman behind them. "She has news about Jentien."

Celeste went still. Kiale cleared her throat.

"I'm part of his squad, and he told us what the Ambient have been doing the same day his partner went missing." Celeste kept her face still, but her breath caught in her chest. "He asked us to pick up where he left off, talking to anyone we thought might be sympathetic to what's happening while he went to look for Isalie."

"What happened to him?" Celeste breathed. Maretha stepped forward and placed a hand on Cel's shoulder.

"He stormed into the commander's office the next morning, and stormed back out, shouting about everything he told us. The commander knocked him out, and he was hauled away. No one has seen him since."

They'd both been taken. Celeste took a breath in and let it out slowly, trying to keep her panic at bay.

"I'm going to get him back," Cortlen announced. Maretha's hand tensed on Cel's shoulder. "I'll get another uniform and look around. I'll find him."

"I can get you some help," Kiale added. "After what happened to him, there are a *lot* of Stills in the Inners that are starting to realize things are not as simple as the Ambient have made it seem."

"And then what?" Maretha asked. "Say you do find him, how will you get him out? How will you escape the Ambient?"

"I served them for years, I know my way around," Cortlen told her.

Maretha shook her head. "We just got you back; please don't do this."

He held a hand out to her, and she stepped into his embrace. Cel's heart twisted, thinking about Jentien and Isalie in the Ambient's prison, where she'd never feel their embrace again.

"It was Jentien who brought us back together, Mare." He kissed her brow, his eyes closed tight. When he opened them again and gazed down at her, he gave her a gentle smile. "I can't let him rot if I can help it."

"Please, don't risk yourself. I couldn't bear it if I lost you again. The kids–"

He shook his head. "They won't lose me again." He shot a regretful look Celeste's way, and then smiled back down at his wife. "If I can't get to him, I'll come back, and we'll find another way."

Kiale stepped around them. "I'm going to search until I find him, and there are a few others who are willing to risk themselves for Jentien."

"You don't know where he's being held?" Celeste asked.

"Not *yet*," Kiale replied, "but no one saw him leave the spire. He must be there somewhere. We haven't been able to get to the prison, but my friends are looking everywhere else. If they don't figure it out by the time we get back, I'll search the entire spire myself."

Celeste nodded, and held up a finger to bid Kiale to wait so that she could rummage in one of the bags she'd brought from her shop. She gathered the leather bag containing glass vials of ground crystal and held the flap open. Kiale peered inside, and then cast a quizzical look at Celeste.

"Try not to jostle them; they're combustible. If you get into trouble, one of them will create a small explosion. If you run into an Ambient, throw them all."

CHAPTER FIFTY-EIGHT

Isalie didn't know which was worse: the rain carving through her skin, the burning wheeze of her breath, or the gnawing hunger eating her from the inside out.

She had no idea how long she'd been locked in this dark cell with water dripping down. She huddled in the corner, where she could at least tuck her head between her arms, but the water still trickled down the right side of her head and face. She flitted in an out of consciousness; there wasn't much else to do.

Her eyes rolled to the side, drifting over polished wooden tables and the crystal cylinder. She'd been here before. They would put her inside of it, heal her—a brief respite from the pain—before returning her to the ceaseless caustic dripping. She didn't know how long she'd been down here, or how many times it had happened, but she'd been through this cycle before.

Someone was inside, and the person in the suit walked into her field of vision to pull open a hatch she hadn't seen in the smooth surface of the cylinder.

They waved a hand toward the person lying still, then at the floor. The body flopped in the air so that the head lolled toward Isalie. Their eyes were fixed and staring past her, and they rotated upright like a macabre puppet.

Isalie groaned, the sound painfully vibrating through her chest and throat, before the body dropped suddenly through the hole that had been covered moments before. The square piece of crystal that she realized was a door covering a hatch floated down, becoming flush with the floor again.

Something cold touched her raw skin, and she jolted awake, not realizing she'd fallen unconscious. The crystal cylinder was much closer now, and she realized that she must be inside. She turned her head to the side, gritting her teeth against the pain of her skin tearing again, and watched the leather-clad figure on the far side of the room, holding a clear container of shimmering dust. They opened it, and with as much care as Cel used when measuring out her ground crystal, took a scoop and placed it in a large sachet on the table. Isalie looked at the floor, and then back to the figure.

Her mind cleared as she realized the pain would go away soon. The cylinder would pull the rain out of her skin and lungs, and the healer would bring her back from the brink of death.

But it wouldn't last. Soon, she'd be back in the room, and it would start again. In that moment, she decided that she couldn't stand the thought of the endless suffering Mistress Kiyash had promised. Spurred on by that determination, she looked at the hatch again, wondering what was on the other side. It probably wasn't good, but, even if she didn't survive, at least she wouldn't go through this again. At least she'd deprive Mistress Kiyash of her twisted triumph.

Isalie's fingers fumbled along the invisible seam of the cylinder, thinking back to the crumpled design she'd seen, thankful that she'd taken the moment to steal Ambient Kova's trash. The latch had been replaced by a button carved into the crystal, and she pressed it down, her hand trembling, and watched the lid swing silently up. She heaved herself toward the edge of the cylinder. One arm flopped over the side, braced on the outside to pull the rest of her torso over the edge. It gave out and she slammed onto the cold floor.

The figure at the table stopped, and turned so slowly it would have been comical if not for the fact that Isalie was inching toward the covered hole, determined to make it there before they could stop her. Their head turned in the opposite direction, buying her precious seconds to drag herself forward.

This close, she could see the faint outline of the cover, and shoved her fingers into it. Her nails were the only thing that could find purchase; they tore, but the crystal moved just enough for her to shove her fingertip further in and grasp the edge. Her arms screamed in protest and shook so hard that she wouldn't have been surprised if they fell apart from the strain of hauling herself toward the edge.

"No!" a muffled voice shouted behind her.

She hurled herself over the lip of the hole and fell.

⁓⧫⁓

Jentien's fist sank into the guard's midsection, followed by an uppercut to the man's descending chin when he curled into a ball. He fell to the floor in a sprawling heap, and three more pairs of arms wrapped around Jentien's torso before he could launch at another. He bucked in their arms, making them work to restrain him, hoping that they might show even the slightest sign of hesitation in their task since he had served with all of them.

"Why are you still working with them?" he grunted. "You *know* what they've done." He stared at the brawny woman holding his left arm. "Ywain, you lost your family in the Gloom. What if they're in the Outers?" She blinked, and if Jentien hadn't been so desperate, he would've felt a stab of guilt at giving her hope that might prove false.

He didn't get the chance to say more. His mouth clamped shut, and his arms and legs slammed tight against his sides, leaving him floating in the air. Jentien couldn't move, couldn't speak, could only watch as Mistress Kiyash strode into the room in a flurry of golden skirts. Her green eyes blazed with fury when she came to a stop before him.

"You *Stills* are proving more trouble than you're worth." She shot the guards a scathing look that sent them scurrying from the cell and waved a hand to send the crystal door slamming into place. They were alone, and she turned a feral smile his way. "I plan to give you to my daughter, so that she might produce a direct heir to carry on the Kiyash name. You have enough of a spark to produce strong Ambient offspring." She appraised him with a prismatic flare of light in her pupils. "It's a shame that you spent so long with my current heir. I'll have to ensure that your *idealism* has not tainted my line. After the dissent that you've managed to spread, we must make an example of you."

Jentien strained against the invisible hold she had on him, and she smirked. The gag dropped, and he growled, "*Where is Isalie?*"

"Is that what we're calling her now?" Her smirk spread into a malicious grin. "You'll spend the rest of your life wondering. I will ensure you live a long life, Jentien Themori."

⁓⤳⟡⟵⤶

Celeste paced the dark room, the distant echo of voices in the cavern outside Amal's house like the thoughts chasing each other through her mind.

Where is Isalie? Will they find Jentien? Is he alive? I should be out there with them. Where is Isalie?

It'd been a week since Isalie had gone missing, and most of the survivors had made a full recovery. Several were still undergoing treatment, and Celeste was starting to doubt that they'd be able to leave the makeshift tent. There was nothing more for her to do but wait.

She *hated* waiting.

Amal shuffled into the room with Nel on his heels. Celeste rolled her eyes and turned away to continue her pacing. She didn't have the patience to deal with Nel right now.

"Any news?" she asked the room.

"None," Nel replied.

She pivoted on her heel and strode their way again, letting her gaze linger on their face. There was nothing smug or condescending in their expression, only sympathy.

"Perhaps you should go home," Amal suggested. Celeste turned, prepared to protest, but Amal didn't let her. "You've done everything you can here, and you haven't rested in days. Go sleep in your own bed, and then come back if you need to." Her stomach dropped, picturing her empty house. Amal noticed, and in a gentler tone, said, "It would be the first place Jentien would look for you."

She turned away to hide her sob, holding her hand to her mouth to keep the sound from escaping. Without turning again, she nodded and stormed out of the house.

The sun was high when Jentien was dragged into the courtyard at the base of the Kiyash spire by an invisible tether. Today, a plinth had been erected in the massive open space at the foot of the spire with a post in the center, looming ominously over the crowd.

The buzz of voices cut off as Mistress Kiyash ascended the steps, the sunlight glinting off her flowing opalescent gown with long, belled sleeves and high neck that gave her an imperious air. The prismatic glow of the crystalline spire behind her lent her its light, arranged to present the picture of Ambient power and dominion over the Stills before her. Jentien spotted a few Ambient in the crowd as well, including the furious countenance of the Mistress's daughter.

Jentien also caught the angry and confused faces of more than a few Stills, watching as he floated up in the Mistress's wake. Bound and gagged, he was a battered prisoner on exhibition for all to see.

"Friends," Mistress Kiyash began, her low voice carrying across the open space, "I gathered you all to address the rumors that have been spreading. I'm here to reassure you that these rumors are false, spread by a troubled, angry mind."

Jentien floated forward until he was directly behind her. "This man has poisoned your ears with lies meant to undermine the order that we strive to maintain in this most difficult of situations. Cut off from the rest of Vortheim, with no chance for aid, we must all pull together to ensure that we survive the deadly Gloom surrounding us.

"We Ambient strive to provide what aid we can to the people forced to live in the outer city. We've seen many of those displaced by the storm lose their minds to grief, to the wild Ambience of the storm, or the pain of their ordeals.

But this man," she leveled a disgusted gaze at Jentien, and he scowled in return, "who has infiltrated the highest ranks of our Ambient Guard, has shown that his only purpose is to sow discord in the society that we have made. He has driven a wedge between Ambient and Still, to turn us against each other, so that he and his malcontents might take what we have. He would drive us into the outer city with those not fortunate enough to count themselves among his small number."

The crowd began to grumble, murmuring their disdain and incredulity, eyes fixed on Jentien. He gazed at the crowd, his heart sinking more for every frown, scowl, or shock on the faces he knew. He spotted Kiale in the crowd, and her face was solemn. Ionna snarled in bitter triumph, and Wist stood close by, glancing between the redhead at his side, Mistress Kiyash, and Jentien, before looking away. For a moment he could have sworn he saw a familiar dark head of hair and bright blue eyes, and then the crowd shifted, and Jentien realized that he'd missed the words spoken next, riling the gathering into a frenzy.

"...our duty to protect against his rancorous lies, to make an example of people like this, whose attacks on our city's balance has the potential to throw us all to the storm!" Mistress Kiyash arranged her face into a firm, if remorseful, expression.

When she turned to face Jentien, he caught the flash of satisfaction that contradicted her words before she hid it again. She strode to the other side of the post, dragging Jentien with her, and gestured to the back of the plinth where Commander Rallac appeared.

Jentien twirled in the air to face the post with his arms above his head against the top. The hold on the rest of his body disappeared, but his hands wouldn't budge. Rallac wouldn't meet his eye as he walked forward with a whip of knotted rope in his hand.

"Sir," Jentien whispered, "don't do this." The man's face was a blank mask. Jentien would gain no ground there, so he raised his voice, trying his best to pivot toward the crowd. "Your families are suffering–"

His shout was cut off by an invisible gag wrapped around his head again, tight enough to choke him.

"No more lies," Mistress Kiyash announced, loud enough for the crowd to hear. "Any suffering has been caused by your deceit! Proceed."

The whip cracked, and Jentien snapped forward from the impact of the tip against his back. It took him a heartbeat to feel anything, then pain roared through him. Another crack sounded, and he gritted his teeth when the whip cut through his ragged shirt, the chill of the morning hitting his exposed flesh. Another crack, and another, all in the same place, and Jentien gritted his teeth behind the gag to keep his agonized scream inside.

He was grateful for the gag, for being incapable of more than grunts and groans and muffled cries. He lost count of the whip cracks as he leaned against the post. Blood ran down his back, soaking the remnants of his shirt so that it stuck to his skin around the whip marks, and the gag fell away.

The next strike hit in the center of his back where the pain was worst, and his scream echoed off the walls surrounding the courtyard. He sagged against the post, barely keeping his feet beneath him, and screamed again.

He waited for the next crack, but it didn't come. Mistress Kiyash appeared before him, once again the remorseful, stoic leader of Olunei, with no trace of the malevolent delight she'd shown only to him.

"Let that be a lesson to anyone who seeks to destroy what we have built. We are united in common purpose, and we will not allow anyone to tear us apart."

The binding holding him to the post disappeared, and Jentien fell in a heap to the plinth until he was lifted by two sets of arms and dragged toward the spire. The crowd's angry murmurs were muffled by cool crystalline doors that closed behind them.

He shifted his head and looked up into bright blue eyes filled with fury and sorrow. Shock dulled the roar of his pain when he recognized who they belonged to.

"How?" Jentien grunted when he shifted and pulled the torn muscles of his back.

"I owe you, golden child. Now let's get you out of here."

CHAPTER FIFTY-NINE

"Keep quiet," Cortlen hissed.

Jentien couldn't help the whimper that escaped him when Cort and Kiale set him against a wall near the servant's hall. Kiale looked behind them, and Cortlen prowled around the corner ahead.

"You shouldn't be here," Jentien groaned. He kept still, afraid to make the throbbing any worse.

Kiale frowned at him. "It was the best opportunity we've had, sir," she replied. Cortlen appeared again, nodding to Kiale before they hauled Jentien up. He clamped his mouth shut, but the pain escaped in a loud groan.

"We don't have long before everyone files back in," Cortlen whispered. "We need to get him out of the district before they're back at their posts, and then we can smuggle him out."

"Your family, Cortlen. Go back to them." Jentien tried to help, to get his feet under him, but the movement sent a fresh jolt of agony through his back, and he sagged again.

"Not yet. I made a promise to get you out."

Jentien's breath caught in his throat, his mind immediately picturing Isalie tear-streaked and terrified with worry. He pictured their tearful reunion, gathering her in his arms despite the pain. He cast a hopeful look at Cortlen and read the remorse there. His hope flared out as quickly as it had appeared.

"Celeste is worried about you," Cortlen told him, his voice soft. "Now stop talking."

Jentien didn't see the route they took, nor did he understand Cortlen and Kiale's muttering when he lost himself to the pain in his back and the greater pain of his loss. Iz was still missing.

They emerged from the spire into the sunlight. Cortlen directed them through the streets of the Ambient District while Jentien lulled between them, groaning every time they had to adjust his weight between them. He let himself drift into unconsciousness to escape the aching hole in his heart.

When Jentien opened his eyes again, he was lying on his side in the dim light of a warehouse in the Inner City, staring at a wall of crates and three pairs of legs in guard uniform. He started, remembering where he was and the danger they were in, and then the doors across the room opened.

"What are you doing here?" someone called as the door swung shut behind her.

Jentien's blood ran cold. Tulia Kiyash strode forward, the heels of her boots clicking on the stone floor. Jentien caught sight of a pale blue gown coming to a halt before the others. "My, my, what do we have here? Where *exactly* do you think you're taking my new toy?"

Revulsion twisted Jentien's stomach, and he tried to sit up. The pain in his back was too much, making him flop onto the ground, eliciting a low chuckle from the Ambient woman.

"Leave now, before we're forced to hurt you," Cortlen said.

She chuckled again. "I find it sad that you think you *could.*"

Jentien forced himself to scoot against the crate he was next to, ignoring the fire in his abused back. Her vibrant green eyes locked onto his, full of hunger. Cortlen reached for his belt to draw his sword, but the leather crumbled and the blade clattered to the ground. Kiale and Tsunal found their belts removed as well, as if an invisible blade had cut through the thick leather. A large pouch clattered a short distance from Jentien, and two vials rolled out, the shimmering dust within illuminating.

Tulia laughed, watching Cortlen and Tsunal scramble for their weapons until she flicked a hand to the side and sent them flying across the room. Jentien watched the contents of the vials glow brighter, and remembered Celeste's trouble with the volatile ground crystal.

Cortlen didn't hesitate; he threw himself at Tulia, who flicked her wrist upward, tossing him over her head to crash into the opposite wall. Kiale sprinted across the room toward her belt, and Tsunal stood frozen, watching as this Ambient threw her head back and laughed.

Jentien leaned forward to grasp a vial, and his agonized growl drew Tulia's gaze. Jentien threw the vial, screaming when his flesh tore again. The vial crashed into her, and the dust within flashed as bright as the sun. Glass shattered and flew outward, propelled by a blast that blew Jentien's hair back.

If he hadn't been braced against the crate, he would have been thrown through the air like the others. Instead, he watched, horrified, when Kiale and Tsunal slammed against crates and stone walls.

The light winked out, and Tulia was a burnt heap on the floor. Jentien's stomach churned again, the scent of cooking meat filling the small space.

Tsunal regained his feet first and limped to Jentien's side. He collapsed next to Jentien, and a worried frown furrowed his young brow.

"Sir, are you all right? You just made an Ambient explode!"

Jentien just grimaced as he tried to sit upright and failed.

"We're going to get you out of here," Tsunal assured him. "I made sure we're on Outers rotation," he said. "All we have to do is walk him through, and then we can get him to your people."

"Let's get him in the crate," Cortlen grunted. He knelt in Jentien's eyeline with blood streaking down his face from a myriad of tiny cuts. "It'll be a smooth ride, if you can keep quiet. I'll get you home."

Getting into the crate was pure agony, and Jentien welcomed the darkness that embraced him. He was jolted awake again to find himself surrounded by canvas cloaks in a small, dark space.

"We're coming to the tunnel, sir," Kiale's voice whispered from somewhere beyond the crate wall. "Don't move."

Tsunal greeted the gate guards, who gave a terse order to show their passes. A familiar voice called out from the other side of the tunnel entrance.

"Is it true Themori was trying to start a revolution?" Lawgra asked, his voice angry. Jentien heard the waver in it.

Kiale answered. "It seems so."

"What will they do with him?"

"No idea," Kiale snapped. "Are you going to let us through?"

"Go," Lawgra said, as irritated as Kiale.

They started to move again, and Jentien let out a held breath. They had a long way to go, and he could only hope he stayed quiet long enough to avoid giving them away.

The house was too empty. Celeste couldn't stand being inside, and had spent the last day in her workshop, parsing out different measurements of ground crystal. Small vials that could be concealed in the palm of her hand, to larger bottles filled to the brim. When she ran out of dust, she started the fragile process of manufacturing more, pouring all her angst into sharp focus and precise movements, grinding crystal down into the finest grain she could without it combusting.

So, when the door to her workshop slammed open, she nearly destroyed this section of the Outers when she jumped and scattered grains across her worktable. They began to glow, so she cast the leather tarp over them to smother them.

Thankfully, there was no blast, and once Celeste assured herself that the threat had been neutralized, she rounded on the doorway. Two figures in guard uniforms were struggling to pry open a huge crate with the Kiyash seal burned into the wood. Celeste grabbed a crystal shard from another table and brandished it at the guards as the lid came free.

"Who are you?" Celeste called from across the room. A hand appeared on the rim of the crate, and a familiar cry of pain made her heart stop. The crystal clattered to the floor while she ran forward, propelled by instinct toward the bearer of that voice, no longer paying attention to the guard who stood to one side to let her pass.

She leaned over the edge to find Jentien in a heap of blood-soaked cloaks, his beautiful face twisted into a mask of pain.

"Jentien!" Celeste cried, reaching down to hook her hands beneath his arms. He cried out again when she hefted him over the side. Cloaks tumbled out with him, stuck to his pale skin.

The guard in the street replaced the lid on the crate and began to drag it away as the second ripped their mask and cloak off and let them tumble to the floor. Cortlen helped her lift Jentien over his shoulder.

"Where should I put him?" he asked.

"This way," Celeste replied, and led him into the house.

She pulled a taper from the kitchen hearth to light a few candles along the way. "Put him on the sofa. What happened?"

Jentien groaned, rolling on his side when Cortlen put him down. Celeste thrust the taper at the dark-haired man and pushed the sodden hair off Jentien's face. His skin was clammy and pale, his eyes screwed shut above gritted teeth.

"He was flogged as an example. We intercepted him before he could be taken into the spire, but the Ambient will be looking for him." A wicked smirk twisted his mouth. "He killed Tulia Kiyash." Celeste turned to Cortlen, her mouth dropping open and her eyes wide with shock. "He threw one of those vials you gave us. It won't take long for them to piece together what happened and come for him."

"Tsunal went to the Undercity," Kiale said from the doorway. "We can't go back."

Celeste gathered some bandages and set water to warm over the kitchen fire, stoking it higher. She found yarrow, eucalyptus, and other herbs she used in her salve and let it steep in another bowl. "In that room," she pointed to the guest room, "find a glass jar on the shelf by the bed and bring it to me."

Kiale nodded, and moments later reappeared with the jar. She gave it to Celeste, who nodded at Jentien as she considered the white substance inside. "Turn him onto his stomach, please." The salve had been made to combat the rain, but had healing herbs as well—chamomile to reduce swelling, garlic to combat infection, plantain for both—but against the amount of damage he'd sustained...

Jentien winced, keeping his eyes shut as Cortlen and Kiale eased him onto his stomach with one arm draped over the edge of the sofa. Celeste waited for the water to warm before pouring it into a large bowl.

She hissed through clenched teeth when she peeled the cloak from his back, making him writhe and groan. Fresh blood oozed from where the clots had been disturbed. Celeste used clean bandages to staunch the bleeding, careful not to apply too much pressure, and then pulled the cooled herbal concoction forward, dipping a new bandage into it.

Jentien screamed when she cleaned the wounds. Cortlen and Kiale held his thrashing body down while Celeste gritted her teeth and ignored her anguished tears. When he went limp, Celeste continued until the wounds were clean, dried them, applied salve to ease the pain and promote healing, and collapsed onto the floor, hugging her knees and sobbing.

She cried until she was spent, and clutched Jentien's limp hand in hers, settling next to the sofa to wait for him to wake.

CHAPTER SIXTY

Jentien didn't rest well, his dreams a mix of pain and fear and heartache. He chased Isalie through a dark storm of burning rain while whips cracked like thunder overhead. He heard Celeste's voice through the noise and felt her grieving sobs like stabs to the heart.

He clawed through exhaustion to consciousness, and squeezed Celeste's hand, grateful for her warmth. A groan borne of heartache escaped him.

"Jentien," Celeste whispered, her voice thick with the same heartache. "I've got you."

"I'm sorry," he mumbled. "I couldn't... Iz..."

Cel kissed his cheek. "Don't," she whispered. "You did everything you could. I know you did."

He tried to shake his head, but it shifted his back, and he shied away from the pain that shot through him.

"You *did*," Cel insisted. "The Ambient are to blame, and we will make them pay."

Jentien looked at Celeste's face, the picture of grief and fury, a mirror to his own. He spotted Cortlen past her and gave him a meager smile of gratitude. "Cort, I owe you."

He shook his head. "No, golden child, now we're even."

"Sir," Kiale said, stepping into his line of sight, "we need to gather who we can. We killed the Consul's daughter; the Ambient *will* retaliate."

"These people aren't ready for that," Jentien grumbled. "They don't have weapons; they don't even have protection from the rain."

"I don't know about protection," Cortlen said, "but Kiale and I managed to grab some weapons when we smuggled you out. It's something, at least."

"Against the Stills, maybe," Celeste said. "Against the Ambient?"

"What about those arrows and spears you've been making? Or a few of those vials you gave us? It worked before."

"I don't have enough," she replied. "Not nearly enough to repel twenty Ambient."

"It might be enough to give them pause, and to show their hand. We can only hope our ranks would swell if they showed just how far they'll go to maintain control."

"That's *if* we can ensure people's safety in the rain. We don't want them to get to the Undercity," Kiale said.

"The leather needs to cure before I can make more cloaks," Cel said, "and I've exhausted my supply of crystal."

"Then we use what you've made to hunt the beasts," Jentien said. "Station as many people as you can near the tunnel to warn us if the Ambient come. Take Stills to the Undercity in the meantime, use the tunnels that we clear for overflow."

"We could do that, if we have hunters to guard them, but how will we feed that many?" Cortlen frowned as he considered. "We could take the gruel pots from the dormitories." His face lit with savage excitement. "And if the monitors and their guards don't like it, Elders help them if they stand in our way."

Kiale grinned. "I like that plan."

"No one will need to go into the rain," Cortlen added, "but the problem then becomes one of numbers. The Consul won't let the death of her daughter, nor the rescue of her scapegoat go unanswered. The Ambients' forces *will* come. If we had more Ambient Guard here, we *might* have a chance."

"Then we need to get more," Jentien said. "With you, Kiale, and me here, we can make sure that anyone who wants to fight learns how." He turned to Cel, offering an apologetic grimace. "We need to talk to Nel."

For the first time, Jentien watched a smile break out on their face. It was too eager, too aggressive, but Jentien appreciated it all the same. Elders knew they'd need that kind of enthusiasm if they had any hope of surviving.

"Finally," Nel said. "It was only a matter of time before something like this happened, and the lines between us and them became clearer." They grimaced at Jentien in apology when he shifted uncomfortably. "Sorry you're the one in the middle, and about..." they waved their hand to indicate Jentien's back, "that."

"If it makes people take notice, it's worth it," Jentien replied.

"Our hunters have been dispatched to the most abundant source of crystal in the tunnels to guard the miners, to get you more supplies," Nel told Celeste. "They've only encountered a few smaller beasts, but the weapons you made sliced through them with hardly any effort."

"Cortlen and Kiale offered to train volunteers in the guards' techniques," Jentien said, "As far as the Ambient go, if we can get more crystal, maybe your weapons will be useful against them, Cel."

"*Maybe,*" Celeste emphasized. "They can block projectiles, and we can't assume arrows or even the ground crystal would be effective against them."

"If we fire enough arrows, they won't be able to block them all," Cortlen suggested. "The Guard don't have heavy armor; if the arrows pierce Gloom beast hide, they'll pierce leather."

"You get me more crystal, and I'll make you more arrowheads," Celeste said.

"When do we leave?" Jentien asked. He shifted in Amal's dining room chair, the new scabs on his back pulling, making him wince. The pain lingered like it had been etched onto his bones, or the soul beneath.

Nel shifted, and the sudden creak of their chair made Jentien flinch, hearing the echo of a whipcrack. It'd been two days since Kiale and Cortlen had smuggled him out of the Inners, and there were times that he'd forgotten the pain waiting to assail him every time he moved.

Only because the pain in his heart—a tearing, gaping hole—was so much worse. And the fire that Iz had started had become an inferno that might destroy him if he didn't direct it somewhere.

Celeste caught his flinch and frowned. Her locs swung about her shoulders as she shook her head, leveling a glare his way.

"You're in no condition to go anywhere," she informed him. "You can barely sit up, let alone fight off a beast."

"I need to do *something*, Cel." He met her glare with one of his own. "I can't just sit here."

"If you move around too much, you will permanently damage yourself, and then you won't be able to do anything *but* sit."

He knew she was right, but he couldn't stand the thought that he needed to sit still while people risked their lives against the beasts, and the Ambient could be bearing down upon them. "I'll wait another day," he conceded, "and then I'm going out there. Even if I'm only an extra pair of eyes."

Celeste ran her hands over her face, clearly frustrated as she muttered under her breath. Nel chuckled but gave Jentien a slow nod and a smile that seemed to say that they approved of Jentien's insistence.

One day, and then he'd get back to work.

CHAPTER SIXTY-ONE

"That beautiful genius," Jentien muttered to himself, giving his shoulders a gentle roll. The pain in his back had subsided over the course of the previous day, thanks to the salve that Celeste had applied several times.

Nel gave him a curt nod. "She is."

They were following a group of miners and seasoned hunters with Cortlen and Kiale, all armed with spears bearing the crystal points Celeste had made for them. The tunnels were vaster than Jentien had pictured; they'd been walking for more than an hour, and had passed many branches barricaded with stone, wood scraps, and anything else they had on hand as barriers against wandering beasts. The hunters guided them with unerring precision around one corner, down another branch, and then out into a wider tunnel.

"Some of these tunnels," Nel said, noticing Jentien peering past another barricade, "lead to underground rivers fed by the rain runoff. The people that were..." they cut their eyes to Jentien, "freed... followed one away from the spire."

Jentien ignored the pause but couldn't ignore the pulse of agony that came because of it. "Could we find a path there?" he asked. "Go through these tunnels to get through the spire from below?"

"No," Nel replied. "There are routes that *could* open onto the tunnel leading to the Inners, but that would alert the Ambient about the Undercity. The prisoners escaped through an opening an Ambient made in a wall. Even if we found one and strong-armed an Ambient to open it, none of the tunnels we've discovered connect that far into the city. The waterways likely do, but braving that water would be a death sentence."

"It's not diluted by the water that's there?"

"Not enough," Nel replied. "We should come to the crystal vein soon."

A long arcing path later, the tunnel opened into a larger cavern with several large pillars stretching from floor to ceiling. The far side of the cavern was shrouded in darkness that the lanterns couldn't breach. Large crystal deposits glittered in the lantern light where it jutted out of the rock, and veins of the same substance cut through the walls.

They walked forward, the lantern-bearers checking the perimeter of the cavern for hidden beasts. Once it was clear, the miners laid the canvas bags they'd slung over their shoulders on the floor, and got to work. The sharp ping of their pickaxes hitting stone echoed around the large space.

Jentien wandered toward one of the branching tunnels and the distant roar of surging water. Jentien gripped the spear in his hand, catching Cortlen's eyes near another tunnel mouth. He kept an eye on the darkness ahead, alert for any sound other than the pickaxes.

Time passed slowly while he waited. His scabs itched, and the muscles in his back protested the longer he stood. Nel wound through the miners, checking on their progress before heading Jentien's way to offer a waterskin. Jentien took a deep draught and handed it back.

"Thanks," he said.

"You all right?" Nel asked.

Jentien quirked an eyebrow. "Do you care?"

Nel smiled at that. "For your own sake?" They shook their head. "No. But for Cel, and everything you represent for the Stills?" They shrugged. "The miners need about an hour more to fill their bags, then we'll head back."

A faint sound caught Jentien's attention from farther down the tunnel; a vague splashing noise. He grasped the spear with both hands in a defensive position. He heard it again and turned to hiss at Nel, who readied their spear, too.

"Something's moving in the water," Jentien whispered.

"Likely a beast," Nel agreed. It sounded like the splash of a heavy foot, followed by a grumble. They motioned toward the cavern behind them, and a low whistle through their teeth summoned Cortlen and a couple of the hunters.

"Gloom beast," they whispered, "too close to leave it alone. Standard hunting formation. Jentien, get in the back." Jentien didn't argue as the others pressed forward. Nel had command here, and he knew he'd be a liability, but he certainly wouldn't let whatever they came across get past him without a fight.

They crept forward, leaving the lanterns behind to preserve their quiet approach. Every step took them closer to the water which was loud enough to mask their footsteps. Only the sound of splashing rose above the roar, and the occasional grunt or snort of the large beast.

The end of the tunnel became visible because somewhere ahead, something cast a pale white light. Nel, Cortlen, and Kiale snuck around the corner, and when the hunters had gone around as well, Jentien finally approached. He peered past the others to see mist rising above a swift river cutting through the rock of a large cave.

Across the river, providing the soft glow, was a forest of fungi clinging to the walls, ceiling, and stalagmites. Standing at the edge of the river, batting at something stuck against a stalagmite jutting over the edge of the stone bank, was a Gloom beast the size of a horse.

Jentien caught a flash of claws when it extended a large paw forward again. The movement was tentative, like a cat poking something strange to see if it would bite. Their group fanned out to block the beast's exits, leaving it with the river before it or the wall of spears behind.

The beast went still and lifted its head, sniffing the air. It turned their way, and Jentien spotted the elongated face of a horse with fangs like a wolf and a mane of silken hair hanging from its neck. It bared its teeth and let out a snarl, its shoulders rising as it turned to face them.

Before it could pounce, Kiale and a hunter loosed crystal-tipped arrows that sank into its flank. It grunted in pain and stepped to the side, just as Cortlen and Nel surged forward to stab it with their spears. The crystal sliced through the hide at its shoulder and below its ribs before it whipped around and slapped Cortlen's spear out of his hands.

Nel fell back, slashing with their spear to keep the beast at bay. Another hunter and Jentien thrust their spears forward to keep the thing in place for Kiale to sink an arrow in its eye.

The beast slunk backward, and a pained howl split the air. Nel approached it as it flailed and stumbled, and in one fluid movement, thrust their spear into its chest. When they pulled the spear free, black-red blood poured out of the wound, and the beast dropped to the ground.

Jentien panted, wincing at the pain in his back while Cel's scolding rang in his head. They kept their distance until the beast stopped twitching, and then the hunters began harvesting what they could. Cortlen stepped to the edge of the river to get a look at whatever the thing had been investigating, and Jentien followed Kiale back toward the other cavern.

"Jentien." Cortlen's grave call from the riverbank froze him in place, flooding him with cold terror.

He tensed and pivoted toward the river, walking forward with as much trep- idation as he'd approached the beast. Nel was standing next to Cortlen now, and everyone's eyes were focused on whatever had been pulled out of the rush- ing water by the beast. Jentien peered at the sodden scraps clinging to stark red burns covering pale flesh. Cortlen gently turned the body over, and Jentien winced at the burns covering most of the face.

Isalie didn't move when Cortlen and Nel dragged her body from the river. Jentien didn't feel the sting of the water against his skin when he fell over her cold body.

His heart stopped beating, the breath whooshed from his lungs, and the pain in his chest dug deeper and deeper with claws that shredded the slim hope that he'd clung to.

CHAPTER SIXTY-TWO

She fell through darkness for so long that she forgot what anything else felt like. When she splashed into the burning, rushing water, she forgot how to breathe as she tumbled over and over, carried wherever the river took her. She came up for air by accident, and wondered just how long it would take to drown and end her suffering.

That's when she'd slammed into something hard, and her ribs cracked.

The water was worse when she stopped flowing with it. Now, it pummeled against her, peeling what little skin she had left away, pinning her to the rock. She'd tried to drag herself out of the water and got as far as hefting her torso and a leg up before collapsing, leaving one leg dangling over the edge.

She'd thought of Jen and Cel, feeling her heart swell even as it stuttered in her chest. Her chest swelled with pride when she pictured Mistress Kiyash's face discovering that she'd lost her plaything, despite the way her breath rattled and tasted like blood.

Her thoughts circled back to Cel and her confidence. She'd shared that with Isalie, giving her the strength to find herself. She thought of Jentien and how her soul had sung when he'd finally returned her love tenfold.

It hurt to smile, but Isalie did as she let herself fade, trusting that Jen and Cel would pick up the fight where she'd left off.

She's so cold.

Jentien clutched Isalie to his chest, unwilling to let anyone else carry her. It didn't matter that he was tearing open his wounds with every step. He felt nothing but Isalie's ice-cold skin.

"Jentien," Cortlen called again, but Jentien was already shaking his head. "Let me help, at least."

"No."

"Your back—"

"It doesn't matter." There was no anger in his voice. That raging inferno had gone out, leaving him hollow. Because he was holding his heart in his hands, and she was cold and still.

Now, the only thing he could do was keep walking. He needed to take her to Celeste. Celeste needed to know.

Cortlen sighed but fell back to give Jentien space. Jentien kept moving, clutching Iz's limp body tight.

And nearly dropped her when she took a shallow breath.

Back and forth across the stone floor of the cavern, Celeste paced with her arms folded over her chest, waiting for Jentien to come back.

He probably hurt himself, she thought. She glanced at the tunnel entrance as she passed. *I shouldn't have let him go.*

She couldn't have stopped him, she knew, but it didn't stop her worry. They'd already lost Lee, and she couldn't lose Jentien, too. She passed the tunnel again and stopped at its mouth, considering plunging into the dark after him. The salve sat heavy in the bag slung over her shoulder.

Celeste took a step forward, and then Jentien was there, rushing toward her. Tears streamed down his pale face, mingling with the sweat pouring from his brow. And in his arms...

"CELESTE!" Jentien bellowed, clutching a pale, burned body.

Tears rimmed Celeste's eyes when she recognized the shape of her brow, her nose, and her chin. Horrid burns covered every inch of her body and her hair had burned away from the right side of her head.

"No," she whispered. She ran forward until she almost collided with Jentien and took Isalie's frail body in her arms. Jentien collapsed onto his knees but kept his eyes trained on Celeste. "No."

"She's breathing," Jentien panted. Isalie indeed took a breath, but it was too shallow, and gurgling. "Cel, please," he begged.

Celeste didn't say another word before she turned and ran toward the medical tent.

Jentien allowed Cortlen to haul him to his feet and support his weight so that he could follow Cel. The gathering crowd parted for her, leaving a wide lane for Jentien. He'd been on the verge of collapse, but he couldn't have given Isalie to anyone else.

Inside the tent, he found Celeste stripping the last rags from Isalie to reveal even more burned flesh beneath. She was too still, and too pale beneath the livid marks...

"Jentien, help me." Celeste's voice was calm and commanding, and it pushed Jentien's horror aside. He pulled off her boots one by one, not allowing himself to dwell on the pock-marked surface. Her wool socks had dissolved, leaving her skin to melt against the interior of her boots, and he grimaced as that skin came with the boots. But Isalie didn't stir, and her wounds didn't bleed enough.

"Cel," he said, "is she..."

"Help me wash the water off," she replied.

Jentien took bowl after bowl of untainted water and rinsed every exposed inch of Isalie's body. He didn't speak while he waited for each shallow, difficult breath. When they finished, he helped Cel carry her still, limp body to a crystal box.

Celeste moved away and Jentien didn't take his eyes from Isalie's chest. *Rise and fall.* Bottles clinked and rattled, Celeste muttered to herself, and water splashed. *Rise and fall.* Isalie's breaths were coming slower and slower.

Cel appeared again with thick leather gloves holding a steaming bowl of water that glistened like diamonds.

"What is that?" he asked.

"Ground crystal in warm water. I'm going to soak these cloths, drape them over her, and pray to the Elders that it helps draw the water out of her wounds." She sighed and reached into the bowl, draping the cloth over Isalie's body. Then, she tucked it between Isalie's legs and arms to form a tight shroud around her body before rolling her onto her side to wrap it around her back.

"And those?" Jentien gestured to glass vials holding ground crystal.

Celeste sighed. "Prism."

Jentien's eyes widened in shock. "Isn't that dangerous?"

She picked up a vial, crossed to the makeshift stove at this end of the tent, and lit a long taper. "I've been using it to treat the people she rescued. Anyone who could recover has." She winced at him. "She was almost drowned; she's going to need a lot more time with it."

Celeste placed the vial next to Isalie's head and lit the contents with the taper. Smoke poured out of the neck of the vial, and Celeste shut the lid of the chamber. "Once the hallucinations start, we'll pull the crystal out."

"How will we know she's hallucinating?" Jentien donned the mask Cel handed him as smoke began to fill the tent, pouring out of the filter.

Celeste just stared at the tendrils of smoke writhing around Isalie, and the rise and fall of her chest.

CHAPTER SIXTY-THREE

Blood rained down on Isalie's face, leaving burning trails of tears on her cheeks. Rainbows danced before her face, reflecting from the walls of her cell, from the lights floating above her head, and from eyes in the center of a head of blonde hair.

A low voice called to her, shaking the walls, burrowing into her head like a worm through the earth.

"Tell me what the Stills know. Tell me what their plans are."

No, she thought, because she couldn't move her mouth to form the word. She couldn't move her arms or legs; she could barely feel them anymore. I won't tell you anything.

"Tell me who's sympathetic to Jentien's mutiny."

No. She wouldn't say his name to this monster. Their eyes turned as red as the blood covering her eyes. She tried to scream, but there wasn't enough air. Her mouth was filled with water. She couldn't breathe... couldn't... breathe.

The voice screamed like a Gloom beast. Claws dug into her skin and her mind. Pain scorched through her lungs, and hot liquid spewed from her mouth. She coughed, trying to gasp for breath, trying to move her body, but the Ambient's hold on her hadn't stopped. She was trapped, she was dying, she was drowning.

Smoke roiled out of the cylinder when Celeste threw it open. Jentien held Isalie's seizing body before she could fall out, and Celeste grasped the smoldering jar with her gloved hands to thrust it inside a stone bucket of water before slamming a heavy lid onto it.

"Cel!" Jentien screamed, and she raced to pull Isalie from the chamber. They laid her on a cot nearby, and Celeste paused long enough to shut the chamber—to keep as much of the smoke inside as she could—before turning back to where Jentien clutched a thick blanket around Isalie.

The seizure stopped, but her chest didn't rise again. Celeste and Jentien held their breath, waiting for Isalie to breathe, and Celeste's lungs began to burn before she did. The first inhalation didn't have the heavy rattle, and it wasn't as shallow as it'd been before.

Jentien went to remove his hood, but Celeste stopped him.

"Not until the smoke dissipates," she said.

He nodded once and stared at the slight color in Isalie's pale skin and the blood oozing from her wounds. Celeste placed a jar of salve in Jentien's hands and picked up one of her own.

"We need to cover her with this, then wrap her to keep her warm," Celeste whispered. She couldn't say it any louder for fear that her voice might crack, just like her heart.

Celeste held her breath as she spread the salve on the right side of Isalie's face, where most of the skin had peeled away. The hair on that side had fallen out, and the wounds extended down the rest of her body.

Jentien cursed under his breath over and over while they worked, until every wound had a healthy layer of salve over it. Celeste draped thick blankets over Isalie, and then glanced at the stove across the tent.

"Help me move her," Celeste said, and grasped the head of the cot.

Jentien took the other end, and they carried Isalie closer to the stove. Most of the people Isalie had rescued had recovered from their wounds and found places to sleep. Only a few were still here, and only because they needed more time for their burns to heal, nothing as dire as Isalie's condition. They'd have to wait for her to come through this... or not.

Celeste *hated* waiting.

Flames licked her skin from head to toe, and the smell of woodsmoke and cooking flesh filled her nose. Her feet and face were the worst, and she wished she could see what was happening to her.

It may have been cowardly, but she was grateful that she couldn't.

Her mind wandered in and out of memories. Jentien's voice called her name as he chased her through Lacorsia. Celeste trailed her hand across Isalie's body. Then a swirl of crystal walls, water flowing down them and through them, washed her away as a dark cloud swallowed her. She disappeared into the black void just as lightning flashed, and everything went white.

The smoke had dissipated, and Jentien sat next to Isalie's cot with Cel as Nel strode into the tent, blinking at the bright light of the Ambient globe overhead, their face grave.

"The Ambient Guard came to the gate."

"What happened?" Jentien asked, though he didn't take his eyes from Isalie. He thought he'd seen her eyelids flutter.

"We've taken some of the dormitories, and though the monitors and guards have started to barricade the others, they can't hold them indefinitely. The monitors we ousted fled to the tunnel, and some of the Stills harried them all the way there, demanding answers about the escaped prisoners. The guards had to bar the gate, but reinforcements came. Our people held them back and put up a barricade."

"Cortlen and Kiale?" Jentien asked.

"They're armed and ready. Distributing Cel's cloaks and the few weapons we have as we speak."

Jentien nodded. There, another flutter, and his heartbeat stuttered. Isalie's eyelashes had been burned away, but he was sure that he'd seen her lids move. "I'd station your best archers in the nearest buildings to keep their bows and strings dry. Break the windows facing the tunnel and prepare them for the Ambient to arrive." Jentien's hand hovered over Isalie's shoulder; he was hesitant to touch her.

"How is she?" Nel asked.

"We don't know," Cel answered.

Isalie's chest rose and fell, and then another inhalation came a bit faster, and another even faster. The pulse in her neck picked up its pace, and Jentien watched the muscle in her jaw tense.

"The barricade won't hold for long," Nel warned from the tent entrance. "And when the Ambient come, there won't be much we can do to stop them."

Jentien didn't reply as Isalie's eyelids fluttered again and her mouth opened in a silent scream.

CHAPTER SIXTY-FOUR

Isalie's scream came out in a gurgle, her throat too swollen to let more out. She couldn't move, even though the feeling had come back into her body, and all of it was in agony. She saw a flash of teal and black, and warm brown eyes before bright light blinded her. She squeezed them shut again, and pain flared through the battered skin of her eyelids.

I've lost my mind, she thought. She'd expected to see the cold crystal walls of her cell, but she'd seen Jen and Cel instead. If she wasn't in so much pain, she could have believed that she heard their voices gently beseeching her to open her eyes. But she'd felt this way before, when she'd walked out into the rain after a phantom of Jen, and in her cell. Her mind had given up again, letting go of the painful reality surrounding her in favor of something more pleasant.

The voices persisted, and when something touched her arm, she flinched away from it and a flicker of memory of bashing against something hard after tumbling through suffocating darkness.

"Iz," Jentien called, his worried voice like a knife to her heart, "we're here. You're safe."

No, she wanted to say. *If I open my eyes the rain will get in. If I believe you, I'll break, and then I'll tell her everything.*

"Lee, we've got you." Cel was calm and reassuring, but Isalie knew that it masked her anxiety.

"Please," Jen pleaded, "come back to us."

"It's up to you, Lee," Cel told her. "You're strong enough to pull through this."

Jen sobbed, and she hated to imagine the pain etched onto his face. It would be the pain she'd seen when she found him. And Celeste, who'd believed in her and given her the confidence to find her own strength, was right beside him, trying to do it again.

She couldn't stand the thought that she'd leave Jen in this misery for the rest of his days, or the thought that she'd let Cel down. So, she opened her eyes, braving the pain and the light. For them.

Isalie's eyes were bloodshot, a sea of red around the dark blue irises that locked onto Jentien's face. The air left his lungs in a rush, and he lurched forward, his instinct to pull Iz into his arms dissolving when he remembered her wounds. She opened her mouth but only a strangled noise came out, and her eyes widened in fear and confusion. She strained to speak, her mouth forming words, and then she coughed, choking on that effort.

"Lee," Celeste said softly, "don't try to talk. You need to heal."

Iz shook her head, her eyes wide and insistent. The blanket covering her arm shifted as if she was trying to lift it. She winced but pushed harder. Jentien held his hand over the blanket, torn between keeping her in place and avoiding her wounds.

"Iz, you need to stay still," he begged her.

She ripped her arm out of the blanket and clutched Jen's sleeve with weak fingers. She strained toward him, and he realized that this wasn't just fear or pain. She needed to tell him something.

"What is it?" he asked, leaning closer.

She choked out a few syllables before she started coughing again. "–am...con...stor." She shook her head and let it loll back. Her throat worked painfully, struggling to swallow, to form words, to move air. Tears fell from her eyes, tracing through the salve.

"Cel," Jentien turned to her pained face, "do you have anything to write with?"

Isalie's eyes shot to Jentien's, and her brows drew together with a look of relief. Cel went to her bag on the other side of the room and rustled through it, returning a moment later with a charcoal pencil and a torn piece of parchment.

Jentien held the pencil to Isalie, who grasped it as gingerly as she could. It scratched across the paper in long, jerking movements.

Her arm dropped to the side when she was done, and her body relaxed, her task done. Jentien turned the paper around and blinked, trying to discern what the scratches meant. Cel leaned close, peering over his shoulder.

"Ambient," she said, pointing out the letters, "con?" She mouthed the letters to herself, working out the puzzle of Iz's scrawl. Then she stilled, and her eyes went wide.

"The Ambient control the storm."

Celeste's lungs burned after sprinting through the Undercity to the surface with Jentien beside her. It had been anguish to tear themselves from Lee's side so soon after she'd awoken. But she'd insisted, and Maretha and Amal had agreed to watch over her as word of their discovery spread beyond the market. Now that they'd painstakingly donned their suits, cloaks, and masks, she held the makeshift door aside for Jentien to climb through and followed.

There was a break in the rain, though the clouds hung heavy and dark over-head, and Cel knew from experience that they didn't have long before it started again. Her mind was still reeling with all the pieces of the puzzle coming togeth-er. The segregation from the Inners, the inexplicable way the storm seemed to target the Outers while the Inners was untouched, the shoddy equipment...

It'd always been a control tactic. However they'd managed it, they'd kept the entire city under their sway and left the Stills with no recourse for survival other than what the Ambient provided.

Is it all a sick game for them? Celeste wondered.

She didn't have time to speculate further, because they arrived at the court-yard with the tunnel entrance. The buildings around the edge were mostly dark, looming above like silent sentries waiting for conflict to erupt. Celeste spotted archers lurking inside broken windows as Jentien had suggested.

The barricade at the mouth of the tunnel was still in place: a mess of crates, doors, and part of a wall from within the depot. It wouldn't hold long against the guard, Celeste knew. Nel was right; if the Ambient came through here, they wouldn't stand a chance. But why hadn't they yet?

"What's the plan?" she asked Jentien, whose eyes were scanning the cowled faces gathered around the courtyard.

"We tell everyone what we know so they're prepared, and let that information spread through the Outers. We rally everyone here against the Ambient—the sooner the better, though our odds of success increase if we take time to recruit as many people as possible—and then we push into the Inners. They can't stop all of us."

"I can handle the gates," Celeste asked. "What if people don't believe us?"

Jentien looked around, and his eye caught on a figure near the gutted depot. Celeste followed his gaze to see Yesrien speaking to Nel, Pelom, and a small group of people.

"If the guards don't join us, you use your bottled crystal to destroy them. As for people not believing us–" Yesrien locked eyes with Celeste, then Jentien, and nodded. "It's not just us anymore, is it?"

He smiled, hope and anger simmering beneath the surface.

"No," she said with an answering smile. "It's not."

CHAPTER SIXTY-FIVE

Isalie couldn't stand the smell inside the tank. It felt like hours since Jentien and Celeste had run out of the tent, leaving Maretha and Amal with instructions to get Isalie back inside now that the smoke had dissipated. It hadn't taken long for Isalie to loathe the smell of herbs, fat, and blood that surrounded her. It was a struggle to remain still despite her weakness, knowing that Jen and Cel were on the surface.

Worse than having to stay in the tent were the looks Maretha and Amal gave her whenever they peered in at her. She knew they cared, but she couldn't stand the gentle, reassuring smiles. She couldn't stand the soft voices laced with pity.

There was so much more to say about what she'd been through, and what Mistress Kiyash had told her, but every time she opened her mouth to speak she choked on the swollen tissue in her throat. She glanced at Amalricus, his wrinkles set even deeper as he gazed toward the path leading out of the Undercity, and, overwhelmed by the urgency of getting her information out, tapped on the glass.

Amal's eyes widened, his white brows almost disappearing into his hairline, and pulled open the cylinder.

"Are you all right, my dear?"

"Rai–" the first syllable stuck in her throat. When she tried to force out the next, her throat spasmed, inducing a coughing fit. For one terror-filled moment, she was drowning in the dark again. With tears in her eyes and blood trickling from her mouth, she rolled onto her side to keep from drowning in blood.

"Maretha!" Amal shouted. He hovered near her with a cloth to wipe the bright red away from her mouth. "Slow breaths, Isalie," he said. "Through your nose, in and out."

Every breath shuddered through her burning lungs, the coughs tearing out of her until she at last forced the air through her nostrils.

In and out, she thought. *In and out.*

Maretha barged into the tent, terrified, and surveyed the scene. Then, with a calm smile on her face and an authoritative tone that brooked no argument, she said, "Back into the tank, and I'll brew you some tea. Celeste left us herbs."

She and Amal hefted Isalie onto her back, leaving the cloths draped over her for modesty. Isalie pinched her thumb and forefinger together and moved her hand back and forth. She pleaded with her eyes for Amal to understand her shaky pantomime of writing.

His brows lifted in understanding. "Maretha, the paper and charcoal."

Maretha picked them up and handed them to Isalie. The paper fell from her grasp, weak and unsteady as it was. A leather-wrapped board appeared for Amal to prop the paper against.

Her grip was so weak that the pencil marks were faint, and the scars covering her hand contorted her fingers into odd angles to make her letters awkward and jagged. She managed to scrawl them regardless, and the pencil dropped to her chest when she finished.

Maretha deciphered it first. "Cort wondered why the Ambient hadn't come for the Outers yet, but if this is true," she looked at Isalie, who gave her the faintest nod of confirmation, "then they don't have to come at all."

Thunder boomed overhead, and the rain began its uneven patter. Yesrien's intense gaze didn't move from Jentien, and he resisted the urge to take a step back. She had the same fire as Isalie without the compassion that had always tempered it. Yesrien's had been burned away by what she'd been through. Dread crept through him as he wondered if the same would happen to Iz.

His words resonated with her, he knew, as he watched her jaw clench and her fingers curl into fists at her sides. She glanced around, leveling her direct gaze at everyone who seemed skeptical of Jentien's assertion that the Ambient were controlling the rain. They slipped their hoods over their heads not only to protect themselves from the downpour, but also to escape her fury.

"I believe you," Yesrien said. "I've seen the lengths they'll go to. What can we do about it?"

"We gather as many as we can and we take the Inners," Jentien told her. The others glanced uneasily at each other behind Yesrien. "We have the numbers to overwhelm them if we work together," Jentien insisted. "Celeste can blow the gates open, and we head inside. Word is already spreading; we'll have even more on our side."

"Will we?" Jentien recognized Pelom's voice among the others. "Most of them are loyal to the Ambient, or willfully ignorant of the strife the Ambient are causing. Plus, *all* the Stills are terrified that they'll lose their place. Not many will be willing to speak up, even if they do believe us."

"Then we show them," Jentien pushed. "Yesrien, you can tell them." Her scars were livid against the skin on her neck and chest.

Celeste tensed next to him, and Yesrien's reply was acidic. "You want me to parade around the Inners, showing everyone my scars as proof of my treatment? Why do you assume any of them would care?"

"If we can sway even a few of them, that's more than we had before."

A scream split the clamor of falling rain, and he turned to find a cloaked figure writhing as they threw themselves under the cover of the warehouse. Jentien reached forward and found that the rain had burned straight through the cloak around their shoulders and the hood beneath the cowl.

Celeste peeled the cloak and hood away, revealing skin disintegrating before Jentien's eyes. Celeste splashed water over the wound before slathering them with salve. It was only when their screams subsided that Jentien heard the others.

He whipped around, spotted a handful that hadn't been able to get out of the way when the rain picked up, and tore out of the warehouse. Droplets hammered against the top of his head, heavy despite his hood and cowl. A woman screamed from a heap on the open ground, her gloves and cloak already in tatters as Jentien reached her. He tried to help her to her feet, but she screeched when he put pressure on her arm. He scooped her up, ignoring the pain in his back and her cries, and ran back to the warehouse to deposit her on the ground at Cel's feet.

Two others tried to follow him into the rain for the people stranded there, but the moment they were exposed, their cloaks began to disintegrate, and they fell back to wrench their clothing from their bodies before the moisture could contact their skin. Again and again, Jentien darted into the rain, carrying or dragging people to Cel's care, ignoring the searing heat in his feet.

Keep moving, he told himself as he turned once more. *Last one,* he thought, seeing the holes through his gloves when he hefted their arm over his shoulder. Jentien forced himself to take a step forward, and another, to follow the shouts from the warehouse.

"Jentien, get *in here!*" Cel bellowed, and her voice pulled him forward.

He crashed to the floor and closed his eyes behind the crystal lenses as hands pulled at his clothes. He tried to wave them toward the last man he'd dragged in, but his hands were slapped away, and Cel's voice boomed over him.

"Strip them, like the others! Where is that water? I need it *now!*" Cold air struck bare skin, and the small area of intact skin on his hands prickled with gooseflesh. The rest was a mess of confused agony.

Jentien bit back another scream when the boots peeled away from his blistering feet. He had relief for the space of two heartbeats before water splashed onto him, cold enough to dull the pain as it washed the last of the rainwater from him. Cel stripped his cloak and mask off next, checking them for holes that didn't seem to be there. He opened his eyes to find Celeste hovering over him, her brow creased and her mouth drawn into a tight frown.

"Such a brave fool," she grumbled while she patted him dry. "Are you ever going to stop taunting death?"

Jentien flashed her a weak smile. "No," he mumbled. Screams rose in the distance; more people were caught in this terrifying new manifestation of the Gloom.

Celeste half-turned toward the sound but paused halfway. "The spire is glowing," she said.

"What does that mean?" Jentien asked.

Celeste's gaze lingered on the spire when she turned around, then scooped a handful of salve. Her warm fingers smoothed it over the worst of his wounds until all that was left was a dull ache. His back burned, but it wasn't from the rain. Celeste touched her lips to his and tucked a long piece of hair away from where it had fallen across his eyes.

"I don't know," she said, "but the timing is suspicious."

The people he'd pulled out of the rain were rolled in blankets, slathered in salve, and being dragged away from the open doors to get them away from the rising mist. Jentien looked at the darkened sky and the singular glow of the spire like bottled moonlight.

"Your cloak stopped it. The rain didn't burn through."

Celeste narrowed her eyes at her handiwork again. "It seems so," she murmured.

"We don't have enough of your cloaks to cover everyone. Tell me you have some idea of how we can get around the rain now," Jentien said, eyeing the remains of the Ambient-made cloaks.

Celeste stared at him, her face blank. "I don't."

CHAPTER SIXTY-SIX

ANGRY VOICES ECHOED IN the cavern outside, and their questions and concerns echoed in her ears. She tried not to look at anyone that wandered nearby, and she was grateful when Maretha banned the gawkers from the tent. Now, they were lined up outside, and their incessant questions wouldn't stop.

She couldn't get the image of Mistress Kiyash out of her head, and the smug smile on her face. She couldn't get the cloying darkness or the suffocating crush of water out of her mind, out of her body, or out of her spirit. The echoes sounded like her screams bouncing off the walls of her cell.

Isalie only saw the face of Mistress Kiyash. She only felt the crumpled body of the Ambient man fall from her grasp, and the rain searing her skin, leaving its ghost behind to haunt her.

She'd touched the raw skin of her face once; the pocked, sticky surface left a bloody sheen on her fingers. The horror lingered on her fingertips like salve, and she hadn't worked up the courage to feel her scalp, to find out if she even had hair left. She was too much of a coward for that. She was too much of a coward to face the people that Maretha shooed from the tent entrance for the third time in as many minutes.

So, here she lay, too afraid of the cramped chamber to stay where she could heal, choosing instead to have her wounds wrapped in salve-covered bandages to protect them from the hood she needed to wear instead. It was a small comfort to hide her face, especially from the impulse to feel the extent of the damage to her head.

"Please," Maretha urged, her voice as weary as Isalie felt, "she needs rest, and she isn't ready to speak to anyone."

"We just want to tell her how grateful we are—"

"She knows," Maretha said. "When Isalie is ready, we will let you know. Until then, the best gratitude you can show is to give her *time*."

A beat of silence, and then, "Well, when she's ready, please let her know that we're all out here, praying to the Elders on her behalf."

If Isalie could shed a tear, she would have. She'd spent them on her worry for Jen and Cel, on her pain, and mourning the ability to breathe on her own. She'd only been awake for a few hours, and it was already too much.

Maretha walked toward her with a sympathetic smile. "There are so many people that want to thank you," she explained, with a glance over her shoulder. Feet shuffled on the ground outside, accompanying the murmur of voices. "I told them you weren't ready yet."

Isalie looked toward the other end of the tent, where Jen and Cel had left. Maretha seemed to understand, and her sympathetic smile dropped into a worried frown.

"I haven't heard anything yet."

Every muscle in Isalie's body screamed for her to get up and chase after them. They needed to know that they had no protection from the rain, that they couldn't win against the power the Ambient wielded. Isalie needed to know that they weren't dead already, dissolving in the street just like she'd dissolved in that cell.

Maretha caught her eye again and seemed to read the rising resolve on Isalie's face, because she positioned herself next to the cot.

"Please, don't trouble yourself. As soon as we hear anything—"

That's when the screaming began. This time, it wasn't Isalie.

The tent overflowed with injured that had been caught outside when the rain began. The worst had been placed in the tank, but everyone wore masks after inhaling the deadly vapor.

The smell of herbal salve and coppery blood was everywhere now. Isalie couldn't help but resent their presence; their moans and wails were too like her own, and their injuries and misery were a mirror that she couldn't face. The fact that *no one* had seen Jen or Cel didn't help her nerves, either.

"We can't get more salve," Maretha said for the tenth time in the past few minutes, weary and exasperated. "Celeste may have more at her workshop, but it's unreachable through the rain."

If Jen and Cel are alive out there, Isalie thought, *there's no way to get to them.*

An angry cacophony rose above the painful wails inside the tent before a group burst through the entrance. They cornered Amal where he stood with his sleeves rolled up, applying the last of the salve to a teenager who'd been lucky enough to escape with minor wounds on their arm.

"What's happening out there?" one man demanded when Amal looked up. "Even the worst of our cloaks could protect us for a while; now it's all useless, and our people are dying!" He swept his arm around the tent to indicate the wounded.

"The Ambient control the rain," Maretha blurted. "Isalie," she pointed toward the cot, and Isalie wished she could shrink away from all the angry eyes that turned her way, "was told by Mistress Kiyash herself that they've been making it worse. Apparently, they've succeeded."

Everyone who hadn't been looking her way did now. This was the whole point to her efforts in the Inners, but now, the thought of giving them the proof they needed sent a thrill of fear through her. Her skin flushed, her stomach dropped, and her blood ran cold. Sweat prickled her skin, irritating it more.

The man at the front of the group took a step in Isalie's direction, but Maretha stopped him, her small arm corded with muscle as she held the much larger man in place.

"Isalie is in no shape to answer any of your questions after what the Ambient did."

Another man pushed past the first, slammed into Maretha, and rushed for the chamber. When he passed Isalie's cot, a chorus of angry protests filled the air. He flung the door wide and thrust his head inside. His sharp inhale sounded like a snake's hiss, and his emaciated chest expanded once, twice, before he slumped to the ground with a beatific smile on his face as chaos broke out through the tent.

More emaciated figures in scraps of cloaks burst inside, knocking over patients, throwing the angry crowd aside, and pulling Maretha away from the chamber to get at the Prism smoke that was billowing out of it. Someone grabbed the injured woman from inside and threw her on the ground. It was bedlam near the tank, and Isalie couldn't tell if these were Prism addicts or people that needed healing that fought to climb inside.

A body flew backward into Isalie, and she crashed onto the hard floor. Maretha was next to her, covering her head and neck with her hands to avoid the trampling feet. There were too many people, too much movement for Isalie to track.

A club swung above her, and she heard the crack of bone and a scream. Nel stood between her and Maretha, and brought a club down onto another person's head when they lunged.

"Stop!" Nel bellowed. They dove into the crowd around the tank, untangling limbs and shoving languid bodies back into the arms of people in the crowd. One by one they were removed as the Prism entered their lungs and they stopped fighting. Nel removed the last one from the tank as Amal helped Isalie onto her cot.

"Take them to my house," Nel commanded. "Get rid of anything they can use as a weapon and tie them down if they try to leave."

Most of the crowd dispersed, and they were left with the pained moans of anyone who'd been knocked to the floor. Maretha's usually calm face was drawn in a scowl that persisted as she and Amal lifted the woman into the chamber again, then checked on each patient. When she came back to Isalie, the lines on her face were more pronounced, and her shoulders were slumped in exhaustion.

"Do you need anything?" she asked. Isalie shook her head once. "Fucking Prism," she cursed. "I recognized most of those people as addicts; I guess they followed the crowd of injured to get down here. We're going to need guards now."

Maretha turned away to rummage in a large bag that she'd shoved into a corner. She came back with a wooden box small enough to fit in her palm, worn at the corners as if it'd passed through many hands.

"I don't want you to try to talk if you need anything, so give this a shake if you do."

Isalie grasped it, focusing on the dark brown wood grain to keep her eyes away from the red streaks on the skin around it. She rotated it slowly, and the contents slid from one end to the other, reminding her of wind rustling the leaves in the tree outside her room in Lacorsia.

She clutched the box to the cloth draped over her chest and turned her head to watch for Cel and Jen.

"Is the spire still glowing?" Jentien groaned. Most of the injured had gone silent, and he still hadn't worked up the courage to ask Celeste if they were alive.

"No," she replied. She'd been frowning so long that it looked etched into her skin. He shifted toward her and leaned his arm against hers in silent support. He wanted to hold her, but the flare of pain in his back reminded him that he shouldn't. "It's been dark for a few minutes, but I don't know if that means anything."

She leaned away to let him know she was about to move, and when he'd steadied himself, she rose to her feet and strode to a nearby wall. The warehouse was empty save for a few sealed crates. Cel pried open one of the lids and rummaged pulled an Ambient-made cloak out.

Without a word, she crossed to the entrance and flung it into the street, watching it billow open and settle onto the ground. Jentien got to his feet and joined her to watch darkness spreading over the cloak with every drop of rain that hit it. When one corner settled in a puddle, it dissolved before their eyes like hair held to a flame. The opposite corner was intact; just a normal cloak meant to withstand Olunei's storm.

"The rain is back to normal." Celeste turned with a grim smile across her face. "Let's get these people home."

CHAPTER SIXTY-SEVEN

Watching Jen limp through the streets wounded Celeste. Seeing the bodies of so many wounded being loaded onto carts was something else entirely.

It was the emptiness that had hollowed out her heart when she lost her parents. It was a failure to protect her people, and it was a slap in the face from the Ambient.

As if she needed any more reason to stop them.

Their trip through the streets was harrowing; they ducked from one shelter to the next, the able-bodied holding crate lids draped with cloaks above the cart to keep as much rain off them as possible. All available hoods were on the injured as well, which left the rest of them exposed. Celeste fought the urge to look up repeatedly, focusing instead on putting one foot in front of the other, and on propping up Jentien's weight so that he could move under his own power. Fool that he was, he'd refused to take up space on a cart when he could walk.

The Elders must have been smiling down on them, because they made it to the decrepit building that marked the entrance to the Undercity. New puddles had collected throughout the interior, though, slowly eating away at the floors and into the foundation.

We'll have to use some of our drinking water to wash it away before it starts leaking through, Celeste thought. It was just one more task on her mounting list. She hoped the crystalline roofs on the buildings outside would hold.

The carts were abandoned outside, and the wounded placed on blankets to slide them across the ground through the hole. Jentien limped through, and Celeste had to force him to sit down rather than helping the rest of the injured inside.

"I swear on Isalie's beautiful head that if you move, Jen, I'll make sure you can't get up again."

He flashed her a wan smile, his face pale and dripping with sweat. "Understood," he breathed.

When the last of the injured was through, the entrance was blocked again, and they began the arduous journey into the depths of the cavern. They didn't make it far before voices echoed up the path, and people surged from below. When Jentien's feet finally gave out, he fell into Nel's outstretched arms.

"Did you lose anyone out there?" they asked. Jentien hissed when they threw his arm over their shoulder, but they just turned back down the trail, leaving Celeste to follow.

"I don't know yet," she replied. "What about here?"

"We brought a *lot* of people down that were stranded in the ruins, but I think most will survive. We had an incident with some Prism addicts, but it's taken care of. Isalie is fine. She's out of the tank, wearing a mask. Maretha is taking good care of her."

Jentien grunted again, and the tension inside Celeste eased just a bit. Maretha was fierce and protective; that's why Celeste had asked for her help. Isalie had reunited families that had been wrenched apart, inspiring gratitude in the rescued and vengeance in Nel's followers. They'd all been circling since Isalie had been found, and Celeste had no doubt that this new development with the rain had set them all moving again. Maretha was the perfect person to stand between them all.

With every step forward, Jentien dragged a bit more. His ruddy tan skin was chalky and coated with sweat, pain apparent with each step. Nel shifted his weight onto their shoulder and Celeste ducked under Jentien's other arm to lift him off the ground before he could drag them over the steep edge of the switchback.

The cavern below shone with more lights than she'd seen in a long time, illuminating figures moving like a hive of buzzing, angry bees. Getting to the ground floor did nothing to dispel the comparison as people rushed between tents, gathered in the center of the market, and swarmed around the makeshift hospital.

Jentien slumped in their arms, his resolve giving way to pain. "Move!" Nel shouted.

The crowd parted, leaving the way open for the injured behind. Entering the tent, she locked eyes with Maretha, who grimaced in greeting and leaned over a woman lying on one of the cots.

There were too many masks, too many figures draped in blankets and slathered in salve. Celeste lost herself in the sea of misery and pain until one figure caught her eye. Celeste knew it was Lee by the way she leaned toward them, and by the small wheeze of breath that Celeste heard as if it was the only sound in the riotous tent.

"He's going to be all right, Lee," she called. "We'll bring him over, stay there."

Isalie shifted her weight away from the edge. Nel dragged Jentien out of Celeste's grasp so she could scoot an empty cot closer to Isalie, and plopped him onto it. Blood seeped through his wrapped feet, and his back had reopened.

"He'll be all right," she repeated, both to herself and to Lee. "He played hero, pulled everyone out of that cursed rain, but he'll be *fine*." A tear ran down her cheek, having escaped her careful control, and she wiped it away begrudgingly. There wasn't time for her to break down; she knew that if she started crying, she wouldn't be able to stop.

Isalie pulled her arm free and reached for Celeste, toward Jentien. Celeste grasped it, and Jentien, eyes clenched in pain, slid his fingers into Celeste's. She was the tether between them, and took comfort in the fact that they both still lived.

CHAPTER SIXTY-EIGHT

Isalie couldn't sleep, but it wasn't the unending chorus of piteous moans that kept her awake. Jen's feet had burned almost to the bone, and the rest of his skin had never been so pale; he looked like a specter compared to his usually ruddy glow. He was breathing steadily, though, and she trusted Cel's assurance that he would recover.

Celeste sent Maretha home to her children with Cortlen after he reported no movement from the Inners. She worked tirelessly to keep the injured comfortable, re-apply salve and sachets of spent crystal, and rotate them into the chamber. Every spare moment, she was at Jen's side. Isalie dreaded the frown that dug deeper into Cel's face whenever she checked him.

Maretha returned an eternity later and touched Cel's shoulder, relieving her of duty. Cel plopped onto a chair between Jen and Isalie, smoothing his hair away from his face once more before she slumped against Isalie's cot.

"I can't take much more of this," Celeste told them when she sat. She draped her arms over the edge of the cot and gently touched their hands. "What am I going to do with you two?"

"Just stay with us," Jen croaked. He kissed each of their hands, taking care to avoid the worst of Isalie's injuries.

Cel shook her head. "If you two keep throwing yourself into the rain, I certainly won't."

Isalie chuckled, but a strangled noise came out in place of her normal laugh. Jen's eyebrows drew together, and his frown deepened. His reaction dampened what small levity she'd felt the moment before.

He'll never be able to look at me, she thought, knowing that she couldn't stand that pain in his eyes. The thought twisted through her, burrowing deep into the pit of her stomach.

"No promises," he replied without taking his eyes off the mask hiding Isalie's face, "though I hope Iz, at least, can stay out of the worst of it. I would be an idiot if I asked how you're feeling," he said to Isalie, "so I'll just say I love you, and I will thank the Elders every moment for the rest of my life that you came back."

"If you could both refrain from being taken by the Ambient again, I might be able to breathe," Celeste huffed.

Isalie touched Jentien's shoulder, feeling a thick scar there, and a guttural growl ripped out of her throat, sending her into another coughing fit. She sucked in a breath, too angry to care that her vision blurred again. Had Mistress Kiyash done this?

Jentien stared at her, his mouth a thin line and his eyes welling with tears. "I'm fine, Iz, please don't worry about me. Not when you..."

Don't say it, she wanted to say. She turned her face away. There would be no getting past what had happened to her, she knew, not when her skin would bear those marks for the rest of her life.

"You two are going to be the death of me," Celeste grumbled. "You both need to rest and heal, because we have a lot to do." She kissed their joined hands before pushing herself off the floor to pull Jen's cot closer. It took some effort, but together they got him onto it, close enough that he could hold Isalie's hand.

"Thank you," he said, gazing at Celeste with such adoration and gratitude that her determined façade broke. She turned her eyes toward the roof of the tent and inhaled a sharp breath. Then, she sat on the edge of Jen's cot and kissed him.

"I'm going to help Nel and Amal put some precautions in place to make sure no one else is blindsided by the rain. Then, I'm going to take a couple of people to my shop to gather the rest of my tools."

Isalie leaned forward, trying to protest, and Celeste moved to her cot. She placed a gentle hand on Isalie's chest to hold her in place, and flashed her confident, toothy smile that made Isalie's stomach flutter.

"Everyone here needs my help, Lee. I'll be careful, but I can't sit by and watch people suffer when I can do something to help." She narrowed her eyes at Isalie, and then at Jen. "It's something we all have in common."

CHAPTER SIXTY-NINE

CLEVER CELESTE WENT TO work even before she had all her materials. First, she outfitted everyone risking walking under the open sky with bags full of scraps—torn cloaks, masks, stones—to hurl into the open with strict instructions to watch for it to dissolve before they stepped foot outside. Second, she handed out what cloaks and masks she had left to the few souls assigned to retrieve the contents of her workshop and those that would watch for any incursion by the Ambient.

It took an entire day to move Cel's equipment from her shop. There were two more downpours of deadly rain, and Isalie heard many terms used to describe it: the ruin, the blight, even the end, but the word that most people moving through the tent used was the Fall. That word resonated with Isalie because it was the fall of rain, of death from the sky, but it also felt like the fall of any hope she'd harbored that the Ambient could be stopped.

When Cel had the tools that she needed and the materials Nel's people provided, she went to work. Isalie caught sight of her just outside the tent, bent over a table, instructing others in the manufacturing of salve. She glanced inside often, Isalie noticed, her eyes stopping on Jen and then herself, as if to assure herself that they were still there and still breathing.

The first batch of salve was divided among the worst of the patients—Jen and Isalie included—while Celeste moved deeper into the cavern to pulverize crystal to fill the sachets inside the masks.

Isalie didn't envy what the injured were going through. She knew firsthand how terrifying it was to feel the moisture pulled from her lungs. When the droplets mingled with her breath again, they burned like they had the first time, like drowning all over again.

She still wore her mask, though she'd felt a shift in her breathing in the past few hours. Without the mask, it had been like knives stabbing her chest every time she drew breath. With the mask, the pain was less. Now, the stabbing was more of a dull throb, and though she still couldn't draw a full breath as she had before that cell, it didn't reduce her to spasms when she tried.

She couldn't bring herself to remove the mask, even though there were others that needed it, and even though she yearned to see Jen and Celeste without the distortion of the crystal lenses. She knew that once the hood was off, people would be able to see her face. They'd see the monster that the Ambient had made her. She didn't want to see it herself.

So, she stayed on the cot, inside her mask, hiding from the truth for as long as possible. When Celeste wandered over, her eyes sunken and her shoulders slumped in exhaustion, Isalie refused her offer to help bathe and apply more salve.

Celeste's brow furrowed. "We need to take care of those wounds, Lee."

Isalie shook her head again and looked past Celeste to Maretha. Lifting a bandaged arm, she shook the rattle Maretha had given her, drawing Jen's attention as well. Maretha rushed over, wiping her hands on a cloth.

"What do you need, Isalie?"

Isalie mimed scrubbing a hand over her skin, and Maretha nodded. But she paused when she noticed Celeste's frown.

"Is something wrong?" Maretha asked.

"We need to clean and dress Isalie's wounds again," Celeste replied. "I offered to do it, but–" Isalie shook her head again, cutting Celeste off. "She doesn't want my help."

Maretha peered at Isalie, who willed her to understand that she couldn't have Celeste and Jentien see her as Maretha had.

"I can help her," Maretha offered.

"You have other people to tend to," Celeste insisted. She turned back to Isalie. "Why don't you want my help?"

Isalie couldn't tell her that she didn't want Celeste to look at her the way she looked at all the other victims. She couldn't say that she hated herself for causing the anguish she saw on Cel and Jen's faces every time they looked at her skin.

Celeste stared at her, and to Isalie's surprise, Jentien interjected.

"Iz, I carried you from that cave, and Celeste and I peeled your clothes off. We cleaned your wounds and dressed them; we got you into that tank. We see the marks on your skin, but we see *you* beneath them. We love you, and there is nothing that could change that. There is *nothing* that could make you any less beautiful."

Isalie hesitated, trying to draw courage from his words. When she finally nodded, Maretha walked away, leaving the three of them staring at each other. Celeste dropped onto the cot.

"When you're ready, Lee," she said.

Isalie nodded again, and Celeste reached forward to grasp the mask. It wasn't as painful this time when it peeled away, but Isalie sucked in a deep breath in fearful anticipation. It caught in her throat, and she suppressed a cough for as long as she could before it tore through her throat and lungs.

She doubled over into Jen and Celeste's arms.

"We've got you," Jentien murmured.

"Easy now, Lee," Celeste said.

Their voices and their steady presence calmed her racing heart, and she managed to take a breath through her nose. The cough stopped, leaving a coppery tang in her mouth as she sat up. Jentien used his sleeve to wipe her mouth, leaving a bright red streak behind. She expected to see tears, frowns, or pitied horror. But the only thing she found in each of them was the love she'd always seen.

Isalie cleared her throat. "M…" The word she needed was like a stone in her throat, and she cleared it again. "Mirr?"

"A mirror?" Celeste asked. Isalie nodded, and the frown she'd expected turned down the corners of Cel's mouth. "Lee… I don't know if I have one." Her eyes darted to Jentien in a silent plea for help.

Isalie narrowed her eyes. "Mirror," she croaked. Her resolve wavered when they exchanged another glance, but Celeste rummaged through her huge leather bag. After extricating a hand mirror from within, she gently placed the mirror in Isalie's palm. The livid streaks on it had faded, she noticed, already the pale pink of scar tissue. She took a shallow, deliberate breath—all she could manage without coughing—and held the mirror in front of her face.

There's hardly any skin left, Isalie thought. The right side of her face looked like it'd been skinned, and the red blotchy mess that was left ran from her scalp to her collarbone and down her arm. The hair on that side was gone, and what was left on the rest of her head was matted and stained with salve and blood.

They even took my eyebrow. The ridiculous thought consumed her, and her stare fixed on the place where her brow should have been. She snorted, suppressing an anxious laugh. *They could have at least taken both, instead of leaving my face even more lopsided.*

Isalie let the hand with the mirror drop into her lap. Her other hand rose to her chest to feel the rise and fall of it. She looked up at Celeste, raised her one remaining brow in question, and tapped her hand to her chest.

"Cough?" she wheezed.

"I hope it will go away soon, if you keep the mask on. Faster, if we could keep you in the tank for a while."

Isalie shook her head. She didn't want to go back in there. It was too much like her cell, and she couldn't stomach one more moment confined like that.

She didn't think she'd survive it.

CHAPTER SEVENTY

THE FIRST DEATH HAPPENED in the middle of the night, when the cavern was quiet enough for the man's rattling coughs to echo beyond the confines of the tent. He'd breathed too much mist in, and there was nothing anyone could do to drain the blood from his lungs fast enough. Two hours later, a woman rescued by Nel outside the entrance to the Undercity stopped breathing. It was more peaceful than the first, and more horrifying for the fact that no one had seen her slowly worsening in the commotion from the first death.

Isalie had watched Nel's face slowly drain of color when they'd come to check on the woman, and watched their friends drag them out of the hospital when they started hurling profanities at the top of their lungs. Their screams slowly diminished as they were pulled out of the central chamber altogether.

Isalie couldn't lie still in the silence that followed. She sat up with a fresh mask covering her face and swung her legs over the edge of the cot. Bandages covered her wounds from head to toe, with a soft robe over everything.

"Are you all right, Iz?" Jen asked. He rolled onto his side to face her with a wince.

She nodded and pointed to her pillow, shaking her head.

"I couldn't sleep much either." His mouth twisted into an angry frown. He'd taken the deaths almost as hard as Nel. "I'm glad you're strong enough to sit up."

Isalie nodded and glanced at the chamber. The blood had been washed clean, but Isalie shuddered, remembering the splatters that had been there when the first man died.

It could have been me, she thought. *It should have. Why did* I *survive?*

She'd sat in the rain for days and had nearly drowned in the runoff. No one survived what she had. She looked around the space, her vision distorted by the crystalline lenses, and wondered how many more of these people would die because of the Ambient.

Isalie scooted to the edge of the cot and gently peeled the mask off. The air didn't hurt as much as it had even hours ago, and she took another careful breath. She couldn't afford to succumb to coughing fits every time she inhaled, and if she was going to keep drawing breath when others wouldn't, she'd make sure every breath counted.

"Iz?" Jen asked. "What is it?"

He sat up, too, and placed his feet on the floor next to hers, nudging her knee with his. Isalie didn't reply and looked around the tent at the injured. She took note of every wound, every ragged breath so much like her own, and the fire she'd thought doused roared back to life in her chest.

When she rose, she didn't waver, though it took every ounce of strength to stay upright. She needed to talk to Amal and Nel, to tell them about the towers so that they could act. She couldn't just lie here while more people died, when she could do something to stop the killing.

Jentien grasped her hand before she could move, and when she looked down at him, he read the thoughts on her face. He didn't protest when she took one halting step away from him, only rose and followed.

She'd seen that fire in his eyes, too. Together, she hoped they could set the Ambient's world ablaze.

Her fingers were black with charcoal when she leaned back in Amal's dining room chair, waiting while Amal read her words aloud for everyone. Most of the council were huddled around his bony shoulders, but Arru hadn't moved or taken her eyes off Isalie.

"Kiyash is channeling the Ambience through the crystal spires to manipulate the storm," Amal read. He continued, ignoring the gasps of the other Olugar. "She doesn't have permission to draw enough power to stop the Gloom, but she has enough to ensure that the Inners are untouched and to make the rain worse." He looked up with his eyes narrowed. "Permission from whom?"

"It doesn't matter," Nel growled. "If she's using the towers to redirect the storm, we know what we need to do to stop her."

"Do we?" another Olugar asked. "We don't know how to stop what she's doing, let alone what the repercussions would be. Do we truly want to destroy the only place in the city that has any relief from the rain? If we do anything, we should take the Inners for ourselves."

"We destroy the spires," Nel said. "She can't control the storm if she can't use them."

"She can't control the storm if she's dead," Jen said. His voice was low and deadly in the rage that simmered beneath the surface, and the room fell quiet. Nel nodded, other members started speaking in low, urgent voices to each other, and Arru continued to stare at Isalie.

Celeste pushed away from the wall she'd been leaning against. "It's possible we could destroy the towers, but they might be the only thing keeping the Gloom at bay, with or without Kiyash channeling power through them. Arru, can you tell us a bit more?"

"A bit," Arru said. Everyone in the room looked at her, but she continued to gaze at Isalie. Not her marred skin, but into her eyes. "The towers are natural Conduits for the Ambience. Coupled with an active flow of power, they will repel the Gloom. The walls around Lacorsia are a perfect example. They keep the Gloom surrounding the Spirit Mountain from spreading into the capital because the Malachi reinforces them with power that is channeled through spires across Vortheim."

"Could the Malachi be the one supplying power to Kiyash?" Amal asked.

Arru nodded. "Yes, and it would make sense for her to be wary about drawing too much from them. I must point out that not all the crystal requires Ambience to be effective; it has its own Ambience in a way that we don't understand. The roofs in the Outers aren't powered, but they still resist the rain without being destroyed. The network of crystal beneath the city is vast, and the towers above ground are an extension of it. It's possible that they could maintain the protection we have *without* Kiyash empowering them, but only if we leave them intact."

"Which leaves us with no option but the assassination of Kiyash and the Ambient," Nel insisted.

"How do we get through the rain?" Amal looked around at the hesitant frowns of his fellow councilors. "Now that we know there is only one way forward, how will we succeed?"

"I can take down the gates," Celeste said. "I can get us through, but it will take time."

"What about the guards stationed in there?" Jentien asked. "We don't need many to overwhelm them, but the same applies to them. We can do it, but it'll cost lives."

"My miners have been working to expand the tunnels," Nel offered. "Leave it to me."

"Good," Amal said. "What of our people? Do we have anyone that could hold out against the Ambient Guard?"

Jentien nodded at Nel. "Cortlen has been training everyone willing to fight. It's a small group, and, assuming we can break through to the Inners, we'd be overwhelmed quickly. I think the only chance we have is to talk to the Guard and convince as many to join us as we can."

"That's risky," Nel interjected. "I doubt they'd go against the Ambient now that they've altered the rain."

"It might just be the catalyst we needed," Jentien said. "Some of the people caught out there were guards, and they just saw that the Ambient are willing to sacrifice them to get to us. I think it'll give them the push they need."

More plans were offered, some discarded while others were discussed in depth, and Isalie sat at the edge of it all again. Arru sidled around the group to Isalie's side and placed a tentative hand on her arm.

"I am so thankful to see you up and about," she said. "I worried that you might not recover."

"Thank you," Isalie rasped. Her throat tightened around the words.

"You brought my daughter back to me," Arru said. "I thought she was lost, and then there she was, bloodied and battered, but alive. When she told me all that had been done to her, it almost killed me. I thought I'd been angry before." She scoffed. "I had no idea what anger was."

Isalie nodded. That feeling had pushed her to ask for this meeting, after all.

"There are people who want to thank you for the lives that you gave back to them. I know you've been recovering, and will need more time yet, but I wonder whether you might consent to meeting some of them?"

Isalie hesitated. After the glimpse she'd seen of herself, she didn't know if she could handle whatever reaction might await her from even more people. The pitying smiles the Olugar were giving her were enough.

Arru pushed ahead. "You got out. You know better than any of *them*," she gestured to the room behind her, "what's happening behind the Ambient's doors. I think it's time that more people knew. I think it's time that we shake the Stills of Olunei awake."

Isalie envisioned a crowd assembled to gawk at her with her face on display. For the people that lived with such a weight on their shoulders that they couldn't lift their heads to see the world for what it was. Nor the oppressive hands holding them down.

She nodded, and Arru smiled at her.

"I'll tell Yesrien first," she assured Isalie. "She's already working to rally them, but she isn't the one who freed our people. That was you, Isalie."

Tears filled Isalie's eyes as she watched Arru walk away. It took a few moments for the other voices in the room to filter back in.

"Nel, you oversee the tunneling, and keep a fighting force with you," Amal said. He was standing with his arms braced on the dining table with a crude map laid out for everyone to see. Nel pointed to a spot next to a long, straight line stretching across a river; the demarcation between the Inners and the Outers. "Hopefully, the miners can make quick work of it, if we're as close as you think we are."

"Cortlen and I will put out the call for training," Jentien added. "We can go through some basics, and hope that we have enough numbers on our side to avoid confrontation with some of the Guard."

"Isalie and I will speak to the people," Arru said. Everyone turned to peer at Isalie, who wanted nothing more than to fade into obscurity again. "We'll get you the numbers."

Jentien peered at her, ready to object if Isalie made the slightest sign that she wanted him to. Celeste nodded at her, and Isalie felt a surge of confidence.

Isalie suppressed a cough before it could explode from her throat. "Everyone needs to know."

CHAPTER SEVENTY-ONE

I can do this.

Isalie stared out at the faces assembled near the medical tent casting furtive glances her way. She couldn't blame the wide eyes and gaping mouths. They didn't do anything to help the anxiety gnawing at her gut, but she sat with her back straight atop the chair Nel had carried from Amal's house.

The council was here, too. It seemed everyone in the Undercity had come when Arru called for a meeting. Yesrien stood at her side, tall and imposing in a way that reminded Isalie of Mistress Kiyash. She shuddered when Yesrien turned that intense stare her way.

"I'm sure you know by now that the Ambient have abandoned their pretense of benevolence toward the Stills," Arru said. Her voice boomed over the crowd. "They tampered with the storm to unleash something far more deadly. It's as good as declaring war."

Arru waved her hand toward the tent behind them, the perfect backdrop for the message she hoped to spread. "Even now our people, including a few Ambient Guard, cling to life. Victims of Ambient cruelty, of their malicious power, of the rain that can eat through everything but the protection that our own Celeste Zynse has provided to so many of us over these long years of oppression."

The people standing close to Celeste reached out to touch her arm or shoulder in silent thanks.

"We have allowed this treatment for too long. Our numbers have always far surpassed theirs, and yet we let the Ambient take our city when the Gloom rolled in. We allowed them to set conditions for their 'help,' and abandoned our homes in the Inners to live under constant threat from the rain that they pushed our way! While they lived in comfort and safety, we struggled to breathe!"

A collective gasp rippled through the gathering. Isalie watched their faces contort into anger, confusion, and doubt.

"They can't control the Gloom!" someone shouted.

"Then how do you explain the rain?" another retorted.

"If they wanted to kill us, why not just do it?" A few people repeated this sentiment, along with a cacophony of rebuttals.

Yesrien stepped forward and whistled to get everyone's attention. "Because we're no better than cattle! We clean and we care for them, and when one of us outlives our usefulness, we're thrown in crystal cells so that they can experiment on our bodies! I spent *months* suffering, breathing in poison mist to prove how fast a person's lungs would give out when exposed to the rain for twenty minutes a day. And then an hour, and then two hours. Every time I thought I'd *finally* die they healed me and stuck me back in that cell."

Yesrien's chest heaved and her face flushed as she glared at the crowd, as if daring them to argue with her assertion. No one did.

"The only reason I'm here, the only reason so many of us are here, is because one woman defied them."

She pointed at Isalie, who forced herself not to shrink away from the renewed attention of the crowd. A breath shuddered in her chest, threatening to bring a cough with it. She held her breath to stop both.

Thankfully, Yesrien spoke again, pulling the attention back to herself. "If *one* woman can do that, imagine what *all* of us could do if we stopped hiding. Imagine all that we could achieve if we stepped out of the storm and into the light!"

Yesrien turned her back on the crowd. When she peered at Isalie, there were tears in her eyes and gratitude on her face. She crouched in front of Isalie's chair and took Isalie's hands in her own.

"Thank you," she said, but this wasn't for show. This was a quiet statement just for her savior. "I can never repay what you've done for me."

"No," Isalie croaked, overwhelmed by the grief on this powerful woman's shoulders. "You don't need to thank me."

People were moving forward through the crowd with Maretha in the lead. Scarred and battered people, surrounded by their loved ones in a procession that ended behind Yesrien. One by one, each of those families moved to the front of the line to offer their heartfelt thanks, all while Isalie fought to stay upright under the weight of their gratitude.

Isalie tried to focus on the faces in front of her, to mutter a response to each person that grasped her hand, but she kept glancing at Arru's satisfied grin. Her own satisfaction that she could finally be of use, even as an attraction to be gawked at, helped her keep her composure when the last of the families moved away to stand near the front of the crowd as a centerpiece to Arru's call to arms.

"Your friends and neighbors, your families, your *children*," Isalie struggled to put more power behind her words, "shouldn't have to live like this. No one deserves to be treated this way." It didn't matter that her voice was strained and quiet; the entire gathering had gone silent, and her words carried. "The only way that we stop it, the only way that we are *ever* going to find justice for the atrocities visited upon the Stills of Olunei, is to fight!"

Her voice echoed throughout the Undercity in the silence that followed. And then, one of the people she'd rescued stepped forward.

"I'll fight," she said. She looked at Isalie through one milky, scarred eye and one grey eye, and nodded.

"I'll fight," a man in the front of the crowd called out, stepping forward to join the woman.

Jentien stepped forward, with Cortlen close behind. "I'll fight," each said. Tsunal and Kiale joined them with the rest of their squad on their heels. Nel joined them, and their faction members filed out of the crowd to stand at their side.

More and more stepped up, until 'fight' rang through the air in a steady chant. The thunderous call echoed through the cavern and beat in time with Isalie's heart. She stood as well, knowing that she would do whatever it took to see this through, even if that meant marching into the heart of the Inners and facing Mistress Kiyash again.

The time of the Ambient was over.

CHAPTER SEVENTY-TWO

IT TOOK TWO DAYS to organize volunteers to train with Jentien and the other guards. Every time he closed his eyes, he saw Isalie's discomfort at being a prop for the Olugar's uprising. The self-conscious embarrassment had been written on her face until it became the grim resignation that she'd worn since. He hated that Isalie was a mascot for their rebellion, but Isalie embraced the role, and the blaze that she'd ignited in him had spread like wildfire among the Stills.

"Golden child, are you with us?" Cortlen asked with a slap on Jentien's shoulder.

Jentien nodded, but he didn't take his eyes off the far side of the cavern. "I'm here," he said.

"We have a lot of work ahead of us, so let's get started."

"Sure, Cort," Jentien replied. He finally looked at his friend.

The older man gazed at him for a moment longer, then wrapped his arm around Jentien's shoulders. "Don't worry, with us teaching them, these people will be ready to march in no time."

Jentien cast a skeptical glance at the collection of people who'd never held a weapon before, most of whom were emaciated from lack of proper nutrition, and nodded slowly. "It's not them I'm worried about."

Cortlen stopped at the front of the group and glanced back toward the tunnel that led to the main cavern. "Isalie is going to be fine, Jentien. Maretha is with her, and I don't know that I've ever seen someone with such resolve in my life."

Jentien took a deep breath and quirked the corner of his mouth in a reluctant smile. "You're right, Cort. She'll be fine."

Cortlen slapped his shoulder, making Jentien wince.

"Sorry," the man muttered. "Are you ready to get these people into shape?"

Jentien nodded again, crossed his arms behind his back, ignoring the stretching scabs, and straightened. He stared at the group, waiting for them to notice him, casting a disapproving frown until the cave fell silent.

"When I am in front of you, facing you, you will be silent," Jentien said. His voice was low, but it carried. "We're fighting to take back your home. I expect discipline, or we've failed already."

The recruits straightened to match his posture, and their eyes filled with purpose. Jentien nodded at them, flashing a small smile of approval.

"Let's begin."

Celeste looked over the tables filled with glass vials and crystals, at the small group she'd assembled to help her grind the volatile substance, and smiled. The first day she'd lectured them about the importance of precision and focus, and then demonstrated the technique several times. She'd had concerns about delegating this delicate process to anyone else, but she'd chosen well. There hadn't been any accidents so far, thank the Elders.

She had to admit that she would never be able to produce so many vials of the combustible granules if she'd been working alone. With miners working day and night to gather more, she would have worn out her arm before she got through enough to make a difference.

Amal wandered toward her, watching over the shoulders of her masked helpers as they slowly and carefully ground the crystal with their stone pestles.

"Not too close, Amal," Celeste called to him from her head table. She stepped back and pulled her mask up to rest atop her unruly locs. "You don't want to breathe that in."

"I wanted to see what you've created," he said.

Celeste peered at the array of vials small enough to fit in the palm of her hand. "Impact charges. We'll attach these to spears and arrows. The finer granules are volatile; when they impact..." She mimed an explosion with her hands and grinned at Amal.

"That's terrifying," he whistled. "They won't explode on their own, will they?"

Celeste grimaced. "If they're jostled too much, maybe. Jen and Cortlen have spears and arrows with similar weights attached for training, but I told them whomever they decide to give the explosives to *must* be careful." She grinned. "I wouldn't give one to Nel."

Amal chuckled. "No, careful is not one of their personality traits. We can use these to break into the Ambient District?"

"Yes, with a few detonations. With any luck, *Mistress* Kiyash will be nearby when they go off."

"Hmm," Amal said. "And if we can't get to her? She could hide inside her spire."

Celeste's grin hardened. "Then I'll reduce it to rubble around her."

Amal put his hand on her shoulder, and her expression softened before he left her to her work. She watched him saunter away, past a cookfire where Maretha and Isalie were preparing meals for the volunteers. The smell of roasted meat filled the air, making her stomach grumble.

Celeste turned her thoughts to the spire, and how she could improve the explosive power of the crystal on such a large scale. Amal was right; they needed a plan to destroy the Ambient if they holed up in their crystal spire. She watched the flames dance in the fire pit, and a log collapsed on itself.

She looked out at the tables again, at the rows of vials, and the lanterns set at the corner of each. One on the nearest table was too close to the lantern, and she rushed forward to carefully lift the vial with a gloved hand as it began to glow. The masked woman looked up from her work, and then at the vial Celeste had moved, and her body went still.

"Even the lowest heat will eventually cause your vials to explode," she called out. "Keep the crystal away from your lanterns, please!"

Her helpers nodded and murmured their understanding, then slid their vials as far from their lanterns as they could. Celeste placed the cooling vial back on the table she'd taken it from, and walked around, offering suggestions on where to improve before she took her seat again.

She glanced at the fire again, at the glowing embers beneath the flames, and then at a large flask on her table. An idea struck, and she smiled as she pulled a piece of parchment and a charcoal pencil out of her bag to work through its execution.

It needed to be precise; to estimate the time it would take for a controlled heat release to ignite the crystal from inside the flasks to create an explosion. But, if she got it right, the Kiyash spire would fall.

⁂

Isalie smiled as she handed a plate to one of the new recruits, with flat bread coated in a tangy sauce, vegetables, and meat topping that she and Maretha had made. The only time her mind had calmed in the past two days had been when she was cooking, and she was thankful that there was something tangible that she could do to help the cause.

The rest of her time she'd followed Amal and Arru into the Outers to showcase the cruelty of the Ambient and drum up more support. Despite relishing the transformation from confusion to indignation or rage she was witnessing on so many faces, she couldn't stand the gasps of horror when she removed her mask, so she planned her next meal in her head while she kept her face blank. Or, she pictured the look on Mistress Kiyash's face when she finally saw what Isalie had inspired in these people.

People still stared a bit too long when they accepted their meals from her, but she could just turn away to prepare another plate and ignore it. She couldn't stand for too long, still, and the walk from the Undercity to the Outers was enough to induce coughing fits and painful gasps, but her strength was increasing every day. She wished Jen or Cel could accompany her on these trips, but they had important jobs to do. And Isalie wasn't sure that including Jen was the best idea, since he'd adopted a scowl whenever she was used as a spectacle.

Cooking, however, was something that she could do. It brought her joy to find creative uses for the dwindling supplies they had down here, reminding her of the days she and Jen had spent wandering Vortheim. She hadn't known there would ever be a time that she would miss endless hikes and perpetual danger, but, after all that she'd been through here, she would give almost anything to be alone in the countryside with him again.

Isalie looked up, spotting Celeste hunched over her table with a pencil in her hand, and smiled to herself. There was one thing she *couldn't* give up.

Would she come with us if we could escape this place? Isalie wondered. *What would it be like, the three of us out in the world?*

Isalie shook the thought aside; there would be no escape, even if—no, *when*—the Ambient weren't in control of Olunei.

"I can't believe this is going to happen," Maretha said, hands on her hips as the last of the recruits wandered off to eat. "I've lived in the shadow of the Ambient my whole life, and I never stopped to wonder if it was right."

"I spent a lot of time thinking about it," Isalie said, "and it brought me a lot of grief."

"I can imagine," Maretha replied. "It's sad to think about everyone back home, knowing that if they only stood up for themselves, they might not need to live like paupers."

"Where are you from?" Isalie asked.

"A small city in the southeast called Atheis, in the middle of nowhere. Known for its artifice, but little else. I've known inventors like Celeste, geniuses who push the boundaries of the imagination to bring safety, joy, and comfort to people like us."

She snorted. "Or they *would,* if the Ambient didn't co-opt their inventions for themselves. All intellectual property is subject to Ambient approval and ownership." Her mouth twisted in a bitter frown. "My brother protested once, wanting to keep his invention for the Stills. The Ambient took it anyway, and my brother was thrown in prison for a year."

"That's terrible," Isalie whispered.

Maretha nodded. "He wouldn't talk about what happened, but he was never the same."

Isalie wondered whether her parents dealt with anything like that. They were paid well, offered status that most Stills couldn't dream of, but most of their products went to the Ambient and their guards. Were they only allowed to provide Jentien with his armor because he was a Sentinel? What would their life have looked like if they hadn't agreed to the terms the Ambient set?

In the capital, Isalie imagined any resistance to Ambient rule would be put down as swiftly as it began. And if it gained any traction, if it progressed to what it was in Olunei, there were so many Ambient that they could level the districts the Stills were relegated to.

Why hasn't Kiyash done that to us? Isalie wondered. She certainly had the power to destroy everything, so why was she bothering to change the rain?

"If something like this happened in Lacorsia," Isalie said, "the Stills would be slaughtered."

"That might happen here," Maretha pointed out.

Isalie nodded. "It might."

Maretha looked toward the back of the cavern where Jen and Cortlen had taken their recruits this morning. Isalie followed her gaze, wishing Jen would appear to wrap his arms around her and hold her tight. Every time he left, she had to fight the clawing panic in her chest as she wondered whether he'd come back. It was worse than her fear of tunnels, worse than the fear she'd experienced in the cell.

She glanced at Celeste, grateful that the woman she loved was here, at least, where Isalie could keep an eye on her.

Maretha sighed. "All we can do is see this through," she said.

Isalie didn't respond; she just watched Celeste scribble furiously, and said a silent prayer to the Elders to help them survive this.

CHAPTER SEVENTY-THREE

Isalie stood stiffly in the tunnel leading to the Inners, just past the second portcullis, grateful for the mask that hid her face from everyone surrounding her. One week in the Undercity. That was all she'd taken to recover from her injuries, because they couldn't afford to wait any longer. One week, because the dreary day dawning somewhere above her head was the day that they would attack.

The barricade they'd erected against the tunnel to the Inners had partially disintegrated in the stronger rain, letting the Ambient Guard push through after three days. Cortlen and Jentien's archers, armed with a mixture of normal and crystal arrows and a couple impact charges, had kept the Guard at the mouth of the tunnel. A short time later the Fall began again, and had been coming at irregular intervals since.

Jentien and Cortlen, along with the other Ambient Guard defectors, had split the most promising recruits into teams poised to surge into the Inners. Their first task was to recruit more of the Guard to their cause after they made it through the tunnel.

Celeste pulled a vial of powdered crystal smaller than her palm and glanced back at the bulk of the Stills' forces, winking at Isalie. Beside her, Jentien stood with a thick section of Amalricus's front door, cut into a thick tower shield to protect them from the blasts necessary to break through the barriers in the tunnel.

"Brace!" She waited a moment for confirmation that they were ready. Isalie turned away from the bright flash that would follow and covered her ears.

The explosion rocked the tunnel before the iron portcullis clanged to the stone floor. Isalie turned back to see Jentien and Celeste moving forward, Jentien always just in front, waiting for an attack from the guards they'd seen retreating toward the Inners. Isalie stepped over the fallen portcullis a short time later with Cortlen at her side, a similarly repurposed door strapped to his arm to protect Isalie and the others.

An arrow thunked into Jentien's shield, and Cortlen brought his forward just in time to deflect another. The guards were putting up a fight, but it wasn't enough to keep the Stills from moving forward.

"Why aren't the Ambient here?" Isalie wondered aloud. "They could stop us with a wave of their hand, or collapse the tunnel and kill us all."

Cortlen snorted. "They probably think the Guard will stop us, and don't need to get their hands dirty. Have you ever known the Ambient to take Stills seriously?"

"I think the explosions are pretty serious," Isalie muttered.

"Brace!" Celeste called from farther down the tunnel. Isalie ducked behind Cortlen's shield and covered her ears again.

Another explosion shook the tunnel, sending loose pebbles onto their heads. Isalie cast a wary glance at the ceiling, hoping Celeste was right, that the whole thing wouldn't come crashing down on them.

Jentien shouted just as a arrows rained down, and Cortlen angled his shield to catch as many as he could. Someone behind her screamed in pain. Too many arrows were finding their mark in Cortlen's shield, and she imagined Jentien's as well.

"There's too many!" Celeste shouted. "We can't move forward!"

Isalie peeked around the shield just as Celeste threw another vial, but Cortlen pulled her back before the flash.

"Down!" he yelled.

"We have to get to them!" Isalie insisted. "Jen's back—"

"Stay close!" Cortlen demanded. He lifted the shield just enough to push forward a step, then let it slam onto the tunnel floor.

Isalie waddled forward to stay behind the wood, watching more arrows fly past and skitter on the ground. Cortlen lifted the shield again, grunting as he shoved forward.

"Cort, stay back!" Jentien called.

It was a slow process, but step by step, Cortlen moved them forward until his and Jen's shields formed a wider wall. Celeste clutched Isalie's arm, the bulky leather satchels and bandolier of smaller vials strapped across her chest making the movement awkward. Their fighters had spears with impact charges affixed, but no one else had the huge shields Jen and Cortlen had. They'd be torn apart if they tried to get any closer.

Jentien grunted as another volley hit his shield. "Well, you're here, Cort, what now?"

Cortlen chuckled through gritted teeth. "I was hoping you'd have an idea, golden child."

A loud crack preceded the guards shouting and Nel's wild laugh.

"Need some help?"

Isalie and Celeste shared a look, then peeked out from behind the shields. Nel was on the other side of the nearest portcullis, slamming a club down on a guard's head. Another body stepped out of the hold just wide enough for one person to step through, onto the stone slab pinning another guard to the ground by their leg. The pinned guard screamed, and another person stepped out. A short, bloody battle ensued, white Jentien and Cortlen surging forward with their swords to stab through the portcullis at the guards pinned against it.

More guards were fleeing, trying to reach the next portcullis and close it, but Nel pulled a spear from someone still in the tunnel, the crystal dust attached to the tip glittering in the light from the Ambient orb.

Nel hurled the spear with enough of an arc to slam down at the feet of the last guard in the line, sending them and the two nearest them flying forward. Jentien called for their archers to move up, joining them while Nel's team surged forward, using another spear to keep the guards away from the portcullis lever.

The rest of the guards scattered, far enough that the Stills' arrows found their marks in the straggler's legs, but the leaders made it to the second to last portcullis and slammed the lever down to block their retreat.

Nel jogged back to them, panting with a wide smile on their face. "Celeste," they said, "I have a few more gates for you to take care of." They clapped Cortlen's shoulder and glanced toward Jentien at the far end of the tunnel with his archers.

Isalie, Cortlen, and Celeste moved forward, joining Jentien at the portcullis, finding the last two were down and the guards were gone. The ground rumbled beneath them, making Isalie gasp, thinking this was the moment the Ambient decided to collapse the tunnel and send them into the burning river below. But the rumbling stopped, and nothing had changed. Whatever they were doing, it was somewhere beyond the tunnel.

Cortlen ushered the archers back, getting his shield in place in front of Celeste so Jentien could join Isalie. Jentien pulled Isalie close and kissed her forehead before searching her for injuries.

"I'm fine," she insisted.

"You should go back," Jentien said.

"No. I've been away from you two for two long. If you and Cel are going in, I'm going too. I'll stay away from the fighting, but you need more people recruiting if we hope to stand a chance against the Ambient. I can do that."

"Brace!" Celeste yelled.

Jentien pulled Isalie close again, ducking with her behind his shield. This time when the blast came, Isalie wasn't afraid. She felt protected.

"Okay, Iz," Jentien murmured in her hair. "You tell everyone what's really happening here, and we'll get to the Ambient. Cort and I are taking our fighters to the Ambient District. We'll keep their attention on us, and Celeste will take her team to blow holes in their precious wall."

"And you send more fighters when she sends up the signal," Isalie finished. "Hit them from multiple sides."

Pride swelled in her chest right alongside the fear that kept her heart racing and her breaths quick and shallow. It had nothing to do with the damage her lungs had sustained, this was the shock of her body preparing for battle. This was the surge she'd felt when she ran from the Gloom beast, and the rush of facing off against Mistress Kiyash after she'd robbed the bitch of her test subjects.

She felt alive and powerful, even as her hands trembled with trepidation. The Ambient thought they'd made her a victim, but she was determined to be their downfall.

Celeste turned her face from the last gate as it exploded into the sunshine of the Inner City's main square and stepped aside to let the fighters through. Jentien touched her arm when he passed, and she longed to hold him back. She watched him rush into the open air, bracing herself for an attack to rain down on him.

He blinked in the bright light, his shield up as the rest of his group filed in around and made a wall of wood and metal. Celeste didn't take her eyes from him as he peered around the space beyond what she could see.

The seconds stretched on, and no attack came. The square was silent but for the stomp of feet on stone and the shifting of weapons and shields.

Jentien's eyes locked onto something or someone she couldn't see, and Celeste stepped out into the light. The Guard was waiting for them, but she saw that some of their resolve was shaken. They couldn't ignore the Ambient's oppression any more, not when the Stills continued to file out behind her.

Jentien's eyes darted around the square, from armored body to armored body of a wall of silent Ambient Guard. His ranks closed around him, and in those seconds, his eyes never stopped moving, trying to find the biggest threat, the weakest point, and the first place to strike.

There were no Ambient in the open, but that didn't mean they weren't there. Every street was barricaded by stone, as if the Ambient had pulled it from the ground and shaped it to fit between the buildings from base to roof, save for a small doorway in each. He locked eyes with his Commander Rallac, who took a step in front of his rank of guards on the top of the wall.

The Stills were trapped.

Rallac's voice called out. "If you do not disperse, we will use force to disperse you."

Jentien glanced around at the people with him, all unshaken by the threat. He nodded at Cortlen, and then stepped out from the shield wall, pleased to hear it close behind him. Cortlen, with his military background, had taken the more experienced of their fighting force and drilled day and night to provide this mobile defense.

"We no longer recognize the authority of the Ambient and their Guard," Jentien shouted. His voice carried over the square, and he noted the shifting feet and nervous glances cast toward his commander. "We're here to free the Stills from the oppression of the Ambient in Olunei."

"Go back to your homes," the commander bellowed. "You are an integral part of Olunei's survival, and we would take no pleasure in your removal from the Inner City."

"Ambient propaganda is not going to work," Jentien called back. "We're here to liberate *all* our people, not just the citizens of the Outer City. If you're tired of the leash the Ambient have on your lives, join us!"

The nervous glances continued, though many faces hardened after his last declaration. He opened his mouth to say something else, but the commander shouted before he could.

"You all know what's at stake if we do not hold the line here! Do not allow the disgruntled few to sway you from your purpose."

Eyes fell away from Jentien in a look he knew all too well. The guards who wouldn't meet his eye were the very people that had backed away from his probing questions about their willingness to side with the Olugar, because they had families here that they wouldn't risk.

Jentien glared at the commander. "How many families have you threatened to force these people to stand with you?" Jentien took a few steps forward, closer to the nearest guards at the southeastern end of the square. "How many of your families are in danger because of the threat that we represent to the Ambient?"

"By all means, please continue to stir up trouble," a drawling voice called out. Ambient Rotre appeared behind the commander, a billowing white shirt crisp beneath his violet tunic and matching pants. His raven hair floated on the breeze, and a lazy smile broke out on his face. "We Ambient have sheltered the few that we can from the looming storm, and *this* is how you repay us?"

Two other Ambient stepped atop the bulwark, minor Kiyash Tethers that Jentien hadn't interacted with. They sneered down their noses at the assembled crowd from the Outers.

"You haven't given us shelter, you've poisoned people with Prism!" Isalie called from behind Jentien. "This is the least that you deserve in repayment."

Jentien groaned inwardly, though he kept his features neutral. When he glanced over his shoulder, he found Isalie, Yesrien, and Celeste moving around the wall of shields until they were even with Jentien. He turned away to witness the horrified looks on the faces of the Stills.

"This is what they're doing to us," Isalie said. Her voice was low and tremulous, but it carried in the deafening quiet. She gestured to her scarred face.

"One duplicitous woman does not prove anything but their desperation," the Ambient countered. "For all we know, she could have done this to herself to persuade you to join their hopeless cause, after spending months here under false pretenses and threatening innocent people."

He stepped to the edge of the barrier, surveying the square below like a general atop the ramparts of a castle. He stepped off and landed easily ten feet below. The Guard made to follow, but he held his hand up, stopping them in their tracks.

He swaggered forward, and Jentien resisted the intense urge to hurl one of Celeste's spears into his chest. He smiled at Isalie as his eyes roamed her face, her neck, and her hands.

"Go back to your homes. This is your last chance to avoid punishment for your insurrection."

"Our lives *are* a punishment," Jentien argued. "The Ambient use us as experiments and toy with the Gloom to make it worse!"

Rotre took another step forward, his smile vanishing as Jentien continued, incensed by the casual dismissal and threat.

"They've knowingly separated families! Any one of you could have someone you love in the outer city, or below the Kiyash spire, suffering until their bodies give out, only to be healed so the process can start over!"

Rotre's face twisted in rage as he came to the center of the square, mere feet from Jentien. With the guard out of earshot and his face hidden, he all but spat at Jentien's feet in disgust.

"You will not leave here alive, Themori. Not you, and not your pathetic lover." He barely moved his head, but his wrathful glare fixed on Isalie. "This is your last chance to get the rest of these unfortunate people back to safety, or they *will* be consumed in the conflagration that I will unleash upon you. And then, I'll march into the Undercity and lay waste to the last haven the Olugar have."

Isalie sucked in an angry breath, and Rotre cast a smug look her way. "The people I *poisoned,*" he sneered the word, "are willing to do just about anything to get more, including telling me how to get to your hidden sanctuary."

"Mistress Kiyash–"

Rotre interrupted Isalie. "Eventually saw the merit in my endeavor." A small movement made Jentien glance downward to Rotre's hands as he clenched them. They bore the same scars as Isalie's face, as if they'd been dipped in rainwater. "Direct infusion of a substance with natural Ambient properties by the Still populace, to jump start their evolution, to help them adapt to the Gloom as the beasts have. Once I've dealt with this paltry insurrection, I have an entire wing of the prison ready for more subjects."

Jentien stood firm, grasping his sword when Isalie shifted. Rotre struck first.

The breath fled from Jentien's lungs, leaving him gaping like a fish out of water. The overseer merely smiled when Jentien fell to his knees and clutched his neck. He looked at Iz and Cel, their twin looks of horror, and the steel in Isalie's eyes before black spots marred his vision.

"This man would sow chaos where harmony is needed!" Rotre shouted, turning in a slow circle as he pointed at Jentien on the ground. His words became muffled through the roaring in Jentien's ears. "Again and again, he has chosen this path. Now, it falls to me to hold him accountable, to halt the vile poison he continues to spew–"

An arrow slammed into Rotre's leg, and another narrowly missed when Rotre waved his hand in its direction. A spear hurtled into one Ambient chest on the wall, the resulting explosion from the impact boring a hole in the woman's chest and sending the nearby guards flying. Cortlen roared, his spear arcing down toward Rotre, until another wave of his hand sent Cort flying.

Heat and pressure threw Jentien onto his back. He sucked in air as his throat opened, and when the roar died, he heard an agonized scream in its place that faded to a low hiss. Hands grasped him, touching his chest, his face, his head, and then Iz's voice drowned out the hissing noise.

"Jen, please, open your eyes. Tell me you're okay!"

He opened his eyes as she asked, not realizing he'd closed them, to find tears streaking down her cheeks. She dand Cel slumped over him in relief, muttering things he couldn't hear over his gasps.

The other Ambient was nowhere to be seen as the guards flung by the impact charge shakily regained their feet. Cortlen got to his feet and called to the Guard on the wall, his voice echoing.

"The Ambient are ruthless killers! They care only for their comfort and status, and we Stills have had *enough.* These people have reunited families, have fought for *your* freedom, and all they have to show for it are scars. Jentien Themori was your brother, and you all watched as the Ambient punished him. Isalie Wylshard saved Stills from being test subjects for the Ambient's experiments with the Gloom, brought us evidence of all that the Ambient have done, and you turned your backs on her!"

Celeste and Isalie helped Jentien sit up, and he stared wide-eyed at the pile of ash where Ambient Rotre had stood. He turned a questioning look to Celeste and the missing vial of crystal from her bandolier, and she gave a quick nod to Isalie.

Isalie didn't take her eyes off Jentien, her mouth set in a thin line that drained the blood from her lips. Her eyes were steely and full of conviction. They'd both killed Ambient now, and there was no turning back.

Cortlen gestured to the recruits in the square, and to the pile of ash. "The Ambient are few, and we are many. We have the tools to take them down, no matter their strength, no matter the Ambience that they wield against us. You," he pointed with his crystal spear tip to one guard, and another, and another, in a sweeping arc to encompass everyone assembled, "can either join us, get out of our way, or be destroyed along with them."

Isalie stood again, and all eyes turned her way. She said one quiet word, but it rumbled like thunder.

"Choose."

CHAPTER SEVENTY-FOUR

Isalie's echo faded. The only movement in the square was the slow trickle of ash blown by the gentle breeze. Then, the wall of bodies atop the wall shifted. One guard stepped away from the edge of the barricade and disappeared. As if that had been the signal the rest of them were waiting for, everyone on either side disappeared after them.

Isalie wondered what they'd chosen, if *any* of them had been moved by Jentien's words, or Cortlen's, or if she'd broken through the stranglehold of fear the Ambient had on everyone by hurling that vial at Rotre's smug face.

She was still trembling, she realized, as she stood tall and stared at Commander Rallac. The older man stared back at her, though his eyes darted to the tremor in her hands and his lips twitched.

Isalie wondered if he knew that this wasn't the tremor of a fear-stricken woman who'd suffered at the Ambients' hands. This was rage. Barely contained rage that had no target to be unleashed upon.

She dropped her gaze to the ashes as the wind picked up to scatter them. All that was left of the Ambient flew away, as if he'd never existed. She wished some piece of him remained, so that she might tear that piece apart with her bare hands.

Shouts rang out from behind the stone, and then the sound of impacts, the clash of blades, and more shouts. It went on for minutes—or hours, as Isalie waited with bated breath. She turned to see Cortlen and Celeste help Jen to his feet.

The rest of their forces assembled around them: Nel's people, every one of the recruits, and even Amal amid a horde of ordinary citizens. They formed a wall of Stills waiting with Isalie to see what became of this confrontation.

Silence fell, and then a doorway at the base of the barricade opened. A handful of guards filed out to stand in a loose cluster near the stone edifice. Another opened, and another, until each of the doors stood wide, and more guards than she'd seen atop the walls stood with sheathed weapons and their shields hanging loosely at their sides. Ionna and Wist started across the open space, leaving the rest behind them.

Isalie fell into step with Celeste and Yesrien, and the entire shield wall shifted forward behind them, reforming at a signal from Cortlen. The rest of their company remained at the far side of the square, hopefully far enough to avoid any altercation that might begin.

"Cort," Ionna said. Her face was blank, but there were tears in her eyes. "We thought you were dead."

Isalie scanned the guards behind her, taking note of the bruises, scrapes, and other minor wounds they'd sustained. She hoped this was a sign that they would fight for their freedom, too.

"I found my family, Ionna." Cortlen turned the corner of his mouth up in a rueful smile. "They were here the whole time; I looked for so long, and they were right here."

Ionna's mouth twitched, and she glanced over her shoulder. "The commander took about half of the guards to hold the Ambient District," she said. "I don't know how many of those will stay with him; most of us are shaken. Another quarter left, but the rest..." She shrugged. "The rest of us are with you. We believe you." Her eyes darted to Isalie's face, which grew hot under the redhead's scrutiny.

Cortlen smiled and strode forward to clasp Ionna's forearm. Jentien held his hand out to Wist, who clasped it and shook it once, smiling at Jentien before giving Isalie a nod.

When they pulled away, Ionna glanced between all of them. "Are we marching on the Ambient District, then?" she asked.

"Yes," Jentien said.

"They've fortified the walls," Wist said.

"We can get through," Jentien assured them.

"How?" Ionna said. She narrowed her eyes in suspicion.

Celeste touched her bags. "We have it covered."

"Tell us where you need us," Ionna said, exchanging a glance with Wist that Isalie couldn't read. "The Ambient have lorded over us for too long, and there are a lot of people here who want to know if their families were hidden from them. Like you, Cort." Her eyes softened when she looked at him, and when he turned his back to address his fighters, regret and longing colored her features.

When Jentien moved toward her, Isalie's eyes snapped to his face. He smiled at her, flooding her body with warmth.

"You saved me, Iz," he said, cupping her cheek in his rough hand. "Thank you."

"I won't let them take you from me again," she whispered. "You'd better come back to us."

"Elders willing," he replied. He brushed his lips over her forehead, then touched them to hers in a light kiss.

"*I* am willing it," she said. She stared at him, letting him see that she meant it. "If you don't come back, I'll find a way to follow you into whatever afterlife there is, and I will drag you out of it or die trying."

His eyes blazed with passion and love. It was the look he'd had the first time they'd made love, and she realized now that he hadn't *stopped* looking at her like this. Not after she'd come back from the dead, not once during her recovery. He wasn't looking at the scars. He was looking at her.

He leaned forward and kissed her, and he was so gentle that she couldn't stand it. She needed more, so she leaned in and grasped the back of his head to deepen the kiss.

Jen gasped against her mouth, and she smiled. "You *are* coming back," she whispered again.

"I'm coming back," he agreed, pressing his forehead to hers.

"I'm glad that's settled," Celeste interjected. Isalie pulled away enough to sling an arm around her shoulders, and Jen did the same. "I didn't know that it hadn't been, but I'm glad all the same."

Jentien kissed Celeste, too, and Isalie waited. Her heart was so full it felt like it might burst from her chest. When the two of them pulled away, Celeste turned to Isalie.

"You are going to stay safe, too, Lee." There were unshed tears in Cel's eyes as she gazed up at Isalie. "You're going to get these people to safety and stay there. Don't come looking for us, do *not* put yourself in danger. If anything happens to you, I will raze the city to the ground and let the Gloom have whatever is left."

"Believe me," Isalie sighed, "I know I'm no fighter. I won't put myself in any more danger than Amal or Yesrien."

"Good," Celeste said. She glanced around, and, finding her people waiting for her, she pulled away. "Take this." She shoved a vial into the pouch on Isalie's belt. "I need to get started. Jentien, watch for the flare, and when the Ambient forces are distracted, tear them down. Be careful, and I'll see you both when it's done."

Jentien pulled Isalie close, and they watched Celeste jog to the others covered in bandoliers and satchels. She spoke to them, her hands gesticulating, and the group separated to follow their designated fighters.

Jen sighed. "She'll be all right, too," he said with a squeeze of Isalie's shoulders. "The Ambient don't know the plan; there's no reason her group should encounter any resistance if we make enough noise."

"And you?" Isalie asked, only turning away once Celeste was blocked from sight. "The Guard that left will tell the Ambient you're coming. What's *your* plan?"

Jentien looked around the square at the ranks of Stills awaiting commands. "We'll stop in every barrack and dormitory we pass and gather as many as we can. And then..." He took a deep breath and cast his gaze to the tall spire at the center of the Inners. "We take the fight to the Ambient. There are so many of us that they'll have no choice but to surrender or die."

"Kiyash will fight to keep control over everything," Isalie said. "And she'll be looking to punish you."

"She can try," Jentien retorted, "but we'll swarm her spire like ants. She may squash some of us under her heel, but more will be right behind them."

"That doesn't give me confidence that you'll keep your promise," Isalie said.

He chuckled, but there was a hard edge to it, and kissed her again before pulling away, half-turned toward Cortlen. "I swear by the Elders, and on the love that I have for you and Celeste, that I *will* come back. Nothing can keep us apart, Iz."

Celeste gazed up at the clear blue sky, something she hadn't seen in decades. She dreamed of it sometimes, and the warmth of the sun above was more glorious than any dream or memory. She hoped it would remain when the Ambient were gone.

Armor-clad figures circled her and Ranois, the young man named she'd appointed as her second. They scouted around every corner, leading them along a circuitous route to the wall separating the Ambient District from the Inners. It felt like they'd been walking for too long, and every time they paused, she strained to hear any sound of battle from the gate. Their flanking attacks and explosive distractions would only work if they happened *before* the Ambient destroyed their forces.

The Inner City felt hushed, as if anticipating the coming change. Celeste craned her neck up to peer at the dormitory looming far above and wondered how many people were inside, and how many of those might join their cause.

They paused, waiting for confirmation that the next street was clear, then stepped into another alley that gave them a clear line of sight on the farthest corner of the wall. Beyond that corner, the wide river surged with runoff from the Gloom's storm before it was swallowed by the roiling black mass.

Another pause where the alley opened onto a wide thoroughfare at the base of the tower, and then the group rushed onto the lush lawn, past stone benches and fruit trees. She hadn't seen a park since she was a child; the parks in the Outers had all been consumed by the rain within a week of the Gloom rolling in.

They encountered no resistance. Maybe the Stills had been warned to stay inside, or maybe the Ambient had collected them in anticipation of the insurgence. Whatever the reason, Celeste was relieved to make it to the wall unscathed.

She crouched in the grass, ignoring the impulse to run her hands through it, and reached inside her satchel to remove one of the flasks. She nodded to Ranois, and he extracted a glass globe with extreme care from its leather padding. A long wick trailed from the neck of the flask, ready to be lit to maximize the explosive effects of the crystal.

"Set it a few feet from this one," she ordered. "Be careful. If you jostle it, the crystal will detonate."

He nodded, and several fighters followed him, taking positions with their backs to him to survey the city. Celeste placed the flask against the base of the wall with the wick against the ground. After making a small pile of tinder surrounding the wick, she pulled her flint and iron from her bag and struck them together until she made a spark.

The spark caught the tinder, and soon the wick was alight. The flame danced along the twine until it caught the coals inside and began to glow. She pulled Ranois' arm, seeing his flask glowing as well, and urged everyone away. It would take a few minutes for the flasks to prime, and they needed to be ready to move.

"Let's find somewhere to send up the flare," Celeste whispered. She couldn't bring herself to speak any louder. It felt like disturbing the hush over the city would bring the eyes of the Ambient down upon them.

CHAPTER SEVENTY-FIVE

Isalie followed Kiale into the dormitory she'd shared with Jentien. Stills huddled around the rows of dining tables in the center of the room. There were a few familiar faces—Elarna, Creno—but most were strangers, and all of them were terrified. Even the Ambient Guard scattered among them were afraid.

Kiale walked toward a group of guards at the front of the crowd, but they reached for swords, and the Stills huddled behind them cowered. Seeing this, Kiale halted in her tracks and held her hands out in front of her.

"We aren't here to hurt you," she said gently.

"The Ambient will know you've been here," someone called from the crowd. "If we don't stop you, we'll be punished, too."

"After today, they won't be able to do a thing," Kiale shouted.

"You can't stop them!" a woman cried. "They're too powerful!"

"We have weapons to use against them," Kiale said. "We have the numbers to overthrow them. We *will* take the city back and protect the Stills. If everyone joins us, maybe we can end this without bloodshed."

"I saw that woman turn an Ambient to ash," one of the guards called out, pointing at Isalie.

She stepped forward, ignoring the horrified gasps that followed. "I did, because he would have killed the man I love if I hadn't. If we don't end them, it's only a matter of time before all the Stills end up like me." She gestured to her face, locking eyes with Creno. "The Ambient have been experimenting on us. I rescued people from Mistress Kiyash, and she punished me for it."

The crowd grumbled. It started as an angry denial, but Isalie saw more faces filled with fear and doubt. Bolstered by this, she pushed ahead, her shout tearing at her throat.

"I survived! I fought back, and now, we're here to stop them. If we band together, there's nothing that can stop us!"

"What about the Guard?" Elarna called. "We can't fight our own."

"Then join us!" Kiale shouted. "Let them see that we stand together, and maybe that will be the push they need to abandon the Ambient!"

"But… the Ambient have kept us safe from the storm," a man in front called. He wore the uniform of the Kiyash house staff, the same colors Isalie had worn. "If we go against them, won't the storm just roll through the city?"

"What about the people suffering in the Outers?" Isalie retorted. "Mistress Kiyash has been toying with the Gloom to make the storm more deadly. Who's to say she won't turn that storm on the rest of the Inners next? If, Elders forbid, you make a mess of her laundry, what's to stop her from throwing *you* in the cell I was in? You would sit in the rain day in and day out, dying slowly until they piece you back together and start again!"

The man stared at her, taking in every visible injury in the silence that followed her words. Creno stepped forward, their eyes glistening as they looked at Isalie.

"My friend, I will join you. Anyone who would hurt someone like this should be punished."

Isalie clasped their hands with a grateful smile. "Thank you, Creno."

Kiale addressed the crowd again. "We have lost so much, and we can't sit by while the Ambient take even more. Please," she addressed the crowd, "follow our people to safety. If any of you can fight, come with me to the Ambient District. Help us stop the injustice. The time of the Ambient in Olunei is over."

⁙

Jentien lifted his shield to block another volley of arrows. His back and shoulders screamed in protest with every *thunk* against the wood. The moment the onslaught ended, he called out to his forces around him.

"Push forward!"

He dashed from the cover of the dormitory with his fighters behind him, keeping his shield high. As more arrows flew from the high windows in adjacent buildings, he didn't turn when he heard a cry before someone crashed to the ground. He couldn't take his focus from the arrow streaking toward him, and he tucked his head behind the shield he thrust up to catch it.

He ducked around the next corner, leaning against the warm stone wall, panting and wincing. The tension in his back muscles was worse with the shield. Jentien scanned the windows above him in the building across the street, and when he didn't find movement, he let the shield drop.

More of his people dashed around the same corner, out of the line of fire. They'd been making slow progress as they neared the gate to the Ambience District, hampered by loyalist guards after gathering too few sympathetic to their cause.

The loyalists didn't have the numbers to stop Jentien and his people, but they didn't need them. The buildings were natural choke points, so while the Stills tried to navigate the narrow passageways, arrows rained down upon them. A small host held the streets so the archers could pick them off at leisure. Even without the Ambient to back them up, the Guard could hold off the Still forces indefinitely.

"We need a new strategy, golden child," Cortlen panted when he slammed against the wall behind Jentien. "We won't get through this way."

"I know," Jentien grunted. "Cel needs more time."

An arrow slammed into the shoulder of another Still that careened around the corner, and she went down in a heap. Jentien leapt forward and grasped her arm, ignoring her shriek of protest to drag her out of the way. Cortlen and a few others blocked the pair with shields, and Jentien gritted his teeth as the woman's weight pulled on his marred back again.

"We can go in the buildings one by one and deal with the archers," Jentien suggested.

Cortlen grimaced and wiped a trail of sweat from his brow before it could drip into his eyes. "It will take time, but it might be the only way we move forward."

"Groups of six, go floor by floor," Jentien called to the growing host around him. "Pair off and search every room. I want at least five of you waiting on the ground floor in case anyone tries to run or reinforce the archers. Go!"

"I'll tell the other groups the plan," Cortlen said. He adjusted his shield and moved in front of Jentien to glance at the street beyond. Two arrows flew toward him, clattering on the cobblestones when he pulled his head back. "Wish me luck."

Jentien clasped his shoulder. "Elders watch over you, Cort. I'll try to keep them distracted down here."

"Don't do anything stupid," Cortlen said with a wink.

Cortlen disappeared, and Jentien hoisted his shield to follow.

Celeste shucked the heavy leather bags, placing them in the shade of the dormitory across the square from the section of Ambient District wall, and leaned forward as the crystal started to glow. *It's working,* she thought. *This is going to work.* She nodded to one of her archers, who pulled an arrow from their quiver. The head was wrapped in thin paper soaked in a crystal powder infusion. It would flash through the sky, telling Jentien it was time to send reinforcements.

She spotted the uniform of an Ambient Guard as the intense redhead from earlier stepped into the open square.

Celeste gritted her teeth. "Hey!" she hissed, hoping her low voice wouldn't carry too far. "Hey!"

The redhead squinted in Celeste's direction and jogged forward, glancing back and forth for anyone who might've seen them. She made it to the shadows Celeste was hiding in, and stood next to her, following Celeste's gaze toward the base of the wall.

"Shouldn't you be with one of the other teams?" Celeste asked. She cast a glance at the former guards defending her flank, who were peering at Ionna curiously.

The woman shook her head. "Is that glow what you're waiting for?"

Celeste nodded and glanced sidelong at the woman. She was chewing on her bottom lip with her brow furrowed, and her eyes darted toward the far end of the square. Her hands clenched into fists before she stretched her fingers wide. A fighter pulled flint and steel from a pocket and looked at Celeste for confirmation to light the arrow.

"Something wrong?" Celeste asked. The woman stilled and turned to face Celeste. The hair on Celeste's neck stood on end when she gave a brief smile that didn't reach her eyes.

"I never thought I'd see this day," the woman said. "The Ambient are powerful; most Stills wouldn't be stupid enough to go against them." She sighed. "I guess I'm nervous about being on the receiving end of Mistress Kiyash's wrath."

"Seen it in action?" Celeste asked. She put her hand on her bandolier, and the woman tracked the movement before wincing at Celeste.

"Yes."

Celeste narrowed her eyes. "When?"

"Often enough," the woman said. She glanced over her shoulder at the tower again. "What happens if that thing is disturbed?"

"Where are the guards you had with you?" Celeste asked, nodding to the fighter. "Jentien and Cortlen need all the fighters they can get; why are you here?"

The woman smirked. "She said you were smart."

A chill ran over Celeste's body, and she watched a team of Ambient Guard file into the street around them as the steel struck flint. The redhead drew her sword and leveled it at Celeste's chest.

"I'm going to ask again: What happens if that thing is disturbed?"

Celeste glared at her. *Click.* "It's too late now. The only thing that will happen if you disturb them now is ensuring your death when the wall falls."

The Still fighters pulled their weapons and clashed with the loyal guards, one of which wrenched the bow away from Celeste's archer before snapping the flare arrow in two. Another guard reached for the strap of Ranois' bag, and Celeste shouted loud enough to make the fighters pause when all eyes turned her way.

"Don't!" Celeste shouted. "One wrong move and we all die. Put the bag down *gently*."

The guard looked at the redhead for confirmation, and, after a long look at Celeste, she nodded. "Do what the woman says." She pointed at the bandolier on Celeste's torso with her sword. "Let's get that off, so we don't have any accidents. As for the rest of you, if you don't want to see this woman's blood on the ground, lay down your arms."

The vials in Celeste's bandolier rattled when she pulled that over her head, and she watched her fighters set their shields and swords on the ground.

The redhead smirked at her. "Now, if that thing," she pointed at the flask at the base of the wall, "is so dangerous, I think one of you needs to remove it."

Celeste's eyes widened and her mouth fell open as cold fear drenched her. "No," she said, shaking her head, "that's suicide. The crystal is unstable in its granulated state, and when heat is applied–"

"I don't care," the redhead interrupted. "Mistress Kiyash wants her home protected, and that's what she'll have." She looked over the small group Celeste had taken with her and settled on Ranois. "You."

He turned a terrified gaze Celeste's way, and she stepped forward until she was halted by the point of the sword at her chest.

"No, you can't." Celeste glared at the redhead. "He won't survive, and the wall will go down anyway." Dread and guilt settled in her stomach, and she couldn't help the pleading edge that her next words held. "Please, don't do this."

The redhead pulled the cloak from Ranois's shoulders, thrusting the heavy leather into his hands.

"It looks hot; you'd better protect your hands."

He stared at Celeste, his lip quivering and his eyes wide. Tears rolled down his cheeks. When he glanced at Ionna and her guards, watching the points of their swords inching forward in a clear threat, his lips set in a firm line and he turned toward the wall.

"No," Celeste whispered. She took another step toward Ranois, arm outstretched to stop him, and the redhead's sword dug into her chest below her clavicle.

"He'll keep moving if he wants to spare the rest of you," she growled.

"No!" Celeste cried, pushing against the sword, disregarding the pain.

Her body halted against her will. The redhead's smug look became deferential, almost fearful, when she noticed the figure striding toward them. Celeste had never seen Mistress Kiyash in person before, but she'd heard the description enough times to know that this striking blonde with the bearing and demeanor of the Malachi themself must be her.

"Celeste Zynse," Kiyash purred, "I have been looking forward to meeting you." She glanced at the wall where Ranois was crouching next to the flask. The tremor running through his body was visible from here. "I haven't seen such genius in a Still in some time. I'm curious to see what you've concocted here."

She waved her hand lazily in the air, and the small breeze that had been flowing through the street disappeared.

The hold on Celeste's body released, and she threw herself forward. She didn't care that it was already too late. She watched the crystal glow brighter when Ranois disturbed the flask, she watched his eyes go wide as the explosion started. She expected to feel the heat of the blast wash over her, but she stopped short at the end of the building when she slammed into an invisible wall.

She pressed against it as the inferno raged beyond. Celeste screamed, still trying to save the young man that had followed her to his death. She didn't care that he was already dead; she was responsible, and her guilt pushed her to slam her hands against the air again and again until they bled.

"Very impressive," Mistress Kiyash said behind her.

Celeste turned away from the hole, Ranois' ashes indistinguishable from the fine crystal powder floating in the air, with tears streaming down her cheeks and her breaths coming out in ragged, angry gasps. She glared at the leader of the Ambient's placid smile, and before she knew it, she was sprinting toward her. Her fingers curved into claws, ready to tear the calm smile off her face.

She stopped short again, this time when the redhead tackled her to the ground. Celeste screamed and writhed, unable to contain her fury, unable to stop while Mistress Kiyash smiled down at her.

"Impressive," she said again. She turned and strolled away as Celeste was lifted bodily from the street and hauled after her.

CHAPTER SEVENTY-SIX

"WE CAN'T LEAVE OUR families behind!" a squat woman insisted. Most of the Stills had been evacuated to the dormitories furthest from the fighting, but the small group before her had refused. "If you won't help us, we'll get into the Kiyash spire ourselves to look for them. That's where the prisoners you rescued were held, right?"

Isalie grimaced, picturing these people trying to fight past the Guard and the Ambient. They'd be slaughtered. She'd promised Jen and Cel that she wouldn't go near the fighting, but could she leave these people to blunder around until they were caught?

"I'll take you," she said, "but you'll follow my lead."

"Are you sure you want to do this?" Kiale asked again.

Isalie nodded, even though every instinct told her to run in the opposite direction. She *hated* running. "Come with me."

They moved into the streets, letting Kiale lead the way and scout for danger at every intersection. Isalie was expecting an attack any moment, so when an explosion shook the Inners, she flinched so hard she crashed against the wall of the building they were standing next to.

"Celeste," she whispered, sharing a concerned look with Kiale.

They were close, and the urge to check on Cel warred with the instinct to flee. She *shouldn't* be this close to the fighting. But, where were the reinforcements that were supposed to be filing into the Ambient District? Shouldn't there be more Still fighters this close to the wall?

"Kiale, something is wrong."

"Come on," she said, stepping lightly forward with her sword raised.

Another two blocks revealed the wall of the Ambient District, with no one in sight. There was a jagged hole in the wall, and the ground was littered with chunks of crystal and glittering ash. Isalie looked at the small group Stills with her, hoping that none of them took off on their own.

"We wait until I'm sure we won't be spotted," Kiale growled when someone urged her forward.

Isalie backed against the wall, out of the hot sun. She almost stumbled on something softer than the ground she'd expected, and the clinking of glass toughing glass made her leap to the side. Two leather bags, the larger one empty, were against the base of the building. She touched the familiar leather, then looked around for any sign of Celeste. These were her bags, and she wouldn't have left them here. She would have taken them into the Ambient District, to destroy the Kiyash spire.

"Celeste," Kiale muttered when Isalie slung the bag over her shoulder. "Elders. There's no distraction."

There was no choice for Isalie, now. She had to press forward, for the Stills, for Celeste.

A contingent of Ambient Guard ran through the intersection at the end of the street, and Kiale pushed Isalie against the wall before they were spotted. Isalie tried to calm her breathing, but a cough welled up in her throat. She held it as long as she could, her neck and chest spasming, but it burst out in a fit that had her on her knees, covering her mouth with shaking hands to suppress the noise.

Kiale looked from Isalie to the street where the guards were, her eyes wide with terror, her mouth set in a grimace. "Isalie," she whispered in warning.

Isalie held her breath and the cough stopped, though her lungs screamed in protest. The street was quiet again apart from the distant sounds of battle. Kiale poked her head out, and a voice echoed toward them.

"Stop!"

Kiale turned and whispered, "Run!"

Isalie was already out of breath, but she pushed away from the stone and followed the others down the street toward the hole to the Ambient District. There were a few dormitories between them and where she'd seen the guards; surely, they'd be able to lose them.

Kiale pushed to the front of the group, sword drawn as she jumped over the rubble on the ground where the wall had been. Shouts of surprise preceded a grunt from Kiale, and steel clashed beyond the opening.

Isalie grasped the arm of the nearest person, trying to pull them to a stop, but they shrugged her off.

"Elders' eyes," she cursed. Then she ran as fast as she could after them and threw herself over the threshold, bracing for an attack.

Kiale was there with a bloody sword in hand and blood soaking the sleeve of her sword arm. "Come on!" she urged, and when the last was through, she led them away from the pile of bodies she'd left behind.

"This way," Isalie croaked, stifling another cough. "We can angle around the buildings to keep the spire and the street out of sight."

Isalie flinched when she heard the distant shouts of more guards, and picked up her pace, guiding Kiale along the paths she'd explored such a short time ago. It felt like another lifetime.

Fire roared down the alley behind Jentien. He threw himself through a door and kicked it shut just as the flames licked his leather boots. He lay panting on the floor in darkness until the orange glow went out.

"Fucking Ambient," he growled when he rolled over. He planted his hands on the ground and pushed himself up, his back on fire as if the flame had caught up with him. He stumbled to the nearest chair and told himself that he'd sit just long enough to catch his breath before he went outside, or long enough to ensure that whatever Ambient was out there gave up the chase. Every second that passed made it harder to get up.

He'd already pushed himself too far, and he knew he couldn't keep this up for much longer. Soon, it wouldn't matter that he couldn't stand letting his people, or Celeste, or Iz down. His body would do that for him.

"Elders' eyes," he cursed when he leveraged himself out of the chair. He trudged toward the door, stooping to pick up his discarded sword and shield, just as the door slammed open and a silhouette blocked the light beyond.

Jentien stood quickly, ready for the fight his instincts told him was coming, but stopped when the figure stepped forward out of the shadow.

"Jentien," Baelen Kiyash called, shaking.

Jentien couldn't tell if it was anger or fear, but he suspected the latter. He let his sword drop but kept his shield up. "Baelen," he replied. He stood a few paces away, his chin held high even as his lip trembled. "You shouldn't be here."

"We must defend our home from traitors," Baelen said, and Jentien could tell from the steady and deliberate tone that this was something he'd memorized, something he'd been told to say. Sweat dripped from his pale blonde hairline down his neck.

Jentien stood from his crouch and sheathed his sword. He'd thought Baelen would see how insidious his people's efforts were, how much this change needed to happen. To see him here, ready to strike down Stills...

"We are only trying to defend our lives," Jentien said gently, suppressing a horrified shudder. "You wanted to help, that's what you told me. That starts by understanding that the Mistress is hurting us. She's *killing* us."

"She had to," he spat. "You attacked us! I thought you were my friend!"

"I am," Jentien said. "I will always be, but her cruelty started long before today. I will not stand by while the Ambient destroy my people."

"Then I have to kill you," Baelen said. He frowned and looked down at his hands as flames licked along his palms. When he looked up, Jentien saw unshed tears shimmering in the firelight.

"No, you don't." Jentien put down his shield. No matter what happened here, he wouldn't harm this young man. "You can just hide, stay out of our way, and I will make sure that none of the children are hurt. This isn't your fight, and I will make sure everyone knows it."

Jentien's eyes darted to the open door behind Baelen, to Nel's shadowed figure creeping forward. They had a bloody dagger in their hand, and they widened their eyes at Jentien, and then Baelen. It was a clear gesture to keep the young man busy so that he wouldn't notice the danger.

Jentien shook his head slightly. It was enough to make Nel pause. "All we want is peace," Jentien said again, taking another step forward. Baelen backed away; another step closer to Nel. "Stop!" Jentien yelled. Baelen flinched, Nel paused in the act of raising their blade, and a gout of flame shot from the boy's hand, narrowly missing Jentien.

"I'm sorry," Baelen gasped, terror in his wide eyes.

"Please, don't do anything we'll regret." Jentien took another step, and the boy brought his hands up again.

Jentien stared at Nel over Baelen's shoulder. He turned as Jentien and Nel lunged for him, and lightning shot through the air.

⚡◊⚡

Celeste didn't remember the section of the city the Ambient had taken for themselves. Tall crystalline spires stretched into the clear blue sky, refracting the sunlight into a myriad of rainbows from every surface. It felt like she was inside a rainbow. She hated every second of it.

Her arms were bound behind her, a gag was tied so tight that she was losing feeling in her lips, and the rest of her people were being shoved along in front of her so that she bore witness to their terror.

She heard fighting close by, but her shouts were ineffective through the gag. If Jentien *did* hear her and come to her rescue, he'd either be killed or captured like she'd been. Lee would lose them both. Her heart twisted when she thought of Lee, hiding somewhere in the Inners with no idea that the plan had failed. She couldn't bear to consider that Lee would go through that again.

A battalion of Ambient Guard blocked the street leading to the gate behind them, forming a physical barrier against any of the Olugar's forces that might make it that far. The district was bustling, but there wasn't any urgency to the Guard's movements. This was an orderly maneuver, not the desperate attempt to stop an uprising that Celeste had hoped for.

Things must be going very poorly for the Stills.

Mistress Kiyash eyed an older man in Guard regalia. "Update," she demanded.

"The Stills are held in the street, and we are slowly pushing them back, Mistress."

"Slowly isn't good enough," she said, quirking an eyebrow. "I want them eradicated."

"Yes, Mistress." He hesitated, and Kiyash leaned forward, waiting for him to continue. "Your nephew slipped away from the Guard, and he was last seen pursuing Jentien Themori. Ambient Kova went after him."

Her lips quirked up in a small smile, and she peered at the gate. Celeste recognized the zeal in her eyes, the same that Nel had had while planning this coup. She wanted Jen, for whatever reason, and that realization sent a shiver down Celeste's spine.

"And his spy?"

"Hasn't been seen," the man replied. "Either she's hiding or she's not here."

"She's here, somewhere," Kiyash drawled. "I want Themori captured, *not* killed, am I understood?" The man nodded, and her small smile grew into a wicked grin. "Once we get our hands on him, the other will come to us."

Isalie's heart felt like it might hammer out of her chest. They'd found their way through empty streets to the Kiyash spire's servant entrance and found it unguarded. That made Isalie even more nervous than she already was, but the Stills were too eager to find their families to listen. The door slammed open, and Kiale trailed behind the rest as they rushed inside.

It shouldn't be this easy, Isalie thought.

She stepped inside, ready to throw herself back through the door, but the servant's quarters were as deserted as the outside.

"Where do we go?" a woman asked, pausing at the door leading to the servant passageway.

Isalie considered. The obvious answer was the cells beneath the spire, but if they managed to find everyone, they'd need to find their way to the ground floor again. She didn't think taking a hostage would work again, nor that they would leave the prison unguarded, even if they'd left the back door open. If they were anywhere else, Isalie had no idea where to start looking.

"This way," Isalie said, taking the lead. The prison was the best choice.

A commotion behind them made her swing back toward the outer door just as it slammed shut. Yesrien and a few Stills Isalie didn't know were there, holding the door shut while someone pounded against it.

"Barricade the door!" Kiale shouted, and the Stills leapt into action. Yesrien and Kiale levered the closest cupboard onto its side, and the others stacked tables and benches behind that.

Yesrien swung around to face Isalie with a terrifying smile on her face. "Looks like we had the same idea."

"You shouldn't be here–" Isalie began, but Yesrien cut her off.

"Neither should you. But the people we talked to said their friends and family were taken to keep them in line, and we both know where the Ambient would put them."

Isalie nodded and led the group back to the wall, leaving the commotion at the outer door behind them. The wall swung open silently as it always did, just far enough for Isalie to peer into the hall beyond. It was empty, and apart from her ragged breathing, it was silent. She pushed the panel open wider, pausing before she stepped out, but when nothing happened, she waved the others forward.

Every footfall sounded like an avalanche to her. Soon, they were at the head of the stairs, and Isalie stared into the dark, her heart pounding in her chest. It hadn't stopped at any point today, but now it fluttered, as if it might give out at any moment.

I don't know if I can do this.

Kiale paused next to her, looking first at Isalie, and then at the stairs. Isalie tore her gaze from the yawning chasm the stairs seemed to become. Kiale moved in front of Isalie.

"I'll lead us down," she whispered to everyone, lifting her shield and sword. "Stay close and stay quiet." To Isalie, she murmured, "Just tell me where to go."

Isalie nodded, not trusting her voice. She pointed down the hall, and they moved as quietly as possible, with Isalie tapping Kiale's shoulders to send her down the appropriate fork in the tunnel. Soon, they came to a familiar chamber, and Isalie pulled Kiale to a stop.

"There," she whispered. The smooth crystal walls glinted with the light of the Ambient orbs. Isalie wondered how many people were trapped behind the hidden doors. "The cell release is in the room beyond."

They inched forward and spotted a hunched figure in the back of the first cell. And in the next. Isalie was horrified to see that most of the cells had at least one occupant. The woman trailing behind let out a sob and slammed her fists against the cell at the end of the first tunnel. A young girl sprang to her feet and stood opposite the woman, tears streaking down her face as she silently screamed. There was no water dripping down on them, thank the Elders for small mercies.

Isalie rushed into the junction room with the crystal panels, but there was no Ambient in sight. Yesrien joined her, and Kiale stalked toward the other tunnels, alert for danger.

"It took an Ambient to open the cells before," Isalie said. "We might be able to get some open with Celeste's vials, but I don't know what it would do to the people inside."

"Shit," Yesrien growled. She knelt, looking below the table, and at the underside of the plate. "That *can't* be the only way. Maybe if we destroy the panel it'll let them out?"

Isalie grimaced. "Try it," she said, and shepherded the Stills away from the chamber. She hunched against the wall, covering her ears and closing her eyes. When the blast came the hall shook, and the Stills screamed. She opened her eyes and rushed into the chamber, coughing in the smoke left behind.

The plate was untouched. Yesrien jogged forward, cursing when she noticed the same.

"*Elders!*" she shouted. She fisted her hands in her hair hard enough that Isalie worried she'd tear it out by the roots. Yesrien's face was red, her teeth bared in a snarl, and she stared at the plate as she strode toward it, angry enough to tear it apart with her bare hands, Isalie thought.

"Yesrien," she called, but the incensed woman didn't hear her.

"*Fucking Ambient!*" Yesrien screamed and grasped the plate, trying to tear it from the table.

The chamber shook again as doors slid open at Yesrien's touch, and screams echoed through the halls as dozens of terrified people spilled out of their cells. Yesrien looked at her hand in confusion, shared an incredulous look with Isalie, and then ran toward the screaming.

Isalie watched reunions with happy tears in her eyes, but she knew the explosion and ensuing cacophony of voices would call someone before long. She couldn't bring herself to tell them to stop because she'd *been* them. If she'd had the breath to do it, she'd have been screaming from the moment she'd fallen down that hole. She might not have stopped.

Instead, she waved to Kiale to get her attention and told her to round everyone up. They couldn't move through the spire like this, so they'd need to get everyone through the tunnel, and pick up any other prisoners on the way. If Yesrien could open the cells, she could open the way out.

They moved slowly, corralling the frightened people whose cries had subsided into sniffles and moans. Yesrien stayed in front of Isalie, placing her hand on every plate they passed. Kiale searched through the branching tunnels, reporting no Ambient in sight, and finding no other prisoners beyond the main tunnel they were in.

Isalie was grateful for that small mercy, at least.

The tunnel opened into a room with two familiar cylinders, and a shiver ran up her spine. Between them was the hole she'd fallen through, with the river of burning water a distant hiss echoing from the darkness.

She pushed through the terror this room inspired, crossing into a new tunnel worked from stone. Her pace increased, as if her body knew that she'd find freedom this way. She glanced over her shoulder, letting the relief she felt show on her battered face.

They kept walking, and slowly, Isalie's relief was overwhelmed by the feeling that something was off. It took a few moments to realize what was making her feel that way.

"We should have seen the handprint by now," she muttered. She glanced back again, her brow furrowed as she searched for the spot in the rough wall that would lead them out. She knew they hadn't passed it; they would have seen it.

"Did we take a wrong turn?" Kiale asked quietly.

Isalie shook her head. "No, this is the right way." She halted and let some of the group file around her before turning back to run her hand along the tunnel wall. The stone was rough and cool in her hand, and her frown deepened every moment she didn't feel the indentation beneath her fingers. When she'd gone most of the way toward the prison, she stopped again.

"It's not here."

CHAPTER SEVENTY-SEVEN

Jentien's body seized, but he held onto Baelen. He *couldn't* let go; his muscles spasmed from the lightning coursing through him. He'd felt something like it in the Gloom, but this had been a glancing blow, searing the outside of his thigh when he'd lunged. Nel was turning toward Baelen locked in Jentien's embrace, and Jentien couldn't move or speak. All he could do was watch Nel smirk and grab their knife from where they'd dropped it.

No, Jentien thought as his teeth ground together. *He's a child!* A grunt was all that came out, and Baelen froze, stunned as he watched his death approaching.

"You're too soft for this," Nel told Jentien.

They raised their knife to Baelen's throat just as a hand clamped down on their wrist. Jentien would have sobbed in relief if he could have when Cortlen pulled Nel back.

"Themori is the furthest thing from soft," Cortlen grumbled. He released Nel's wrist.

Jentien collapsed and groaned as the shock wore off. Cortlen pulled him off Baelen and took a length of rope from his belt to bind the boy's hands. Jentien slowly pushed himself up and gazed at Baelen.

"You saved me," he whispered, staring wide-eyed at Jentien. "They would've killed me."

"Our fight isn't with you," Jentien said.

"Yes, it is," Nel protested. "This is *war*. We don't have the luxury of leaving any Ambient alive, no matter how young. They'll all grow into the monsters that their parents are. They will *never* recognize that Stills aren't bugs to crush under their heels."

"Not unless we show them," Jentien agreed. To Baelen, he said: "I promise no harm will come to you if you stay out of the way. Please, for the sake of our friendship, let me protect you. Let me protect as many of you as I can."

The young man nodded and stood. "Tell me everything," he said.

Jentien gave him brief explanations of everything that Iz had uncovered, everything that'd been done to him, to the prisoners, and to Isalie. Baelen looked more perturbed the longer Jentien spoke.

"Dad told me you'd been arrested, that I wouldn't see you again, but he wouldn't tell me why. I assumed he didn't think I'd understand, but now, I think he—and the rest of the Ambient—were just lying to me." His face crumpled. "You're the only one who ever told me the truth."

Jentien pulled Baelen into a hug while the others looked on. The war continued outside, and Jentien knew they couldn't delay much longer.

"What do we do with him?" Cortlen asked.

"No matter what you do," Nel interjected, "it won't be enough. He can break any bond, destroy any cell, and murder anyone you set to guard him. We can't afford to leave people behind, and we can't take him with us."

"Yes, you can." Baelen stepped out of Jentien's embrace. "I can't hide while my family is doing these awful things. I said I wanted to help, and I meant it. I'm going to get you to the Ambient District, and I'm going to tell the Ambient to stop."

Nel scoffed. "They won't listen to a child."

"I'm not just a child, I'm the heir."

Nel glared at Baelen, who stood his ground, to his credit. Finally, Nel nodded.

"If they don't listen to you, maybe it'll give them pause when they see their heir in our custody. Fine, but if anything happens to us, you'll be the first to die."

Nel turned away, sticking their head out the door to survey the street. Cortlen joined them after a wary glance at Baelen.

Jentien stepped between Baelen and the door, stopping to face him and level him with an earnest stare.

"I will do everything in my power to keep you safe, Baelen. If things go wrong, run."

Celeste shifted her shoulders again, pulling against the ropes binding her wrists as her eyes darted around the courtyard. Ten Ambient were gathered at the far end, leaning forward to listen to Mistress Kiyash's angry whispers. That left Celeste with several guards standing over her, glancing back and forth between their prisoner and their commander.

She was tied to a wide pole set in the center of the courtyard, and her stomach turned when she took a deep breath. The coppery tang of blood filled her nose; she tried not to picture Jentien strapped in this very spot as a lash came down on his bare back over and over. How this place *still* carried that gory scent, she didn't know. Perhaps one of the Ambient had preserved it, somehow, as a reminder of what would happen if anyone disobeyed their orders.

"I don't care *what* you need to fight through, I want Themori *alive!*" Mistress Kiyash's voice rumbled across the courtyard, drawing more than Celeste's gaze toward her.

There was madness in her eyes that lasted a second, but Celeste felt the ground rumble beneath her before it was locked away behind the calm, superior countenance that washed the madness away. If Celeste hadn't been so terrified, she would have taken some satisfaction in watching the other Ambient take a step away from their Consul.

"What of the mice below?" Mistress Kiyash asked, her voice controlled again.

A thin Ambient woman straightened. "Trapped in the laboratory. The exit was sealed as ordered, and the spy is among them. Cizal will have her soon."

Celeste's stomach dropped. *Lee.*

"Well done," Kiyash answered. "I'll be along to fetch my prize shortly, and I'll have Themori where I want him. Both of his lovers are in my grasp, and with the three of them out of my way, this little rebellion will flare out as quickly as it began."

"No, it won't," Celeste muttered.

Kiyash's eyes cut to Celeste, and a small smile pulled the corner of her mouth upward. "Oh? You think the rest of the Stills will continue without their leaders?"

Celeste straightened her back against the pole. "Yes. Your tyranny ends today."

Kiyash spared her Ambient a knowing glance before she stepped forward, crossing the courtyard in a few long strides while her crimson gown flowed around her. She stood over Celeste now, smiling down at her.

"You and the other two are the backbone of this attempt. If I want to stop its momentum, all I need to do is snap its back and the rest will crumble."

"We pushed it along," Celeste retorted, "but the rest of them know the truth. Lee tore your dirty secrets out of the shadows and held them up to the light. Every *one* of us will fight until our last breath to see you brought low."

Mistress Kiyash crossed her arms and gazed at Celeste, whose blood pounded in her ears. Lee was trapped, Jentien was walking into a trap, and Celeste was tied to a pole. She could only distract this terrifying woman for the precious moments that she deigned to listen. There had to be more that she could do…

"I applaud your spirit," Mistress Kiyash said. "And I thank you for letting me know that while Jentien Themori has been the public face of this disappointing interlude, your Lee is the real catalyst. How fortunate, then, that she has delivered herself back into our hands."

Fury filled Celeste's body, and she tore against her bonds as if the maelstrom inside her could break them. "Even if we fail today, I will see you *dead*," she spat. "Our people will rise again. We are *not* your playthings."

Mistress Kiyash laughed. "That is exactly what you are."

Celeste seethed, straining against the ropes that tightened when Kiyash glanced at them. Celeste's chest constricted, driving the air from her lungs until she slumped against the post. Mistress Kiyash crouched next to her; the crimson train of her dress flared out behind her, spread evenly as if placed there by one of her attendants.

"We watched the Gloom spread toward Olunei from the Malachi's palace in Lacorsia. Why do you think we built the spires in the first place?" She chuckled. "It wasn't to protect the pathetic Stills running this backward city. The Malachi appointed me to make use of what would otherwise be wasted. It was only a matter of time before Olunei and its citizens were consumed. So, we took it upon ourselves to study the effects of the Gloom, to study the effect it had on the Stills."

It wasn't possible for Celeste to feel any more disgusted than she already did, but she would have screamed if she'd been able to breathe. Mistress Kiyash smiled triumphantly when she continued.

"The Malachi gave this city to me. We cordoned off a portion for our use, with the Malachi themself funneling Ambience into the crystal to repel the Gloom. The other spires can repel the worst of the chaos, but these allow us to catalog the effects of exposure, to note how the Gloom is altered by our constructs versus the constructs flowing with Ambience. And the Malachi allows me a portion of the power they have graciously bestowed upon my city for my own use.

"What I didn't expect was you. Our experiment continues, but while our efforts against it have continued as hypothesized, you have become the focus of new observation. Thank you, Celeste, for taking our research in a direction that we didn't anticipate."

She craned her neck to gaze upward at the glittering spire above their heads. It sparkled in the sunlight, serene, as if Celeste's entire world wasn't crumbling around her.

This isn't right, Isalie thought. She knew the handprint wasn't there, but she couldn't help but run her fingers along the cool stone wall. *This is a trap.*

No sooner had the thought crossed her mind than a light flared in the tunnel from the direction they'd fled. A small radiant orb hovered over the palm of a woman with ebony hair falling around the grim determination on her face. Her grey-blue eyes spared a surprised frown for the crowd they'd assembled, then pierced Isalie, holding her in place.

"There is no escape here," the Ambient woman said, her voice just above a whisper. "Come with us, and these Stills will be allowed to join the Guard in the courtyard to bear witness to the Mistress's judgement." A small host of Ambient Guard flanked her with swords and shields at the ready. There wasn't a sympathetic face to be found, especially when she spotted Ionna's hard stare over the Ambient's shoulder.

"I'll come with you if they can leave," Isalie countered. It was an empty request, and Isalie knew it. There was no use resisting; there was nowhere else to go, but she had to try.

"You have no leverage with which to make demands," the Ambient spat. "You *will* come quietly, and you will be taken to the Mistress. You killed my brother, so it's only by the grace of Mistress Kiyash that I haven't already killed you." Lightning crackled from her fingertips to punctuate the threat.

Isalie sucked in a breath seeing the similarity between her and Ambient Rotre in the shape of her eyes and her black hair. "No," she whispered, shaking her head. One hand clutched the leather neckline of her bodysuit, and the other snaked into the pouch attached to her belt beneath her cloak. A small glass vial rolled between her fingers.

There's only one way out of here now, Isalie thought as her mind retraced the steps up to the main floor. If they could make it there, they might have options, but they'd need to get away from the Ambient and her Guard. *I can't send these people into the river.*

"We'll come," Kiale interjected, stepping through the crowd. "These people had nothing to do with the battle."

Isalie fumbled with the vial, willing herself not to throw it at the Ambient's feet. The air crackled around her. Isalie stared at the woman, and then at Ionna behind her, her fear burning away in the heat of her anger.

"Bind them," the Ambient ordered. Ionna started toward Isalie, but the Ambient stopped her, taking the length of rope from the redhead's hands. She pulled Isalie's cloak off, glanced at Isalie's hand in her pouch, and wrenched it out. Isalie twisted her wrist to free it from Rotre's grasp, hard enough to jostle the contents of the vial.

The subtle glow of the granules was easy to miss when Rotre used the Ambience to pluck the vial out of Isalie's hand and tuck it into the pouch on her waist. But Isalie had seen it processed so many times, had seen it explode in the face of an Ambient, and she knew it was only a matter of time. Rotre waved a hand and Celeste's bag slipped over Isalie's head, floating through the air before settling over the pouch with the glowing vial.

"I would love you to give me a reason to kill you now," Ambient Rotre hissed. She wound the rope around Isalie's wrists hard enough to make her gasp. "The Mistress wants you alive. I want to see the life leave your eyes."

Isalie stood still while Rotre finished tying the bonds, then ran her hands over Isalie's pockets. She pulled another small vial out and smirked.

The Guard moved through the Stills, confiscating Kiale's weapons and tying ropes around anyone who looked healthy enough to fight back. Most of the group moved ahead of the guards, with Isalie between them and the Ambient, then they all shuffled through the tunnels again.

CHAPTER SEVENTY-EIGHT

THE OLUGAR'S FORCES WERE dug into the buildings ringing the district, having fought for every bloody inch between the Outers and here, but their momentum had stopped. The crystal arrowheads tore through invisible shields that stopped normal metal and stone, but the Still archers didn't have enough to keep those shields down. Even without the Ambience, there was no taking the gate, where most of the Guard were holding against the siege using mundane means.

Now, after hours of trading arrow volleys, Baelen's presence had stalled the Guard, and word was spreading that he'd been captured. Jentien strode forward with his left arm through his shield and his right hand clasping Baelen's shoulder in front of him.

The Ambient District gate loomed ahead, and the streets were eerily quiet after the clamor of what felt like days of fighting. A handful of Olugar fighters surrounded Baelen and him.

There wasn't much in this world that Jentien believed Mistress Kiyash would make concessions to the Stills over. He hoped he was right, that the boy was one of them.

"I don't like this," Cortlen grumbled from the front.

Jentien glanced at his friend, catching sight of guards loyal to the Ambient in the windows above them. A door in the gate opened when he turned back, and Commander Rallac stepped through with Ardaf Kova just behind him. Kova's eyes went wide when he saw Baelen.

"If this doesn't work, we run," Jentien replied.

"Where?" Nel demanded.

Jentien didn't need to turn around to know their retreat had been blocked as they moved forward. Seeing how many of the Guard had remained on the Ambient's side was like a blow to the chest. "Baelen, if they attack, go with Cortlen. Find a way through." He looked up, locking eyes with his commander. "We've come to ask for peace negotiations!" Jentien shouted.

"Peace?" Kova spat. "You're using my *son* as leverage for your mob. Release him now, or I will tear you apart!"

"Please!" Baelen shouted. Jentien tightened his grip. "All they want is to feel protected, Dad! That's all any of us want!"

"Baelen—"

"You will take me to the Mistress!" Baelen interrupted. "I am offering my assurance that these rebels will receive a chance to voice their demands, under my protection." The young man drew himself up, holding his head high as he peered at his father with as much authority as he could muster.

Jentien squeezed his shoulder again, but this time, it was a show of support and reassurance.

Hurt flashed across Kova's face before he nodded. "As you command, Master Kiyash." Baelen let out a heavy sigh at his father's reaction, but kept his posture rigid.

Jentien waved his shield above his head, making the Guard jump. Before they could react further, Jentien lowered his arm, and watched as the Guard's eyes moved upward to the windows of the flanking buildings where the bulk of Jentien's forces waited with arrows nocked. Rallac moved aside to make a lane for the Olugar to march through.

Isalie waited at the bottom of the stairs, watching the prisoners shuffle upward until most of the Guard and Stills were out of sight. Kiale stood with her, though Yesrien had already gone up. Ambient Cizal Rotre and two guards were behind them.

They were out of time. Isalie wasn't a fighter, she wasn't brilliant like Celeste, and she had no idea how to do anything but put herself between danger and whomever she needed to protect. So, when the last foot disappeared and the Guard pressed in on the two of them, Isalie caught her foot on the first step and tumbled.

Kiale was there in an instant, just like Isalie knew she'd be.

"Isalie—"

"Get them out," Isalie whispered, cutting Kiale off. "When you see the signal, get them out."

"What?"

"Get moving!" Ambient Rotre snarled.

"Sorry," Isalie said. She coughed, and the breath wheezed in and out of her lungs.

"How are *you* the face of this rebellion?" Rotre demanded. "Pathetic."

Isalie could only gasp for breath once the coughing fit subsided. Kiale scowled but didn't say anything. When she tried to help Isalie up, Isalie pushed Kiale forward, answering her curious frown with an urgent widening of her eyes.

Kiale nodded and rushed up, leaving Isalie to struggle for every step. Her performance was helped by the very real difficulty that she was having as her cough came again.

"What is wrong with you?" The Ambient flared her nostrils in disgust.

"I went into the river to escape your hospitality," Isalie choked out. "My mask helps, if I can?" She held up the mask with a shaky hand, turning to block the others.

The Ambient waved her permission, glaring all the while. Her hands bound, Isalie pulled the mask over her face one side at a time. When it was finally in place, she took a few deep breaths and looked up the stairs to see that Kiale was gone before she slowly started moving again.

More than once, someone shoved her from behind when she took a few steps, and Isalie used that excuse to stumble again. She wanted to let Kiale and Yesrien get some distance between them and the Ambient at Isalie's heels. Hopefully, they wouldn't encounter more in the halls. Hopefully, one of the prisoners would know where to use the servant's halls to escape and they could fight off the guards that went with them. Hopefully, Isalie could neutralize the threat behind her and find her own way out.

Afternoon light shone in the stairwell as they neared the top, and shouts echoed in the hall ahead. Isalie came to a stop, and the Ambient reeled when she slammed into Isalie's back.

"Move, you stupid *Still*." She shoved again.

Isalie hunched forward, clutching the rail, then kicked backward into the pouches on Cizal Rotre's belt. Rotre slipped, stumbling into the guard behind her, tipping both into the one below. All three tumbled down the steps, and Isalie pulled herself up the stairs two at a time, using the railing to propel herself faster.

"You bitch! Do you really think you can get away from us?"

She reached the top step as the world erupted below her. The floor buckled, and she scrambled forward on hands and knees. The walls crumbled around her, and all she could do was pull the hood of her cloak over her head and shelter it with her arms before the crystal slammed down onto her.

CHAPTER SEVENTY-NINE

"It warms my heart to see that your plan has failed," Mistress Kiyash purred.

Celeste leveled her with a glare that had cowed so many Stills. She hadn't heard any sounds of fighting in too long. Their endeavor had failed, and she was just waiting for what came next. It made her skin crawl.

"I must say, I'm disappointed," Mistress Kiyash sighed. "I thought, of all the Stills, *you* would understand my pursuit in understanding the Gloom."

"Me?" Celeste asked. The ropes were still too tight, but if she didn't struggle, they didn't constrict further. They seemed to sense every slight twitch, as vindictive as the Mistress herself.

"Yes," Mistress Kiyash laughed. "You are one of the brightest minds I've seen in an age. You've found a way to adapt to the Gloom that I never considered. The necessity of understanding and surviving the Gloom is greater than any of us." She tapped a slender finger against her temple.

"Elders curse you."

"I'm sure they do."

The ground rumbled behind Celeste, and Mistress Kiyash whipped her head around, amusement replaced by a mask of cold fury. Cries rose across the square. Stills huddled against each other, Ambient rushed to the Mistress, and Celeste craned her neck but couldn't see anything more than the crystal wall glinting in the golden light of the afternoon sun.

Mistress Kiyash took a step forward, then stopped in her tracks and pivoted on her heel. The cold fury became a manic smile that split her mouth wide, and she instead rushed away from the spire.

Celeste turned and locked eyes with Jentien, who stood just behind a young man with pale blond hair and features like Mistress Kiyash. Jentien didn't spare the Mistress a glance as he advanced but reached up to grasp the young man's shoulder and pull him to a halt alongside Cortlen.

Celeste's face crumpled in pain when she shook her head. Jentien's expression didn't change, but Celeste watched the same pain dance across his eyes. Their plan had failed, and Jentien had just walked into the lion's den.

She searched his body for one of the vials she'd given him, and when she looked up, he gave her one miniscule nod, seeming to read the question in her eyes.

"The Stills request a negotiation for peace," Jentien called out. "We've brought Master Kiyash—unharmed—as a show of good faith."

Kiyash cocked her head to the side as she considered Jentien. Just another specimen in her grand experiment.

"I appreciate that you haven't harmed my nephew," she said, "but I fail to see how that could possibly serve as an incentive to negotiate for anything. Every Still that has participated in this little coup will fill the cells below my spire. Every Still with an association to the traitors will have their rations cut by half until I decide that they have proved themselves worthy of my forgiveness. Everyone else," she bared her teeth, "will live the rest of their lives grateful that I allow them to live as they did before you destroyed the balance."

Jentien still didn't react beyond his jaw clenching. The young man in front of him, however, cast a look over his shoulder at Jentien, seeking confirmation of what he'd just heard.

"Your cruelty has been exposed," Jentien said. "We don't need you anymore. We can find our own way in the outer city and leave you to your paradise. If you won't make concessions for our survival, we will do that ourselves."

"Without the inventive Celeste Zynse, I think not." Jentien's mask of determination fell away, and his eyes shot to Celeste. "Yes, you see the problem. I'm not willing to let such a precious resource out of my grasp."

"Olunei is an experiment," Celeste ground out. The ropes tightened again, driving the air from her lungs again. "We're... all research subjects."

"Correct," Mistress Kiyash said, "and Celeste has made surprising strides to combat the Gloom's debilitating effects. She has surpassed our projections of protection the Ambient can provide, becoming the most important aspect of our experiment." She turned aside to include Celeste in the conversation. "I had hoped to invite you to join us once your efforts were brought to my attention, but I think we can all agree that's no longer an option."

"You won't take her," Jentien growled.

"My dear, we've been abducting people since we came here. Everyone who stumbles into the outskirts of the Gloom surrounding Olunei is brought here. Those lightning strikes? They're our lassos, snaring anyone stupid enough to come so close to the edge of a Gloom. Then, we deposit people wherever we'd like."

"Separating families? That was part of your experiment?" Jentien's body vibrated with rage.

"Our experiment must have controls to compare to. People live so differently across this great continent of ours. How else could I ensure that a subject's reaction to the rain wasn't an artifact of their environment or previous exposure?"

A strangled cry erupted from Celeste's mouth, since she didn't have the breath to scream. Jentien pulled his sword, but stopped short when Mistress Kiyash looked his way. He strained against his invisible bonds as much as Celeste struggled against the ropes.

Mistress Kiyash stepped between them with her back to Celeste, close enough to kiss Jentien if she leaned forward. Her voice still carried when she spoke to him. "You may suffer from a limited perspective, believing that I am here to elevate myself above the Stills out of some sort of superiority complex, but I do not." Her voice hardened, and Celeste could almost see the smile drop off her face to become that cold, calculating glare that sent a shiver down Celeste's spine.

"Our home is dying," Mistress Kiyash continued. "The Gloom is devouring everything. If the Malachi cannot keep it at bay, if they cannot find a way to stop it, *every* city in Vortheim will be like Olunei. *Every spirit* that lives here will suffer. It will not end there, but will spread over Celuthia, consuming unsuspecting continents like Trylia, Friga, and everywhere else. There will be *nothing* but wild Ambience. There will be *no survivors* but Gloom beasts. We must determine how to live with the Gloom if we are to survive."

"Why are the Stills the only ones to suffer, then?" Jentien spat. "If all of us are in danger, shouldn't we *all* learn how to live with it?"

Mistress Kiyash scoffed. "Stills are the most vulnerable of us, but in that vulnerability is ingenuity and drive to survive. Celeste is the perfect example of that. As the storm's intensity increased, our protection increased, but eventually failed. Our power is a bandage, but Celeste's inventions have stood against the full power of the storm. My experiment will continue for as long as it takes for us to find a way to combat the Gloom."

"I won't do it," Baelen said, stepping forward until he was face-to-face with the Mistress. "You won't live forever. If we can't find a way to live together while you're in power, I will make sure it happens after you're gone."

She stood still for a few moments, and then she threw her head back and laughed. The spire glowed brighter behind her, and the ground vibrated again as the Mistress began to glow with it. Baelen stepped back, his eyes wide in shock and fear.

"Foolish child, I will never give control of this city and this experiment to you."

"B-but, I'm your heir."

"Yes, you are. The only Conduit child born in the decades since we came here. The Malachi has given me more than just access to their power through the spires. They have also given me the knowledge that has kept them in power for centuries. All that's needed is a vessel powerful enough to contain them. You are to be *my* vessel."

Celeste's stomach turned. If they couldn't stop her, there would never be a way to unseat her. She could live forever, torturing generations of Stills in the slim hope that they could find a way to stop the Gloom from the inside.

"No," Baelen said. He stepped back, then let out a terrified cry when his body stopped in mid-air.

"My sweet nephew," Mistress Kiyash cooed. "You have no choice." She waved a hand toward Tsia, who strode forward and bowed her head. "Take him to one of the cells below. That will contain him long enough–"

Whatever she was going to say was cut off when Ionna streaked past Celeste, blood dripping from a gash in her side and an arm hanging at an unnatural angle.

"Mistress! The prisoners have escaped, and the spy collapsed the entrance to the prison with some sort of explosion."

"Elders' eyes," Mistress Kiyash cursed. "Where is she now?"

"Buried in the rubble when one of the halls collapsed."

"NO!" Jentien bellowed. His face turned red as he strained against the Mistress's hold. Celeste thrashed, tears streaming down her cheeks and her vision going black. She couldn't breathe, Lee was gone, Lee was gone...

Another thunderous crash, and then another as the spire rattled. People screamed in the courtyard and started running. Mistress Kiyash gaped at the spire and shook her head in disbelief.

"What in the name of the Malachi was that?"

CHAPTER EIGHTY

SHE COULDN'T BREATHE WITH the weight on her chest. It was the river again, she was drowning. Isalie tried to shift, but there was no space around her. The walls of the spire were pinning her to the floor that was still beneath her somehow. The only thing that had saved her was the mask over her face, filtering the air. She would have laughed if she'd been able to move her chest that far.

I hope Kiale got them out, she thought. *Cel...*

She twisted her head as far as she could to see the slab of crystal a finger-length above her. A smaller chunk the length of her torso was pinning her right arm against her side. She had no idea when her bonds had come apart, but her left arm was free, and her legs wiggled from side to side.

"Elders," she wheezed, "I need some help, here."

With her left hand, she shoved the slab while rolling to her right. The slab moved a bit, so she gritted her teeth and shoved harder, her feet scrabbling against the floor to scoot her away from where it would impact. The slab fell with a muffled thump as something in her left arm popped, and the rest of her crystal cage ground against itself with a terrifying screech.

Isalie froze, waiting for the rest of the rubble to crush her. It remained in place, and the rest of her body was free. Carefully, trying not to push against the roof of her prison, she flipped onto her stomach so she could look around.

Bits of crystal were wedged near her head, propping up the larger section above her. To her left was the slab she'd just escaped, and to her right was an opening large enough for her hand. She reached through the hole and found nothing beyond.

"Thank you," she said aloud. To the Elders, to fate, to herself, to whomever might be watching over her. Reaching forward, she hissed as her left arm screamed in protest, but she didn't have time to nurse her wounds. She used her right arm, grasping the head-sized piece of crystal nearest the opening and rolling it out from under the slab until the hole was a bit wider.

Isalie worked as quickly as she dared, ignoring the pain in her arm when the rubble was too stubborn to move with one hand, ignoring the cuts that jagged edges of the broken wall left in her arms and wrists. The floor became slick with her blood and still she worked.

The slab shifted and screeched, and the hole she'd made shortened a fraction of an inch. The panic she'd kept at bay raged when she imagined her worst fears coming true as the tunnel she'd made closed its mouth around her.

She'd fought that fear once, but being caught in the imaginary beast's jaws was a far cry from picturing it. She fought to control her ragged breaths, coming faster and faster, expanding her chest as she kicked and pulled against the floor to worm her way through the opening. Isalie had to press her head against the floor to clear it, and then her shoulders wedged her there. She could feel the slab pressing down and imagined that the pressure increased until she started to wheeze and cough.

She heard Jentien's voice in her head and closed her eyes to imagine his hand in hers. She replayed Cel's words, telling her how strong she was, that she didn't need anyone to save her.

Her breathing calmed, and she pivoted one shoulder back so she could bring the other one forward. She scrabbled forward with her toes and fingertips, pulling her hips free when the rubble shifted again. The slab brushed against her calves and Isalie whined just before her feet came free. She flopped onto her back as the slab slammed down and the floor cracked where she'd been moments before.

"Elders," she hissed. The cracks splintered toward her, and she scooted away from them.

The floor rumbled, and she stood to run, dodging more debris as she sprinted down the hall, away from the collapse before it could swallow her again.

She emerged into the foyer amid a scattering of debris, the outer perimeter of the spire still standing while the innermost section lay destroyed in her wake. Light glared in the upper reaches of the spire. Mistress Kiyash's voice carried through the open door, and Isalie seethed, looking around for a weapon. She stooped to grab a shard of crystal before stumbling toward the door.

"No, no, NO!" Jentien screamed. He'd only just gotten Iz back, then forced them into this losing battle. He should have protected her. He shouldn't have let her go alone; he should have protected her...

He still couldn't move, or he would have torn Mistress Kiyash's throat out with his bare hands. She'd taken Celeste, she'd doomed all the Stills to suffer endlessly, and she'd *taken Iz*.

Mistress Kiyash's shocked denial cut through his misery. "No…"

Jentien opened his eyes and followed her wide-eyed stare to the spire. At the base was a figure walking toward them, hunched and bloodied. They lifted their head to look around, and Jentien saw straw-colored hair matted with blood on one side of her head, and scarred skin on the other.

His heart stopped, and if he could have collapsed, he would have.

"Iz," Jentien moaned. "Iz!"

Isalie's eyes snapped to his, and her face crumpled with relief. She took in the rest of the courtyard, taking a step toward Celeste before she locked eyes with Mistress Kiyash and straightened.

"No," Jentien called when Iz stepped forward. "Get out of here! Iz, run!"

Isalie didn't listen, but walked forward, past Celeste, toward Kiyash as Jentien's body flooded with terror.

⁂

"You should have died," Mistress Kiyash spat.

Isalie chuckled, her anger giving her the strength to stalk forward even though all she wanted to do was fall to her knees and wrap her arms around Celeste. Or run to Jentien and fall apart in his arms.

She couldn't do either of those things while Kiyash was free.

"I should have," Isalie agreed. She was shocked to hear that her voice was steady. She gripped the shard in her right hand to keep her mind off the pain in her dangling left arm. "Part of me wishes I had. It would have been much easier than this."

Mistress Kiyash let out a humorless chuckle. She stood imperious even now, when everyone stared at Isalie like an Elder come back to life. The Stills with shock and reverence, the Ambient with awe and fear.

"I can rectify that for you." Mistress Kiyash held her hands out toward Isalie, and the same light that flashed through the Gloom arced through the air.

Jentien and Celeste screamed as Isalie ducked aside. She crashed onto her injured shoulder and swallowed a scream. Another flash made her roll to the side.

"I have the Malachi's own power at my disposal." The light of the spire dimmed as the light surrounding the Mistress flared, her pristine crimson dress flaring when the wind picked up. Ambient light enshrouded her, and she lifted off the ground. "I *am* the Ambience. You are *no one*."

The ground beneath Isalie's feet rumbled, and she sprinted toward Kiyash moments before a stalagmite stabbed upward in the space she'd been. Another was close enough behind her that she rocked forward onto her toes, and Isalie threw herself to the side to avoid the next.

"Stop!" Baelen roared. He struggled, seeming to break free of invisible bonds. He reached toward the Mistress, his hands clawed as if to grasp her and drag her out of the air, his eyes glowing with the same light that enshrouded her.

Mistress Kiyash grunted, the boy's efforts giving her pause, until she glowed brighter still, and Baelen tumbled back, gasping. Voices throughout the Inners called out in terror as the perimeter of towers dimmed, like the spire's inherent light had dimmed when Kiyash brightened. The storm spread, and the Gloom roiled beyond the far boundary. The Ambient present were looking between their Mistress and her heir, only Ardaf Kova daring to approach his son to help him to his feet. The Stills rushed toward her, picking up swords, arrows, even rocks, letting them fly toward Kiyash. She didn't move, but every weapon stopped short of her, her body trembling a bit harder with every deflected blow.

Jentien picked up his discarded bow and nocked one crystal-tipped arrow, arcing it through the shield to sink into her shoulder. Kiyash screamed in pain, cast her arms toward the crowd of Stills and Ambient, and everyone came to a halt. Jentien floated toward Kiyash, and Isalie came after him, until they orbited her.

Kiyash cast her arms toward the storm and the cloud ground to a halt just before it hit the Ambient District. It roiled upward as if hitting the wall of a glass container, and spread along the edges, encircling them.

She's taking power from the towers, Isalie noticed, watching Kiyash hold the storm at bay now that she'd realized what she'd done. Her face flushed with the effort, and Isalie felt the hold on her slip. She was still suspended in the air, now behind Kiyash as she redirected the bulk of her power to keep the storm out. Isalie rotated her wrist and fumbled with the shard in her hand until the tip stuck out like the blade of a dagger.

The spire flickered again, and the storm seeped through the barrier. People below them began to move again, Kiyash's concentration focused on the Gloom, and gouts of fire joined the arrows flying toward her. The Ambient had joined the Stills' assault, seeing the danger they were in. The attacks glanced off the shield Kiyash was still maintaining, and Isalie realized she could move her arm. With a scream of righteous fury, she slammed the shard into Kiyash's neck. Kiyash's eyes went wide with shock as she wrapped her hand around the shard and stared at Isalie.

The storm rolled around them when she and Jentien fell with Kiyash onto the ground. The prismatic glow in the Mistress's eyes sputtered. Isalie struggled upright, over Mistress Kiyash gasping on the ground. Blood trickled out of the corner of her mouth as she snarled at Isalie.

Isalie looked at Baelen, who looked so much like the woman at her feet. "Unless you want to end up dead, I suggest you get to safety. The Gloom doesn't care how powerful you are."

Jentien called out. "Baelen, get everyone inside!"

The young man shouted over the confused voices rising in the courtyard. "Ambient, get everyone under cover! NOW!" His voice rumbled, and the Ambient started to move, gathering the Stills.

Kiyash tried to pull the shard from her neck, but Isalie slammed her hand onto her shoulder, sending it deeper. She choked on the blood pouring from her mouth. "You're... nobody."

"That's why you'll lose," Isalie said. Thunder cracked behind them, and the first patters of rain began. The Ambient Guard filed inside the spire along with the Ambient, but a glance showed Isalie that they stood just inside the doorway to watch.

Jen rushed to free Cel. They stood with the Stills from the Outers, everyone who'd worn their cloaks and carried their masks in pockets from habit, to watch Isalie speak. The crystal lenses were blank and impassive, as if the Elders themselves had come to Vortheim to stand in judgement.

"I'm no Ambient, and I'm no warrior. I'm one of many oppressed by the Ambient, but I have the physical scars to prove it. *They* are my weapon." She leaned closer. "I could be *anyone* that has suffered. I will always be here, because I am the same as everyone here. And there are more of us than there are of you."

Rain spattered Isalie's back and fell onto Kiyash's head for the first time, and the woman screamed. Isalie watched blood run down the Consul of Olunei's face with the rain.

Kiyash crumpled to the ground, and the light retreated from her eyes as they closed, back to the spire. Pressure undulated in building waves from the crystal structure, sending everyone around her to their knees while Isalie stared in a daze. The pressure snapped, and the glow surged outward. It passed above the heads of the people on their knees, and Isalie knew she couldn't get out of the way in time. Two voices spoke in her mind when the wave reached her, separate, but somehow the same.

"The Gloom."

Something inside her erupted, like a dam of energy bursting, and the wave dispersed around her harmlessly. Isalie watched, dumbfounded, as it surged up the walls of the spire, dousing its glow.

Jen and Cel called her name, and then she was in their arms, staring down at the Consul's corpse, wondering how she'd survived.

CHAPTER EIGHTY-ONE

Isalie's heart hammered in her chest as she breathed faster and faster. Her body shuddered, and she moaned.

No more, she thought, writhing against the hands that held her down. Those hands pressed firmly, and she arched her back and cried out as the throbbing pulse between her legs shot through her body in the wake of the orgasm.

Celeste hummed against Isalie's thigh, flicking her tongue against Isalie again. "I told you to lie still, Lee," she murmured. She climbed up the bed to drape her body over Isalie's. Her violet locs spilled over Isalie's chest, tickling her sensitive skin.

Jentien grunted before he rolled toward them and slung an arm over Celeste. "Doing what she's told isn't Iz's strong suit, Cel." He kissed Isalie's shoulder when Celeste slid up Isalie's other side, and then scooted down the bed to wrap his lips around her nipple.

Isalie rolled toward him, moaning again when his teeth gently tugged her in his direction. She chuckled, heaving a satisfied sigh when he released her and flopped onto his back. Celeste laid her arm across Isalie's midsection from one direction, and Jentien from the other.

Her body felt boneless, as it had for more than a day now that everything had settled. Mistress Kiyash had died a week ago, and Isalie, Jentien, and Celeste had spent most of that time arguing over a new balance for the citizens of Olunei along with the Olugar leaders and Baelen Kiyash, acting as the new head of the Ambient. Once they'd hammered out the details and the Ambient had healed as much of their wounds as possible, Isalie had insisted they retreat to the Outers to recover.

There hadn't been much rest since they'd come home, but Isalie had to admit that she felt better than she had in a very long time.

"Don't we have somewhere to be?" Isalie muttered. She wasn't sure she'd be able to get out of bed, but she had a nagging thought in the back of her head that told her she was missing something important.

Jentien snored softly the way he did when he was on the edge of deep sleep, but Celeste sighed and rolled away, pulling her arm free of Jentien's.

"Yes," Celeste grumbled. "I need to talk to the Olugar and the Ambient today about reconstruction and the plan to distribute more cloaks and masks." Celeste sat up, and Isalie trailed her fingers up Celeste's bare back. "Mmm, that feels nice."

"I'm sure they can wait another hour," Isalie said.

"I'm sure they could," Celeste replied, her eyes twinkling over her shoulder when she glanced down at Isalie. "But since I made them wait a day longer than they'd like, I think it's time for me to get out of this bed and back to our new reality."

Isalie looked past Celeste to the window. The sky outside was gray, and fat droplets of rain were pouring down.

"I wonder whether we'll see the sun again soon," Isalie said.

Celeste narrowed her calculating eyes at the window. "The even dispersal within the radius of the outer towers seems to have lightened the burden for the rest of us. It'll take more time to track the patterns, but the simple fact that we had an hour of clear blue sky yesterday gives me hope."

Isalie smiled. So many Stills that'd been relegated to the Outers hadn't seen the sky in decades. The smiles on their faces and the joy that echoed through the streets yesterday would stay with Isalie for a long time.

The memory also drove her to put Jentien's arm aside and sit up, joining Celeste in her search for attire. "I'm coming with you," she said when Celeste turned a curious glance her way. "I want to see what's happening out there."

"You want to say a few choice words to the Ambient," Celeste muttered.

"I do," Isalie laughed. "Though I've had a hard time saying them to Baelen."

"The boy is adorable," Celeste said with a begrudging nod.

"If you're trying to make me jealous," Jentien grumbled as he sat up, "it's working."

Isalie crawled over the bed and flopped onto Jentien's chest. He grunted, and Isalie smiled as she pecked his cheek.

"Get up and get dressed, then," she said, unable to help the smile that broke out on her face. "You can chaperone us. Make sure we don't make any inappropriate advances on the young man."

"We can't," Baelen said, his voice cracking on the last word. He cleared his throat and started again. "We can't make any more cloaks or masks, and we can't rebuild the city with the Ambience."

"And you can't get anyone out?" Jentien asked. "Or call for help?"

Baelen shook his head. "We have orbs that *should* talk to the palace in Lacorsia, but they went dark. Maybe the surge destroyed the enchantment. It would also explain why the Gloom grows whenever we use the Ambience above ground."

"There's been more success in the Undercity," Arru added. "The crystal veins in the bedrock seem to deter the Gloom's effects, though great uses of power could still cause the spread above ground. Perhaps even below. Until we determine the limits, the Ambience should be used sparingly, if at all."

"It's a good thing you have us Stills to show you how to adapt without your power," Celeste said.

Baelen smiled, but the other two Ambient in the room scowled. He cast a glance their way, and they rearranged their faces into neutral expressions.

"How are the Ambient and loyalists responding?" Jentien asked after a pointed look around the room.

Isalie followed his gaze, taking note of Ionna among their ranks. She had serious doubts about Baelen's ability to keep everyone in line without using his power. Hopefully, the fact that they wouldn't survive without everyone's cooperation would give him more authority.

"Fine," Baelen replied. "Some won't listen, but that's what the prison is for."

"Our biggest problem now," Amal said, "is water and food supplies. Our first priority should be to utilize the Ambience to provide more crops and light orbs."

Ardaf Kova nodded. "We can produce orbs that radiate sunlight, but the process is slow since we can only use a fraction of the power it normally takes. We should have enough to cover the Undercity in a few weeks."

"Then let's focus on the caverns we've hollowed out for this purpose before we spread the light anywhere else," Amal said. "With Celeste's help, we can keep them watered and have something other than meat and gruel to sustain us."

"I'm working on a filter for the water," Celeste said, "including the runoff from the rain. I think it should be possible to extract the Ambience, rendering it potable again. Arru and a few Ambient are helping me, and with so much crystal debris from the spire, we should have enough to sustain the population in the next day."

"We've organized hunts in the tunnels," Nel said. "There are still plenty of beasts roaming down there, and the meat will keep us fed while the hides provide more cloaks. I think we should work on expanding the tunnels into the Inners, so that we have protected access to both sides of the river."

"Assign a few teams to that endeavor," Amal told them with a nod.

"What are we going to do about living space?" Isalie asked. "Are we going to allow people to relocate to the Inners? Some of the reunited families could certainly use more space than the dormitories in the Outers allow."

"My volunteers have begun taking requests for relocation as they distribute the full city rosters to every dormitory and house. If we run out of space, we'll hold a lottery to see who can move."

"The Ambient District is also at your disposal," Baelen said. "We have more space than we could ever use."

Jentien flashed him a proud look, and Baelen smiled in response. Isalie's heart warmed to see the exchange. It gave her hope that the Stills could coexist with the Ambient, given enough time.

They'd leveled the playing field. Now all they had to do was survive the Gloom.

THE CHARACTERS
FROM

THE

GLOOM

SUNDERED

WILL RETURN!

Acknowledgements

This book was straight from my soul, and it took a lot to get here. Thank you so much to my amazing husband, I couldn't have done this without you. Not without your patience and love, not without your endless insights when I rattle off story ideas without context, not without your child wrangling expertise. Most of all, thank you for the support you've given me while I doubted and mistrusted myself. I love you. My wonderful, funny children, thank you for letting mom write. Mom and dad, thank you for believing in me and listening to me talk about the entire process.

For everyone that helped me to make this book so much better than I thought it could be. Woody Johns of Copper Coin Editing, I think we've finally figured out those dashes! Thank you to my beta readers, for your feedback that helped me shape this story and its characters. For my cover artist, Marybeth Mondok, you've done it again.

Lastly, and most importantly, thank you, fabulous reader. I couldn't be here without you. I hope you'll continue with me as more stories in Celuthia unfold.

About the author

DANA C BRENTSON has been enjoying fantasy storytelling since she was small, whether in books, movies, or video games. As an adult, she began to create her own stories, which blossomed when she started to explore tabletop gaming. You can follow Dana on Instagram, Threads, and Tiktok @dcbrentsonauthor Find out more about her and her other works by subscribing to her newsletter www.dcbrentson.com

instagram.com/dcbrentsonauthor

amazon.com/stores/Dana-C-Brentson/author/B0BBPTJQ93?ref=sr_ntt_srch_lnk_1&qid=1745086170&sr=8-1&isDramIntegrated=true&shoppingPortalEnabled=true&ccs_id=1a285bde-8e52-454e-81bc-8b2cb8e4f1bb

tiktok.com/@dcbrentsonauthor

goodreads.com/author/show/22517460.Dana_C_Brentson